Florid

C000127882

Rod Usher has been a journalist
for over twenty years, and is a
former chief sub-editor of *The
Sunday Times*. His first novel,
the highly successful *A Man of
Marbles*, was published in 1989.

Rod Usher

Florid States

This edition published in Great Britain in 1999 by
Allison & Busby Limited
114 New Cavendish Street
London W1M 7FD
http://www.allisonandbusby.ltd.uk

First published in Australasia in 1990 by
Simon & Schuster Australia

Cover illustration by Cristina Paradís
Cover design by Neil Straker Creative

A catalogue record for this book is available
from the British Library

ISBN 0 7490 0427 4

Printed and bound by Biddles Limited,
Guildford, Surrey.

ACKNOWLEDGEMENTS
This book is totally fiction, but I would like to thank:
the many people with schizophrenia who have agreed to talk to me
so openly over the years; Dr John Lloyd and Margaret Leggatt for sound advice;
Dr Harry Derham for providing research papers on postnatal depression;
Philippe Tanguy, once again, for his great enthusiasm and editing skills,
so ably assisted by Katri Hilden; and Angela for her critical eye
and endurance.

To the memory of my dear son Damien
(17.3.1969 – 12.9.1989)

And for Jane and Jacob

Psychoses are mental disorders of such severity that they affect the whole of an individual's personality and interfere with his understanding of the world to the degree that he is said to be divorced from reality.

Of course, no-one is in perfect touch with reality.

Frederic Neuman
American psychiatrist

Part 1

Sometimes Ned Quinn could not instantly remember his younger brother's name. Usually he could find it, fast enough, through one of those associations that build up like silt over half a lifetime. For instance he might think 'curly hair, take care'. . .and this would bridge some synaptic gap to give him 'Carl'. He would cover up the brief pause this indented into conversation by looking over his listener's shoulder distractedly, or else by patting his pockets as though for cigarettes. Small holes in the autobiographical memory were part of the price. If ever he got completely stumped, well, people just thought what they thought.

In calmer moments than the present he sometimes wondered whether the application of electricity might not also have impeded his olfactory sense. Most smells were new to Ned each time he inhaled. Mint, sun-dried cotton clothing, a dunked gingernut biscuit, a geranium, they always came to him startlingly fresh: small hits of pleasure. Petrol, ammonia, dogshit on the sole, a stray armpit on the train … these, too, were reborn and reborne on unpleasant winds. It was a matter of sinuses rather than synapses, but at least *this* could be kept private. Apart from which, olfactory amnesia was probably more blessing than curse.

Right now, however, conversation was too deep for such trifling matters, although there was some odour around him. The smell of nervousness?

Ned Quinn was leaning against a splintery hoarding, splashed with rock-concert fliers. It boxed a giant dental excavation, the ground gaping and root-drilled for the start of yet another skyscraper. High above him the chain of the slender crane that would raise the building hung slack, an evening breeze bending its links into a slight curve against gravity. A union flag set itself proudly from the chain in the cool capitalist air.

He was sweating.

The unseasonal perspiration on his forehead, in the evening breeze, guaranteed his public privacy – which was crucial. Ned often sought safety in numbers if he could not be absolutely certain of being alone at the flat.

The city was beginning its evening purge. Commuters hastened to the tube station opening, which sucked them up like a vast vacuum cleaner. Occasionally – perhaps because he was a strongly-made man in jeans and windcheater, going nowhere – a glance would be thrown Ned's way, then hastily retrieved. If someone had stopped to ask him the time, or for directions, he would have had to cut dead the conversation with The Others, would have needed to haul his line of sight back from distance.

He had agreed with the voice he called Two that no attempt on his life was likely this particular night. 'But complacency is an enemy's ally,' Two had said. So he remained alert; an awareness in the corners of his eyes, in the small unseen hairs that prickle, in the involuntarily clenching muscles of calf and jaw.

Ned was complaining that Two's tone never varied. Somehow Two could not come forward with an argument that wasn't fed by some waspish perspective of negativity or doubt. Ned had tried to have it out with Two many times, but there was always a law-of-averages possibility to what Two said, accompanied by a shrug which implied only a fool could ignore his advice. 'After all,' Two had boasted quite recently, 'I'm your lighthouse, my role is entirely to alert you to the dangers. You're at the helm.'

And indeed in times of danger, times when Ned Quinn admitted in the residual canyons and crevices of his mind that he was vulnerable and in need of prudent counsel, Two would always be on hand, somewhere just behind his left ear, insisting in that well-spoken way of his. 'Instead of Two, you should call me W ...' he'd advertised aloud only yesterday, '... W for Warning!' Ned had been sitting in Carvallo's Cafe, working on The Treatise. His sudden laughter had blown the froth of his cappucino over his black beard.

He much preferred the talk of One. One was an intellectual, not a manufacturer of conspiracies. And her voice was almost hushed, neutral. With One Ned could not ignore the sotto voce imperatives, the soft urgings to achievement, the quiet triumphalism, but at least she and he could calmly debate the approaches to a problem. It was no coincidence, Ned felt, that she was always on his right hand. With One he could spend many hours in fruitful discussion of The Treatise, how it should be presented, how the disbelievers and paid dissenters would seek to impugn it or to divert it to their own unhealthy ends.

But Two would always contrive to interrupt. Right now, as usual, he was on cue. 'Alright,' he was saying curtly, 'put me down as paranoid if you like, but there *are* plans afoot to stop you. It's your neck, but your beloved Treatise will hardly be able to put the world back on the rails if you're rubbed out.'

'For Chris'sake!' Ned hissed out of the corner of his mouth. 'Keep your effing voice down! If One and I can discuss the predicament without raising our voices, why can't you? The last time you and I had a shouting match I was sectioned. This time let's not make it so easy for them, eh?'

A uniformed shop-girl turned her head back at him as she hurried past. Ned realised that he'd slipped again, that he was talking aloud. He and One could go for hours, days, totally inside their heads. It was invariably smartarse, doomster Two with whom the slanging came blurting out of his mouth. Often he would not even know that he'd erred until a passer-by stared, picked up a stark phrase. From there it was only a hop and a step to Dr Logan and those godforsaken clinical catch-alls such as 'Palpable loss of lucidity'.

Ned was unaware that he had also spat these last four words aloud. A suited man with a briefcase passed close against the hoarding, quickly looking up at the cold scaffolding to avoid Ned's eyes. The man thought he'd overheard 'Culpable loss of your city', mistaking Ned for another of those loons from ASP, the Anti-Skyscraper Protestors.

Ned allowed a pause, bit his bottom lip to ensure that One and Two were contained while the peak hour swallowed up the businessman. He'd made it clear back at the flat that the three of them would communicate silently. How often had he come unstuck because of their failure to do this? An added difficulty was that the three of them would be going all at once: One talking about her grand designs, Two forever cautioning, and him, mere Ned Quinn, trying to sort the three of them out.

It was a mistake to have left the flat. He and One had been fine-tuning The Treatise for, what, two weeks? Two's voice would chip in regularly with his sensational claims about bugging, about periscopes, about thought assemblers from the Eastern Bloc embassies across the lake, bouncing sound-waves off its surface and into Ned's bedroom. . .Well, at least *that* had been acted upon: with aluminium foil from the kitchen stuck Blitzlike over the window, robbing the room of natural light.

Not really such a big price to pay, One had joked while Ned unrolled the silver paper. Such a blackout would have been much harder for the first Socrates: there was no electricity then! Socrates The First, *he'd* been able to reach enlightenment in darkness, hadn't he?

Ha bloody ha, Ned had said. In truth he did not believe Two's allegation about the soundwaves, but The Treatise was too important to risk spoiling for a happorth of foil.

Yes, it was a mistake to have left the flat. But there had been 'The Milkman', claiming that those full bottles had been at the door near a fortnight, peering through the security grille in the pretence of needing to know whether or not

Ned wanted to cancel, whether he'd been on holiday. Same kind of stunt with the 'Electricity Board', this weasely fellow who purported to be reading the meter. When he'd called, Ned and One had been discussing what the new Socrates would wear at the Press Conference – old Athenian or modern Australian? It was low-secrecy stuff, so Ned and One had continued to talk in the kitchen. The so-called meter man had hurriedly noted down the figures, getting no answer to his question about why the windows were blacked out.

Worst of all were the neighbours. The old girl in flat six had babbled to him about the smell of the milk, said she'd take it up with the agency. And the heavily made-up woman a floor down, the one immediately below him, she'd left a note under the door alleging 'non-stop pacing' through the night these past two weeks, and had the cheek to offer Serepax so he, and she, could get some decent sleep. (Feeling mischievous, Ned had been half inclined to reply with a note of his own: 'Socrates abhors Serepax'. But of course Two had instantly seen all sorts of dangers and risks in this.)

In this way Ned had come to the present pass, where he was spending less and less of the daytime at the flat, choosing to discuss the final preparations on the anonymous open road. Amid the throng.

The first Socrates would have approved; he also was a pacer.

Both Ned's voices – she of the right hand who had first informed him that he was the reincarnation of Socrates, and he of the dire warnings in the left ear – had repeatedly made themselves heard on the dangers of the role he was taking on. The first Socrates, One explained, had been fitted up and given a dud trial. He had told his judges that he had merely used his philosophical gifts at the behest of the gods, 'whose authority I regard more than yours'. Fine words bravely spoken, but, One pointed out, he was ordered to drink hemlock. 'No wonder,' Two had delivered in that booming radio announcer's voice of his, 'no wonder I'm forever warning you about what you eat and drink. You can put much more subtle killers than hemlock into a milk bottle nowadays!'

The Treatise itself was, superficially, a simple document. Its weight was carried, she of the quieter voice had finally convinced Ned, not in its advocacy of peace and tolerance and non-violence, all those things that clergy declaim each Sunday, but in its juxtaposition of certain key words. These combinations, rediscovered by One and whispered so cogently, triggered reactions of acceptance in all who heard them. 'Socrates had them; you have them; you are the returned Socrates.' One's proposition was as uncomplicated as that.

Ned had struggled against both One and Two when they had first come to him again quietly, what was it, three weeks ago? Tried the usual tricks: singing loudly, turning up the Walkman so the earphones fairly gouted rock 'n roll, smoking joint after pungent joint, gulping down beer after beer, even putting Blu-Tack in his earholes. No matter how much he desensitised himself, tried to drown them in activity or stupor, the voices always won out in the end – first cajoling, arguing between themselves, eventually shouting. It was useless to try to stop them once they were in full flight. He ceased the smoking and drinking, even stopped the regulation doses of Modecate. Unable to beat them, you joined them.

It had taken only a matter of days for One to remove any doubts that Ned was second-time-around Socrates. At her instruction, he had written out The Treatise at the kitchen table. He would have felt better had The Treatise been typed, his handwriting going through a shaky stage at the moment, but ballpoint and aerogramme paper it had to be. Ned had read the ten pages of wobbly, blotched text over and over and over – so often that Two had argued he should make the task of infiltration that much harder for the Eastern Bloc embassies by memorising the whole thing and destroying the original. Ned had ignored Two, made the mistake of telling him he was deluded, for which Two paid him back by just breathing in his left ear for twenty minutes, something which never failed to leave Ned cursing, occasionally stamping his left foot, neighbours or no neighbours.

The Treatise, when read aloud, was no threat to Martin Luther King, Ned complained more than once. Having part done university Honours English several years ago, he felt he could have produced a far more inspiring text if he'd been left to his own devices. It was almost bereft of adjectives, and made no use of the oratorical device of keyline repetition. Churchill would have torn it up. But One asserted that it was its hidden Socratic structure that was going to win over the masses, whether or not they cared to be won. The position of each word was as crucial as the placing of the decimal point is to mathematics. Subliminal, she insisted. He would see for himself at the Press Conference, she assured him.

Ned still had his doubts about harnessing the media to The Treatise. Two, of course, saw limitless possibilities for foul play at the Press Conference; he suggested that Ned should read The Treatise from a secret television studio outside the city.

The five o'clock crowd was teasing out now, although the traffic was still solid. Any minute Two would start to get jumpy. Ned could anticipate his carping. Two would point out that without the crush of people acting as a mobile shield, Ned was more vulnerable to a silenced and silencing shot from a hotel window, or a rooftop, or else to a car 'accidentally' lunging onto the pavement and smearing any idea of a returning Socrates all over the rock-concert fliers of the hoarding ... This fear of attack was another reason why Ned had been standing more than an hour in front of the excavation site: apart from the protection against eavesdropping, his back was also guarded by the ugly hole in the ground.

Still, the three of them had never managed to agree on exactly whom it was who was out to subvert The New Socrates and His Treatise. 'There are countless groups,' Two had said sibilantly into his left ear. 'Where, for instance, will the big political parties be left when The Treatise has been televised throughout the world? Who needs a Prime Minister when you've got a new, pro-active Socrates? And what about big business? If suddenly everyone stops drinking cans of fizzy cola … we're talking multinationals here! And you can bet your bottom dollar they'll *all* be looking for the solution to this threat, as no doubt they'll regard The Treatise given its discomfiture of both Keynes and Marx. I'm bound to point out that the solution is the mere elimination of one Ned Quinn, nobody. No offence intended old mate.'

One was more subtle; she would simply repeat the last words of the first Socrates as the hemlock coursed about his veins and his friends looked on in mental agony: 'Crito, we owe a cock to Aesculapius. Pay it and do not neglect it.' The code was patently thin: he, Ned Quinn, humble highschool teacher, must deliver The Treatise, like an outstanding debt, to the world.

Apart from the feeble attempts of 'The Milkman' and the 'Electricity Board' on his flat, however, Ned had no clear sightings of these forces of evil. And while he mostly resisted Two's exhortations to ever-tighter security, One's non-stop reinforcement of the weight of their campaign sometimes penetrated to the point where his whole head hurt. She wouldn't let him forget for a moment the transcendence of the mission, as she insisted upon calling it.

Ned hunched his shoulders forward and moved out from the hoarding and into the lines of the homeward-bound. Just before the station, at Two's urging, he quickly crossed the road as two strolling policemen, hands clasped at their backs, loomed on the pavement ahead of him. Ned chided himself as he did so; this was being ridiculous in a democratic city. 'Fuck you, Two,' he snapped in protest at the nagging voice as he dodged between the lines of cars waiting at the lights.

'Fuck you, too!' swore a taxi driver who thought Ned was addressing him. Turning to his back-seat passenger he demanded: 'What'd I do, for Christ's sake?'

On the train Ned hung on a strap and kept his head down, concentrating on the floor. Being tall made you conspicuous. One had said that the first Socrates had also been a tall man. Although he had found no evidence of this at the library, the thought had made him smile, and did so again now. He caught himself and switched off his face. A quick look around reassured him that no-one on the train had noticed. Most people had their heads in newspapers.

Three stops out he alighted, handed in his ticket. Two was immediately into his left ear as he walked down the asphalt to the underpass. 'Approach the flats from the north today. Routine's the last thing you follow in these circumstances. Okay, okay, so it's a wasted two-block walk. Just do it for my peace of mind will you?'

Ned was tired. His gastric juices were eating at him the way Two's voice did to his head, acidly. He'd better cook some food. 'No!' Two interjected before Ned had time even to remember the virginity of his fridge. 'Take-away's safer! Yes, old mate, again.'

One sounded as if she was Socrates' mother: 'Patience, Ned. Not so long now before the truth is out and we're recognised for what we are …'

Ned nodded and approached from the north, exhausted though he was. He slowed almost to a halt when he saw the panelvan of the block's managing agents parked in the street out front, its logo of crossed keys and interlocked initials. 'Don't be silly, Two,' he said aloud. 'Kidnap is too much like hard work for estate agents. I paid the rent, when was it, last Thursday?'

As it happened, the suited young man from the agents had been looking for him. He was squatting, about to slide a piece of paper under the door to the flat when Ned approached.

'Mr Quinn?'

'Yes?'

'I'm glad I've caught you. I have to discuss some lease matters. Can we go inside?'

Ned flinched as he heard a distinct click. He exhaled again as he realised it was the snib closing on the door to flat six.

He didn't answer the young man but stepped in front of him and inserted his key. Two's curt voice told him to back into the hallway, keeping his eyes on the man. It made him move awkwardly, but he did so.

'The rent's not …'

'No, no,' the well-dressed young man said, hesitantly following him inside, 'it's the noise. Complaints about loud voices, some swearing. The woman below claims there's a stamping sound at night …'

He stopped. He had followed Ned into the kitchen. Ned looked at the stranger's face, then studied the room himself.

Trying to see it as the other would, he could accept that it was a mess: half-finished pizzas, see-through plastic tubs with congealed Chinese vegetables. The door to the small fridge was open, light on, motor throbbing overtime, the whole room chilled because of it. Inside there was only one yoghurt carton, on its side.

'Look, I think you should go,' Ned said, on Two's instigation. 'I've been engaged in some very important research work, extremely important, and I just haven't had any time to devote to domestic matters for a while. Don't worry, a big cleanup is about to begin.' He couldn't help a splutter of laughter at the double meaning. 'As for the noise, any complaints should surely be made in writing? As I say, I've been working long hours, late hours, but you can tell the woman below I'm nearly finished. I wish she'd realise that some people have more important things to do than sleep their lives away.'

'I dunno what's going on here,' the young man said, formality and grammar falling away under pressure.

'You don't need to,' Ned smiled paternally. 'Just stay alert, read the papers, watch the television, and one day you will have something quite remarkable to tell your grandchildren.'

The fellow from the rental agency could not think of the appropriate reply. He went briskly out to the landing, down to the van with the crossed keys. Ned watched from the kitchen window as it pulled away from the kerb. He went back to the landing, locked and safety-chained the door. He made a mug of black coffee and sat down to re-read The Treatise for the umpteenth time. He restrained the urge to pace, to stamp his foot in anger when both One and Two interrupted simultaneously. His trialogue was barely more than a mutter.

It was seven pm when the police came. The rental agents must have supplied a key because from the kitchen Ned heard its smooth slide into the lock. There was a thump as the safety chain caught short the opening door. Sitting at the table he hissed at One and Two to be quiet so he could hear what was happening.

There were some voices, departing footsteps. Silence. Returning footsteps. More muted conversation on the landing. Then a grunt, immediately followed by movement as the boltcutters destroyed a link in the safety chain.

Jennifer Duncan's short letter was never meant to have been posted. It shouldn't even have been written. But it was. She composed its few lines up at the house while they were letting time slide. Country people, friends passing the untelevised hours at the end of a manual day.

It was a fifteen-minute walk from Jennifer's cabin to the Vickers' house. Her own feet had worn the up-and-down track and she was both proud of it and reassured by it. After four-and-a-half years, she could follow it blind. The track, she thought as she walked up it alone, had been drawn a bit the way sheep made theirs across pasture; by instinct, not theodolite. It had taken a long time and a lot of whistling for her to be at ease in the bush at night, particularly where the track descended to the Condamine, the river with its great hands of sighing willow and its throat-clearing frogs. Even the stars had been hostile at first, winking unkindly at every start, scurry and crashing departure provoked by her footsteps. Now, after all this time, the track was as one of her own arteries.

On summer nights such as this, Jennifer would reach the house to find Henry Vickers out on the verandah, feet on the rail, eavesdropping on the nocturnal bush. Or he would be reading by the kerosene lamp at the kitchen table he had slabbed out of a tree with his chainsaw. This hot night he was inside, ribs like xylophones down his bare torso, stubbled face held by a book entitled *Earth Wall Construction*.

When Jennifer arrived about eight pm Lorna was in loose underpants and an old black T-shirt of Henry's, big enough for the swell of her ripening motherhood. This night Jennifer wore jeans and a bottle-green T-shirt. Beneath it her breasts flattened a little against her body, unlike those of her younger, soon-to-be-lactating friend. Lorna had often asked why, in such a private place as Overton Valley, Jennifer covered herself up. The answer was partly red hair, pale skin. 'You wait 'til you're my age, girl,' Jennifer would chide.

Their differences, the two women had long ago agreed, probably explained why they got on so well. The dissimilarities started with skin and went deeper. Jennifer was taller by five inches, foxy hair corkscrewing below her shoulders, the same colour freckled across her arms and legs. Lorna had once asked if she could join up all the dots on Jennifer's shoulders to see if they made a picture. Even Jennifer's green eyes had understatements of copper. Whereas Lorna was dark-skinned with straight black hair, short as a man's. Henry cut it with the kitchen scissors, called it squaw style.

Jennifer was six years older than Lorna Vickers and her face revealed that she had been to certain limits. Lorna's, on the other hand, had an unblooded, wide-eyed air; and it radiated the self-confidence of partnership.

It was Jennifer's solitariness that was to be the impetus for the letter.

She entered by the back door of the yellowgum house, put her torch on the table and looked over Henry's shoulder at his book. He smiled up at her. Lorna was lying, six-month belly upwards, on the couch in front of the stone chimney. She was stroking the head of the circled iron-grey cat.

'Could you be puttin' the kettle on, Jenny,' she purred in her brogue, never mind that she had spent only the first few months of her life in Ireland. Lorna claimed her only regret about marrying Henry was having exchanged O'Rourke for Vickers, something she insisted she would not do were they to re-run the film. On St Patrick's day she always pinned a few gumleaves to herself: 'Me Queensland shamrock.'

Jennifer lifted the kettle from the Rayburn to the sink and drew water, the heavy iron base hissing as she replaced it. The night was almost as hot as the stove.

She flopped into a wickerwork chair next to the couch. Lorna was slowly fanning the air above her belly with a notepad, as though to cool the child within. 'I think he's going to come out looking like a large cashew,' Lorna laughed. She always referred to the unborn as a boy. Henry dismissed this as wishful thinking, but Kate, their small daughter who had not long gone off to sleep, had piped up that a girl would be just as good, wouldn't it? Lorna could hardly demur.

'I wish we hadn't finished that jigsaw last night,' she sighed. 'Henry says they're like a quickie, great while you're having it, but you can feel a bit empty after you've finished.'

Jennifer laughed: 'Better quick than never.'

'Ah, so forgetful, Mrs Duncan. Smelly socks off, the old in-out, then smelly socks back on again. Whereas the silent jigsaw, now it at least has a start, a slow middle and then an end, all of which can be managed at your own speed.'

'Yes, Lorna, but hearts aren't put together like jigsaws, which you well know.'

Lorna had been fishing for such an affirmation.

Jennifer had not been looking at her. Using her legs as a table she had been rolling a joint. Now she sucked down two draughts of the compost-smelling smoke, then offered the cigarette. Lorna glanced over her shoulder. Sure enough, Henry had looked up from *Earth Wall Construction*.

'No,' she sighed. 'Henry and I decided today that I'm off until after this fellow's born.'

Jennifer waved the cigarette at Henry. He shook his head 'Solidarity,' he said, and turned back to his book.

Lorna heaved herself up to attend to the kettle. 'Anyway, the jigsaw's complete, I'm too restless to read. But I do have an idea. Bit of a wee lark,' she added in the forged accent that could madden or charm, depending on when she chose to use it. 'It came to me this afternoon when Kate was having her nap and I was lying here reading *Grass Roots*. It struck me that there must be plenty of good people who read the magazine.'

She put a cup of tea on the table next to Henry. He kept reading but lifted a hand, which she briefly held and squeezed before she returned to the sink and carried two cups back to the couch, placing them on the polished floor-boards.

'So I thought … why not send one of those letters off? Just for fun?'

'No thanks,' Jennifer answered, firmly enough for Lorna to frown. 'Only desperates resort to the lonely hearts columns, even if *Grass Roots* readers might be my sort of desperates.'

'I knew you'd go all sensible on me,' said Lorna, pushing out her lower lip. 'I got to thinking that I'd probably do it, though, say if Henry got kicked to death by the cow or felled a tree onto his head, something awful like that.'

Henry looked up from his book. 'Just checking to see if you were listening,' Lorna grinned.

'And then I got to thinking about the wording. How would I try to sell myself? I mean, would I say "Spunky Irish widow seeks loving bushman …"?'

Jennifer, lightened by the cannabis, rocked forward in her chair, spluttering. Behind them Henry coughed drops of tea onto his book.

'You see the problem,' said Lorna. 'Of course Ned Kelly's dead, and that Irish widow stuff is not *really* me, is it? Then I wondered how would Henry have advertised me, after all those years he worked at the agency? Fascinating, isn't it?'

'You're not for sale,' said Henry, taking the bait. 'But if you were, I'd put in something like "Good bitch, on second litter. Working animal but also a pet. Needs obedience training. Best offer".'

'Droll, very droll, Henry Vickers. And don't you be worried about me getting some offers, never mind that you've tried to turn me into a balloon.'

'We're back on sex,' complained Jennifer.

'Good clean monogamy,' said Henry, turning away again.

'Nothing's more boring than monogamy,' teased Lorna.

'Sure is,' grinned Jennifer.

'Well then,' Lorna had her friend trapped, 'let's just pretend, shall we, that you're putting an advertisement in the next issue of *Grass Roots?* Now what, hypothetically, does it say? That's the interesting part, I reckon, someone trying to summarise their self-perceptions in three or four lines. Go on, Jen. At least it's something to do while this baby grows!'

Jennifer groaned indulgently. 'The games grown people play! Give me some bloody paper then, something to write with.'

As Jennifer began advertising herself Lorna paced a few laps of the couch, palms pushed into the small of her back, arching against her belly. Seeing that she was distracting both reader and writer, she walked to the front of the big room and out to the verandah.

The bush the Vickers overlooked was virgin, although in the darkness Lorna was robbed of the land's rush to the river and the tall gums' climb back up the steep slope towards the house. There was so much unseen business going on out there. Little Kate had asked for a night walk on her third birthday last week. Henry's torch had pinioned possums in goggle-eyed innocence on the guttering and had held a koala midway down a white-skinned gum, a baby tight on its back. The beam had been pricked by the spikes of an echidna, snout-to-ground, and had brushed the backs of departing rabbits and roos. Kate had been so excited that she was talking and singing to herself long after Henry had tucked her into bed.

Lorna smiled into the blackness. Around her, moths were touching up the verandah windows with nymphomaniac lust for the light of the two kerosene lamps, one on the table next to Henry, the other hanging on a wire from the ceiling above the couch.

'What are you leering at?' Jennifer asked testily as Lorna

came back through the flywire door. Lorna knew her friend well enough to differentiate nerves from annoyance. She put out her hand.

Jennifer hesitated, then gave her the piece of paper. Henry was looking up from his book as Lorna read it aloud: 'Earthy type, non-materialistic, 38, no raving beauty (red hair), once burnt, wants to write to and perhaps meet a man who is gentle, strong, warm, intelligent. No Leos, please! Sane letters answered. J. D., Roadside Delivery, Overton Valley, via Walrae, Queensland 4057.'

'I really like that, Jen,' Lorna said, her voice serious. 'It's a good mixture of honesty and ... No, it's really good, don't you think so Henry?'

Henry shrugged. Lorna thought she noticed a slight blush on her friend's cheeks; maybe it was just the heat of the night?

Jennifer anticipated. 'And the answer's No, we agreed that it was a game.' Her voice softened. 'You're right, though, it *is* a difficult thing to do. I prefer jigsaws.'

She reached up and deftly removed the sheet of paper from Lorna's hands, rolled it into a tight ball and landed it on the pile of ash in the wide fireplace. Lorna screwed up her face.

Jennifer's voice was now devoid of wistfulness: 'Let's have your list for Walrae. I'm fetching for half the valley tomorrow, the Joneses, Mary and Pete, the Cochranes, Arvi and Sue, the Gills.' It had become a habit that they referred to the relative newcomers, such as themselves, by first names; the families who had always been here wore their surnames like life-membership badges.

Lorna crossed to the stove and took her shopping list from between two cannisters on the shelf above it. She handed it to Jennifer then tiptoed and kissed her on the cheek. Jennifer smiled. She retrieved her torch, patted Henry's shoulder, then stepped out into the murmuring.

The sun woke Jennifer next morning, as usual rousing her

warmly through the uncurtained windows. She guessed it was about seven o'clock, considering the time only because today it was her turn to make the valley's shopping run to Walrae

Her cabin was one large room cut into a slightly less steep slope of the valley than Lorna and Henry's house. It was the first place Henry had built, roundpole stilts holding up its front to the river and the morning sun. The back opened onto the breathy climb to the ridge which capped one side of the valley that ran on and on towards the coast until it lost itself in the Darling Downs.

Her bed was a double mattress on slats of wood, two sheets. She rose from it naked and stretched her arms and shoulders, rotating her head. Collecting a cake of soap from beside the sink, Jennifer stepped out the back door, plucking a towel from a line slung beneath the iron-roofed open verandah. Walking around the cabin, yawning, she ambled the two hundred or so metres down to the Condamine. Where two planks bridged the gap between the bank and the horizontal limb of an overhanging gum she knelt and scooped handcups of clear water over herself. Standing again she travelled the soap over her long limbs, under her arms, between her heavy-thighed legs. Then she dropped feet first into the river, its water dark and tepid, continuing to rub her hands over herself to remove the lather.

The Condamine moved her pliant body downstream to where a rope dangling from a willow's branch provided the grasp to regain the bank.

Jennifer wrung her hair then turbaned it in the towel. The climbing sun began drying her back as she returned slowly to the cabin. She made an attempt on her wet red hair with a comb in front of the mirror. Before pulling on a burgundy T-shirt above her jeans she rifled the chest of drawers and found a bra – for the sharp eyes of Walrae. She wore unlaced sandshoes on her feet, no socks. Dressed, she took from the coolsafe a billycan of milk from Lorna's cow, sniffed it, poured some onto a bowl of muesli.

As did the Vickers, Jennifer ate in a deckchair on the verandah overlooking the Condamine. By now the sun had scoffed the overnight dew and was sending out dry tongues of heat. The day would be Dante hot.

Over the verandah Jennifer inspected her Seven Sisters, sometimes also addressed as The Magnificent Seven. The marijuana was now about one-and-a-half metres high. She had planted ten seedlings this season, mulched them with riverweed. Three had been uprooted on revealing masculinity in their foliage, Jennifer apologising to the widows.

After a cursory cleanup, she went out again, this time going underneath the propped-up front of the cabin where she kept the animals' food and many of her own supplies. Strings of garlic and onions were hooked below the beams; a long line of capsicums hung on a string to dry, like elves' socks. From a bin Jennifer took a tin of wheat and went up past the vegetable garden to the chicken run.

She'd made the run herself, digging away a bit of the slope and using scraps of wire netting, two old doors, several sheets of corrugated iron, bush poles. There was not a right angle in it, but the hens laid well. Henry said the only reason Jennifer rarely lost birds to the foxes was that they were unable to recognise the construction as a henhouse.

Her Saanen goatling Splash bleated greetings, which Jennifer copied, going over and scratching the tight whorls on the animal's dainty head. Splash had another Jennifer Duncan building: two sheets of corrugated iron on a pair of 44-gallon drums. She also had a running tether: a wire from the shelter to a steel spike which was moved every few days.

Jennifer filled the goat's water bucket and fed her some seeding spinach from the vegetable garden. Chores finished, she rubbed her hands on her trousers and moved towards a bulky shape off to the right, casting the first shadow over the day.

Parked away beneath some gums on the slope, it faced

down towards the Condamine and the wide dirt track dictated by its bank. Big stones under the Holden utility's front wheels guaranteed what the handbrake couldn't. If it failed to start, Jennifer told herself, she would have to abandon the trip, or be dependent and call upon Henry to bring down his tractor.

Her plan was to revert from internal combustion to horse and cart, as many of the newer arrivals in Overton had done. But the utility had been part of the divorce settlement she was carefully nursing and it clung heroically to existence.

Reaching Walrae in a horse and cart would take most of a day, but time was one thing the people of Overton Valley, old and new, had enough of.

Walrae lay forty kilometres from Jennifer's cabin. Apart from a kilometre of bitumen on each side of the township, the road was all dirt. The track that penetrated the valley ran off this, the Walrae–Dirranbandi road. After twisting and turning, rising and falling, cooling itself in several creeks, the valley track petered out into the bush along the Condamine past the Vickers' house. Henry and Lorna had not seen more than half a dozen cars go past their place in the seven years they had been there. Anyone who blundered off the Walrae–Dirranbandi road by mistake turned back long before, usually calling at the first house, the Cochranes', to be re-directed.

These rare, brief intrusions acted to unite old and new against 'outside'. If you happened to meet an older valley inhabitant you could pass a good half hour, given decent pauses, discussing a strange car.

Jennifer opened the door of the Holden, seated herself and turned the ignition key. The petrol gauge moved but the engine remained mute. She'd developed the habit of speaking to the utility, but without the warmth she used for her Seven Sisters. She patted the dusty dashboard: 'Come on, let's soldier into Walrae, shall we?' Then she got out, kicked the rocks from under the front tyres, hurried back in. Choke out; column shift in second ... ease off the handbrake.

The utility lumbered forward, slowly at first but soon rushing headlong down the rough slope to the river track. Jennifer bit her top lip, waited, quickly lifted her foot from the clutch. The Holden gasped. It shuddered, farted smoke ... and started.

Jennifer was applying both foot and hand brakes, plus hauling the wheel to the left to bring the utility onto the river track. There she eased the choke in and allowed the engine to compose itself. She patted the dashboard again.

'Over to you, eh? Paperwork's complete.' Typically clipped, Ned thought, smiling up from his chair at the man who had overseen five applications of electricity to one side of his cranium. Had he ever seen Dr Logan in anything other than a blue suit? Even when the good doctor had, as apparently frequently happened in his line of work, been called back into the city from home at weekends? Had he ever spoken more than six words without resorting to a full stop, as though fluency was bubonic? Ned had overheard one of the psych nurses refer to 'Scissors Logan'; he knew the nickname's origin must have been behavioural, not surgical.

Ned liked him: a man who rationed his words had more time for pure thinking. A specialist with some Scots blood and one of his degrees from Edinburgh would err on the side of frugality, understatement, canniness. Given that he was the person who fed current through the thin wall of Ned's skull, conservatism was for once welcome.

'You go forth and gamble, eh? Fixed but fragile. But then crossing the road's a risk.'

Logan's sharp injection of recklessness knocked the stuffing out of Ned's imaginings. The doctor saw that he had stripped the patient's smile like skin at an autopsy, but he and Ned Quinn had been fighting from the same trench for eighteen years, since that first full-frontal assault when Ned had been nineteen. Their ensuing engagement with Ned's schizophrenia was one of strategic retreats, rein-forcement of defences, long truces where ground was neither gained nor given. And, of course, losses. After this amount of shoulder-to-shoulder, euphemism would have been offensive.

'You've kept me enough as it is,' Ned sighed. 'How long, two weeks?'

'Takes time when it's Hippocrates versus Socrates.'

This was the first outright joke Ned could recall coming from Dr Logan, and the latter did seem to have surprised himself.

Ned laughed appreciatively, but also blushed: funny in hindsight, funny in someone else, unremarkable if merely fanciful or ego-tripping ... but he had actually *owned* this consuming delusion. He sometimes put his all into one big madness; most people led lives that were a vast array of small, passable insanities.

'You could have been God,' Dr Logan offered.

'It beats me,' Ned held Logan's eyes, 'how grandeur and persecution seem to be bedfellows in my episodes, in many people's. It would be easier if one or the other got the upper hand.'

They were in the sunroom of the Magdalen Clinic, Ned in an armchair, a novel by Chinua Achebe folded open on his knees. His grey trousers and navy blue shirt had been brought in by his younger brother Carl two days after Ned had been removed from the back of the police van.

'Didn't mean to mock,' Logan said, lowering himself to perch on the arm of a couch. He reached out and gently touched Ned on the shoulder. 'I've great respect. Great. You're managing, ninety-five-per-cent-plus managing.'

The intended compliment made Ned look away.

Dr Logan read aloud the title of the book: *Things Fall Apart*. Apt!'

Ned smiled again. 'Hadn't thought of it, but yes, I s'pose that's what happens: things fall apart; the centre cannot hold. It's a Yeats line, but I don't think he had heads like mine in mind.'

'Yeats? What's the poem?'

'The Second Coming.'

Both men laughed.

'Least,' Dr Logan smiled, 'your grandeur manifests in the philosophical, not the Biblical.'

Ned shook his head. 'Same horse, different jockey. When my cerebral centre will not hold I *do* think I have the right recipe for the world.' Any embarrassment had gone from his face, but his voice was flat.

'Less glum,' Logan persisted. 'You've held pretty fast recent times.' He opened a manila folder, and read over the top of his glasses. He closed it. 'Fourth shut-away in more than eight years? Enviable.'

'Yes, but you're implying, particularly when you say "managing", a role for willpower over chemistry, and you the man of science! We've had this out often enough. When the voices succeed, when I palpably lose my lucidity …'

'Florid psychosis. Socrates and Treatises.'

'Spare me the demented detail.'

'I'm against "demented". Pejorative.'

'What would you prefer: "Software malfunction."?'

'Why, yes, yes I would,' Logan said enthusiastically. 'Long as it doesn't connote reprogramming by experts. We doctors have enough God-problems.'

'I guess "software malfunction" is less gaudy and gross than "florid psychosis". But I'd stick with your clogged filter analogy for the purposes of general consumption if I were you. People can relate it to their kitchen drains.'

'Poor Ned?'

'Sorry,' Ned smiled at the older man, 'too early for a pity trip. But the point is that you of all people wouldn't be the one I'd pick to be putting the gloss of willpower over failure of the reality filter, whatever it is that temporarily stops sorting out the goats in everyday perception. You who have always explained to me that the tripwires are chemical, invisible to me as the beams on those automatic doors. If there's an element of will, why is the solution no better than brains on toast?'

Ned touched the middle of his forehead. 'Ground Control loses touch with Major Tom somewhere, but don't give me any shite about it being re-established because Tom *wants* it to be. What's a man's will against an involuntary chemical process, or lack of, inside his head? You can't replace a blown fuse with hope. That theory's like saying a trapeze artist needs only to *think* that he can't fall?'

'I'll wager it's a factor.'

Ned grinned. It was old ground, and Dr Logan often managed to wind him up. This conversation had almost become a signing-off ritual between the two men: for Logan it had taken on a departure-lounge formality; for Quinn a peace conference that confirmed ceasefire.

As usual, they would not get down from the esoteric to the essential until just before the end, when it was time for Ned to walk out. Then it would be blunt talk about management of Modecate and other Major Ts, as Ned called them; tranquillisers, not astronauts. Talk about sleeping patterns, about side-effects, sinister spinoffs like tardive dyskinesia, which could spasm the strangest muscles, send your tongue on wild exploration around your mouth as though all your teeth had food stuck to them.

Dr Logan cocked his head and raised those ginger eyebrows. 'I want to have a bit each way. You've said that sometimes, early in an onset, you *can* shut off, put the voices on such low volume that they fade right out. Maybe turn stereo to mono, cut one voice out of it?'

'So the chemistry isn't fully imbalanced at that time, surely that's all?' answered Ned. 'Like a ship that lists almost to capsize then, at the critical point, for some reason, rights itself. But at that all-or-nothing stage the captain can scream his lungs out from the bridge, or sit silently preparing to go down; it's beyond his will or influence.'

'Maybe so. Probably. But managing also involves knowing when to take the ship out. When to leave it safe by the dockside.'

'I know the next word you're going to say.'

'Oh?'

'Stress!'

Dr Logan smiled. Nodded.

He might as well have said pudding, Ned thought to himself.

Walrae sits in the middle of nowhere, doing nothing. The only time when there is noticeable activity is when the players from Cunnamulla, a few hundred kilometres away, are in town for the annual competition for the district Shield. Then, after the thocking sounds of cricket on the near-grassless 'oval', Walrae is suddenly liquid shouts of 'yahoooo!' and 'whoooheee!' coming out of Hamilton's Hotel on the corner opposite the station, the alien noise bouncing off the concrete grain silos, quickly dissipating into the silent plain.

The flatlands surrounding Walrae are a darker red than Jennifer Duncan's hair. They dance off to the horizon, begrudging country measured in unfenced square kilometres. Vast tracts of it are required for cloven-footed farming, a small parcel quite useless unless fate has dealt an ace below the baked surface: bauxite, uranium, precious metal.

Apart from Hamilton's and the railway station, Walrae has a garage, a Post Office, a general store, and McConnachies' Farm Supplies, where you can buy cattle dip, Blundstone boots, sunglasses, fencing wire, a tractor, a water tank, car radio, Lifesavers, layers' pellets, flyspray … The town's stock-and-station agent's office opens only on saleyard days.

Nowadays the Walrae general store carries, along with all the tinned and packaged foods, curry powder, rennet, herbs, yeast, dried fruits. Lance, the owner, takes orders and they come up on the train with most other goods. He refers disparagingly to these commodities once unknown in Walrae as his 'city' lines.

Jennifer did not reach Walrae until after eleven am. She had called first on the Jones family, her nearest neighbours after the Vickers. Only Hilda Jones was home, together with the chickens that highstepped in and out of her kitchen. Bert and the two grown sons were often away cutting timber, contract work.

The valley through which the Condamine curls is relatively lush, but Hilda's face often reminded Jennifer of the plain upon which Walrae squats and from which the Overton ranges rise: eroded and overcooked. When Jennifer called Hilda was, as always, in blue overalls.

'I'm makin' stew,' were her opening words, as though this was greeting enough for the first woman Hilda had seen since Lorna Vickers and her little girl had walked over ten days ago with some peaches. Perhaps it was meant to soften the lack of invitation to enter?

Jennifer had learned not to ask questions; it made Hilda screw up her eyes.

'I'll get the list,' Hilda said, disappearing inside. Jennifer sat on the front bumper of her utility, every tic of her body noted by the yellow-eyed kelpie that had announced her.

Hilda reappeared with two enamelled mugs of black tea. She sat on the raised doorstep, the overalls allowing her to splay her legs like a man. The tea was strong and cloyed with sugar, which Jennifer didn't take and Hilda hadn't asked about.

'Be warm enough in Walrae today.'

Jennifer tasted the hot metal of her mug as she nodded agreement. She was just a little bit afraid of the older woman, of the ropey blue veins in her fatless brown forearms, the way words escaped slowly out one side of her mouth when she held a cigarette paper on the other.

Hilda pulled a square of cardboard and a pencil from her bib pocket, handed them over. 'Bag of flour,' she said, and watched as Jennifer wrote. 'Tin of kero, three packets of Capstan ready-rubbed, four 1.5 volt radio batteries, pack of Bushells. And if McConnachies' have got it, some iodine.' She reached back into her overalls and when Jennifer had finished handed her a red purse.

Hilda got up and went back into the darkness of her kitchen again, no details of which Jennifer could make out from where she sat in the bright sunlight. Jennifer took the opportunity to flick her cloyed tea behind her, giving the dog a start.

This time when Hilda returned she carried a large brown paper bag, which she held out. It was full of almonds in their shells.

'Hey, thanks,' said Jennifer. 'I love 'em. But listen, you don't have to give me anything for getting your stuff. You people have been kind enough, especially that scrap iron Bert found me.'

'I'd like to,' answered Hilda, expressionless.

That seemed to be it. Jennifer thanked her for the tea and said she hoped to be back about five.

Her second stop was only a few kilometres further down the river track. Mary and Pete were 'new', they'd been in the valley only eight years. Their house was built just above the flats on an elbow in the river, a two-storey place of heavy vertical timbers infilled with mud bricks. Pete had coated the bricks with a brew one of the Cochranes' sons had passed on: linseed oil mixed with cow dung. As well as waterproofing the bricks, it gave them a patina of age. Pete said new things stood out too starkly against such an old landscape.

When Jennifer called he was away tending his hives in the ironbarks higher up the valley. His honey was popular in Walrae, but it did not always provide enough to support a family of four, frugal though they were. The talk was that Pete had another crop hidden somewhere.

Mary was chopping wood when Jennifer's utility nosed up the rough offshoot of the track. Jennifer noticed how the big young woman's breasts jumped as the axe clunked down. Mary straightened slowly and smiled. As the Holden's engine ceased its struggle and the silence rushed back Jennifer could hear the playful yells of Silas and John, who were taking turns to sail out over the river on a rope, letting go at the top of its arc and dropping, knees-first, into the Condamine.

Both boys called greetings, waved for her to come and watch. They often visited her at her cabin, running messages, or sent there by Mary for help with school correspondence when her own artistic flair or Pete's practicality were insufficient. Jennifer waved to them and called hello, her voice drowned by a trio of sulphur-crested cockatoos jagging through the trees, screeching their indignancies.

Unlike Hilda, Mary was fluent, but Jennifer held up her hand to the offer of tea. 'Maybe on the way back.' If a person wanted to, and had the time to get from place to place, he or she could be offered a good twenty cups of tea in a day in Overton valley.

After collecting Mary's list Jennifer made three other stops: at Arvi and Sue's, at the Gills' and at the Cochranes', the last of whom ran pigs on fifty hectares about a kilometre up from the Walrae–Dirranbandi road.

When at last she shut off the Holden outside the Walrae Post Office, the engine making several last harrumphs after the key was turned, Jennifer remained in the fiery cab while she wrote three lists from all those she had collected, one for McConnachies', one for Lance at the general store, one for the hotel. After delivering each list to be made up, she returned to the Post Office to collect the valley's mail.

The arrangement that the Overton people had with Australia Post was that each Friday the man in the red van who whirled in a flattened tornado of dust down the Dirranbandi road would leave letters in the communal box at the start of the track. If someone was in town earlier they could also collect letters. None of the valley residents wrote or received many.

It was on a Friday, three weeks after Jennifer's trip to Walrae, that Lorna asked Henry to take her down the track to the letterbox. She would normally have taken her horse, with Kate up behind, but she had stopped riding for the baby's sake.

The weather had been dry as shellgrit for those three weeks and Henry was exasperated: the windmill which raised water from the Condamine up to their fenced vegetable garden had sheared a bolt. It lay on strike in the first light breeze for days. He wanted to work on it.

'We've only had one letter in three bloody months, and that was grizzle from your mother.'

'Look, love,' Lorna cajoled, scratching Henry's stubble, 'you're meant to indulge the pregnant whim, right? I'm just itchy about the mail; can't help it.' She had one arm hooked around the back of his neck.

Henry rubbed her belly and laughed. 'I make myself sick the way you manipulate me, billing and cooing.'

'Bullshit, you love me like this,' Lorna whispered in his ear, victorious.

She was silent as the Land-Rover reached and grabbed its way down the track. They saw Jennifer digging in her garden on the hillside as they passed below the cabin, Lorna reaching over and tooting the horn. In the back Kate was bubbling away in her own half-heard language, her dark eyes climbing and descending trees in the hope of furry animals.

Henry put his wife's silence down to discomfort on the lurching track. 'The boy'll be a good swimmer,' he said, nodding to her stomach. She didn't answer.

Lorna got out quickly enough when they reached the end of the track. As she swung up the letterbox lid her head jerked back.

'Jesus!'

Henry had the door open and was half out when she sensed what he was thinking. Billy Cochrane had once found a tiger snake dozing in the empty box. Billy, born with an oxygen-starved brain, had urinated on the snake then run back home, booming laughter into the tall trees all the way.

'It's okay,' Lorna shouted. 'It's okay.'

Henry saw the source of her astonishment, a wad of letters.

'That's amazing,' he said as she returned to the idling Land-Rover.

'Not really,' said Lorna, quietly.

'Who are they for?'

'All the same,' said Lorna, 'eighteen of them.'

'Oh, no,' growled Henry.

Lorna nodded ruefully

'Mummy naughty,' chipped in Kate from the back seat, picking her father's tone.

'Are you going to tell her?' Henry demanded crossly. 'We don't want an army of city tomcats sniffing their way up the valley.'

'Course I'll have to give them to her,' Lorna answered, regaining her composure. 'Anyway, *you* were a city tomcat once, mister! I must say, I didn't think there'd be more than one or two replies.'

'How did you do it?'

'Well, Jennifer actually posted the letter herself,' Lorna grinned, 'even if she didn't know it. I took her advertisement from the fireplace, wrote it out again, sent it off to *Grass Roots*. I just told her that we were renewing our subscription.'

'You lied.'

'Sort of. It's only a joke. 'Course, it's her own business. But another man …'

'Are you giving them to her now, on the way home? I want to watch.'

'No, no.'

Lorna did, however, ask Henry to stop when they were

back below the cabin. Jennifer looked up from her digging. Lorna cupped her hands.

'Tonight? Eggs?' she yelled up the hill.

Jennifer waved and nodded. Above the Land-Rover she watched a reel of king parrots thread colours through the evening sky, their thin chatter underselling lavish plumage.

By the time darkness was easing into the treetops Lorna was noticeably jumpy. Henry, however, was his calm self. He had finally got the windmill going again, its big tin blades now freewheeling in the gentle breeze that always came to the valley at nightfall. About seven pm he had returned to the house and washed. The shower was an outside arrangement, a bucket with holes punched in its base and hung from a pole, big coils of black rubber hose providing free warmed water.

Lorna didn't want to eat. Henry fixed himself and Kate goat cheese, carrots and lettuce to go with Lorna's solid bread. He noticed that Jennifer's letters had been removed from the table, winked at Kate who tried unsuccessfully to return it, making them both laugh.

When they had cleaned up he took Kate to the verandah and told her a story, after which they just sat and listened to the birds making preparations in the trees. Eventually he carried her in to Lorna, who was reading on the couch. Kate kissed her mother twice; on the mouth for herself, on the navel for her brother-to-be. Henry finally piggybacked her into her bedroom, its log walls bright with fingerpaintings.

Jennifer walked up the track in the dark, the night sitting on the hot-skinned land like a salve. It was about 8.30 when she arrived at the house.

'Christ I need some rain,' she announced, placing a billycan of eggs by the sink. 'My vegetables are so limp. I must have coolied a hundred buckets up from the river today. '

'A windmill will last a few lifetimes,' Henry offered.

Jennifer ignored the advice. 'Were you lot calling in on Mary and Pete this afternoon?'

'No, we went to get the mail,' Henry replied, his cheekiness magnified in the lamplight. He caught the red signals in Lorna's black eyes as she mouthed a swearword at him.

'Whatever for?' Jennifer was putting the kettle nearer the middle of the Rayburn. 'You written away for something?'

'Actually, there were some letters for you.' Lorna managed to control her voice as Jennifer crossed to the couch, cocking her head to one side. Lorna began rubbing her large belly.

'Well?'

'Look, Jen, you're going to be furious with me.'

'What's going on here?'

'I was feeling a bit off ...'

Henry butted in. 'Lorna took that ad you wrote out of the fireplace, copied it, sent it off to *Grass Roots.*'

'You rotten little worm!'

Lorna could not read the anger level.

'And you got replies? How many?'

'Eighteen!' blurted Henry, laughing.

'Jesus!'

In the long pause left by Jennifer Lorna had the sense to say nothing, not even an attempt at apology. Her eyes went from the sleeping cat to her friend's feet, as though to transfer part of the blame. Eventually she forced herself to look up. Jennifer was shaking her head, the tip of her tongue resting against her top lip.

'Well,' she finally said, 'we might as well have a look at them, I suppose. I'd forgotten all about that little bit of silliness.'

'Thanks, Jen,' Lorna exhaled, 'we can just chuck 'em on the fire, if you like? I've been feeling terrible.'

'I'll bet you're also squirming to read them, knowing

you. I'll make the tea and we'll divide the pile: nine each. Unless you want to sample some, Henry?'

'Thanks, but ...'

'He's too cynical,' said Lorna enthusiastically.

Two hours later, Henry long having departed for bed, the women had divided the correspondence into three piles: frightening, sad, and interesting, the last being Lorna's choice of word.

When they had finished there were three letters in the first pile, thirteen in the second, only two in the third.

The frightening ones, long-distance boasts and promises of sexual violence, were quickly cremated in the stove, the fear not quite leaving with the flame. There was reassurance in the knowledge that the nearest of these senders was postmarked Sydney.

Jennifer said she would acknowledge the sad letters, as promised. Individually, it was hard not to feel pity for the men who had written them, but, as Lorna said, when you had read three or four in a row ...

'Thirteen men and not one spine,' Jennifer concluded, shuddering involuntarily.

'Poor bastards,' said Lorna softly.

The one she had chosen from her pile as interesting was from a man called Eddy in Brisbane, who described himself as 'out of cities, pollution, paper marriage, motor cars, television, nuclear weapons and the National Party'.

'Out of money, too, I'll bet,' Jennifer had interjected as Lorna read.

She had also disliked the way Eddy from Brisbane signed off. Too smooth. 'Tell me more, tell me more. Maybe we're ships in the night, maybe Anthony and Cleopatra. Who knows?'

'Well,' argued Lorna, 'perhaps a little bit slippery, but he does claim to be as clever with his hands as he is with his mouth, which he'd need to be if he's to visit ...'

Jennifer let this pass.

'I get the feeling that behind that glibness there might be an ageing hippie who's looking for some Earth Mother to suckle his wishy-washiness. T'aint me, babe.'

Lorna smiled. 'You don't have to plough Eddy in so deep. You must admit, though, hasn't this been more fun than jigsaws?'

'The joke's on me, I s'pose.' Jennifer was looking at the night-blackened windows to the verandah. Her voice was soft and serious. "I know you were only clowning when you did this, but it does, well, it opens the wounds a bit. Shows up the ostrich approach to loneliness. In some ways you could put me in there with those thirteen washcloths in the middle pile.'

'Oh no, Jen! You've got guts, and strength and character ...'

'And all the uninterrupted time one needs.'

'Your voice is sarcastic, Jennifer Duncan, but there's still light in your eye.'

Neither of them was quite sure what Lorna meant by this, but Jennifer did not try to deny it. Lorna knew something had cut close to the quick in the other letter, the one Jennifer had sifted from her pile and read quietly before showing it to her.

Lorna stretched both arms high and yawned loudly. 'Bed, sweet bed. Take both letters home. Eddy might look better in daylight.'

After they had emptied ashtrays and carried cups to the sink, Jennifer patted Lorna's stomach. 'Shut down that mischievous mind of yours and get this boy some good rest.'

Then she collected her billycan and headed for the thin trail back to her cabin.

Jennifer had pulled her clothes off roughly and fallen straight into bed. She had felt drained, although it was nothing to do with having toiled so long in her garden. Sleep had taken her easily.

She woke to the sound of Splash's bleating up the hill, barely focusing her eyes before her hand reached around the floor for the letters. For a moment she thought she had dreamt them.

She found the letters, picked up Eddy's, pulled the sheet up over her breasts and re-read it. It was quickly back inside the envelope. She flung it across the room and it flapped against the wall and died, sliding down behind her sewing machine.

Night relaxation, a few joints, Lorna's enthusiasm for the whole silly exercise, all had wilted in the crisp daylight. She could throw the other so-called interesting letter to the wall too, hurry out of bed in answer to Splash's very real demands. The goat was imprinted upon her.

But she didn't throw the letter. She opened it, said aloud, almost as a precaution: 'I wonder if this fellow comes from another planet?'

Dear Jade,
I doubt that's your name, I just fitted the A and E into your JD, and it felt alright, less impersonal than initials. I suspect that on paper you are a Judy or a Jennifer, but that Jade at least fits a facet of you?
I read *Grass Roots* by chance in the day room at a hospital. God knows how it got to be there, in

suburban Melbourne. Or why I noticed your advertisement, furtively tore it out. It sits here on my desk, trans-
planted to my flat. All around me is concrete, asphalt,
mean windows onto more fixedness.

It's a few days since I read your advertisement.
Should have replied straight off … it would have been
more down-to. But tonight I got hooked, reeled in by
the black sky and the stars. That's one bit of fixedness
from my window that I don't mind, although of course
it's all really very mobile. I mean fixed in the sense of
permanence. Sometimes I can fly off into its immensity
and become as hard to find as one particular grain of
sand on a beach. I'm there, but just try to prove it! And
while I'm making my swoops and sweeps (allowing a
grain of sand an id) through the black and brightly
speckled sky, I'm not here in the cold city, propped up
by books, television and my gift – solitude.

There is some camouflaging going on here, JD, as I
imagine you may be guessing. The above flights are of
imagination, those drugless trips that enable us to
swallow less-than-perfect Fate. On occasions, my mind
is taken down roads that lead to brick walls.
Later …

Don't worry, I'm a verbose schoolteacher, not an
occultist. I must have stopped looking through the
window at the night when my neck started hurting.
Funny how a stiff human muscle can make a flight of
fantasy crash back to earth. It was the sound of your
valley earth in Overton that so appealed to me, no
offence intended. I used to teach at a country school in
northern New South Wales. For various reasons I've
lived in Melbourne in recent years, emergency
teaching, and what's called integrating. For other
various reasons, nowadays I introduce kids to shaping
woodwork rather than English, for which I was trained.
More dust, less stress.

I miss the bush. Often I would taste it. Yep, literally. Just pinch up a bit of clean ground if I liked the look of some country, wherever I happened to be standing. Stick it on the tip of the tongue. Amazing variety of flavours!

I feel from your ad that you are involved with the soil, if not an Earth Mother. I sense also that you've been a mother literally, although you don't mention offspring. I hope I – a stranger – am not here scampering lightly over scars?

I don't know why I'm answering you in this gawky, discursive way. I don't even know why your advertisement gave me a twang, but it did, JD. A sense of some loss (mine, not yours). Perhaps it was that 'once burnt' line. I too am a one-time loser. I'm now 37 on the outside, older, but not wiser, within.

Say good day to your good earth for me, JD. I think you'll know whether or not to write back.

If you do, the above c/o address is my younger brother Carl's. He'll pass it on. I'd like to know all there is to say about your surroundings, all you want to say, and no more, about yourself.

Ned Quinn

Jennifer's smile, as she quickly got out of bed, was lit by the sun. She placed the letter on the floor next to the mattress and hurriedly dressed in shorts and her bottle-green T-shirt.

Splash snickered rebuke as Jennifer strode up the hillside. She had grown to expect that each day began with head-scratching and a bit of babytalk. Jennifer, if late, was particularly maternal this morning. Her hammer's blows rang brightly off the rock faces higher up on the ridge as she moved the tether spike several metres down the hill, feeling the hard goat pellets under her feet.

She fed the chooks and renewed their water. Later in the day she might walk down to the Joneses' and ask Hilda if she would like to exchange some eggs for fruit.

Back at the cabin she collected a basket of clothes and a bar of Velvet soap, and walked down to the Condamine, whistling softly. Squatting on the plank jetty she dunked and sudsed underclothes, T-shirts, two printed cotton skirts. She hummed to herself and slapped the clothes hard onto the river's surface for the sake of the thwack they made into the silent morning.

When the washing was spread to dry on the grassy bank Jennifer undressed. Lathered, she made her daily feet-first drop into the black-skinned river. As the current carried her on its downstream arc back to the bank she laughed unexpectedly, the river deflecting the sound into the tall riparian timber.

By the time she reached the cabin again there was already a fine dew of perspiration on her freckled skin.

The billycan of eggs she had taken to the Vickers' last night had been filled with milk in return and she gulped a few creamy mouthfuls. Breakfast was that and a slab of brown bread lubricated with her own blackberry jam. She took it to the verandah, together with a pad and pen.

About an hour later, many balls of paper at her feet, she had finished her reply.

Hello Ned Quinn,

It's Jennifer. I agree, Jade has more style, but I had no choice in the matter. I do have green eyes, though. You should buy a lottery ticket, although intuition isn't something that's always rewarded. I had eighteen answers to that ad, which my friend Lorna Vickers got me to write in fun, then inserted behind my back. It was a joke … at the time.

Yours is the first that I'm answering, mainly because it was the only one I found interesting. Most of the letters were so sad. A few were kinky. You write very well … the words, I mean, not the handwriting.

Lorna and I differed on whether or not you qualified for the interesting pile (there was only one other that did, out of eighteen!). She read you as clever, but 'possibly a mindfucker', which she did not fully explain. Don't know if I agree with her or not, yet. I suppose your intuition appealed to me, seemed almost feminine. That's not meant to be female chauvinistic.

I almost cried up at Lorna's house last night when you guessed that I had been a mother. My daughter died in an accident when she was four. I don't want to discuss that now, and you make it plain enough that there are things you don't want to talk about, or should I say, Sir, about which you do not wish to talk?

I liked the unashamed nature of your letter, although I'm not sure what I'm getting at there. Perhaps that it revealed you are 'open', and yet with a private side?

You asked about my surroundings. I'm bad at detail, but I live in a small wood cabin overlooking the Condamine River, which runs through Overton valley, several whole climates north of you. So you can't drop in for a cup of tea.

The earth here is thick and potent, not like the dry flat plains around the valley, and the trees grow straight and tall. I love this world, especially the Condamine, which accepts my tears, and laughter, equally. Not to mention providing bucketfuls of herself for me and my vegetable garden.

I keep chickens and have a goat called Splash. Most of the people here barter goods, help each other. Occasionally there is friction between the old valley families and the 'news', as they call us, but not often.

What else? I'm not as alone as you might think. Lorna, her husband Henry and their daughter Kate live upriver from me, further along the valley track. I have my own path to their place. Henry once referred to it as my umbilical cord. Like you, he's clever with words.

I visit the Vickers often.

On the strength of your recommendation, I tasted the earth down by the river this morning. It was sort of, ah … earthy! A rather woody taste. I spat it out. Then felt guilty.

I would like you to write again,

Jennifer Duncan

Jennifer looked up to see Lorna entering the back door, Kate in tow. Lorna's eyes danced from pad, to face, to floor, the rejected balls of paper.

'Hand in the till, eh?'

There was no doubt, Jennifer's skin darkened. Lorna laughed. Little Kate joined in. Jennifer couldn't resist them.

'God, Lorna! You make me feel the way my mother did if I'd held a guy's hand, like I'd been raped. It's only a friendly letter.'

'I watched your face last night,' Lorna replied. 'There's something about Mr Quinn, isn't there?'

'I think so, yes. Though God knows what. I have a sort of picture of him, even physically. Which is odd because he says nothing about his appearance. I can see him sitting by a window, black-haired, white teeth … looking out into the night sky.'

'Exciting, isn't it?'

'Oh shut up!'

'Can I read it? Your reply?'

Jennifer handed her the letter. Lorna sank to the mattress where Kate was already lolling, eating an apple.

Jennifer lit the primus stove and put the kettle on its one burner. She stood at the back doorway looking up at the sentinel ridge of grey rock. 'I like that fixedness,' she said aloud.

'What's that?' asked Lorna without interest, her head buried in the letter.

She had soon finished.

'It's a good reply, Jen, straight as an arrow. The two letters have something about them ... they could be between people who have known each other for quite a time. He's a bird of a different feather to Greg Good riddance Duncan, if I may be saying so. I wish you hadn't quoted me, though. It looks a bit ill-considered to be calling someone you've never clapped eyes on a mindfucker. That was me loosemouthing. What if I ever met him?'

'OK, I'll add a PS with your second thoughts.'

'Thanks. How are you going to post it?'

'Oh, probably wait until I need to go into Walrae next, I suppose.' Jennifer spoke as though it was the first time she had given the matter any thought.

'I see,' said Lorna. 'It's odd that he doesn't give an address, uses his brother's, don't you think? S'pose he could be between flats.'

Jennifer sipped her tea in silence, occasionally stroking Kate's black hair, straight, but, unlike her mother's, half way down her back.

'You know what,' said Lorna suddenly, dripping some tea on the floor and wiping it with the toe of her shoe, 'we could take the Land-Rover down to the Cochranes', if you like. Johnny C's going into Walrae tomorrow. Mary told me. Might as well get it in the post?'

'Yes, alright. Do you reckon Johnny Cochrane would mind buying me some shampoo?'

Kate suddenly said 'Goody, goody', and all three of them laughed.

Dear Jennifer Jade Duncan,

Your letter confirmed the picture I saw on reading that bald advertisement. I imagine you as a strong woman, big-boned. Under that mane of red hair you gave away, those green eyes you've confessed to are set in a pale face? Briefly I thought of you as 'alone and palely loitering', as in *La Belle Dame Sans Merci*. 'Her hair was long, her foot was light, and her eyes were wild'. But the poet was talking about a woman by a withered lake and a cold English hillside, not the Condamine and yellow Queensland. Don't know why I've applied this lacquer of sadness.

I sense a woman latently passionate, but within some self-built sanctuary. I'm trying to rein in these thoughts because should we meet I might have a lot of extrication to do, and I'm a shy man.

I have a weakness for tangents. Head men tell you that thought should be sequential, a process of consumption and digestion that carries you from A to B. Well, my train sometimes lurches from A to P to F before reaching B.

When I have reason to I can shut down this neuron reactor. To do so, I've just closed my eyes. What a sight I conjure! A man and a woman, dusty and sweaty. It is a hot day and they have been walking a long, long way. No, they've been working together, turning earth. Suddenly they hug: bodies exchange the clean incense of labour. Recharged, they get back to it. Nothing said. I think now that they had been hoeing, a fine task once you get its rhythm.

It is good to know your warmth, even vicariously. One day we might feel each other's strengths and weaknesses.

Tell me about your river. It's the only way to live in the bush, near water. Without it you don't die of thirst nowadays, but you go a bit crazy. Your eyes need it. Even a stagnant creek or dam. But a flowing river, ahhh! How wide and deep is yours? What does it taste like? What lives in it? Do I hear spotted brown trout? In your next letter please introduce us.

Also tell me of your friend Lorna Vickers. I don't think I'm a mindfucker, or at least only of my own. But I s'pose Hitler would have argued that too.

Shut your green eyes and fill your lungs with early morning air for me. Mine here is flannelled and stale,

love, Ned

She had read the letter standing by the wooden box on the Walrae–Dirranbandi road. Lorna's horse, a big lazy chestnut, was cropping the long grass at the side of the track. Jennifer could have lurched down in the utility, but riding made the journey longer, teased out the threads of expectation.

There'd been four letters in the box. One for Bert Jones, three for herself. She had shuffled them fast, annoyed for so wanting to see the vertical hand of Ned Quinn. Relieved, she had put his letter on the ground, first opening her other two. Both thin cries of loneliness. She would farewell them gently.

She devoured Quinn's letter then re-read it slowly, standing in the dappled afternoon light.

On the ride back up the valley her body swayed to the amble chosen by the indolent horse. Jennifer tried to let the feel of the letter reach her gradually. The pole gums,

their scabrous bark, the negotiating birds, the quietly travelling river, the blood-dark earth … all had colours they
had lacked on the way down, or to which her senses had
been blunted. This Ned Quinn was building a hedge
around himself. The Keats and the cleverness were a
clown's makeup. Shy underneath, as claimed.

Was there really a quieter soul behind the noisy word-
play? Mind you, some of it was very warm; that bit about the
sweaty embrace was more to do with closeness than sex, but
it nevertheless made her scalp prickle. The things she so
enjoyed were also important to him; she was sure he would
love all the bends and reaches of her river. But why was he
teaching woodwork in an inhospitable city? Why did she see
him living in sadness or darkness, more of a pallid loiterer
than herself, when his letters were so vibrant?

She steered the horse in at the Joneses' track. At the
house the yellow-eyed dog barked a lot, but there was no
sign of two-legged life. The horse stood right outside the
open front door, patronising the chain-tugging kelpie with
complete disregard.

Should she dismount and enter the dark kitchen to
leave the letter there? She called out 'Hello?' and 'Hilda?'
but there was no answer, her voice blotted up by the trees
around the clearing. The hens entered and left with
disdain, but she felt reluctant to trespass on Hilda's privacy.
She was about to get down when Bert Jones came around
the side of the house from the direction of the animal
sheds and yards. Immediately she saw that his fly was open.

Bert Jones was grinning metal teeth. He'd be embarrassed when he realised later. At the same time, Jennifer felt
glad to be high on the horse's back.

'I thought no-one was home.'

Bert's mouth and fly leered.

'You after some chickenwire, girl?'

'No, no,' she said nervously, 'been down to the
letterbox.'

'Goin' down there a lot these times.'

Jennifer wondered how he knew. You could not see the valley track from the front of the Joneses' house.

'I stopped by because there's one for you.' She handed the letter down, Bert Jones taking it from her warily.

'How's Hilda?'

'Good.' Bert revealed nothing about Hilda's whereabouts as he tore open the envelope with a curled finger.

'Lost me specs.' He was patting his pockets. 'Here, read it will you, girl?'

Jennifer glanced at the letterhead. 'It's from a solicitor. Do you still want me to read it?'

'Solicitor? What's a solicitor want?'

'Well, it says here he acts for a man called Harris, who bought six heifers from you back in …'

'So?'

'Well, the solicitor, it says here "would appreciate written proof of your ownership of the aforesaid cattle prior to the sale to our client".'

Before Jennifer could continue Bert reached up and snatched the letter with such violence that the horse flinched. Screwed it between his hands like a rooster's neck.

'Up their bums!'

He stomped off around the side of the house without another word.

Left high and speechless in the saddle, Jennifer shrugged and turned the horse's neck.

She passed her cabin and continued to the Vickers'. Lorna came out as she was unsaddling. Nothing was said, but Lorna knew at once that her friend had received a letter from Quinn. Jennifer's face was too shiny for the box to have been empty; there were tricks like an opal's in her eyes.

The horse strolled into his yard, a white rime of sweat templated by the saddle, and the two women walked towards the house, leaving Kate to draw in the dust with her finger, talking softly to herself.

Lorna put on the kettle. 'Nice ride?'

Simultaneously they cracked into laughter

'Yes, you silly woman,' blurted Jennifer. 'Along with two more never-nevers.'

Lorna curled her hands and performed a begging dog. Letter passed over, she moved to the table as fast as her belly would allow. 'Oh do make the tea, girl,' she ordered as she sat. Jennifer thought how different the word sounded in her mouth to the way Bert Jones used it.

Lorna said nothing when she'd finished, but she serious.

'Well?

'I have an inexplicable feeling that I should be careful what I say to you, Jen. Is it because I sense you've reached certain conclusions very quickly about this Mr Quinn, and will resent any doubts I might have?'

'Don't be daft!' Jennifer arrived at the table with two cups. 'I haven't even met the man yet.'

Lorna ignored the yet. 'I'm not sure … He certainly mixes a smooth batter of words, while he's also self-effacing. Intuitive, but …'

'But?'

'There's also a bleakness in there. Maybe he's in jail?'

Jennifer laughed. 'So what are you suggesting that I do? There was no prickliness in her voice. Hearing Lorna's doubtfulness was unpleasant, but it pinned some of her own querulous butterflies. 'Should I stop writing?'

'How much would doing so bother you?' Lorna asked cleverly.

Jennifer knew she knew. Her eyes rested on the treetops outside the verandah. 'At first this letter electrified all the hairs on my neck. Then, after I'd read it a couple of times, I felt so calm … so sure.' Immediately she hoped Lorna would not ask her of what she was sure.

Lorna bit her bottom lip. 'You poor darling.'

Jennifer laughed dismissively, but her cheeks darkened.

'We, or rather you, need a bit more information about this man-to-be, I'd say,' said Lorna. 'I feel responsible. It's great to see you thinking of flying, but I'd hate to see you crash, after what you've already been through.'

'Dear Mother Lorna! I'm thirty-eight years old, and pretty hard-headed. What do you want me to do?'

'Let me show this to Henry.'

Lorna quickly raised her other hand defensively. 'I know, I know … you're a grown woman and all that. But you *are* falling. See? Blushing again. Me, I'm too impetuous. Just for this once I admit it. Henry, well, he's a fine mix of compassion and detachment; he's soft beneath that veneer of hardwood, you know that.'

'It's a bit embarrassing though. Also, he doesn't know what was in the first letters Quinn and I exchanged.'

'Oh yes he does. And don't be looking so shocked. We Irish have got to talk to somebody, and for the life of me I can't get Kate interested in adult romance.'

As though their ears had been burning, Kate and Henry entered the kitchen, the former naked and muddy, Henry in torn shorts, the rolled gold of outdoor work glowing on his chest and long arms.

Kate ran up to the women and proffered the lid of a coffee jar packed flat with glistening mud. 'For your dinner, Jenjen,' she said.

Jennifer accepted it seriously and kissed a fat, dirty cheek. 'I love you too sweetheart.'

Henry prised his boots off. 'Come on chicken Kate,' he called from the door, 'you and your dirty dad are going to get under God's shower.'

Kate went with him. Jennifer and Lorna could hear her say: 'God don't make showers, silly daddy!' And her father's reply: 'Oh yes He do, my girl.'

The four of them ate around the kerosene lamp. Lorna surprised them with an announcement as she carried to the table a big earthenware dish. 'Can I say grace, for once?'

Henry and Jennifer exchanged looks. Grace had never been said in that house.

'I'm easy,' said Henry.

'You're the cook,' said Jennifer.

'What's saygrace?' asked Kate.

No-one answered, but Kate copied the dull 'Amens' Henry and Jennifer offered after Lorna had finished her 'For what we are about to ...'

Lorna plunged into the casserole and into the subject of the second letter while Henry sawed the bread with a craftsman's eye.

'Jen's got another letter from this Quinn fellow, and I, we, would like to know what you think of it.'

Henry chewed all the way to the end of a mouthful. 'It doesn't sound like my business. Or yours.'

'If you love someone then their love letters must be your business.' Lorna had prepared that one while getting dinner.

'I'll happily read it,' said Henry, trapped, 'I just didn't want to poke my nose in?'

Jennifer nodded her assent and handed him the letter. He wiped his buttery fingers on his forearm and angled the paper to the lamp.

'Interesting.'

'What I reckon ...' began Lorna, but Jennifer cut her off.

'I think I'm quite taken with the idea of him,' she said to Henry, her face wide open.

He nodded, chewing.

'He *is* eccentric,' she added, more nervously, 'but a lot of people would say that of the three of us ... stark raving mad even. I'm just a little bit unsure, or rather Lorna is, about whether he goes beyond being, well, different. God knows, if I want a man I want one who is different! Maybe this guy just happens to be something good rising up from bad ashes?'

Henry had not before heard such impassioned talk from his neighbour; he felt both flattered and uneasy.

'It's a bit like being asked to do one of your blessed jigsaws when you know some of the pieces are not in the box,' he said finally. 'But it seems this Quinn has tripped a wire with you. I know how that can feel.' He was looking at Lorna. 'It also seems to me that you two hothearts are trying to put me in the place where your heads ought to be, eh?'

Jennifer grinned and nodded.

'Well, my head wants more of the missing pieces. If my head was writing the reply you're obviously going to send, I'd ask for a photo right off. Send him one of yourself, too. Either of you might get hit by cold water, so why not do it now? Then I'd ask where he's living, about his family, more about why he's switched to teaching woodwork from English, which he obviously knows and loves. I was watching a pair of woodpigeons up near the ridge today, puffing, cooing, bowing and all that formal stuff. You and your Ned Quinn seem to be shortcircuiting courtship. Mightn't be a bad idea at your age! But the eye and the ear and the nose always want a big say, not to mention touch. You're operating outside the senses in a way.'

Henry had finished. Jennifer got up, went round the table and kissed him on the forehead. 'Thank you,' she said quietly.

Kate, who had been dozing on her father's lap, her head nestled into his neck, opened her dark eyes and demanded: 'Tell us about them pigeons again.'

Ned Quinn's new flat was small but lighter than the last, also closer to the school. He'd had another week at home after leaving the clinic – Dr Logan's orders – and had used the time to find a place, move his belongings from his brother's garage, do all the neglected things such as washing and cleaning and putting up shelves for his army of books along two complete walls of his new sitting room. He'd chosen the place for the wallspace.

The flat had a small concrete balcony that protruded from his sitting room. Its view across a driveway was of another, near-identical cream-brick block, one space-saving pencil cypress needling the sky, its base encircled in a ring of concrete. He sat there in a canvas deckchair on this warm Sunday evening, mug of coffee beside him, a manila folder on his knee. On Monday he would start back at the school.

The school had received a letter to the effect that he was suffering from a stress-related skin condition, with an oblique reference to the work environment. A month off, Dr Logan's letter had made clear. The principal had replied to Carl Quinn's address that a junior master would fill in, that Ned shouldn't hurry back, and that they were having the sawdust extractor fan inspected. For Logan, it was most unethical: lying for a patient. But Ned had virtually demanded the subterfuge of him. An act of faith, Logan privately consoled his conscience, with therapeutic value. Stress *was* a factor in Quinn's illness, so the lie was off-white.

Logan had told Ned that his letter was like advice to a ship's captain that there were rust spots on his bow when you knew there was a hole in his hold.

The two of them always ended up talking about stress, much to Quinn's annoyance. Sleep deprivation and emotional trauma were trigger mechanisms, Logan argued. Keep both within reasonable bounds, keep taking the Major Ts, and the onset of full-blown episodes could be relatively infrequent.

Quinn had followed the prescription, notching up long spans without the voices gaining ascendancy. Often it was a close thing; he would withdraw snail-like into his shell. But in Logan's terms he was a half-success story, a rarity.

Logan several times suggested that Quinn return to country teaching, the slower pace of the bush, its quietness and clean air. Ned said that the theory was right, but cities offered the one thing a country town couldn't: anonymity. If he crashed in Melbourne, a city of more than three million people in varying states of sanity, there was room enough for him to pick up the pieces and move to another suburb.

What most annoyed Ned during these talks was that he felt Major Ts were a big enough cross. Why should he also have to avoid life's rapids and steep slopes for the sake of staying 'level'? He refused. As for his sleep pattern, it had a mind of its own. He could influence it by making sure he exerted his body each day, but not much more. Now and then marijuana could float him off in its wobbly arms, but he hated smoking. Surely his life was clandestine enough without stashing little plastic bags?

He had already made concessions. It was Logan who had quietly suggested he switch at the school from English to carpentry, a neglected inheritance from weekends in the back shed with his sawing, nailing, hammering father. Ned had resisted stepping down from *King Lear* to breadboards, but when the woodwork position fell vacant he did ask the principal to let him have it, again with a 'stress' letter from Logan to smooth the way. He continued to be an assistant master in the English department, which meant that he coached small final-year groups with their option subjects.

Another compensation was the poetry he wrote under the name of Ted Gwyn. He and Logan made Jekyll and Hyde jokes about the pseudonym in moments of bad taste. Several of Ned's poems had appeared in small magazines. He did not tell the doctor how much writing poetry can strain a person's seams.

Ned had put some verse in one of his letters to Jennifer Duncan. They had exchanged many since that second one of hers asking him to explain himself more. Barring him treading on one of the snares that he knew lay around her feelings, Jennifer had made it clear that the way was open for him to think about visiting her beloved Overton.

And her.

Dear Ned,

I'll start with the river, the Condamine, as requested. Sometimes I call it Friendomine. When I've finished this I'll walk a few kilometres along its bank to the house of some other friends, Mary and Pete, who will post this today in Walrae, our version of the Big Smoke.

The river does have fish, and they are brownish, but I don't know what they're called. I've eaten them (Mary and Pete's boys offer them in exchange for some help with their schoolwork), and they're good. I'll ask Pete what kind they are and put it on the back of the envelope. I share the fishes' home (when I'm not eating the poor blighters): I drink from it, water my garden with it, wash myself and my clothes in it (no detergents!), watch its movements and listen to it. Some seasons I've seen it rage and roar, which is exciting, but usually it is placid.

I've never tried to explain my feelings for a river before. I suspect that you would have the same sort of friendship for it. The best I can do is to say that I don't like to be away from it for too long. It is more my home than my cabin is. Perhaps that's because it's not subservient to dry rot or white ants or ageing. It has that mobile fixedness thing you spoke of in the night sky. I think.

Of my other friend Lorna Vickers there's not much to say except that I trust her, and there aren't so many that you can. Henry's quieter, more self-contained. What I know of him I like. There doesn't seem much point in describing them further, because I hope you will meet them one day. They and Kate are my family.

Speaking of looks, I'm enclosing a photo Lorna took of me and my goat Splash a few months ago (Splash is the one with the four legs!). I would like one of you. Is that possible? Also, can you fill in some of the ordinary detail of your life? All I can tell from reading between the lines (something *you're* pretty good at!) is that behind your cool there has also been some heat ... I mean of the blowtorch not the fire-side kind. You may not wish to talk to me about this. I'd still like some day-to-day detail.

Do you think about the possibility of visiting us all the way up here? You might argue that I could just as easily travel to Melbourne to see you. But it's *much* nicer here! Besides which, I must be around because Lorna's baby's not far off.

love, Jennifer

Looking back, Ned realised that straight after the arrival of that second letter he could feel a strong pull drawing him to Overton, to this Red Jenny. After a few more letters he'd begun to paint in the landscape, started to summon the sound of various people's voices, to picture what Jennifer's blunt neighbour Hilda Jones looked like. He could see evening light gliding through the tall trees to rest on the tight skin of the Condamine, he could hear the harsh, dry screech of the cockatoos.

Eventually he had sent her the photograph. One where his black hair was long, his beard was bushy and his heavy reading glasses sat well out from his eyes, making it hard to tell whether they were grey or blue. According to Carl's cheeky wife Geraldine, who took the photo while he was flitting through a newspaper, the tortoiseshell frames made his generous Sephardic nose less 'konky'. Geraldine had laughed at his feigned hurt and added: 'But you do at least *look* intelligent.'

The beard was now scissored back almost to burnt stubble, his glossy hair shorter. He'd written on the back of the photograph: 'Hirsute Quinn. Nowadays less hair but konkier', making sure the o couldn't be misread as an i. It was after that letter that Jennifer had started to refer to him only by his surname; he looked more like a Quinn than a Ned, she said.

He had stuck the one of her and her goat to the fridge. In his next few letters he had filled in the spaces in his biographical boxes, as she'd asked. But his own footwork was annoying him, continuing to dance lightly around the real distance that lay between them. Finally, when he found himself hearing the postman in every slight noise from the street, he decided to put a stop to it. He would begin to reverse the magnets so that the fields pushed apart rather than attracted.

What was the point of learning by correspondence if you knew you would never graduate? Now he was in the silly position of wanting to see someone yet having to pretend to himself and to her that he no longer did, of needing to slide off in such a way that the least damage would be done. He had waded into these tricky waters before, had learned the styles of retreat.

His fourth and fifth letters had been pale; nothing clever. He had been warm only in response to the detail of Jennifer's daughter's death in a car accident, which had left her 'deep down the well, fingers barely gripping life's rim'.

He had implied that he'd come through tunnels of his

own and that he'd remained 'hindered from involvements'. After that line had slithered like an asp from his fountain pen Ned had caught his reflection in the kitchen window and muttered to it: 'Euphemistic prick!'

The poem he sent Jennifer with his sixth letter, the first goodbye letter, he called 'Rapids'. He remained unsure whether he had really written it for her – or for himself? Whichever, through its veils of meaning it *had* offered the clear vision of doubt he needed to convey. Predestiny. A way out. What really disturbed him, what stopped him simply writing Jennifer a Dear John, was that hope had bitten him, and would not let go.

Sitting on his high concrete ledge he read a few of the verses aloud to the dusty cypress against the neighbouring flats:

> *If only answers fitted question*
> *Like fingers take to glove*
> *Were all the sun's rays saveable*
> *If only death were love.*
>
> *A wishing verse is not a bridge*
> *Planks of air, not wood*
> *Its feet do not bed into ground*
> *The way foundations should.*
>
> *Could we improvise on the scores*
> *Of fates that call the tune*
> *Or would we, like the river mist,*
> *Be burnt to nought by noon?*

Jennifer must have had wax in her ears, the sun in her eyes. She was dancing some light footwork of her own. Ned smiled as he re-read a passage in her answering letter. 'I have been ticking off the hurdles as you cross them: you're not married, although you had a close shave; you are not in jail; your appetites are no more nor less than mine; like me, there is some sort of defoliant that has worked on branches of you in your past, and you carry those dry twigs silently with you; solitude is a close friend; you have a quirky sense of humour. There is something at work here. And yet … I suppose I'm not picking up your most recent messages on purpose. Please don't worry about 'damage control' Quinn. You don't need to. A simple adios will suffice whenever you wish to send it. But I'm not a weak woman. I want you to know that, and to use it if you decide to. Don't let pity, for self or me, make up your own good mind. There is always a chance that new connections might *burn to nought by noon*. In our case there's a prosaic answer to that one: buy a return ticket.'

After that it had been hard to play winding down games. The heat began to creep back into Ned's letters. He found it more and more difficult to pretend that he hadn't made up his mind to go. None of the hand grenades he'd lobbed in his letters had silenced Jennifer in her hidden cabin. She had even thrown one back in her eighth letter, the one full of pink laughter about the entire population of Walrae pursuing one of Cochranes' sows after it had escaped the saleyards.

The same letter had advised him to double stick his envelopes because she suspected that Bert Jones or somebody else was opening her mail; his letters were looking too thumby by the time they reached her. It was at the base of this letter that she'd asked, as a throwaway PS: 'Why, Quinn, don't you just plainly state the symptoms of your illness?'

He forgot to 'double stick' it, but his next letter went straight through the mist. It was easier for him if he wrote curtly, the way Dr Logan spoke:

Dear Jennifer,
1) I hear voices, as the song says, when there's no-one there.
2) When the illness really bites I get delusions of

danger. Become super-careful. Sometimes look under beds, inside cupboards, behind doors. Over and over. Tend to stay in the 'safety' of one room or place. Like the visiting king, I'm even wary of eating food I haven't cooked myself. While I don't slobber at the mouth or run amok, misconception grips at my entrails. Very draining and real for me. Total mystery for others. Not easy to cope with publicly.

3) Sometimes the delusion can translate into fears for the world. The icing on the cake: I believe that I'm the one with the key to its salvation.

4) Medication usually keeps such slides years apart in my case. A recent 'attack' was my first for three. At other times, when the voices are not overwhelming, I withdraw. Seem to need to be incommunicado.

5) The label for this illness is schizophrenia. It – the label – is one of the toughest symptoms.

6) Cause unknown. Most researchers believe it's chemical. Somehow the brain's filtering system packs up. In my case temporarily. My own doctor likes the view that sufferers may have a structural abnormality in part of the brain called the hippocampus. This small section might be involved in consolidation of memory and processing of sensory information. It may enable the brain to interract with the outside, or reality. Some American researchers have compared cell structure in ordinary hippocampi – where they are aligned in orderly rows like fenceposts – and those of schizophrenia sufferers – where they are in disarray, as though a car had hit the fence.

All of which should make you think hard, Jennifer Jade, about whether you should be corresponding, let alone considering more, with a fellow who probably has bent fenceposts in his hippocampus …

love, Quinn

Jennifer arrived at the Vickers' place about six pm, driving on past her cabin to the turnaround below their house. Her sixth and final stop on her return from Walrae. Carrying the Vickers' bags up the short sharp path through the trees she was tired and ridiculously tearful. She was also happy. It was as though one eye cried sadness, the other elation.

The Walrae postmistress had watched her in a way that fully underwrote her nickname – Molly 'The Ferret' – as Jennifer held her breath and slotted the envelope into the metal mouth of the mailbox. Her last letter to Quinn. It contained a map she had drawn herself, a timetable she'd got from the Walrae stationmaster, and only two words, which she had written on the base of the map: the usual 'love, Jennifer'.

Later, when she cleared the box, Molly 'The Ferret' Davies touched up the envelope, weighed it on her palm, held it to the light. She wasn't the only one interested in the steady flow of letters the Duncan woman had been exchanging with this oddbod in Melbourne. On the back of one of those southbound letters, Molly had informed selected confidants, had been printed 'Rainbow Trout!' What was that supposed to mean to a sane person? Mrs Cochrane had said to Molly she 'spected it was some sort of code. Mrs Gill had told her while passing the time of day that the Duncan woman had got seven letters from this man. 'Eight,' corrected Molly.

Just before she reached the Vickers' house Jennifer pulled herself together, brushed the back of her hand across her face. After Quinn's second letter she had not shown any more to Lorna or Henry. Jennifer had calmly resisted Lorna's inveigling, *she* would make her own decisions. More so she felt that it was unfair to Quinn – a breach of confidence and trust. She and Lorna still talked about him a lot, but Lorna was aware that the information she was now getting had been passed through Jennifer's sieve.

As Jennifer was a few paces from the door little Kate came running out of the house to greet her, charging into her legs and gripping her jeans.

'Guess what?' the small face looked up at her breathlessly.

'What my sweet? Why so speedy?'

'Mummy's having a baby. I think he's a bit hurting.'

'Jesus!' gasped Jennifer, dropping the shopping bags to the ground. At once she saw that she had frightened the child. 'It's alright … it's fine … it's bloody marvellous! You just surprised me, that's all. We thought mummy's baby was still a few weeks off. Quick, take me to see her.'

Jennifer had helped deliver Kate, too. She swept her up, left the shopping where it was, and hurried into the house. Adrenalin flushed away any remaining melancholia.

Lorna was on the high double bed, Henry sitting on the edge of it beside her. Cool as always, but obviously glad to see Jennifer. When Kate was born he had driven into Walrae at the first sign of labour to fetch Josie Hamilton, nurse-turned-publican, from the hotel. Although the round trip had taken three hours, they were back in plenty of time. Josie had co-opted Jennifer – to help and to boss – but clearly Josie's memories of midwifery had been clouded by time and by alcohol. In some ways it had been harder than it would have if Lorna had just produced Kate on her own.

In recent months Lorna, Henry and Jennifer had agreed that this was the way it would be with the second one, without Josie Hamilton if things looked as though they were going well. Kate was asked if she wanted to be present. She did. She had seen a calf being born; this would be better.

It had been … what, nine years? … since Jennifer's own waters had broken. She went to the bed and kissed her friend on the forehead, squeezed her small damp hands. Lorna's contractions had begun about the time Jennifer had been setting off from Walrae. They were increasing steadily now, the intervals less frequent.

'Dry water and clean towels!' said Henry, standing up, military pose, mocking Josie's fumbling instructions last time. 'No, soft water and hot towels! I mean wet water and dry towels!'

They all laughed, Lorna feebly. The three adults had read two books on home births, one by a mother, another by a doctor. They felt confident.

Kate had been briefed enough so that she would not panic at her mother's expressions of pain. Those rolling eyes of the labouring cow she had watched with Henry had frightened her, Kate admitted. The arrangement was that she would go off to her room and play if she found it upsetting.

Jennifer went out to retrieve the shopping. She made a cup of tea for herself and Henry then disappeared out back to shower. She scrubbed her hands and forearms hard, tying her wet hair back tightly so that it would not get in the way. Kate stared and wanted to know why the hair between Jennifer's legs was red, and how a baby 'did fitted in there'

When they were all together again in the big bedroom Lorna had said in one lull in her pain: 'Aren't we all cool and collected then?'

'Well, we're appearing to be,' said Henry, holding up his right hand for them to see the self-induced tremor.

Lorna was nearing the four-finger stage, the cervix dilated to about ten centimetres. The contractions were coming every two minutes, Lorna's self-control stretching with each one. She would let out short, sharp cries, her face screwed up, then smile as the surge passed like a wave breaking then sliding up a smooth shore. Henry was breathing with her, as they'd practised, trying to make her muscles work for rather than against arrival.

The rapid contractions lasted thirty-five minutes, Henry and Jennifer caressing Lorna through them. Jennifer thought to herself that midwifery was like being an air-traffic controller nursing down a pilot. She mustn't think now about her lack of qualification: they'd all discussed the risks and benefits over and over, the clinching fact being that millions of the world's women brought forth children without benefit of medical intervention.

When the baby's head began to appear Lorna was ohhing and groaning and laughing all at once as pain meshed with expectation. She arched her back, pushing down at the same time, trying to watch between her wide-spread legs. Near the doorway Kate hunched her shoulders and covered her eyes.

Henry was glad that Jennifer was doing the cajoling and ordering; he had started to feel weak in the legs and he was sweating. Twice he had to bite his lip to stop himself crying.

It was he, however, who shouted 'hooray!' as the baby slid into the world, accompanied by a long, low moan from its mother.

He was a small boy. Very small.

'I reckon he can only be a four-pounder, Lorna, nothing like Katey.' Tears were now glittering Henry's face, zigzagging into his stubble for cover.

Lorna was still breathing hard, trying to focus through her lightheadedness on her baby, which Jennifer was holding upside down. Lorna had heard through the euphoric haze two tight little cries, she had seen the sparrowy chest move.

Jennifer waited for the umbilical cord to stop pulsing.

She tied it near the baby's belly, cut it with the sterilised scissors Henry passed.

Then she handed the naked baby to Lorna, who was reaching out for the blotchy little thing, more like a winter frog than a human. She held him to her breasts.

No sooner had he touched her skin than everything changed. With the ringing acuity of new motherhood, Lorna knew that something was wrong. She quickly lifted him up from her chest. 'He's not breathing!' She repeated it, this time as a screech.

Jennifer reached for the baby. She had already made the routine inspection of his mouth and had felt clearly the start of respiration through her hands around his slippery chest, her fingers secured in the little cavities of his armpits. Hadn't some redness started infusing his cheeks?

As she roughly pushed one of Lorna's legs aside and put the baby on the bed she saw Henry picking up Kate and carrying her out of the room.

The tiny mouth opened easily and she blew a stream of air down his throat. Waited. Pressed her palms gently on the diaphragm. Blew again. As her head descended she could see blueness tinge the fine, immobile lips.

Lorna was whimpering, her head thrown back on the pillows, her eyes staring at the wall behind her. Jennifer ignored the final heaving contraction as the placenta was expelled.

Henry was back now, wiping Lorna's wet face with a towel.

'Stop, Jennifer,' he said flatly, putting his hand on her shoulder. 'He's not for this world.'

Lorna's hand went to cover her mouth. Great sobs burst from her, punctuated by sharp intakes of breath.

'Let me take him,' Henry said to Jennifer.

'No!' Lorna shouted, struggling to rise up on her elbows, slumping back.

Henry nodded. He placed the dead baby back on its

mother's large breasts, the nipples dark against the taut white skin. The little head she stroked had small paint-brush hairs and was not much bigger than an apple. She kissed the wisdom wrinkles of his forehead over and over.

Jennifer was sitting at the end of the bed, her face in her hands.

'Where's Kate?' Lorna asked suddenly.

'In bed, she's alright,' said Henry. Tears were again eroding his cheeks.

The three of them sat in silence for several minutes. Everything spent. Eventually Henry stood and said again: 'Let me take him.'

This time Lorna did not resist. After kissing the baby on both cheeks she handed him up then rolled over to face the night-black windows as Henry left the room.

At the doorway Henry whispered to his wife's back: 'He was loved for every second of his life. That's ...' His voice broke.

After a pause he said quietly: 'We'll bury him tomorrow.'

'I suppose his little lungs weren't big enough, strong enough ...' Jennifer spoke as she went about cleaning Lorna, sponging and towelling the smooth insides of her legs, sliding out the bloodied sheets and replacing them. Her friend was limp as she hugged her, pulled her to herself, kissed her cheek and neck.

When Lorna was quite clean, tucked up and lying still, she gathered up all the towels and sheets and sponges and carried them out to the kitchen. Henry went back in to Lorna and pulled the door closed behind him. Jennifer sat at the empty table, exhausted, forehead to palms. She looked about the room, but there was no sign of the dead child.

When Henry came back into the kitchen Jennifer had stopped crying. She stood up as he crossed the room, and he put his arms around her, cried into her still-wet hair.

Straightening, he held her by the shoulders. 'You were wonderful, Jen. Wonderful. I think Lorna's in shock. She's just lying there quiet as a wounded dog, very tired. He was so small, wasn't he? Poor little blighter of a son. I think I'll just sit with her and watch her till she falls asleep. Why don't you stay the night? You look a wreck.'

Jennifer smiled wanly. 'Thanks, no. I'd like to go back to the cabin. I'll leave the car here and walk.'

'I'll come and get you in the morning. We'll bury him,' Henry said.

Jennifer walked out into the blackness, a corner of the sky weakly lit by a slice of lemon moon. Where her track dipped down the slope right to the river's edge she stopped and sat down on the curl of bank. She cried and cried, the noise broken by her hiccuppy splutters, subsumed into the cacophony of a million grieving frogs.

Part 2

The banging on her cabin door woke Jennifer. It was, by the angle of the brittle sunlight glaring in at her, midmorning. She had lumbered into sleep only as daylight was scaling the far ridge of the valley. At first the knocking seemed to be within her head, then she heard Henry's voice.

He entered once she'd called hello. 'We're ready to bury him, and you should be there,' was all he said, his voice thin but not wavering.

Jennifer, who stood toga-wrapped in a sheet, was suddenly wide awake.

'Henry, I know how you feel, but we shouldn't bury him. You know that. There has to be a post-mortem. We'll have to take him to Dirranbandi Hospital, there'll be an inquest. We should notify …'

Henry's hand stopped her. 'We know the law, Jennifer. Lorna and I are going to break it, but we'll understand if you can't be part of that. No drama. Our boy is going to be buried today, in the bush, as he is, where we choose. No pathologist's knife or microscope is going to retrieve him, no clerks or coroners or policemen are going to come near him, let alone a funeral director.'

Jennifer saw the resolution in his eye, heard it in his voice. Then it changed, the warmth returned.

'I've made him a little coffin. I was awake watching Lorna all night but I got out to the workshed at first light while she was asleep. Now she's sitting up in the kitchen, determined as hell. I've dug a grave down by the river, and we're planting a tree.' He paused, then added lightly: 'If all this is breaking the law, fuck the law.'

'Give me fifteen minutes.'

He was gone.

Jennifer dressed in turmoil. Her heart agreed with Henry's. Home birth, home death. The thought of Henry driving the bub all the way to Dirranbandi, where he would be put into a fridge until all the right people and papers were assembled ... No, a bush burial was right.

But surely there would be repercussions? Everybody in Overton, in Walrae, knew Lorna was pregnant. The whole valley would get to know what had happened, nothing surer. Word would creep out, the law would stride in.

She wondered whether the tiny child might have to be dug up? But on balance, Henry and Lorna were right, the simple end justified the illegal means.

The chooks and Splash gave her evil eyes for feeding them so late, her mind galloping as she clambered around the steep hillside. There was another issue to be considered: would Josie Hamilton have kept the child alive? Was the crucial defect in the boy, or was it in her amateur midwifery?

The only person who could really answer the question was a coroner.

She ran back to the cabin and tried to arrange herself, fiercely brushing her undisciplined hair, cleaning her teeth, swapping her T-shirt for a badly ironed white blouse, which she tucked into a black skirt. Then she hurried out into the sharp sunlight and onto her track. There was no question of raising her doubts with Henry and Lorna. The baby's death seemed destined to remain a splinter in her conscience.

Lorna was wearing an old checked smock which hid the shape of her body. She was sitting in a cane chair in the shade near the back door when Jennifer arrived. Kate was standing beside her, resting her head on Lorna's shoulder. Jennifer bent down and the three of them circled arms into one silent hug.

'Henry's down there already,' said Lorna. 'I said we'd

wait for you. You'll have to help me a bit.'

There was no point in saying she should not be out of bed. Jennifer had one arm firmly around her waist, Kate clung tightly to her mother's free hand, and the three of them measured their way down a steep side path to the river flats. 'Where Henry wants him is such a nice spot,' said Lorna, panting, 'I want to be buried there myself.'

'Not now, mummy.'

The two women smiled and reassured.

Henry was standing with his back to them, staring at the Condamine. In the middle of the grassy flats, about twenty metres from the river's lip, he had dug a neat, deep hole, cruelly short. His long shovel stuck up from the mound of black excavated earth. At the top of the grave, the river end, a sapling had been planted – an almond Henry had grafted himself, about Kate's height.

Jennifer settled Lorna gingerly on a rug on the grass. She noticed that Henry had found one of his old pale blue business shirts, creased from years folded at the bottom of some drawer. His one gesture to funereal formality, apart from the fact that he had shaved. The shirt looked ludicrous above his baggy khaki work trousers and earth-coated boots.

No-one said anything. Kate sucked her thumb. All of them could hear the river travelling quiet as a thief where the willow leaves drooped into it.

Henry went over to the shade of one of the willows and returned with the coffin in his arms. Although the timber was unplaned gum, Jennifer saw that it had been tightly jointed with wooden pegs, not nails. No handles.

He stood next to the little almond tree facing the three of them, the coffin looking so small and light on his forearms. Jennifer looked down at her friend sitting on the rug, her legs tucked under her and to one side. Lorna's eyes appeared to go straight past Henry, losing their way in the fusion of trees, the dance of the day's heat.

'There's not much that can be said,' Henry began

croakily, his eyes holding Kate's. 'We have got to say goodbye to your brother, to our son.' He tried to smile at Kate, but his mouth just bent. 'We can't understand why he lived for such a short time, but, as I said last night, he died loved, and he died innocent. So his short life was a pure one. When we need to we can come here to this spot to admire that truth.' Without pausing he knelt and placed the box in the grave, his head and shoulders briefly disappearing into it. He stood to attention next to the tree again. 'So, we name you Robert Vickers, and we put you here in this earth. This small tree will grow, and we will know it as Robbie's tree. It will blossom and bear for you. We hope your soul can hear the river's, it yours. Goodbye, Robbie Vickers.'

His face was wet but his voice had held up. Henry looked to Lorna to see if that was enough, if she wanted to add anything.

'Amen,' was all she said, her eyes turning away again to the blurred trees.

Henry began shovelling the dirt into the grave, letting the first few scoops slide slowly off the blade so they would not drum the wood. When he had nearly finished he called Kate over, hugged her, got her to help him with the last of the black soil, to pat it down with her hands. After the convex mound was smoothed he went down to the river and washed his hands, cupped water up over his face and neck. He ripped the pale blue shirt off, not bothering about the buttons, and used it to dry himself. He returned carrying two river-rounded stones and put one at each end of the raw patch of earth.

The others were still standing, Jennifer's arm under Lorna's. Henry picked up Kate in one arm, took the rug in the other and walked ahead of the women up the path. He disappeared fast on his long thin legs; Jennifer and Lorna struggled behind, the younger woman's cheeks blanched.

By the time they reached the house Henry and Kate had

already set out the cups and saucers, plus bread, biscuits, cheeses, stewed fruits. It was only when she saw the table that Jennifer realised that she had not eaten since lunch in Walrae the day before. 'That looks good,' she said, adding to Lorna, 'eat something with us, then bed.'

Lorna agreed. 'I'm knackered alright. I feel numb-headed, drugged.' She sipped slowly at the tea Henry poured. Kate ate quickly then left the table to chase a cockerel away from the open back door. She stayed out in the sunshine.

'I'd like to clear something up, Jennifer,' Henry began as soon as Kate had left, his voice dissonant. 'Let's get it straight from the start that there was nothing wrong with the delivery. It was smoother than Kate's. I re-read the books last night, and we did everything right. It was because he was so premature – foetal failure in utera, they call it. Whatever, there was nothing going to save Robbie. The wizzardry and electronics of an intensive care unit might have, but Lorna and I decided against that, not you. Anyway, the point is, and Lorna and I talked about it this morning, you must not blame yourself in the slightest way. If there are any legal consequences over the burial, then that's our problem too, Lorna's and mine. Agreed?'

Jennifer nodded her thanks for the speech, which sounded so cumbersome after the talk from his heart by the river. She looked to Lorna, but her friend's eyes were glazed.

Over the next few days Jennifer kept pretty much to herself, although she would go up to the house at night to do some cooking and cleaning. She would entertain Kate, bringing her back to the cabin to stay with her for a few nights.

Lorna remained in her room. Jennifer often went in to see her, bring her cups of tea, spongebath her, but Lorna wouldn't say more than a few polite words. Henry said it was best to leave her to recover at her own pace.

The subject of Ned Quinn was never raised.

Ned Quinn stood by the side of the wet road at four am. Occasionally headlights would pick him out of the blackness, eyes squinting, thumb raised, then dump him back into it. This was the time of day when the interstate transports were kings of the road, and they were his best chance.

It had taken a day and a half, allowing some hours spent in a roadside motel, to hitch between Melbourne and Sydney, the northern outskirts of which he now stood astride, his brand new pack at his feet. The pearly drizzle did not bother him; he was glad of it. Although it glossed his hair and beaded his beard, it put pressure on drivers to stop, to take pity. He had remembered this from his university days.

In the fortnight since Jennifer's last, two-word letter he had made several decisions, and had managed to get nearly all the jigsaw pieces into place. Now he was travelling north, travelling light, meandering up to Queensland at a pace that was deliberately not in his control.

School had been the easiest part. The stand-in teacher wanted the work and Quinn was owed long-service leave. His English group was fully fledged and he had smoothed the rough edges from his carpenters; the holidays were only six weeks off anyway. His brother Carl's eldest son, Andrew, needed 'breathing space', and would move into the flat while he was away. Ned had locked his car beneath the flats, its rotor button removed for good measure in case his nephew got ideas. His brother couldn't understand what he was doing, why he wasn't driving north. Neither could he really explain his decision to hitch. 'The golden past,' he told Carl. 'Mid-life crisis.' Carl had learned not to ask too many questions of Ned.

Just as the drizzle was thickening into rain he caught an International Harvester. He'd seen the indicators winking, heard the engine notching down through the cogs, the angry spit from the airbrakes. It was 150 metres past him by the time the driver halted it. Grinning whitely through the tail-lit drizzle, Ned trotted after it, pack hooked over one shoulder.

'Kempsey?'

'That'd be great.' He followed his pack up into the cabin and wrestled his way out of his wet jacket.

The driver was inspecting him in the overhead light. He switched it on again after Ned closed the door.

'Harry.'

'Ned.'

They shook.

Before he switched off the overhead the driver pulled from the floor on the right of his seat a smooth flat bar, about half a metre of steel. Held it up just long enough for Ned to see it branching from his singleted trunk.

'No offence mate.'

'No offence.'

The truck carried a huge container on its tray. Ned sat silent as the driver worked back onto the road and through the gears. He stopped counting at eight. Once Harry had the truck wound up he reached for the Marlboros behind the sunvisor and adjusted the CB radio. There was a cassette player underneath.

'Brisbane?'

'No. Out west from there. I'm heading for a place called Walrae, other side of the Darling Downs.'

'Been through it, I think. Way to Cunnamulla? Nothin' there.'

Quinn just laughed. He was happy: twenty-two wheels devouring a broken white line, windscreen wipers chopping up the high beams. He felt like asking Harry to put on Willie Nelson, Roger Miller. This was Bobby McGee country.

'Workin' up there?'

'Nah, there's a certain woman lives thereabouts.' Ned laughed at himself for saying thereabouts. 'You know how it is when you reckon you're in love?'

'Achin' balls!'

They laughed. Harry slid a cassette into the slot.

Waylon Jennings.

In years past Lorna had been the counsellor, with all the authority that inexperience allows. They had talked about the daughter Jennifer had seen hit by a car outside a kindergarten. Initially Jennifer had been unable to get out more than Lucy's name, the date. Over months, years, Lorna had learned through all the tributaries that run into a deep friendship that the child had been the mortar for the marriage. With Lucy's death it had begun to crumble, until, in Jennifer's words, fissures opened and it crashed about her and her husband like the House of Usher. Grief had to be lived.

One week after the burial of Robbie Vickers, Jennifer and Kate were sitting cross-legged on the floor rejoining the dismembered leg of a rag doll. Lorna was at the big table kneading bread dough.

'Any more letters?'

Jennifer had been waiting for it, but the question still took her unprepared. She looked up and nodded.

Lorna's face showed its first glimmer of animation.

'How many Brownie points has Mr Quinn logged?'

'Plenty,' Jennifer said with feeling, half-hoping that would be the end of it.

'I've been selfish not to have asked,' Lorna said, punching the dough. Jennifer saw that tears were dropping to the table from her bent head as she worked. Yeast and grief.

'No, that's fine.' This was not the right time.

'Well, enlighten me! I don't want the whole valley knowing more about him secondhand than I do first. Or have you been talking about him to Mary and Pete, to Arvi and Sue?'

'No I have not!'

'Out with it then, girl.'

'We seem to have something good on paper. Sight unseen, I'd say we're off to a good start. He's warm and honest, yet not invasively so.' She paused. 'One thing. Quinn's a bit … unstable, at times.' Jennifer was ashamed for the weakness in her voice and in the word.

'Ha! As if we didn't know that. He sounds pretty much like us to me. I thought we had agreed that he was probably just the right kind of unstable for you? Arvie and Sue called in to see me yesterday and he used the same word. Said that, from what he'd heard, you were postally engaged to some, as he put it, weird dude from Melbourne. Said he was wary about anyone coming into the valley who might upset its balance. They'd come up to say how … to be nice about … my Robbie. I pointed out to Arvi that any man who after half a dozen glasses of his home brew invariably climbs the nearest tree and plays the Last Post on his bloody trumpet can't claim to be a pillar of stability.'

In one sense Jennifer was pleased. She had not heard Lorna string two sentences together since Robbie's death. But how did everybody seem to know so much about Quinn … and yet so little?

'Actually, he suffers something like … well, it's called schizophrenia.'

Lorna let the contorted dough drop heavily to the table. Silence. Then fracture.

'Oh, Christ no! Oh, Jen!'

Jennifer squeezed Kate's hand as her mother began to sob again, gesticulating with her floury arms.

'All my fault. I had a feeling. Only wanted to. Linked you up to a putter.' Lorna was spitting out hacked sentences, pummelling the dough with her small fists. She slumped to the bench, unable to continue.

Jennifer's face was flushed with anger and sudden tears of her own. She was torn between wanting to go and shake Lorna violently by the shoulders, and knowing that her friend was awash with hurt. 'Come on, Kate,' she said wearily, standing. 'You and I are going to put Mummy to bed.' The two of them guided Lorna up from the table and, unprotesting, to her room.

Back in the kitchen Jennifer could see where Lorna's tears had hit the table, leaving bomb craters in the flour. Had Kate not been there her own tears could not have been fought. Sensing how tenuous was her grip, Jennifer sent the child off to fetch her father, who was up the slope working in the shadecloth nursery. Henry's make-do income came from grafting and potting trees and seedlings which he carted by trailer to Walrae, from whence they went by rail to the coast. Jennifer told Kate to ask Henry to come down because her mother was … she nearly said unstable. 'Just say she's got the weeps.'

After Kate had trotted off Lorna called Jennifer to her bedroom. She was sitting up, doing her best to speak through surges of feeling that made her face distort.

'We'll have to tell Henry, Jen. Just in case this Dr Jekyll tries to find his way up here.'

'Oh, Lorna!' said Jennifer, all the air sighing out of her and her shoulders dropping. 'I'm going home. Henry's on his way, I've sent Kate to get him. You just try to get better, I'll look after my own life. Please?'

Before Lorna could attempt an answer Jennifer turned and ran from the room. From the house.

Jennifer stayed alone at the cabin over that weekend. She worked hard in the garden by day, sewed late into the night. As Henry with his seedlings – as with nearly all the newer arrivals to the valley – Jennifer had her own cash crop: babies' nightgowns. The material which came up from Sydney on the train she cut to her own patterns and sewed on the treadle machine against the wall opposite her bed. What made her nightgowns so saleable in Sydney was the embroidery she imposed on the warm ecru cotton: brilliant rosellas, open-beaked kookaburras, braces of king parrots, sulphur-cresteds, possums, even spiky echidnas, which took ages.

Lorna teased her about catering for the pampered progeny of urban greenies, but it was a living. Every few weeks she parcelled up a batch and deposited them with Wally, the perfectly named Walrae stationmaster, and they would clatter to the coast, then fly south. Anyone after a good christening present could do worse than look in selected Sydney and Melbourne babyhood boutiques for Jennifer Duncan's 'DOC' label. She had chosen it, with the help of ex-advertiser Henry, partly for the cachet of apparent medical endorsement, more for the secret acronym: Dreams Of Cash.

As Jennifer sewed the wireless offered staticky company. But she didn't really hear much. It made her smile sadly to herself thinking just how much work an upset person can get through in a day.

But by that Sunday evening she was itchy and irritable. The thing had to be dealt with, you couldn't just pull your head in and hope. As darkness began to discolour the boulders high on the ridge she washed and changed and headed up the track to the house.

Henry was sitting on the back verandah, his legs angled high on the rail. She stood with him in silence, staring into the bush as the night blurred, and unseen birds could be heard booking their branches. After a while they began to talk quietly about Lorna, how it was going to take a long time.

'For you too, Henry.'

He didn't respond, but told her what he'd overheard Kate saying firmly to her toys: 'My baby brother's dead!' How he'd made himself watch as she re-enacted the burial with her rag doll.

'As for your Ned Quinn,' Henry changed his voice and turned to face Jennifer, 'well, as you'd gather, Lorna's told me about it. She doesn't make much sense of anything right now, but I have to tell you I don't like the thought of this fellow coming up the valley. It's a risk. Selfish, small-minded me, but I might as well come out with it. That said, you do what you reckon's best, and I'll live with it. Alright?'

Jennifer wanted to hug him.

Inside the house, she conspired with Kate over tuck-ins, songs, phonetic I-Spy, until it became obvious that Jennifer was procrastinating as much as the child.

When she and Henry and Lorna were at last sitting alone around the lamp at the table, Lorna immediately apologised. She'd been overwrought, she knew, and she'd used language she would have flayed anybody else for. 'Nutter in particular. That was really neanderthal, and I'm sorry. It's not the man's fault if he's ill.'

But just as quickly the softness departed. 'Obviously it would be ludicrous for someone who needs regular treatment to come trucking up here. He could throw a turn and …'

Jennifer cut her off: 'You're already back into that dungeon language!'

She tried to stop herself there, but her anger was up. She managed not to refer to whose idea it had been to forge and send the advertisement.

'Well, Quinn's passed all *my* paper tests, and I've asked him to come up to visit me.'

She got up from the table and walked out to the front verandah. After the abrasion of her own voice against Lorna's the night air was soothing, soft sounds of an underwind through the lower branches of the trees, of moths butting glass, the smooth wood of the verandah rail trustworthy in her hands. She could half-hear Henry and Lorna hitting the subject of Quinn back and forth across the table behind her.

It was on one of these winds blousing through the trees that she thought she heard another noise. Like a distant sawing. She pushed her body tight against the rail. There it was again. This time she knew it. She went inside.

'Expecting anybody?' She thought she'd sounded matter-of-fact.

'Course not … this late on a Sunday?' Henry was dismissive.

'Well, there's someone coming up the track. Four-wheel-drive, I'd say. That breeze is wafting its sound off the river.'

'Christ! Henry!' Lorna's shouts shocked them. 'He might be armed. Shall I get Kate out of bed …?'

'Shut up!' Henry snapped. He was standing at the verandah door, an ear bent to the night. The three of them listened.

'You're right,' he said at last. 'Going very slow. It's not Cochranes' truck … not Gills' ute … Maybe it's Arvi's Toyota, or it could be Pete?'

Jennifer grabbed his arm, jerked his attention back to his wife.

Henry saw it, too. Lorna was rigid, frozen like a rabbit at the end of a beam of light. Terror had locked up her face.

'Stay with her,' Henry ordered. 'Slap her if you have to. I'll nip down to the track and have a look.'

Jennifer went and put an arm around Lorna's ungiving shoulders. As Henry departed he made an odd movement to his right at the doorway. He was quick, but both women caught the light on the clean wood of a new axe handle as he seized it, the one he'd been meaning to fit but hadn't got around to. Jennifer felt Lorna shudder.

She went to the verandah to try to see the headlights. The noise of the engine was steady now, but the bush between them and the river was too dense. She looked for

Henry's bobbing torch, but there was only darkness.

'I hope to Christ he's alright,' said Lorna, her voice back under rein. Her body now had broken from the shock: she was able to grab for her cigarettes. Jennifer flinched at the hint of resentment in Lorna's voice.

She laughed. 'Maybe Pete's been down to Sydney, sold a bundle, come back with the new Landcruiser he's been coveting?'

'Pete's been home all week.'

So the two women sat in silence. The engine noise rose louder still. Jennifer thought to herself that the driver must be going very slowly. A local would push harder than that, never mind that it was dark.

The noise ceased abruptly, conceding all to the darkness. In the silence both women noticed the steady dripping coming from the sink. Almost at once came the sound of Henry's boots on the hard ground outside the house. They thumped onto the back verandah, followed by the clunk of the axe handle.

'Police,' he said at the door, using the toe of one boot to help remove the other. He was breathing fast after galloping up the path in the hot darkness. 'Police Land-Rover ... could only see one ... copper in it.'

'Thank God,' said Lorna, the fear falling from her face. 'And there was me seeing you trading axeblows with a madman.' She let out an embarrassed laugh, quickly diverting any outrage that might come from Jennifer. 'What the hell would a cop be coming up here for at this time of night? We haven't seen one since they were after Kevin Gill over ...'

Just as quickly she stopped. As Lorna sat slowly on the couch Jennifer saw the wet light again filling her eyes.

'I'll do the talking,' Henry said quietly, the sound of boots again heard outside, this time moving slowly. Through the back windows they could see the beam feeling its way across the ground like an insect's antenna.

Then he was there at the back door, a silhouette breathing heavily.

'Senior Constable Worthing,' he introduced himself through the flywire.

Henry, his own breathing back to normal, pulled the door open.

'Henry Vickers.' They shook hands. 'My wife Lorna, our neighbour Jennifer Duncan.'

'Helluva long time since I've been up this far,' the policeman said. There were dark loops below the armpits of his blue shirt. 'Thought I'd lost my bloody way.' Uncomfortable.

'Cup of tea?' Jennifer asked, breaking the stalemate.

'Wouldn't say no. Ta very much.'

'Oh yes, I'm sorry,' said Lorna, taking over from Jennifer.

'Look, I'd like to have a private word with you and Mr Vickers. No offence meant Miss ah …'

'Is it about the baby?' Henry stepped in.

The policeman nodded.

'Well, Jennifer can stay. There's nothing to hide from her. She delivered him.' Henry waved the bulky policeman to the table, where he sat and spread. Behind him, Jennifer noticed that his neck was almost the same width as his head and that it was pitted by acne.

Henry sat opposite him. 'How did you come to hear about our baby?'

The policeman seemed to relax as Lorna brought a tray to the table. 'Look, Mr Vickers, I cover from Walrae to Cunnamulla in the west, nearly as much north and south. A copper's information comes all sorts of ways … a word here, a nod in some pub, chat over a fenceline …

'Ahhh,' he said in appreciation, appearing not to notice Lorna's shaking hand as she poured the tea. 'Put it this way, everyone in this valley would know Mrs Vickers was pregnant, right? Folks in Walrae, too. Well, these people know she isn't pregnant any more, but nobody has seen the little nipper. So there's talk …'

Lorna's head was in her hands at the far end of the table.

'I'm sorry Mrs Vickers.'

Senior Constable Worthing did look embarrassed. An avuncular bull, in his mid-fifties.

'The baby died a minute or so after he was born;' Henry said.

'I *am* sorry,' Senior Constable Worthing repeated. 'The reason I came out here at this hour of a Sunday is that I wanted to be a bit … discreet. And I happened to be coming back from a theft at Dirranbandi.'

Jennifer smiled to herself at the thought that anyone could possibly come up their valley discreetly, day or night.

'The delivery went perfectly but he was premature,' Henry continued his flat monologue, 'very little. He lost colour fast, then just gave up breathing. We couldn't revive him.'

'I see.'

'We buried him the next day, in a coffin I made. Put him where we chose to. It was my wife's and my decision, Jennifer had no say.'

Lorna kept her head in her hands.

'You realise you've done the wrong thing?'

'I'm afraid I don't,' Henry replied, but not belligerently. 'Our little boy died naturally. We buried him naturally, in the bush. We'd do it again.'

Lorna had lifted her eyes just above her fingertips. The policeman saw that three faces were waiting on him. He took in a deep breath.

'As I said, Mrs Vickers, Mr Vickers, I've called here informally. Just a chat on my way back from another job. A bush policeman's got to follow his nose a bit, if you take my meaning. I reckon I could come into some of the houses in Overton, turn 'em over good and proper, and I'd find a small amount of the old Bob Hope. But what would be the point of that, eh?'

He paused, began again. 'Now this is different. You've bent some very old laws. What I propose is that I place the matter into my inquiries pending file. No promises, no guarantees, and there'd have to be a formal investigation if I'm ordered. But I've had some matters in that bloody file for, oh, ten or more years. And that's not counting the ones I've clean forgotten.'

He realised that he had gone on too long.

After another pause in which none of the other three spoke he said, rising: 'So, for now I'll be gettin' back down that twisted track.'

Henry got up and they walked to the door. The policeman held up his hand and stopped him from accompanying him outside. 'No, you get back to the missus.'

'Everything, all at once …' Lorna said plaintively when Henry had returned and put his arms around her.

'You're like a frayed rope,' he said. 'Its going to take time. A long time.'

'I wonder who told him?' Lorna turned away. 'It's only been a week. This valley's got a bloody long nose.'

'It's a creepy feeling, that,' said Jennifer. 'I thought the same thing the last time I was down at the mailbox. I had the strong sense that there was someone watching me. Of course there wasn't.'

Jennifer was in her bed just before eleven pm. None of them had allowed the conversation to go beyond smalltalk after the policeman had left.

She tried to read a book, but couldn't. As she had done so often recently, she dipped into Quinn's pile of letters.

It was like plunging into the Condamine. There was a particular quotation he had used which she had copied out in large calligraphy and stuck on top of the oval mirror above her bed. Its presence also disguised the fact that lately she'd been looking into the mirror more than had been her custom.

Quinn had borrowed the words from Lucio in *Measure for Measure:* 'Our doubts are traitors, and make us lose the good we oft might win by fearing to attempt.'

As she felt sleep feathering down upon her Jennifer thought that if Lorna ever had another baby boy she might suggest Lucio as a good name.

Three days, four trucks and one train later, Quinn arrived at Walrae. He had been told by a driver who was continuing up the coast to Townsville that he would be better getting the train inland; there was so little traffic on some stretches that he might stand there for a week with his thumb poking up at the sun, his brain melting.

He had not been at all nervous. The survival level of hitching, the obligatory explanations and then chitchat, had precluded any contemplation of what lay ahead. Perhaps that was why he had not driven? But now, after the two-carriage train had slouched out from the coast and waddled through the heat-rippled country, he'd had plenty of time to get rattled, to question.

Standing alone on the Walrae platform at midday, offloaded boxes and machinery all about him, he felt awkward and conspicuous. Although the train had stopped for two hours at Dirranbandi and he had showered and changed at the caravan park, he felt crumpled, his senses clogged by days of roadside greasefood, diesel fumes, grey-water coffee, that hypnotic white line which ran like a perforation all the way to the horizon. Wailing Waylon, Slim, Willie, Dolly, Chet … they'd become torture. He longed to feel and hear Jennifer's quiet Condamine.

Some of the drivers' maps hadn't even shown Walrae. One referred to the Condamine as a 'creek', along with the Mungallala, the Balonne, Widgeegoara, Moonie, Maranoa, Bunjil … varicose veins on a huge body of land.

The sun was hot on Ned's bare legs, it was making small snakes in the waves of his hair. He looked up to see an older man, also in shorts, loading boxes onto a hand trolley. Fate and a regional transfer from Dirranbandi had blessed Walrae with a stationmaster called Wal Hunt.

After he had shunted the perishables into the shade of the stone station building, Wally Hunt turned his attention to the cooking stranger. Here was something to talk about at Hamilton's, which was where Wal would soon be heading for his fluids.

'G'day.'

'G'day.'

Wal couldn't really leave it at that. They'd be asking questions at the pub … tall two or three of them.

'Y'cn get rooms at Hamilton's if yr after one.'

'Thanks, but I'm heading out Overton way. Which road's that?'

'Thataway, the Dirranbandi road. Helluva long walk but. Whose property?'

'Jennifer Duncan.'

Wally straightened. 'I'm half expectin' her in today. Look, these've come just now. Her sewin' stuff from Sydney.' He pointed to a well-taped parcel.

'I could carry it out.'

'What, you walkin'? Take you the rest of the day, if not more.'

'No desperate hurry.'

'Well,' said Wal, disconcerted, 'I can't just release people's parcels to strangers.'

'Sure,' said Ned. 'Rules are rules.'

Wally appreciated this.

'Couple those Overton families got th'phone. Cochranes. Gills. Y'cd ring from the Post Office, ask 'em to gwup Jennifer's with a message. Zisaid, she might be comin' forer parcel anyway. She'd be expectin'ya?'

'She'll be right, I'll walk. Thanks for your help.'

Wal leant on his trolley and rolled a smoke. He watched as Ned jumped off the platform and eased his arms into the straps of his pack. He watched as the stranger went into McConnachies', came out several minutes later wearing a floppy cricket hat, sharp white against his black beard, and carrying a brown paper bag. He kept watching as the figure got smaller and smaller on the Walrae–Dirranbandi road, the hat becoming a white dot against the spreading red.

The unfenced land on either side of Ned was flat as an oven tray, cooking on it prickly pear, sawgrass clumps, some contorted sheoaks not much taller than the anthills. He could see his destination in the milky distance where the extended plain buckled into a ridge that looked like a welt from a whip, with purple bruising.

For more than ten kilometres he walked solidly, only his dustpadded footfalls touching the vast silence. He did not seem to have made a big dent in the distance, although the purple of the ridge was turning bluegreen. Behind him Walrae was nowhere again, doing nothing. When the straps of the pack began to bite and a blister spoke to him from one of his new elastic-sided size elevens, he stopped at a stand of lean gums. After removing his boots he glugged down half the large bottle of lemonade from McConnachies'. The round cheese rolls bought early that morning in Dirranbandi looked like flaccid breasts in the mid-afternoon heat.

He would snooze for a while. Looking at Jennifer's map he calculated that he could reach the turnoff before dark. He might find a spot to camp by the Condamine, then walk up the long valley track to Jennifer's cabin tomorrow morning. Unannounced as he was, it would be better not to suddenly appear towards bedtime.

Sitting up with his back against his pack, he fell uneasily asleep under the thin sheet of shade. In time his eyeballs began to move behind his closed lids as he dreamed. In his dream he pictured his long legs stretched out of all proportion as though in a child's drawing. They ran like thin pipe right across the Walrae–Dirranbandi road, the knees bumping up right in the middle. He dreamed he tried to pull them back, tuck them under his chin. But they did not respond, and wouldn't have fitted there anyway. Just lay skinny and inert, limbs fallen from a ghost gum.

A smile fluttered on his face: they'll shrink back in time. No harm done. No traffic on this road.

Then his sleeping face frowned. He could hear a buzzing, a humming. An engine approaching. A motorbike. At once he envisaged its front tyre right at the point of impact with his brittle, stretched knees. The driver catapulting over and over through the hot air in slow motion. The sudden silence before the screams began, before the dust even began its lazy downward float. Now he tried desperately to retract his legs, the whine of the engine growing louder and louder.

Quinn woke with a lurch, knocking over the lemonade bottle. The fat brown blowfly that had been motoring around his sleeping face in decreasing circles jagged off into the sunlight. His legs were bent up under his chin. 'Stupid bastards!' he said to them.

Rearranged and about to set off again, Ned saw what appeared to be a puff of smoke rising in front of the ridge. Cupping his hands around his eyes he watched it billow, realised that it was moving too quickly to be fire. A funnel of dust. After a long wait he began to hear the sound of the engine. Real this time.

On impulse, with the plume of dust advancing, Quinn quickly gathered his pack, his boots and socks, and stepped behind two lean gums. They barely concealed him.

He flung his hat on the ground.

Within a minute the badly tuned Holden ute was beside him, then past, pulling a stretched corkscrew of dust behind it. He had not seen the driver.

As soon as the car had gone it occurred to him how ridiculous he must look, hiding behind trees in the middle of nowhere, boots in hand, lemonade bottle between his bare white feet. Why had he done it? Must have been unsettled by that dream. 'Welcome to Walrae,' he said to the silence that had returned about him. 'A motorbike over your knees and a mouthful of dust.'

He resumed his journey. It was after four pm, and the sun was beginning to ease off.

Jennifer called out 'Wally?', 'Mr Hunt?' No sign of the stationmaster. She pushed open the office door. Up at Hamilton's, she thought to herself as her eyes travelled the racks where the inward goods were stacked. Wal was known for letting 'lunch' shunt away whole afternoons.

She needed the material and threads badly, had sent a priority-paid letter ordering them. There was nothing in the racks, damn it. She'd have to go and see Wal at the pub.

Then she found the parcel, on the floor near the platform door. At the desk she wrote on a pad: 'Wal, have collected it. Thanks, Jennifer D.'

At Lance's general store she bought a few groceries. She had not told the Vickers or anyone else in the valley that she was going to town, an anti-social gesture which would be frowned upon.

She was tempted to cross to the Post Office to see if there was a letter from Quinn. But, being Monday, the odds were a hundred-to-one against. And she did not want to have to deal with Molly 'The Ferret', whom she could see peering at her across the road as she stood in the shade of the verandah outside Lance's store.

As she left the town's token sealed road and hit the dust again Jennifer sang, loudly in concert with the engine. The song was the same one that Wal Hunt could usually be heard mouthing as he wandered crookedly back to the station from Hamilton's in the dying light of day:

Show me the way to go home
I'm weary and I want to go to bed.

I had a little drink about an hour ago,
and it's gone right to my head.

Over and over she sang it. It helped to gobble up the bald, boring countryside. Under the layer of dust the corrugated road kept time through the tyres.

Quinn was sitting on the ground just in from the turnoff, his back against the redgum post that supported the Overton letterbox. Inspecting another blister on the heel of his right foot. The light had mellowed from molten to amber, filtered by the tree canopy. The grass around him was cropped and there was horse dung dropped among it.

He had been struck by the sudden change of geography as the valley opened dull green ahead, rising to grey battlements that serrated above the beeline on both ridges. Climbing one of the trees he had seen the silver line of the Condamine curling away to the left. Soon he would be in it, rubbing away this talcum of dust. Should have bought a cake of soap at McConnachies'.

Gingerly pulling on the troublesome boot, he heard the car. He had not seen it because the trees at the start of the valley block off the road like a bad memory.

Quinn had time only to stand. He was running his fingers through his hair when Jennifer wheeled left onto the start of the track, slapping the column shift into second gear.

She gasped at the sight of the dishevelled man, adrenalin plunging to her stomach. The panic was a much stronger surge of that same rush a few weeks back when she had felt that someone was watching her as she stood at the box reading one of Quinn's letters.

Instinctively she had stabbed her foot on the brakes. The car had almost come to a stall. Now she reefed it into first and jerked up the clutch. She had passed the man and was looking straight ahead, accelerating forward to safety.

A shout scalpelled into her terror.

'Jennifer Jade!'

She braked again. This time the Holden did stall.

In the rear-vision mirror Jennifer saw a man in blue shorts, green T-shirt, big boots. He was clumping to the car, favouring one leg. Then he was standing beside her, grinning in the window with his large white teeth.

Nothing came from her mouth. She was nodding her head, more in understanding than assent.

'Well,' he said quietly, 'aren't you going to get out and shake hands with Ned Quinn?'

And they did. Jennifer, weak in the legs, managed to open the door, grip his big hand firmly. 'Jennifer Duncan,' she said.

He was staring straight into her eyes. No wavering. Then he put a hand on each of her shoulders. 'It's me. I'm here. Dirty, but happy to see you.'

He stepped back. There had been no weight in his hands.

Jennifer realised she was standing there like Noddy.

'I can't think of all the right things to say,' she managed. 'I got a fright. You didn't say …' She paused. 'Welcome!'

'I'm sorry,' Quinn said looking down at his dust-and-hair legs. 'I'd planned to wash in your river, camp the night among the trees, walk up to see you in the morning. I should have written, but your gesture with the timetable was so … strong … that I just said "yes, and I will surprise her, too".'

'You sure did!'

They laughed awkwardly.

Jennifer was only half hearing what he said. His voice was soft, a slight husk. Despite his finding words quicker than she was able to, she could tell he was nervous, which was good. His nose was big. Aristocratic big. What with his black hair and beard cut to a point, he could have been a Sicilian noble.

'I must have passed you driving into Walrae,' she said. 'Tend to drive in a dream.'

He was handsome in a crooked sort of way. And he didn't know it.

'I had a sleep by the side of the road. That may have been it.'

'Well,' she said, realising she was on home ground. 'Shall we go up to my place?'

'Yes please. Soap and Condamine.'

'And, as everybody says up here, a nice cuppa tea.'

She got into the ute while Quinn walked back to his pack by the letterbox. Restarted it and reversed slowly. Without the engine noise she suspected her heartbeat would be audible.

Quinn swung his pack into the back and got in beside her, moving the parcel with her materials so it was between them on the seat.

'That road from Walrae, it seems like you're going to hell. Then you come across this … this growth.'

'No-one in the valley will believe you walked all that way,' she laughed.

His eyes were only for the country, the trees. Which was good.

Where the track first bent down to a broad bend in the river she stopped and turned off the noise. Jennifer held out her left hand. She was feeling quite lightheaded, but slowly recovering from the shock of the new. 'Mr Quinn,' she announced formally, 'meet the Condamine River.'

She stayed in the car while he got out and took a few paces, stood with his back to her. The river was flowing like spilled mercury in the evening light, the trees motionless above it, the earth of its banks dark with moisture.

Quinn stood there a long time. He knew Jennifer would not hurry him. When he turned back to the utility his face was radiant above the dirt that darkened his skin. Then he bent down to the ground, poked up some earth on his index finger, stuck out his tongue and tasted it.

The gesture made all his letters swirl back to Jennifer. Her cheeks coloured, but he didn't notice. Quinn was clowning, nodding like a wine buff in approval of a bouquet. He winked at her as he got back in.

'Listen,' he said, suddenly serious, 'this is your territory, not mine. Anytime at all you can say, "So long, then; it's been nice meeting you, Quinn." Right now if you like.'

He put out his right hand; they shook on it.

'What I do want you to do,' she said as they drove on, 'is not come into the cabin until I've had a chance to, um, organise it a bit. I'll give you a towel and you can get to know the river.'

He grinned at her embarrassment, read the insistence.

At the cabin she backed the ute up the hill, one hand on the wheel, the other holding open the door and her upper body leaning out to look over her shoulder. She blew air from her mouth a few times to push away interfering tresses of red hair.

'Back in a minute,' she said after getting out and chocking the front wheels.

He watched as she ran off towards the small cabin cut snug into the slope. Her bottom was large. Full moons. He liked the way she ran with a long, straight stride, that hair flowing behind her.

On her return Jennifer handed over the towel and yellow soap silently. He thanked her and began off down the hill.

Walking back to the cabin she called down to him: 'You can jump or dive from the little jetty, it's deep there.'

He waved back, just before his body burst through the tensioned skin of the river, sending the water spiders and wrigglers dancing away from the explosion.

Crashing dishes into the sink, Jennifer thought she heard singing. She wiped away crumbs, gathered underwear, picked up papers and stray strands of tobacco, made the bed. She stopped briefly to fill the kettle and put it on the primus.

Finally, flushed with emotion and concentrated house-work, she stood on the verandah and looked down to the river in the trembling light. Quinn was only a shape, but she could see that he was kneeling, washing clothes. She cupped her hands to her mouth and bellowed:

'Okay!'

He acknowledged the all-clear and she went back in. Not long afterwards he knocked at her door.

'Who is it?'

They were both grinning as he stepped inside. Jennifer saw at once that there was nothing of the Sicilian in Quinn. The Condamine had left his skin pale Anglo, emphasised by the darkness of his hair, wavy and wet but now brushed back into obedience apart from the curls at his neck. He had on a grey checked shirt and jeans, nothing on his white feet, which were enormous. He caught Jennifer looking at them. 'Like witchetty grubs, aren't they?' he said of his toes as he wriggled them. 'But at least they're clean now.'

She also saw that he was reading her cabin like a palm, and quickly turned away to make the tea.

'You must be hungry?'

'You're right,' he said absentmindedly, preoccupied with books, etchings, a sock protruding from a cushion on the couch, a note stuck above the mirror.

Jennifer took crackers from a cannister and pasted some with peanut butter, some with Lorna's soft white pepper cheese. She placed them and a few stalks of the snappy celery from her garden on a plate and handed it to Quinn. She asked him how he took his tea and then carried two mugs out to the verandah.

While he wolfed the snack Jennifer rolled a joint above a book on her knees. He saw that her hands had short nails and slightly flattened ends to the fingers. Again she'd send puffs of air from the sides of her mouth to swing away a stray curl of hair.

Jennifer knew that he was watching her, that his eyes were travelling the way hers had. She was glad that he looked away as she lit the cigarette; nerves had made it lumpy and poorly stuck. After a few draughts she offered it, but he shook his head and pointed to his crunching mouth.

'Tell me about the trip up, Quinn. When did you leave?'
There, she had managed to refer to him by name.

Between mouthfuls he recounted his journey north:
slow trucks, fast food, music from the American west, poli-
tics from the Australian right. He estimated that the 1300
kilometres that separated their homes in a line on a map
were more like 2000 by wheel and foot.

The last light was flattering to their faces, smoothing out
age. Or so Jennifer thought, the cannabis helping.

Quinn noticed that she wanted to know his every word
and movement in Walrae. What had Wally told him? What
he'd bought at McConnachies'? He told her, then reached
into his trousers and showed her the small Bushy-brand
pocket knife he'd taken a boy's fancy to.

At first he thought the smalltalk was to cover her unease,
but there were frown lines above Jennifer's nose.

'I'll bet Wally and The Ferret have been breaking the
news, foaming into the phone.'

She saw the puzzled look on Quinn's face.

'Sorry. Thinking aloud,' she apologised, smiling. 'Look,
Lorna Vickers is expecting me about now. I need to talk to
her, and to take her up some eggs. Might be better if …'

'Sure. You go up on your own. My legs are on strike
anyway.'

'Make yourself at home. I'll be an hour or so.' Jennifer
showed him the foodsafe, the tea and coffee, said she
would happily cook a proper meal when she got back.

'You can meet Henry and Lorna tomorrow.'

'Got to break the news, eh?'

She nodded, embarrassed.

Lorna was standing on the verandah when Jennifer came
whistling off her path, the billycan of eggs swinging freely in
her right hand.

The voice cut straight through her mood.

'Jen! Thank God you're okay. I've been so worried.

Henry was about to drive down the track to look for you. I'd told him that if you weren't about he should round up George Cochrane, Kevin Gill, Pete, Arvi ...'

Jennifer's laughter was cold. 'I'm fine. I'm fine.'

'We came down to you early afternoon. You were gone. So was the ute.'

'I raced into Walrae in a hurry,' Jennifer said guiltily. 'Had to collect my parcel from the train. I would've come up earlier but ...'

'He's here!' Lorna blurted.

They were standing in the kitchen. Henry was sitting at the table, watching.

'Somewhere out there this very minute.'

Henry noticed that Jennifer's voice was hard and flat.

'We're talking about Ned Quinn, I presume?'

Lorna galloped: 'He arrived on today's train. Asked Wal Hunt where you lived. The Ferret rang Cochranes' place and Mrs C. sent Clive up to us on his motorbike. He hasn't called at Cochranes or Gills, they haven't sighted him. Mary and Pete ...'

'Lorna! Lorna! Calm yourself!' Jennifer had to shout to stop her.

Henry looked uncomfortable. 'Jennifer's right, there's no value in panic, Lorna. Look, Jennifer, The Ferret told the Cochranes this fellow looked a bit of a fright, and ...'

'Really?' Jennifer made Henry sit straighter. 'What else did dear Molly pass on?'

Lorna couldn't restrain herself. 'You'd better stay the night here with us, Jen. I'd never forgive myself. I know, it's all my fault. Nobody in the valley will be sleeping tonight.'

'This is getting totally out of hand!' Jennifer's voice was now raised to Lorna's heights. 'Ned Quinn is an ordinary bloke who suffers from an illness. For God's sake, he's not a criminal. He doesn't go round chopping people's effing heads off, although I'm starting to think of a few ... How could you two? Of all people?'

Lorna's voice was now quieter.

'Did you know that he was arriving at Walrae station today?'

'Well, I …'

'Did you?'

'No I didn't. But I *had* invited him up. I told you that.'

'I see. So he just arrives. No warning, no letter?' Lorna paused. 'Did you also know, Jennifer, that he purchased a knife at McConnachies' within minutes of getting off that train?'

'Oh, Christ!' Jennifer moaned. 'It's a bloody weeny little pocket knife about this long. You couldn't skin a mouse with it.'

Silence hit the room.

'You mean …?' Lorna managed at last.

'Yes, I do. The lunatic, dangerous, demented Quinn is right now sitting on my verandah. He's had a wash, so he's not quite as gruesome as The Ferret painted him. In fact, I'd go so far as to say he's … attractive. Before I came up here we had a cup of tea and a nice chat. I had a joint, he had some crackers with your pepper cheese. And do you know what, Lorna? You'll find this hard to believe, but he hasn't frothed at the mouth once. Not once!'

She rushed for the door, getting there just as the sobbing burst from her throat.

'Jennifer! Come back and talk,' Henry called.

The blackness and her flooded eyes soon made Jennifer ease to a walk. She stopped and cried quietly, angry with herself for screaming and shouting at her friends. At the river she sat for a while with the unseen frogs.

She thought of Quinn ahead of her. What would she tell him? Would she lie? How would she explain her eyes? Or that she would not be introducing him to the Vickers tomorrow?

A bigger question: one that had hit her like a charge of electricity the minute he'd sat beside her in the ute. Where would he sleep? Would he try to climb in with her tonight?

Oh, God no. Thinking about sex had been fine by remote control. It had even been fun to indulge in the paper innuendoes and gentle flirtings, a hotness that sometimes crept between her legs. But she was nowhere near ready for him, might never be at this rate. Tonight she could as easily make love to an ayatollah.

'Bugger and shit!' she yelled across the water, silencing only a few of the nearest frogs. She stood and dusted herself off, straightened her hair. Stomped on down the track towards another unpleasant scene.

For the first time in four and a half years her little home was not her castle.

Outside her door she stood still and listened. There was no sound. She patted the puffed skin under each of her eyes and entered.

Her gaze fell through the soft kerosene light to her bed. It was empty. Quinn was on the couch, under but not inside his sleeping bag, the bottom hanging over the end. He was too long for the old sofa.

Jennifer tiptoed past him. In the lamplight she could see his lips slightly parted to show the ends of his teeth. His breathing was slow.

She almost touched his forehead, wanted to show how grateful she felt.

Quietly Jennifer undressed and pulled on an outsized T-shirt as a nightie. She left on her underpants, smiling at this strange, rather exciting obligation to cover herself.

Crossing to the table by the window to blow the lamp she saw a note under its base:

> Dear Jennifer, Dog-tired, and relaxed. Your river,
> your goat (we introduced ourselves), your trees
> … all are beautiful. You, too. 'Til morning,
>   love, Quinn

When the sun woke Jennifer, the butterfly had flown: Quinn's sleeping bag was an empty cocoon.

She remembered that on her own first heady morning here she too had risen early to explore, climbing a tree, scaling the bouldered ridge, swimming downstream in the dark river then walking back through the clean timber along its bank. 'That's where he'll be; the Condamine probably has captured more of him than I have.' Stupid statement! 'Whatever we might be beginning must never descend to entrapment. We will travel too lightly across the ground for that.'

On her back with her hands behind her head, Jennifer realised she was composing phrases – just as she'd done in all those letters. But now it was real life. Off the paper, off the wall. She looked at Quinn's few exposed belongings: the green sleeping bag, its cover, a plastic-handled hairbrush on the shelf above the couch, the fat unpacked rucksack. More intrusive was the new scent to the room, the exhalations a sleeping man's body had brought into her cabin, commingled with her own. A one-night odour. She breathed it up like a vixen snifflng the ground where a dog fox has walked.

If he's going to stay a while, you'll have to become tidier, girl. Have to find some space for his clothes, for him not to feel like a couch-guest. In the utility he'd mentioned accumulated leave from his school. How much? Don't think he said. Maybe if we get along, continue to get along …

'Maybe: another banned word,' Jennifer announced aloud, swinging her legs from the bed and getting up. The elastic of her knickers had left a pink line across the flesh of her belly. She dropped them, pulled them over her thumb and fired them across the room. They landed on the dishes beside the sink. She hurried across the bed to remove them, suddenly embarrassed; Quinn could walk in any moment.

She dressed quickly, rolling her khaki shorts down to reduce her legs. No bra, Quinn or no Quinn, but Jennifer put on a white shirt she had embroidered herself, the dark colours of two rosellas in flight sheltering her nipples. Brushing her hair she gathered handfuls to pin atop her head, sitting there like fresh croissants. Or turds, she thought, coming back to earth.

Doing her teeth at the sink she admitted that they were not as white as his. Went back to the mirror and bared them. He was only one year younger, but could have claimed thirty-three or thirty-four. Must have noticed that she'd stuck to the mirror Lucio's admonishment on doubt?

Jennifer conceded to herself that she was excited; also unsure which feelings to deflect, which to receive. It was all quite an assault upon the routine with which she had become surrounded. Her cabin was her castle; her keep was the knowledge that the foundations of her solitude could stand any test. And yet …

For the moment there was a stand-off between these cautious and impulsive forces in her mind. Having fed the animals Jennifer ambled down to the river with her hands in her pockets, looking back up to the ridge and around her as she went. No sign of Quinn.

As she stood on the plank jetty, she spotted him. About a hundred metres upstream at the bend. Crawling on the spot – something she did frequently herself. His long arms stroked with exactly the strength necessary to keep him stationary in the current. Had he lined up a tree on the bank to mark his place? The flow was not swift on the inner edge of the bend but she could see that he was a swimmer, not a thrasher. Better than her. Mind you, he had those huge feet to help propel him.

Quinn now and then stopped and let himself slide ten metres or so, forcing him to exert himself to regain his spot, slipping his arms into the river as though putting on a coat back-to-front. Funny sort of a man, she thought to herself.

He'd seen her.

'Morning.' The voice came softly downriver. He was standing now, only a few metres in from the far bank but the water up to his elbows.

'Come in!'

Momentarily it struck her that he looked like Groucho Marx would have with a full beard and without the glasses. No. He was a lot bigger, stood too straight. She realised she was, as usual, hauling off her clothes. Even though he was a fair way off, she hastened her undressing. The embroidered rosellas flew over her shoulder, quickly followed by the shorts, the black cotton knickers, all landing near Quinn's jeans.

From upriver Quinn watched Jennifer plunge feet first. He saw her unpinned red hair lose its buns and fly upward as she fell. The white outline of her breasts? Then just a leonine head slowly coming towards him as she sidestroked steadily against the current, her arms and legs not damaging the surface.

She stopped near the bank opposite him, duckdiving shallowly to allow the river to pull her hair back. Quinn briefly saw the whites of her bottom just below the water. Then she stood there where the current was stronger, leaning into it, watching him.

Quinn dived and came up swimming strongly. She could see that he was aiming for a point upstream of her, allowing for the current. When he stopped he was breathing hard, about three metres upstream. He leant back, dug his heels into the silty riverbed.

'Morning to you,' she said.

'Sorry I didn't wait up last night,' he smiled, shaking his head hard and making water fly from it like a wet dog. Jennifer could just see the flat coins of his nipples and the sparse black hair where his breastbones met. She was glad to be in deeper water.

'I was so tired. Didn't hear you return. You seemed preoccupied when you left. Alright now?'

She nodded. 'Thanks for your note. I'm going to miss your letters, you know. That couch is much too short.'

Why had she mentioned the bloody couch? He might think that she was disappointed he hadn't jumped into her bed. God she was clumsy! Her naked largeness in front of him had unsettled her. Never mind that it was cloaked by the water. For all she knew *he* might be wearing his underpants, bathers even? Only a few hours ago she had been careful enough to wear a T-shirt and knickers to bed. Now she'd flung off her clothes as she would normally do, without thinking. Up a creek without a stitch.

Quinn saw that she was rattled. 'Don't worry about the couch,' he said. 'I was just too tired last night. I've got a tent in my pack. So many places to put it ... down here, up on the ridge, over in those trees?'

They stood apart in the crooning water. A rush of real rosellas embroidered the omniblue sky above them, chattering of breakfast as they went.

'I don't want that.'

Jennifer had again spoken before grasping what she was saying. The rashness showed in her cheeks.

Quinn lifted his feet from the mud and let the river ease him towards her. He had not intended to come so close but when he anchored himself again they were only inches apart. He raised a strand of wet hair from her right cheek. Then she felt his arms rest on her shoulders and the river pressed parts of them together.

Jennifer let her body relax, shielded now against the

current by his own. She felt Quinn's hands glide slowly down her back and cup under the cheeks of her bottom, lifting her so that only the tips of her toes were in the mud. He tilted her towards him so that their combined angled weight held them still in the moving river.

Afterwards she remembered the instant sense of relief to feel that he was naked.

Quinn felt her nipples against his chest and drew his hands up her sides, stroking the outer curve of each breast flattened against him.

Jennifer's own arms wrapped around the middle of his back. His erection indented into the fullness of her belly, moved against her navel.

He was kissing the curve of her neck. She angled her head to make it easier for him, to stretch the skin there so she would feel the travel of his mouth.

'I hadn't imagined this, Quinn,' she said quietly.

Jennifer straightened her head and leant her torso back, looking up into his face, increasing the bar of pressure against her belly. Unclasping one of her hands from his back she ran it through the wet rat-tails of his hair.

She was about to try to speak again when Quinn leant forward and gently kissed her top lip. Jennifer thought she felt the tip of his tongue. She replied. No gulps of suction and breath. Their kiss was long and quiet like the river itself. Surface and depth.

Neither one was sure who stopped that first kiss. Gracefully Jennifer pulled back from him, slipped from his hands like a slick fish. Reaching into the Condamine she flicked a handful of it into his face.

Quinn gave better than he got, shovelling the heel of his hand at the surface, sending arcs of water leaping at her.

Out of range Jennifer put down her feet again. Now he could see more of her breasts, the dark skin of the aureoles. Her face was serious, the laughter splashed and gone.

'I'm not a tease, Quinn. I want to make love to you; my

body does right now. It's nothing to do with it being too soon, or because I'm unsure. I haven't been so aroused … It's just … Look, I want my head to be empty of everything else when we make love the first time. Everything. And it wasn't. Isn't. Nearly but not quite. I don't think I'm making any sense, am I?'

He was grinning. 'Don't look so worried Jennifer Jade. I'm not going to explode. I'm glad you *do* want me, that we want each other. I hadn't planned to try to touch you. Well, it just sort of …'

'Happened!' She finished it for him, relieved that he had not misunderstood her. 'This bloody river is to blame,' she said in mock petulance.

'Speaking of appetites, I'm famished.'

'Coming up!' she said, turning her back on him and swimming as fast as she could downstream, the current helping her to show off.

He stood and watched, feeling the soft mud between his toes as he dug them in, the softening of his penis as the pressure of blood began to subside.

He did not follow at once but waited some way off as she pulled herself out with the rope, hurried dripping to the scattered clothes, climbed quickly into her shorts. She didn't put on her white shirt but kept her back to the river as she began walking up to the cabin.

Quinn let himself float down towards the jetty. He could see Jennifer's shorts taking the shape of her bottom as they blotted up the water from her skin. A bum he had just been holding. Jesus! She had quite a broad back, her spine set deep into it. He liked the shotgun blast of freckles across its whiteness.

Once she had walked round the side of the cabin Quinn stopped watching, allowed the current and a few kicks to carry him to the rope.

He sat spreadlegged on the bank to dry, the warm hands of the sun firm as Jennifer's had been. The heat from above and from memory made his penis stir again on his inner thigh. He slapped the outside of his leg hard a couple of times, as though to convince himself that this was happening, that he really was so far from cool Melbourne, from the smell of turned and shaven wood, the cave of his modern, third-storey flat. He smiled at the river. 'Queensland's Best-Kept Secret', he said out loud to nobody. It was the title of a song his nephew Andrew sang. Quinn wasn't really sure whether he was applying it to the valley or to Jennifer Duncan.

Writing those letters at night, all those kilometres south, he had not remotely imagined a beginning like that. The contact, those few flowing strides he'd taken in the river. He'd never found it possible to move smoothly towards any woman. How had it been? As far as he could remember, he'd just thought to flick away that strand of wet hair – and then their bodies had met, supercharged under the black blanket of water. He had briefly seen in her eyes that she'd been as much surprised as he had, by the ease of it.

Quinn slapped his leg again and hooted with laughter. It had really happened!

Jennifer was frying eggs when he returned to the cabin, led by the nose for the last twenty metres. Quinn was still dwelling on the sexual river. In places, where it foamed headily under an overhang or in a slow spot, it made him think of Guinness. He had eaten little food on the final leg of his journey.

When he entered Jennifer was sliding one egg after another down the slope of a spatula onto thick brown bats of toast. Coffee was blurping against the glass cone of a dented percolator, fighting the hot eggoil for nasal supremacy. In his letters he had not written of the eternal newness of smells.

She was silent and did not look at him as she went about the finishing touches, grinding a hail of black pepper onto the perfect whites of the eggs – two each – pouring some milk from the billycan into a jug and putting it on a tray.

Their eyes did not meet until she was ready, everything arranged on the verandah table where they would eat. Quinn had quickly swapped his jeans for shorts while Jennifer completed the breakfast. Now he coughed and pointed to the remnant of a red handprint on his outer leg. 'Know what this is?' he asked her. Her face was flushed when at last she looked at him.

She shook her head.

'I had to whack myself to be sure that I wasn't dreaming.'

'Look! Me, too,' she laughed. 'See? I pinched my arm really hard.'

She hooked her right hand up behind his neck. As Quinn's face bent down she kissed him on the lips, let go just as quickly.

'Hurry,' she said, pushing the tray at his midriff. 'You might as well know I can't stand hot breakfasts getting cold.'

As he followed her, and despite the reaffirming kiss, Quinn could tell that this was to be what businessmen and politicians call a 'working meal'.

Neither of them spoke for a while, their knees nearly touching. Quinn was trying to discipline his mouth so that he didn't wolf the blazing orange of the eggs. Finally, when he was manhandling a crust around his plate to lubricate it with spilt yolk, he tried to make it easier for her.

'You had a hard time up at your friends' house last night?'

She nodded, her mouth full.

'That's the iceberg you were referring to when we were … in the water?'

Jennifer put her empty plate on the wood decking of the verandah, gulped on her coffee.

'Word seems to have spread of your arrival, Quinn.

You've lived in the country, you know how sharp its eyes and ears are. Perhaps, in my excitement over your letters, I've been less than discreet. At times I did have the feeling that some of my mail might have been tampered with. I even thought once or twice down at the letterbox that I was being watched. At the time I ignored it as me being stupid, paranoid.'

'How much do you think people know?' He didn't look to be at all concerned.

'Can't tell. After your last letter, after I'd posted you the timetable, I did tell Lorna about the ...'

'Schizophrenia.' He'd stepped smartly into Jennifer's hesitation. 'I've found I need to use euphemisms in some circumstances – something looser like "recurrent perceptual disorder". Sounds more like bad eyesight than full-on loopy.'

'I should have tried it with Lorna,' Jennifer laughed hollowly. 'Took it really badly. And her such a warm, intelligent woman. Since she lost her baby she's been lurching from down in the deep blues to wound up high like piano wire. Poor Henry.'

'I'm a dangerous madman then, am I?'

'Well, at the moment, in her state of mind ...'

'Don't worry Jennifer, I've been called crazy by experts. Stop frowning, my hide's grown thick so that most of the bullets ricochet. And you shouldn't worry about your friend too much. Fear is a strong emotion; even you fear the unknown in me a little.'

'I don't!'

He smiled.

'The thing is, it's not just Lorna.'

Quinn knew nearly all the Walrae and valley names from her letters, both the old and new communities, some of their traits and idiosyncrasies, their small-town tensions. Now Jennifer was rattling off most of the list, spitting the name of the postmistress with particular venom. 'I really don't think Lorna would have broken my confidence,' she said at the end. 'She'd barely have had time to, anyway. But by last night the terrible telegraph seemed to have carried the news to everyone that some dangerous case was about, even that he'd bought a knife at McConnachies ...'

Quinn laughed. 'I s'pose,' he said thoughtfully, 'anyone reading a few of our letters could have found a heavy load for a small mind. The last one, the one I doubted you'd respond to, that would be a real hand grenade. Should we start digging trenches?'

'It's not funny, Quinn. It leaves me feeling very cold ... and ashamed.'

'You don't need to be. But let's be practical for a moment, a bad word is very difficult to turn around in the country. I've found that out before now, the hard way. Farm mud sticks. As I've said, it's largely why I live in a city, against all my instincts. In hindsight, coming here the way I did, on elated impulse, by thumb and by train, was stupid. I should have given you good notice of my arrival, driven my own car.'

He stood at the rail and stared down to the Condamine, his back to her. 'Perhaps the best thing is that I should stay this week. Pitch my tent somewhere, like I said. I can splash about in the river, walk around the place. Then go. We could leave it at that: a surprise visit from an odd pen-pal. No harm done. Your friends and acquaintances soon relieved.'

'Are you asking me or telling me?' Jennifer said quietly.

He turned to face her. 'Asking. Perhaps suggesting?'

'Well, to answer you,' she held his eyes, 'I reckon when you go from here, how long you stay, is a matter for Ned Quinn and Jennifer Duncan. Nobody else. Don't you?'

'I do. We'll see what happens.'

He sat down again.

'I think you should empty your mind some more.'

Jennifer raised her eyebrows then bent her head to the

joint she had been rolling on and off for several minutes. A tremor was disconcerting her left hand.

'What I'm saying,' he helped her again, 'is it's probably time you asked me more about my illness. You've been out there bravely defending me to the world, admirably from my point of view, but in my letters I've given you largely the neuronal kiteflying of the whitecoats. What I suspect must, for God's sake, be nagging inside that fine red head of yours is: "When will he go funny? What will I do? How does he behave? What are the signs?"'

'Quinn!' she laughed. 'You're becoming an invasion of privacy.'

Now she looked away into the trees climbing the slope behind his head. It would be good to be walking alone, thinking. She admired his percipience but also felt an urge to whisper to him that he need say nothing more. She'd cope. This mixed with a tenderness that made her want to throw her arms around him, repay those kisses to his neck.

'To kickstart you,' he said, reaching into his pocket and withdrawing a cylindrical plastic container, 'these are my main buddies. I take a daily quartet. The biggest one, here, is Modecate, which is a Major Tom, sorry, major tranquilliser. My doctor, the fellow on whose doormat I sometimes end up, refers to these as my ship's keel. Like lead, they're also dangerous. Expensive friends. One of the ironies of my type of schizophrenia is that the florid episodes frequently arise because the sufferer stops believing that he or she is ill; stops medication; gets ill. Vicious circle indeed.'

'Alright then, Quinn, here goes.' Jennifer exhaled a deep breath of laced smoke. 'You've explained that your psychotic episodes have been well-spaced, that you also seem to have this need to withdraw at times, and that you take all these pills. But can you tell me what it feels like to you? Not how an episode appears to the outside world, which sees you as off-the-planet, but how *you* experience it?'

He was impressed. She was trying to see it from inside his head rather than how it may or may not impinge on her almost self-sufficient life. 'That's the perfect first question, Jennifer Jade,' he said. The emotion in his voice, the fact that he was again referring to her as he did in his letters, made her swallow.

'It's difficult to describe the fire you're standing in,' he continued, his voice back to the businesslike tone with which he had explained his tablets. 'At the time all you think about is trying to escape it. All fires die out, but then you're left with trying to describe the tree from its ashes.'

He stood and leant on the rail again, this time his back to it and the river. 'I suppose it starts as a build-up of tension. You've seen me fairly relaxed, and most of the time I am. Like everybody else, I have bouts of anxiety, but for me, without medical governors the anxiety can cross the normal limits marked by anger, a row, some other form of natural release. With me the volcano implodes, the lava doesn't escape. Consequently my perceptions and judgments begin to suffer.'

Jennifer was watching him closely. He crossed his arms over his chest and avoided her eyes, instead looking down towards the Condamine.

'What can happen then is that just as my own views are starting to warp and ripple like plyboard left out in the rain … *other* views impose, usually bloody stupid ones. There are always two voices, occasionally more. Gradually their intensity can grow until, apparently, I become incapable of shutting them out. They have a foot in the doorway of my mind. Can be male or female, only rarely recognisable as belonging to anyone I've known. Usually they are opposed. I give them names sometimes – most often labels like "Other One", "Other Two", even "V1", "V2".'

'You poor bugger.' Jennifer by now was relaxed enough from the sprinkling of Seven Sisters to speak straight from her heart.

'I hope that stuff's not stopping you understanding what I'm saying?'

She giggled. 'That's the first time you've showed me the schoolmaster in you. Yes Sir! I'm listening. Truly, Mr Quinn.'

'It gets pretty embarrassing in hindsight. At the time the concentration on the voices is so intense, such a difficult debate, that what's going on around me becomes slight. The outcome, as I wrote, is that reality blurs; frequently I begin to believe that someone's out to get me, that there's a threat to me. Often my mind deludes itself – and here I'm only recounting what those who have to cope with me tell me afterwards – to the extent that I believe I'm some important historical figure. This last time, which was my first derailment for years, I managed to convince myself that I was Socrates.'

'And how do you get back to being schoolteacher Quinn?'

'If I'm in that psychotic state, with delusions of grandeur and/or persecution, usually Logan, my doctor, gives me ECT, electro-convulsive therapy. Shock treatment. Which frightens some people almost as much as the word "schizo-phrenia". They refer to it as "dial-a-voltage", campaign against it in the letters-pages of newspapers. A view which probably gets its currency from *One Flew Over the Cuckoo's Nest* as much as schizophrenia does from *Dr Jekyll and Mr Hyde*. All I know is that for me, whether it re-aligns the fenceposts in my hippocampus or snaps awake my synapses, it works.'

'Do you wake with the sense that your body and mind have been jangling?'

'No. What Logan does is put electricity into one side of the head, the right side in my case. He allows for hair and scalp thickness. The idea is to apply just enough power to induce seizure, no more, no less. The thrashing about that you see in the films doesn't happen. Logan's let me watch him administer it to someone else. There are muscle-relaxant drugs to prevent rigidity and prolonged spasm. I *do* tend to wake up feeling as though I've been poleaxed, but that's the general anaesthetic. For me the main perceivable side-effect is that it causes occasional potholes in my memory, mainly autobiographical glitches.'

He turned back to face her. 'So there we are. I don't think I've ever told anyone this much in one sitting. After the ECT I return to my medication. That needs to be tuned like a radio, adjusted now and then. And I resume normal transmission: Ned Quinn woodwork and erstwhile English teacher. Unfortunately not Socrates.'

'Do you want to stop now,' was all she said. 'Go for a walk?'

He shook his head. 'I guess because of our letters, I'm not finding this as hard as I thought I would. Also because I like talking to you. Your thoughts may be roller-coasting behind that silly cigarette, but it's good to be getting all this out at the start, stripping the wallpaper.'

'I hope you won't expect me to be so honest,' Jennifer laughed. 'Shall I put some more coffee on?'

Quinn felt a sudden urge to touch her, but he didn't.

'Please.'

When she came back outside Jennifer had a frown.

'Do you mind me smoking? I don't during the day as a rule, but …'

'Nup,' he laughed. 'I've tried marijuana many times in an effort to zonk the voices, with little success. When I'm okay, tight control over my head is the last thing I want to relinquish.'

'Not very romantic.'

'I said my head, Jennifer Jade. Anyway, as long as you don't smoke in bed …'

She went back in to look after the coffee.

When Jennifer returned Quinn didn't wait for her questions.

'Sometimes my state seems to peak quite early, and you'd describe me as not much more than edgy, silent, suspicious. I'll perhaps avoid open spaces, trams and trains even. I'll feel compelled to have my back and flanks covered, like some geriatric general still fighting a war. Under siege. Mind you, I'm not belligerent like a general. It seems to be more defensive. I head for the kennel the way a dog does when there's a roll of thunder. At these times I might not end up in a state of florid psychosis, be hospitalised, with or without consent, but I do withdraw into a sort of fortress of concentration, I am very fearful. I suppose if I could see myself I'd think I was pathetic.'

'It seems so unfair, all of it,' Jennifer said. 'That chemistry, or whatever it, is can exact such a price. I'm glad you've told me all this because I'm as ignorant as the next person. I don't feel frightened, but one can see how in days gone by words like "possessed" and "exorcism" and "demon" were used.'

'Ha! Still are. Neuro-chemistry, psychiatry … they pale before superstition … Quinn held up the palms of both hands to her. 'Yes, let's stop for now, or I'll end up thumping this rail like a pulpit.'

'I can tell you there are some *real* pulpit people around here,' Jennifer said, 'and, getting back to where we began, I suspect their ideas about you and your illness belong back in the Salem days. I don't just mean the old families either.'

Quinn offered her his hand. 'Come on, I'd like that walk you mentioned. Take me somewhere special.'

'My pleasure!'

He carried the egg-streaked plates and empty mugs inside while Jennifer got her boots. They had talked well into the day and the cabin was hot and confined, the food smells now lank.

Quinn was wearing the now-off-white hat he'd got in Walrae, Jennifer her broad-brimmed straw; the sun was sharp as broken glass. Splash stood mute in the shade of her shelter as they passed, too lethargic to bleat. In their misshapen yard the chooks fluffed up their feathers and bathed in dry pools they'd fussed into the dust.

As they reached the vegetable garden Quinn stopped. 'I had a look around here this morning,' he said waving at the silverbeet, potatoes, sweet corn soldiering up the incline, the lower plants in each bed benefiting from run-off and thus stronger. 'I'd like to get stuck into it, dig some contours, make it bigger. The fencing …'

He stopped when he saw Jennifer's smile.

'Sorry. I'm being presumptuous. I'm sure it's just how you want it.'

'No it ain't!' She teased the boyish embarrassment from his face. Her vegetable garden could absorb years of sweat. 'And you don't need to worry about being presumptuous or bossing me; you'll hear when you are. It would be good to have some company to work with. I'd probably drive you bonkers because I talk to the plants, to myself. I do need some help to start more fruit trees. I can get them from Henry Vickers, but they need protection here. Possums are the worst. The tree guards I make … well, you've seen the chookhouse.'

They didn't talk as they continued to climb, the slope getting steeper, the cover sparse. After a few hundred metres, patches of bald ground or dandruff shale made the going harder.

'This explains my calf muscles,' Jennifer puffed. 'I spend almost as much time up on the ridge as I do at the river.' They stopped again and gazed down on the merged foliage of the trees below. The Condamine looked cut up from here, like a freshly killed blacksnake. Quinn was not breathing hard. He must be fit, Jennifer thought, stronger than he looks. In more ways than one.

As they approached the ridge the athletic trees that strode the riverbank had wizened to shrunken arthritic scrub, grey and elbowy. Rock occasionally shouldered through the lean soil in large blisters. The grasses that spiked the ground were swordy and fibrous. Immediately above, the ridge's battlements seemed set to topple forward on them in an avalanche of weight.

They reached level ground and turned left onto a path dictated by a cleft in the rock. Jennifer led the way as rubble sometimes made hiccups in their progress. The architecture of the ridge provided welcome shade in places, flash-bulbs of raw sun in others.

Neither of them spoke, the path taking them silently through squares, rectangles and domes of granite so deeply cut that the land falling away on either side was rarely seen. Even the sky was blocked out where the thin path cut under overhanging stone tables, or when it tucked into the base of a house-sized boulder.

Knowing the way so well, Jennifer also managed to keep an eye on Quinn's face. He was awed.

From the cabin the ridgework had looked quite needled, the dentistry of time, sun and rain grinding it to resemble the edge of an old breadknife. But up close it was vast, the erosion and movement had been much blunter than the profile from below indicated. Jennifer was leading him over fallen debris through a small canyon. The narrow path was buttressed by flat-sided monoliths that would suddenly give way in a great slumping to reveal a dangerous gap of green or blue. Circles of whitegreen lichen grew on the smoother rocks, lace doilies flung from a madhatter's teaparty, stuck for eternity. Elsewhere stone piled up like the droppings of a giant Pegasus. In other parts jagged pinnacles impaled the sky. All around were doorways and hollows. Strengths and weakness exposed everywhere.

Their path was now clean sandy soil – from Jennifer's frequent treading Quinn presumed. There were no animal prints.

Looking at the ground, he nearly crashed into her. She had stopped. The grey shade leached out from the rock about them. The air was dry but there was some movement as it channelled through the haphazard openings and closures.

Before Quinn could say anything Jennifer had put a finger gently to his lips. 'Shut your eyes,' she said, 'give me your hand.'

He shrugged and obeyed, following clumsily because the path was not wide enough for them to travel side-by-side.

'Where are we going?' he ventured after about twenty paces, stooping the way sighted people do when forced to walk blind. 'I hope you're not intending to push me over a precipice.'

'You said you wanted to be taken somewhere special,' she said, 'and so you are. When you open your eyes – it's not far now – you'll be in a place I call "The Room". I like to think that no-one else in the whole world knows about it, or not now that there aren't any Aborigines left in these parts.'

At last they stopped, and she turned him slowly by the shoulders. He could tell that they had come off the path: he'd cheated, reached out his free left arm to find the rock no longer there.

'Now!' Jennifer said triumphantly.

Quinn was standing in a big three-sided space, its almost-square walls formed of smooth stone rising to several times his height, with the sky sitting there like a blue ceiling. The fourth side was a full-width window to the opposite ridge and the green valley below.

Jennifer had put him right in the centre of The Room. His impression was that the land dropped away suddenly rather than in a steep slope, that you could step right out into space. The distant ridge looked bleached by the sun hitting it. The Condamine had turned to solid metal. Another light bounced from the tin roof of the matchbox cabin. Far away to the left a pillar of smoke gave the only other signal of mankind. 'Mary and Pete's,' Jennifer said, her eyes watching Quinn's more than the view.

She saw him drink up the distances, colours, lights, knew that his head was soaring like the wedge-tailed eagles that sometimes creamed across the valley on unflapped wings. Patiently she waited for his vision to reduce back into The Room, to notice the soft dusty floor and the ring of round stones encircling dead fire. 'And look here,' she said, seeing that he was back on the ground, 'look at this!' She was running to the far wall. About a metre up was a natural cupboard, where some sweetness in the rock had left a cavity, a deep recess about half the height of a man. Jennifer reached into it and pulled out an old Milo tin.

'Paper and matches.'

She held up one by one a waterbottle, a spoon, a cannister with tea written on it, a jam jar of sugar, a black billy.

He was laughing more with each proud item.

Her hands went in again and she extracted a sleeping swag, tied like stringed beef, and an oilskin groundsheet.

'Voilà!' she shouted, 'a room with a view, and mod cons too!'

'You little kid!'

She nodded agreement. 'Sometimes I spend days and days up here. When night forms a fourth wall, shutting down that view, then you're open only to the stars. Do you like it?'

He shut his eyes.

'How do I get up to the top?' he asked, suddenly alert. 'I want to climb the walls to see the view south.'

'Back along the path on the left. You'll see some hand and footholds, you can climb up there.'

As he left Quinn saw how the path stopped flush at the room, its opening barely wider than his own shoulders. Before leaving he turned back to see Jennifer rolling out the green bag on top of the groundsheet just near the edge to the slope. There was a typewriter ribbon of shade now that the sun had slipped off-centre.

He disappeared, retracing the steps he had taken in blind faith.

In the shade, Jennifer pulled off her boots and her hat and lay down on her stomach on the sleeping bag, hands under chin, eyes gambolling down the hillside. She could feel her heart beating against the resistance of the ground, fast from the climb and from her excitement.

Quinn had found the spot. His long arms and legs made easy work of the footholds in the vertical rock. He scrambled along the tabletops of the stonework until he was standing high above Jennifer, looking down into her room from the back wall. She didn't see him. He shaded his eyes and scanned the flatlands to the south of the ridge. The horizon was somewhere across the plain beneath stacked sheets of corrugated heat.

'So that's the real world,' he said, not so loud that Jennifer could hear, 'and the green valley is an aberration. Australia Fucking Felix, eh Major Mitchell?'

The rock was cooking the soles of his boots. He hurried away out of the sun, feeling and searching with his feet for the footholes on the descent to the path.

Back in The Room he sat on his haunches next to where she lay. Jennifer rolled onto her side, her back to the rock, making room for him in the shade.

He reached down and gently ran his finger along her lips, sealing them.

She smiled at him. 'My head's empty.'

Quinn took off his boots, flung them over his shoulders like wineglasses.

It was about four pm by the slope of the sun; more than half The Room was now in shade.

Quinn and Jennifer lay on their backs a few inches apart, their clothes still discarded about them. A light breeze was working to remove the gloss of sweat from skin, leaving silvery snailtrails where juices had dried. Quinn's right shoulder wore an epaulette of grit where, when Jennifer had been on top of him, it had worked off the edge of the sleeping bag.

They had not spoken for a long while; in fact Quinn had slept for half an hour. Now he ran a finger between her breasts and down across the roundness of her tummy. Jennifer pulled a curl of hair from his neck, twisted it round and round her finger. They were watching a hawk riding high into the blue on a thermal. 'I wonder,' Quinn said at last, 'if that bird feels as floaty as I do?'

He watched as she propped herself on one elbow to look at him. One of her dark nipples became hidden in the folds of the sleeping bag, the other, now smooth and subsided, was only inches from his face. He lifted his head and kissed it again.

She touched her lips to the end of his nose.

'How's that head of yours now?' he asked.

'I feel a bit spinny, to be honest. As though I've had huge surges run through me. Yet I'm more relaxed and calm than I've been since ... I don't know. Strong and tender all at once. Not making much sense.'

'My heart's also incoherent, Jennifer Jade. Blood-drunk.'

'Shall we go now?' She was pulling herself to her feet, looking around for her clothes. Jennifer did not hurry as she had at the river. The heaviness of the white flesh around her middle and thighs was a reality he could like or lump – and she knew he liked. Those eyes of his, which closely matched the colour of the stone walls, were still palpable on her freckled skin. But both of them had skydived into such intimacies, so tasted and tested and pleasured each other, that this cool examination was nothing to be embarrassed by.

'Come on, you lush,' she chided as she was pulling on her socks. 'Get yourself moving, why don't you? We could even do some honest manual work before nightfall to counterbalance all the psych and sex. Hmmn?'

'Why not. A bit of rumination amid the vegetation would round off a perfect day.' He had on his trousers now and was rolling up the green bag. 'But there's one other thing I think I should tell you.'

Jennifer froze with a boot half on. His voice had cut to serious. It was a knack she'd noticed – almost the only thing she wasn't sure she liked about this man – which enabled him to switch in a breath from chat to life-and-death acute. Probably a spinoff from the stark contrasts his illness must impose. She waited.

'Well,' Quinn said reluctantly. 'I want to tell you that for a burnt redhead you're not bad.'

She chucked her boot at him, her face suffused with relief. 'And you, Mr Quinn, you are a silly bastard.'

They walked single-file back along the path, then picked their way slowly down the valley's face. Half way down he reached for her hand.

Near the cabin he watched as Jennifer stopped to collect the eggs. He stood on the outside of the leaning henhouse, his fingers curled like talons through the chicken wire. 'Are you taking me up to meet the Vickers tonight?'

Jennifer was bending over the nesting boxes and craned her neck, like a curious chook, he thought. 'You want to?'

'No, can't say I do. But whatever happened last night will only fester otherwise. It won't be possible for you to hide me here indefinitely, although I must say I quite like the idea. I might as well face the inquisitors.'

'*We* might as well,' she corrected. 'After dinner then. Would you mind moving Splash's tether? There's a big hammer on the drum.'

As she walked towards the cabin with the eggs she tried to convince herself that going up to Henry and Lorna's was the perfectly natural, neighbourly thing to be doing. 'Oh,' she called over her shoulder, 'and some water for Splasho. Plus a cuddle!'

He'd patted the goat, topped up its water and was hammering the spike, enjoying the brittle clang bouncing all around him, when between blows he heard his name. It came in shrieks from the cabin door. 'Quinn! Quinn!'

He flung the hammer and ran, his long strides and the slope propelling him. Jennifer grabbed him hard by the shoulder with one hand, pointed behind her with the other not wanting to look.

Quinn was alight. A snake? There was no movement inside the cabin. Then he spotted the rock. On the corner of Jennifer's bed, a bit larger than a cricket ball. It had come through one of the verandah windows, gouged a piece of the polished wood floor as it bounced, then landed on the bed, a comet's tail of glass marking its path. He smiled wryly to himself, but removed the look as he turned to face Jennifer.

'Good thing we weren't making love on the bed.'

'We can't just laugh it off, Quinn,' she said irritably.

'No, but at the same time I refuse to let today be shattered by a rock.'

Jennifer smiled as best she could. She went onto the verandah and hurled the rock into the trees. Quinn was sweeping up the glass fragments when she returned. She found some old newspaper; fetched sticking plaster from a cupboard.

'There, that'll keep out moth and moz for tonight. Tomorrow I'll have to go into Walrae and get a new sheet.'

'Maybe you should get a couple.'

After they had cleaned up and drunk tea in silence on the verandah, Quinn said he was going to work in the garden. Jennifer had lost her will to hoe, said she would go to the Condamine to wash. 'Then I'll cook,' she said. 'I should also do some sewing.'

Quinn went to leave, then stopped in the doorway and turned. 'Hey!' he called to Jennifer, who was sitting, smoking thoughtfully. He'd pushed a finger into each corner of his mouth, pulling his lips into a wildly distorted grin.

She shooed him away with her hand, but she was laughing again.

Quinn decided to terrace a section of the side of the hill. He would dig narrow beds stepping down the slope, the way he'd seen it done in Malaysia and Japan. If the terraces were lipped they could be irrigated from the river somehow, maybe a hydraulic ram. This would eventually mean doing away with the uphill beds Jennifer had cultivated, but she did not seem to be a proprietorial woman. He caught himself thinking long-term, something he'd spent a lot of time unlearning. 'One spadeful at a time, Quinn,' he said to the ground as he started.

After the spade had hissed into the soil a few times he stopped and grabbed a handful of earth, smelled and tasted it. 'Gold medal,' he told it.

Half an hour later he stopped to remove his T-shirt, then continued with the mattock, pulling the earth down, treading it, beginning a small topography lesson for the hillside. 'This could take forever,' he told himself, smiling stupidly.

Quinn worked until about eight pm, when the sky was merging with the earth again and he was digging more by feel than sight. Where he had cut the slope and pulled the ground level with the mattock he placed loose rocks like large raisins into the doughy soil, kicking them in with the heel of his boot to give the reshaped earth something to grip.

When he could wring no more out of the day he tucked his T-shirt into the waistband of his trousers, hoisted mattock onto one shoulder, spade over the other and headed for the cabin, the muscles inside his back glowing.

At the door he leant his torso in and reached for the soap, his dirty boots anchored outside. Jennifer had lit one of the oil lamps and was sitting at the sewing machine. She wore metal-framed glasses, which made her look like a librarian, Quinn thought. Steam clacked the lid of a pot on the primus and there was the new smell of hot olive oil.

They smiled at each other, then Quinn swung himself out of the doorframe and into the darkness. Jennifer heard him go around the side of the cabin, replace the tools underneath.

He could just see where he was going. At the plank jetty the river looked like molasses. Quinn soaped up and jumped in, but he did not like to be in night water and washed himself quickly. Back on the jetty he rinsed the day out of his T-shirt.

Jennifer was still sewing when he returned in his underpants. He towelled his hair and brushed it before the mirror. For the proposed outing he dressed in jeans and a green windcheater which had IHS across its chest, the Ivanhoe High School initials which frequently drew religious witticisms in the staff common room about In His Service. The students said they really stood for I Hate Skool.

'You can put some of your clothes in the top drawer of that chest, if you want to,' Jennifer said without looking up, 'I've emptied it.'

'Thanks.' Quinn understood the size of the offer.

When he had finished transferring his belongings from the rucksack to the drawer Quinn crossed to the chair where she was sitting. He watched her hands move, catching and losing the lamplight as they re-threaded the machine. He could tell that he was making her uneasy standing over her. With both hands he lifted the mane of hair from her shoulders and put a river-cooled kiss on the nape of her neck. Jennifer squirmed as it tripped down the vertebrae of her spine.

'Smells great.'

'What does?'

'Your neck … the food … the night air. In that order.'

'It's a vegetable casserole,' she said, squinting at her work. 'Won't be ready for half an hour or so. Do you want to light the other lamp?'

Quinn did, and sat on the couch where he had slept so long ago last night. He began reading a book from the shelf above where he sat, *An Insular Possession,* by Timothy Mo. It was inscribed 'From Lorna, with love'. Apart from the constant hiss of the primus and the odd clack of the pot lid the only sounds were from kamikaze moths attacking the verandah windows. There was a different noise when one of them hit the paper taped over the hole.

In time Jennifer packed away her sewing and rose to attend to the meal. Quinn's eyes left his book, the very first words of which had widened them, notwithstanding that they referred to Canton rather than Queensland: *The river succours and impedes native and foreigner alike; it limits and it enables, it isolates and it joins.*

His eyes followed her, the blue denim skirt, white cheesecloth blouse, the single silver earring hanging half-hidden under the mane. He didn't know that Jennifer could not remember when she had last dressed up so. The one earring, plus an old necklace of her mother's, were her only jewels. She'd had to rummage several drawers to locate them, a vanity she managed to disguise to herself on the ground that she was making some room for her guest. She did not put on the necklace but held it up to the light to admire it. Its stones were jade.

They set out on Jennifer's path about 9.30 pm, Quinn having insisted that he clean up the kitchen after they'd eaten. His presence seemed more obvious there in the cabin, Jennifer thought. Much more so than when they were wetly coupled in The Room. She was still overwhelmed by the way they had fallen upon each other up there, how it had been at once unbridled lust and tear-soft tenderness. She'd always imagined this must be an ecstatic state reached by two passionate people over a long period, not something that descended from the sky in a rush of wings and carried you off in its clutches. The very first time. After so long. She would have liked to have been able to sit on her own, or in silence with him, to bask in it, think about what it all meant. But here she was, slightly sore from him, trudging up to a meeting that could only do damage to their day.

This path was also narrow, so Quinn followed, with Jennifer angling her torch beam back for him at intervals. The moon was away, and few stars made it through the weft of cloud.

Where the path dropped to the river, she stopped. 'We could go home? Read in bed?'

'Look, woman,' he said in feigned exasperation, 'I *was* nervous about meeting you. But now that our beginning has not proved to be our end, I'm not worried about a few failures in the outside world, if that's what it's going to be. Lead on!'

When they got to the Vickers' clearing Jennifer reached for his hand. He squeezed it and let go, noticing that it was cold despite the tepid night.

On the back verandah Jennifer hesitated again; there were several voices inside. She was about to hiss to Quinn that their timing was bad, they'd have to slink off, when the talking stopped and Lorna called: 'Who's there? Who is it?'

They'd crossed the Rubicon.

Jennifer pushed open the flywire door and poked her head in without entering.

'Jen!' Lorna cried. 'Since when do you be standin' on the verandah, girl?'

Jennifer did not move. 'I've got Quinn with me,' she said looking back over her shoulder. Then added awkwardly: 'Ned, that is.' She had been taken aback. Sitting with her neighbours at their table were Mary and Pete, plus Kevin and Anne Gill – an unlikely social sextet.

Several seconds passed before Lorna could manage to say 'Yes …'. No more; her face looked slapped.

Henry rescued them both, calling loudly: 'Come on in. Do.'

Quinn shuffled in behind her. The prodigal son, minus the feast, all chairs occupied.

Jennifer was so busy assessing the significance of what was obviously a 'meeting' that she quite forgot Quinn behind her. He had to nudge her elbow, a movement none of the eyes at the table missed. 'Oh, I'm sorry,' she blurted. 'Ned, this is my mate Lorna, Henry, Kevin Gill, Anne Gill, and over there that's Pete, and Mary next to him. They're not far down the valley.'

The men had nodded to Quinn. Lorna and Anne Gill managed smiles of sorts. Dreamy Mary stood and held out her hand. Quinn crossed half the room to shake it. 'How do you do?' he said.

Jennifer blessed every overweight pound of Mary. In fact the gesture, or merely Mary's soft spontaneity, had highlighted the lesser response from the men: a firm hand-shake is the bush passport. The others were now shifting in their chairs, Kevin Gill paying unnecessary attention to his pipe.

Jennifer was stung but she recovered enough to play a pawn.

'Sorry, Lorna, didn't know you had a bit of a gathering, or we'd have come some other time. Maybe we should …'

'No. No,' said Lorna.

Henry had risen and now he placed two extra chairs just to the right of Lorna, where the new arrivals sat. Whatever had been under discussion, the conversation now was extinct.

Jennifer could not stand the glassiness. For the sake of

breaking it she cleared her throat and announced: 'Quinn's been digging in my garden.'

She regretted it straight away. Kevin Gill's eyes said: 'So the man can use a shovel?' His wife's knowing look said: 'I bet that's not the only thing of yours he's been digging into.'

Mary, who, as always, looked relaxed and was one question off the pace, asked: 'Is Quinn a nickname?'

'No.' All eyes turned to him as though surprised that he could talk, that Jennifer would not have to translate for him. 'It's my surname, Mary. But Jennifer has latched onto it more than Ned. As a kid I was dubbed Sequin, after some kid in the playground asked "Anyone see Quinn?"'

Mary laughed loudly.

'I thought you only put sequins on dresses?' Anne Gill said.

'Don't worry about that,' Quinn answered gravely, 'I only wear dresses when the moon's full.'

Mary's laughter was even more raucous.

Her thin, nervy husband stood. 'Come on, we'd better pedal off, Mary. I've got a big day ...'

Henry asked the first question that didn't have a curve on it. 'Jennifer says you're interested in trees, horticulture?'

'Yes,' Quinn answered gratefully. 'I like your table.'

'Just a bush carpenter.'

The table became an object of universal fascination.

Pete was still standing behind his wife. The room was once more humid with silence.

Jennifer tried again. 'I'm going into Walrae tomorrow, if anybody wants anything?'

'You were there only yesterday, weren't you?'

'Yes, Lorna, but we've got a broken window; I'll have to get some new glass at McConnachies'.' She and Quinn agreed later that none of the faces changed at the news of the window, but her use of the plural had its effect, particularly on Lorna's eyebrows.

At last Mary noticed her husband's patting of her shoulder and stood.

'Us too,' said Kevin Gill getting up. 'Thanks for the tea.'

Jennifer decided to join the exodus. 'We won't stay either, only called up to say hello.'

'Oh!' said Mary, as though about to say something momentous. 'Could you get me some fizzy in Walrae for the boys? Silas dared to inform me the other day that he was an underprivileged child. That's what you get back in your face for trying to educate them about the Third World. Anything but Coke, Jen.'

The banality was a blessing.

'Sure, Mary, you shall have it.'

'COD?'

'That'll be fine.'

There were mumblings of goodbyes and thanks, enough to camouflage the fact that none was directed to Quinn.

Jennifer put her head down and hurried for her track. Only the realisation that Quinn would be lost without the torch stopped her from running.

'What a load of pig manure!' she said as he caught up with her. She mimicked Anne Gill's question about his schoolboy nickname: 'Oi thought ya only put seegwins on drairses?'

She laughed into the darkness. 'Why the hell did you get smartarse about wearing dresses at full moon? I mean, a gay Dr Jekyll?'

She held his hand.

'I'd love to be eavesdropping on the Vickers' verandah right now,' said Quinn.

'Not me,' she shuddered. 'That room really stank with suspicion when we interrupted them. That's what's beginning to frighten me. I'd been prepared for one or two people behaving badly, but not the whole valley, as though some epidemic had got their collective reasoning.'

They were not far from the cabin when Quinn said:

'There's a couplet of John Dryden's: *Nor is the people's judgment always true: The most may err as grossly as the few.*'

'I know it,' said Jennifer gleefully, adding more seriously: 'But I've always interpreted it on grosser lines, if you see what I mean, more on the scale of Hitler's Germany than Overton.'

'Ah!' said Quinn, 'but Adolf was a Leo.'

Their laughter crashed into the sleeping trees about them.

'You silly bastard, Quinn!'

They did not light the oil lamp; it was not worth it. Jennifer dropped the still-lit torch on the bed and they began undressing, both trying not to appear to be in a hurry.

'Beatcha!' Jennifer said, plunging in naked. The torch clunked onto the floor, where it lit up Quinn's funny white feet.

Then they were together on the mattress that had never before slept two. The sheets were clean.

Part 3

Shattered-glass dawns, kiln-fire noons, tepid-milk midnights: Jennifer and Quinn began living together under the valley's dictatorial sky, sometimes despotic, more often benevolent.

There was another, less-settled climate in the valley in those weeks. The comfortable tyranny of same tomorrows appeared to be less certain. Jennifer and Quinn paid unconscious heed to fallen feathers, to the shapes of clouds, to the sudden cracking of dead wood. They had no routine between them but were cautious explorers. Each quietly recorded dissonances and harmonies. Usually Quinn would rise early, sometimes with the light, and slip from Jennifer's bed like a dream, dressing silently, pulling his boots on outside then climbing to the garden that was increasingly bearing his stamp. He liked to work in this stolen time when the dew muffled the notes of shovel or mattock and the softer sounds of the hoe. In these cool hours he wouldn't use the axe or drive posts with the sledgehammer; the noise would have elbowed awake both the bush and the big-hipped redhead from whose warmth he had peeled himself.

Quinn was careful never to use the possessive pronoun about the garden he was re-shaping, and he would suggest rather than state plans. It was clear, however, that Jennifer did not mind. He would often see her looking up from the cabin doorway as he divided his time between cutting terraces and putting up tight fences to keep out possums, wallabies, rabbits and other soft-leaf lovers. She had once suggested borrowing Henry's tractor but Quinn had not liked the idea, said he preferred shoulder and blade.

Some mornings she would reach for him; then his absence would wake her quickly. She'd dress and join him, digging and tilling in silence as the land woke slowly around them. At other times she would curl foetally in their bed and think irresistibly of pasts and futures that were best left unspoken. Eventually she would make breakfast and call him down or carry it up on a tray. He could eat endless plates high with buttery toast, and none of it grew on him.

Often they would work together until the afternoon heat made labour senseless. Then they would go to the river, to the ridge, or siesta together in the double hammock Quinn had made and slung in the shade beneath the cabin. He learned that there was a niche between mid-afternoon and early evening which was Jennifer's especially erogenous time-zone.

The day after the difficult night up at the Vickers' house Jennifer had driven into Walrae for the glass. Quinn had offered to come with her but she'd said that people would only gawp at him. She had asked at breakfast whether he wanted anything. 'Yes,' he said through toast, 'four rolls of chicken wire from McConnachies', plus some fish hooks, mixed sizes, and a reel of line.' He fetched his wallet from the drawer she had assigned him, he handed her two $100 notes. 'Here,' he said, 'put any change toward chooks' food.' It was their first discussion of money and he could see that Jennifer was uncomfortable. 'Take it,' he laughed, 'it doesn't buy me any rights. But you don't need to keep me, my bush seamstress. If I run out I can arrange to have money transferred to the Walrae Post Office.'

He saw Jennifer wince at the thought. 'Well,' she said, 'I won't need this much.'

Closing her hand around the money, closing the subject, Quinn said: 'Husband it as you will.'

Quaint expression, Jennifer had thought. The words money and husband so close together had made her swallow involuntarily.

In Walrae she had bought the fencing wire and fishing gear at McConnachies' and the young man who loaded the rolls into the ute said: 'Didn't know you was into fishin', Mrs Duncan.'

'Well I am,' she snapped, at once regretting her tone. It couldn't possibly be him who had rocked her cabin.

From the Post Office doorway Molly The Ferret had watched her progress from Lance's store to McConnachies'. Jennifer waved at her and flashed a dead smile. She had no difficulty in making out the arch of Molly's pencilled eyebrows: 'Stabbed anyone with that knife yet has he?'

At Lance's she had bought orangeade for Mary's boys and the butter and milk she would normally have got from Lorna in exchange for eggs. Carton milk and foil-wrapped butter were part of the price to be paid.

Down at the station she handed Wal Hunt her parcel for Sydney. Wally also kept hens, but their common tongue of layers' pellets, shell thicknesses and problem roosters had dried up. Wally did venture a 'layin' well?' but Jennifer's curt 'thank you' was a full stop.

Jennifer forsook *Show Me the Way to Go Home* on the drive back. Apart from the subliminal reminder of Wally, she had the sense – from the growing conviction that her mail had been read, the rock through her window, the gathering at Lorna's – that she might be returning to trouble. There was even that pervasive feeling of surveillance as she swung left onto the track, slowly because of the sheet of glass on the back seat.

Stopping at Mary's house she had been relieved to see that Pete's truck was not there. Mary came out from the kitchen in her artist's smock, so streaked with oil paints that it too could have been stretched and framed.

'An unexpected surprise.'

'But I told you I'd call,' Jennifer laughed. 'Remember Lorna's place? Fizz for the deprived boys?' She held up the orange bottles.

'Oh yes. Ta,' Mary said, taking them. 'The boys have gone out around the hives with their Dad.' She went inside.

Jennifer strolled around the clearing in front of the house, stretched her legs. Didn't Mary normally invite her inside? Or did she usually just walk in unasked? She kicked the base of a yellowbox. 'Paranoia!'

Mary returned with the money.

'Thank you for last night. You were the only one to offer any welcome to Quinn, to shake his hand.'

'Was I? I'd like to try to paint him, his face is an unusual composition of sharp and soft lines.'

'I could probably arrange that.'

'It's not going to be easy, Jennifer.' Mary was looking into the distance above the river.

'I know,' Jennifer laughed, 'it's a difficult sort of a face. I'm still unsure whether or not he's handsome.'

Mary smiled indulgently. 'I'm not talking about painting.'

'Oh. I see.' Jennifer's voice was almost a whisper. 'I'm going to give it a real go, Mary. Wouldn't you?'

'I don't know, Jennifer. I really don't. Anywhere but Overton, yes, probably. Would you like a cup of tea?'

'No, I'd better push on.' Jennifer was unable to keep the sadness from her voice.

Mary strolled with her to the utility. She looked in at the glass.

'Some dear soul threw a rock through my window yesterday. Landed on the bed.'

Mary shook her head slowly. 'People in glass houses.' Then suddenly: 'My goodness, I hope it wasn't either of my boys?'

Jennifer had started the engine. 'No, Mary. I trust those two little savages.'

As her cabin came into view Jennifer saw Quinn standing on the hillside next to a post at one corner of the new garden. Beside him was another man. All her instinctive foreboding flooded back and she pushed down on the accelerator, ignoring the glass on the back seat.

She left the utility on the track, facing the wrong way, and ran as fast as she could. Then Quinn waved hello. The man beside him turned too. It was Henry Vickers. Jennifer stopped running, tried to hide her panic, to think of an explanation for not having backed up the slope as she always did. The glass! Didn't want to risk the glass!

'Hi,' said Henry, 'Lorna sent me down with some milk and butter, and for eggs if you've got enough?'

Jennifer was relieved that in her fright she had left the provisions in the ute. She stood next to Quinn, who was wearing only shorts and boots. He put his arm across her shoulders; the first public demonstration.

Henry appeared not to notice. He told her that Quinn had been explaining his terracing project, how he'd seen it in Asian countries, how a rectangular crop-rotation plan could be adapted to tiered beds.

'I've been picking Henry's brains on irrigation,' Quinn said. 'What I'd really like to see is a hydraulic ram lifting water up here. The river's got a strong flow, but it is a hell of a lift. Maybe I could have a look at your windmill system one day?'

'Sure.'

The men's talk was soothing. She walked across to the hens' yard and returned with a bowl of eggs. 'You guys want a cuppa? I do.'

"Thanks, no,' said Henry. 'Ned's already offered me one, but I've got work to get on with. I put the stuff from Lorna inside your door on the bench.' He took a few steps with his bowl of eggs then turned. He was about to say something but clearly changed his mind, disappearing onto Jennifer's track and into the trees.

'Nice enough bloke,' Quinn said. 'He's offered to give me some more poles.'

Jennifer pulled his head towards her and kissed him on the lips. 'Nice enough bloke.'

He took her hand and they walked to the cabin. 'Tell me about Walrae,' he called over his shoulder from the step where he was taking off his boots. 'Did you get the stuff I asked for?'

Jennifer had not heard him. He saw from where he sat that as she went about making the tea she was grinning to herself, now and again shaking her head from side to side as though dismissing some internal dialogue. The sun was slatting in through the back window above the sink, igniting her hair and sparking in her green eyes as she moved in and out of it.

'Did you get the wire?' he repeated softly.

'I don't know, Quinn.' Jennifer again ignored the question. 'Being with you is like … being pleasantly uncomfortable. I'm so happy that all the hopes your letters kindled in me have been met, yet at the same time I'm apprehensive, fearful that what seems to be so attractive and good between us is as thin as rice paper. That some force beyond our control will hold a match to it …'

Quinn did not reply. He was sitting on the couch now, absentmindedly tearing at a jagged fingernail and watching her body's movements under her clothes as she banged about the kitchen.

'I don't know,' she repeated, unaware of his eyes. 'I seem to be talking and thinking so … sentimentally. Me, Mrs Once-Burnt! I know I'm doing it, though, so please be patient if I'm boring you witless. I promise I'm not normally garrulous. Why, I can go well over a week without saying a word, other than the odd chat with Splash. I guess it must be a quirky side-effect of starting to fall in love …'

She dropped the lid of the metal teapot. Bending to retrieve it from behind the bench increased the rush of colour to her face. Possibly he had not heard what had just leapt from her undisciplined tongue. Perhaps the crash of the lid on the floor …

Quinn had. She turned straight to the sink, but not before

seeing all his teeth on display, the laughter in his eyes.

He got up and crossed the room. From behind he slipped his arms around Jennifer's waist, his hands moving inside her yellow T-shirt up to her unheld breasts.

"I think I'm falling in the same direction,' he said barely audibly into one ear.

They drank tea in self-conscious silence on the verandah.

Afterwards Quinn went down to the utility, reversed it up the hill as close as he could get it to the vegetable garden and unloaded the rolls of wire. He returned carrying the sheet of glass. The broken window was quickly replaced.

Jennifer lay on the bed reading, avoiding looking at him. Quinn washed his face and arms at the sink and sat on the couch. He reached up to the shelf for his pad and a pen and began to write.

Often he would sit quite still and write for an hour or so in that torpid time when the sun was at its zenith and even the cockatoos were heat-mute. He always closed the pad when he finished, but did not put it away in his drawer. After several such days Jennifer's curiosity was a splinter, but she managed to restrain herself from looking while he was out working.

Two evenings after she had made the trip to Walrae for the glass, as she was kneading dough in the kitchen, Quinn came panting up to the cabin from the river. Face alight, he demanded: 'Shut your eyes. Hands out.'

She extended her floury arms and he slapped onto her hands a large brown trout, its mouth agape.

Jennifer pulled back from its slipperiness and the fish fell. They knuckled heads as each tried to catch it before it hit the floor. That night they sucked on its sweet flesh.

A tear in the rice paper came on the fifth day after they had visited the Vickers. Jennifer had not seen Lorna since then – a long stretch in the pattern of their friendship – although Henry had returned with half a trailer of fencepoles behind the tractor. Quinn had asked how he could repay him.

'Some teacher's advice on dovetail joinery?'

'Done.'

That evening Quinn stopped digging postholes to listen. He could tell by the birds' telegraph that something was coming up the track. Jennifer was in the cabin. He resumed his work, the growl of a motor surging and waning.

At last it cleared the baffle of the trees into open space along the river, and he saw the unmistakable flashing on the side of the police Land-Rover. Quinn leant on his shovel and watched as it came to a halt immediately below the cabin. A large uniformed policeman got out and stretched then reached back inside for a clipboard.

Quinn pulled on his shirt. Just as he reached the cabin door Jennifer opened it. Her freckles stood out against the whiteness of her cheeks.

He shrugged. 'God knows. You didn't hold up the Walrae Post office?'

'I fear,' Jennifer said quietly, 'that this is the beginning of that nightmare I've been dreading over the burial of Robbie.'

They watched as that same policeman, Senior Constable Worthing, disappeared around the side of the cabin, heard his rap on the door. Jennifer cleared the croakiness from her throat and let him in.

'Hello again, Mrs Duncan,' taking off the hat, pulling his arm across his forehead.

'Hello. This is Ned Quinn.'

The men exchanged handshakes and g'days.

'What brings you out here again?' Jennifer asked, waving him to a chair and sitting beside Quinn on the couch.

'A robbery,' Senior Constable Worthing replied bluntly. 'Just like to ask you two a couple of routine questions.'

Jennifer's relief was superseded by puzzlement. She shrugged. 'We don't know anything about a robbery. No one's robbed us … not that I've got much worth pinching.'

'Mr Gill. Kevin Gill.'

'Golly.'

'Some money from a cannister in the kitchen. Nearly $200. Plus his chainsaw from the cab of his truck.'

'So why come here?' Quinn's voice was neutral.

'I've got to investigate a reported robbery.' Senior Constable Worthing made it sound like a stupid question.

Jennifer interposed. 'You reckon it's someone from Overton valley?'

'Well it's hardly likely that anyone from Walrae would bother coming out here for a job like that, is it?'

'But there's never been a theft, a crime, in all the time I've been here. I mean …'

'Exactly.'

'And what,' Quinn had an edge on his voice, 'makes you think I might have done it?'

'Now I didn't say that. But, as your friend Mrs Duncan says, we haven't had this sort of offence occurring in these parts. A stranger arrives, a robbery's committed soon afterwards.'

'How did you know of Quinn's arrival?' Jennifer asked.

'Walrae train last, um, Thursday, wasn't it,' the policeman said with some pride, looking down at his clipboard. 'No criminal record, in this State.'

Jennifer was stunned. Quinn was staring at the floor.

Senior Constable Worthing took their silence as a compliment. 'I keep my eyes and ears open, as I said that time up at your neighbours', Mrs Duncan.'

'I bet they've been working overtime lately,' Jennifer hissed to Quinn beside her.

'So,' said Senior Constable Worthing, ignoring the whisper, as though his right to probe had now been established, 'if you could both just advise me of your whereabouts on Monday afternoon. That's when the stuff went.'

'This is bizarre,' scoffed Jennifer.

The policeman just sat with his ballpoint poised above his clipboard. Jennifer sighed.

'Monday I went to Walrae, bought some things at

McConnachies', chicken wire etc. I went to Lance's store.'

'And you, Mr, ah, Quinn?'

'It's N for Ned, not R.' Quinn, nodding towards the clip-board, refused to allow the trick to pass. 'I was here working in the garden. On my own.'

'Yes. Been doing some fencing up there? How've you been cutting your posts?'

'With an axe. Some Henry Vickers cut to size for me … with his own chainsaw. For God's sake, I don't even know where these people the Gills live. I've only ever seen them once, for a few minutes up at the Vickers'. How would I find their house, rob it, carry a bloody great chainsaw back here on foot, given that Jennifer was in Walrae with the utility? If I had taken it to use, people would hear the noise, and presumably most of them would know that Mrs Duncan doesn't own one?'

He could have kicked himself for calling her that, couldn't think why he had done it, apart from the fact that that was how the policeman addressed Jennifer, with the suspicion of an emphasis on the Mrs.

'I haven't accused you of anything, Mr Quinn. No need to get upset. The chainsaw taken from Gill's truck was his trim-ming saw, only a ten-inch bar, lightweight. Of course, some-body might have stashed it in the bush somewhere. Will you be staying in the valley long, Mr Quinn?'

'No idea.'

'That's not police business,' Jennifer said crisply.

'Perhaps not at this stage.'

'Is that the lot?' Quinn asked, his voice under control.

'Could I have your occupation, age and home address?'

'By what legal right?'

'It was a request, not a demand, Mr Quinn.'

He provided the information curtly, adding 'No criminal record in Victoria, either.'

The air in the room had become oppressive. Jennifer got up to open the verandah door in the hope that a breeze might stir the porridgy atmosphere. Her eyes fell on the stretching heads of the Seven Sisters, only inches below the edge of the decking. The policeman must have walked right past them!

When she returned to stand beside the couch Jennifer's nails were digging into her palms. Her getting up had, however, brought matters to a close. Quinn stood, too. 'Sorry we can't help you any more, Senior Constable, ah, Worthing.'

The policeman had a long look over his clipboard. 'That's it for now then.'

Quinn noticed that Jennifer had changed, that she had somehow switched on all the hospitality that had been so absent before. Why on earth … she was even offering the ox a cup of tea! Thankfully he declined. Now she was accompanying him out the back door. He watched in amazement from the verandah as Jennifer walked on the policeman's left down past the cabin and more than half way to the track. She was chattering, gesticulating: the man might have been her brother!

'What's got into you,' he asked when she returned, 'suddenly sweetness and light?' They were watching from inside as the policeman struggled to turn the Land-Rover on the tight track.

'I notice he's not going up to the Vickers' to ask Henry and Lorna his routine questions,' she said bitterly. Then she laughed. 'He must think I'm the weird one; one minute openly hostile, the next I'm escorting him to his car, saying how hot it must be in those uniforms, how bad the track was, anything that came into my head …' She continued laughing as she grabbed Quinn's hand and led him to the verandah, pointed.

'Christ!' he said.

'Exactly. He walked right past them.'

'For a minute I thought the heat had got to you.' He kissed her forehead.

Jennifer left him and went back outside. He could hear

her clumping about under the cabin, then she emerged below him with a machete. 'Never mind robbery,' she shouted, waving the blade aloft, 'I'm going to commit bloody murder!'

Quinn watched as seven blows felled the Sisters, their serrated foliage swishing to the ground. He went up to the garden and returned with the shovel, began to remove the Sisters' roots. He would carry the evidence off into the bush for burial.

'Good luck doesn't last long,' Jennifer said. She was tying the plants upside down on a long bamboo pole.

'Where are we going to put that?'

'The Room,' she answered.

'Of course.'

They carried the pole Chinese-style on their shoulders, the leaves brushing away Jennifer's footprints as they went, Quinn taking the weight of the load from behind. As they stopped for a breath half way she said: 'I always come up here by a slightly different route so I don't wear a path.'

They were perspiring by the time they had finished in The Room, one end of the pole resting on a forked branch Quinn had propped against a wall, the other in a chink on the facing wall of the corner. Jennifer stroked and arranged the upsidedown leaves like a salesgirl preening a rack of dresses in a boutique.

Afterwards they dozed together in the shade for a while, the marijuana bleeding rank fragrance into the dry air. Quinn lay on his back on the sleeping bag. Jennifer was on the ground at right-angles to him, her head pillowed on his chest, listening to the ship's beat of his heart.

In some ways the second robbery was better than the first from Jennifer and Quinn's point of view. In other ways it was worse.

Because the theft was from Mary and Pete's place, Senior Constable Worthing was not involved. Pete was wild enough about his losses – a set of spanners, wire strainers, wrenches, his Plum axe, the cheap padlock on the shed door crudely broken – but he would have nothing to do with the law, despite Mary's protestations.

The fact that the robbery went unreported did not, of course, mean that it went undiscussed. Pete had kept his mouth thin, and Mary could not recall having told anyone, but the news was disseminated within two days. Young Silas inadvertently lit the match when he was out checking on his father's hives. Gladys Sampson, the spinster who lived in the shed beyond the Cochranes' place, had surprised Silas in the bush and he'd answered her 'howsitgoin'?' with a proud: 'We got robbed!'

The second theft was six days after the first. In that time the rush between Jennifer and Quinn had not slowed, as each had privately suspected it must. The lack of reserve from such adult hearts surprised them both. One night when they were sitting by the lamps, her reading, him making notes on his pad, Quinn lifted his head to see Jennifer looking at him intently. He raised his eyebrows. 'Well,' she said, 'I've been considering it long and hard, and, with the possible exception of those feet, I don't think there's anything I don't love about you, Quinn.' She smiled, more to herself than him, and went back to her book.

Jennifer was aware, however, that Quinn was pocketing something away from her. She surmised that the policeman's visit had gone deeper than it showed. She would catch him staring through solid objects or gazing out at something beyond river or trees. It was a new thing.

The day of the second robbery the weather changed. About four pm all motion ceased, and alarm entered the talk of the cockatoos, crows, parrots and finches. The harbingers were right; edgy clouds began to shoulder in above the valley.

Jennifer and Quinn stopped digging to watch as the rump of a typhoon which had caused widespread damage on the coast marshalled its last hurrah. Jennifer's face was excited as the first fat drops made dust craters in the now-fenced garden. Gift water that they had not carted from the Condamine. The overture included several rolls of thunder from the percussion section, flashes of lightning from the brass. Then the deluge. Allegro. Troppo.

'That's where Wagner learnt his stuff,' yelled Quinn through the salutes of raw noise.

'Bugger Wagner!' said Jennifer, dropping her hoe. 'I'm getting out of here.' She ran for the cabin, the bombardment pasting her hair to her head, her T-shirt to her body, rain working its way into her mouth like a lover.

Quinn walked slowly after her, also wet through, stopping once or twice and holding out his arms. Dripping, they watched the rest of the performance from the dress circle of the verandah. They heard one violent passage clap the iron sheets of Splash's shelter like cymbals.

The storm left almost as quickly as it had arrived, dragging itself across one side of the ridge with dark you-were-lucky mutterings. Only minutes later blue replaced grey. Afternoon looked like dew-wet morning, bullets of light ricocheting everywhere. Splash regained enough composure to start bleating.

They did not make love that night but Quinn and

Jennifer refreshed themselves in great draughts of sleep in each other's arms. Not knowing that a synthetic storm would break next day.

Word of the second robbery came to them, it later occurred to Jennifer, from the best source: a kind heart. It was the first time Hilda Jones had been to the cabin. Apart from the valley parties, when the old families and the 'news' swallowed their differences in drink, and when Arvi would invariably end up slurring the Last Post on his trumpet, Hilda was a stay-at-home. She would go to Walrae once or twice a year. Thus Jennifer was greatly surprised to see her neighbour standing down by the Condamine, looking up at the cabin. Quinn, who had been in the garden, had come in to tell her: 'There's a bloke in overalls down on the track. Look. Been there like that for about half an hour. Shall I go and see what he wants?'

'That's no bloke,' Jennifer laughed, 'that's Hilda. She must be too shy to come up here. Could be she's trying to pluck up the courage to ask for some more Seven Sisters. Hope I haven't been turning her into a drug fiend. You better not come, she's a funny bird is Hilda.'

He watched as Jennifer trotted down the slope.

'Afternoon,' Jennifer said warmly. Hilda revealed a selection of widely spaced and variously coloured teeth.

'Would you like to come up,' she gestured toward the cabin, 'have a cuppa?'

'No, I won't.'

'Haven't seen you up this way for, oh, ages.' Jennifer could tell that Hilda had something to say, but it was stuck behind her frown.

Hilda pinched loose strands of tobacco from a cigarette she had rolled, her eyes on the river.

'Good bit of rain,' she said, as though Jennifer might not have noticed the storm.

Jennifer waited.

'Been a robbery,' Hilda managed finally, 'thought you oughta know.'

Jennifer was grateful. 'That's kind of you Hilda, I appreciate it. But I already knew. That bloody Senior Constable Worthing has been up here questioning us. Because Quinn's new up here, never mind that he doesn't even know where the Gills live.'

'Not that robbery,' said Hilda, flicking a finger tip repeatedly against the live end of her cigarette.

Jennifer cupped a hand over her mouth.

'Pete's shed got broke into. Lock snapped. Tools gone, strainers gone, a good bit of stuff.'

'I see. You've come to warn me that everyone's going to think it was Ned?'

'I reckon they will. Won't be no coppers this time, but. Not with Pete. Think he mighta done it, your bloke?'

Jennifer's laughter bounced on the river. She looked into her neighbour's rodent-brown eyes. 'No, Hilda. There's no way that Ned did either of those robberies. He *has* been sick on and off in his life, but that doesn't make a person a criminal. I swear to you Hilda, he hasn't robbed anybody. Do you believe me?'

'Fair enough.' Hilda looked away, having made this leap, preparing for another. 'It don't look good for 'im, but. Who's listenin' to me? Others ain't goin' to take your word for it, no offence.'

'I know. Look, Hilda, can I ask you something in the strictest confidence?'

Hilda screwed up her eyes and puffed on the tab of cigarette between thumb and fingernail.

Jennifer spoke softly. 'What I'm saying is, just you and me?'

Hilda ground cigarette under heel. She didn't look up, not wanting the flattery to escape from her deepset eyes. 'Yer've known me to be private.'

Jennifer plunged. 'You don't think ... I probably

shouldn't even suggest this ... I'm not saying there's anything at all that I can prove ... but you don't imagine your Bert might have had anything to do with ...?'

Not a flinch.

'Wouldn't be the first time he's nicked. By a longshot. But I'm sure as you are about him up there that Bert ain't done these. He only nick a thing he needs, see. Rather than buy it. And he don't need no tools. He's always needin' a dollar, that's true. But Bert don't have the nerve for goin' right into someone's house, particularly them Gills. No moralty worries, like, but he ain't got the bottle. *I'd* be more likely to rob Gills th'n he would.'

'I wonder who bloody well ...'

'Not saying Bert don't have it in for your feller, mind. Strange, but he says to me even before your bloke come up here how we don't want no loonies in the valley. Ha! He should talk. As though he's Alfred Einstein!'

Jennifer's mind was too busy to wonder what tortures marriage to Bert Jones might entail, but she welcomed an ally, any ally.

'You'll never know how much it means you coming to warn me, Hilda. I was beginning to feel that it was me against the whole valley. Thank you.'

'I'll be gettin' back,' Hilda said flatly. Her eyes were leaking light. She turned quickly and retreated along the track and into the shelter of the trees.

'Christ!' Jennifer swore to herself as she watched Hilda's back dissolve. 'My mail, the Gills, the rock, now Pete. Lorna in a spin. That fat cop pencilling in Quinn's name. No doubt by now Anne Gill and Molly The Ferret have pegged him as a transvestite for good measure.'

She trudged up the hill. What would she tell Quinn when he asked? Was this the moment when the lying would begin? She let her boots kick the ground. Thank God for Hilda. Henry, too. Henry? He need not have given Quinn all those fenceposts. He hadn't followed up his request for

advice on joinery. Maybe he'd been too busy. It was probably difficult to leave Lorna on her own at the moment,
impossible for him to ask Quinn up to his workshed yet.

Quinn was no longer in the garden when she reached the
cabin. He was not inside either. Jennifer was annoyed; she
wanted to talk it out with him straight away. More so, she
wanted to touch him, she needed his warmth. My God, she
thought, am I beginning to lean on him? So what if I am, a
bit. Where is he? She saw the note on the bench: 'J, Gone
for a walk, Q.'

'Bugger you,' she said aloud. Then she grinned. 'I know
where you are!'

She went back out into the sharp sunlight of the drip-
dried day and began climbing in a zig-zag the slope to the
ridge.

When she first entered The Room she did not see
Quinn. She turned around. He was sitting in one of the
stone corners, knees drawn up under his chin, arms belted
around his legs.

'You look like a shrunk sock,' she laughed, relieved. It
was true; how could a tall man have reduced his size so drastically? Quinn resembled a marionette folded for putting
back in its box.

Her laughter must have known something because she
heard it brittle and breaking on the solid walls. She bit her
tongue.

Quinn's face was pale and tight. His eyes bored unblink-
ingly into walls of fortress stone. He said nothing, made no
acknowledgement of her arrival.

'Quinn,' she said, her voice now soft, 'everything's
alright.' She knelt in front of his tucked-up legs. 'Give me
your hand,' now lovingly but firmly, as though man had
returned to boy.

Quinn pulled his eyes from the flatness of the wall with
apparent difficulty.

'Please don't look through me, too. I'm real, Quinn, I'm your Jennifer Jade, and everything has been going so well between us, hasn't it?'

His eyes reduced their range a little, she thought. They were not hard or unkind, just focused somewhere far beyond a Queensland Tuesday.

She asked again. 'Let me have your hand, Quinn.'

He unlocked one arm from around his shins and held it out dutifully. She took his hand gently between hers, bent and kissed the fingers, lifted it to her cheek.

'More bad news?' His voice sounded older.

Jennifer gave him back his hand and stroked his hair. His forehead was cool. 'Don't worry about old Hilda. She's a friend. A real one.'

The corners of Quinn's mouth lifted, as to a joke heard too many times. 'Tell me.'

'Not unless you kiss me. No way.'

Quinn leant his face forward and she kissed him hungrily. But she might as well have blown the kiss on her hand. Jennifer fought the urge to cry.

His eyes had come right back to his face now; he even blinked occasionally.

Jennifer sat back on her haunches, one hand on his bent knee. 'Another robbery,' she said looking at the ground. 'Hilda came to tell me, it was at Pete's house. Down there. The lock broken on his shed door, tools taken. There'll be no police involved this time, Pete wouldn't report it in a fit. But as Hilda says, there's going to be talk.'

He said nothing.

'I've learned a couple of things from Hilda. I'm sure it was her husband Bert who read some of our letters. I also know that he's not the one who has robbed the Gills or Pete.'

She could not think what else to say, took his hand again and massaged the back of it with her thumb. She tried to share his stare out over the edge of The Room where the land fell away and the blue sky filled its absence.

'Quinn?'

He heard the softness of her voice, she could tell.

'You're pretty tense, aren't you? There's a lot of pressure in the air right now. I'm feeling it, too.'

There was some warmth in his brief smile

'I'm with you, Quinn. You know that.'

His gaze was adrift over her left shoulder.

'Are you coming down to the cabin?'

'I'll stay a while.'

'Do you want me to be here with you?'

'No, you go.'

'I'll come up with some food later, shall I?' She was standing now, feeling like the air hostess dispensing platitudes to the frightened passenger before take-off.

Quinn didn't manage an answer. He drew his shoulders in towards his neck and leant his back into the millions of years of rock behind him.

Jennifer went along the passage and turned onto the slope, the ground conspiring to hide quickly the tears that fell to it. She stumbled a few times on the way down.

Inside the cabin again she collapsed on the bed, face down. The very last thing she needed at that moment, on that cracked mirror of a day, was a knock at the door.

Once Lorna would not have knocked, any more than Jennifer would have up at the house. Spirit and body prone, Jennifer immediately pictured the policeman at her door again. Quickly pulling herself up off the bed she wiped her eyes. Her face was set for defence as she pulled the door open, just as Lorna's raised hand was about to knock again. The other hand held Kate's fingers.

'Oh. Hello, Lorna. Come in.' Jennifer bent and picked up Kate, the child's arms scarfing her neck.

'I'm thirsty, Jen.'

'Drink coming up, my sweet. I wish all our wants were as easily filled.'

'Jen been crying,' Kate announced to her mother, although Jennifer's eyes had spoken for themselves.

'Well young lady,' said Lorna, 'I seem to remember *you* crying at times.'

'Cuppa?' asked Jennifer.

'Please.'

'You okay?' Lorna was looking about the cabin, sniffing out Quinn's absence.

'Sure.'

'Why you been crying, Jenjen?'

Lorna rolled her eyes in adult sympathy.

'Alright my girl,' Jennifer said, sitting on the couch and lifting Kate to her knee. 'If you want an explanation, let's have the one about our friends Mr Walrus and Mr Carpenter.'

'Goody!' said Kate, wriggling her small backside into Jennifer's lap. Jennifer sniffled, laughed. Kate mouthed many of the words as she recited the poem about the beach that

would have been perfect. . .if only it didn't have all that sand!
Kate's favourite verse was:

> *'If seven maids with seven mops*
> *Swept it for half a year,*
> *Do you suppose,' the Walrus said,*
> *'That they could get it clear?'*
> *'I doubt it,' said the Carpenter,*
> *And shed a bitter tear.*

Kate giggled, then said with sudden gravity: 'Poor Mr
Carpenter.' She slid off Jennifer's knee and did a Fosbury flop
onto the bed.

The poem had come unexpectedly to Jennifer's rescue.
Any resemblance to living persons purely coincidental? She
tried to see whether or not Lorna had got the gist. If so, she
hid it well. 'I think that's still her favourite, just ahead of
"Michael Finnegan". The other day she asked me why there
aren't any walruses in the Condamine.'

Jennifer was fixing the kettle.

'Where's your Mr Quinn?' Lorna inquired, offhand.

'He got bored digging, I s'pose. Must've gone for a walk.'
Jennifer could not remember having lied to her friend
before.

Lorna seemed to relax. 'I wondered if you and he could
come up for a meal tomorrow night?'

'Better the devil you know, eh?'

'Will you?' Lorna ignored the slight. 'Henry says I've
behaved badly, particularly given that I was the catalyst for all
this. Henry's usually right where it's a matter of my being
wrong, damn his lovely eyes.'

Jennifer gave Lorna a mug of tea and a wan look. So much
was going unsaid between them, something neither of them
was used to. Stroking Kate's black hair, Jennifer was trying to
assess Lorna's knowledge and intent. What was most strange
was that she was unable to read the state of her friend's mood,

what Lorna's blood was doing beneath this surface play. Forced back to that level, she decided that Lorna did not know about the second theft. No doubt at all she would by tomorrow.

'Yes, Lorna, we'd like to come. Or I should say I would. I can't speak for Quinn, but I assume he would, too, despite his first visit. The only thing is, he was a bit off colour when he got up this morning. Possibly a touch of the 'flu. He will probably have kicked it off by tomorrow, but I'll have to let you know, either way.'

Two lies in as many minutes.

Jennifer tried to concentrate on their small-talk, about the Seven Sisters, Henry, Kate … good, safe subjects. Her head, however, was up on the ridge, her eyes seeing Quinn with his back to the wall near where, so long ago now, their bodies had caught up with their paperwork.

Nevertheless it occurred to her that there was little logic in risking somebody else bringing word of the second robbery to Lorna, assuming that she hadn't already heard. And if Lorna behaved badly again upon hearing the news – well, at least she would not have to invent midsummer influenza on Quinn's behalf … That thought made Jennifer shudder, midsummer or not. She took the leap.

'Pete's been robbed.'

'No!' said Lorna. 'Not another one!'

Hilda's information was quickly retold, Jennifer surprised at the relative calmness with which Lorna took the news. Deep frowns and groans and bloody hells, but not the explosion for which Jennifer had braced herself. No hysterics.

'You didn't know about the robbery?'

'Course not. How did you hear?'

Jennifer thought warmly of Hilda by the river. 'Oh, the vixen's the first to hear the hounds bay. I expect it's all around the valley by now, that's why for a minute I thought you had already been told.'

There was a long silence between the two women as they

sat on the verandah smoking. Kate could usually be relied upon to plug any gaps, but she had gone to play with Splash.

'Penny for them?' Jennifer said at last.

'We've never thought about crime, isolated out here.'

'Not until Quinn came, eh?' Jennifer's voice was weighted. 'Mind you, the violence hasn't started yet. Must still be sharpening that knife of his.'

'I didn't come here to have the mickey taken out of me, Jennifer Duncan!' Lorna flashed. 'Don't put your two-and-twos together in my mouth, thank you very much. I came waving the little white flag, but I won't have you pushing it up my nose.'

'Oh I *am* sorry. So you don't think Quinn is responsible for these thefts? I've quite misunderstood you.'

'How the hell would I know?'

'Exactly, but you and Molly The Ferret, Anne Gill, the Cochranes … the whole effing valley seems to be convinced that it has been invaded by a dangerous lunatic. Which means I'm getting rocks through my windows, Quinn's getting tried and convicted without a skerrick of proof.'

'You remember,' said Lorna, 'when Senior Constable Worthing came up to the house that Sunday night about, about my Robbie? How I carried on like a pork chop?'

Jennifer refused to look at her.

'Well, that's what you're doing right now, girl.'

'You're probably right,' sighed Jennifer, still watching the river. 'It's just that the odds are stacked so unfairly. I end up feeling that the valley's a kibbutz and I've announced I'm going to marry an Arab.'

'Marry him?' Lorna was wide-eyed.

'That was just an analogy '

'But would you, if he asked?'

'I haven't thought about it for one minute.' She could hear the exasperation in her own voice. 'It must be obvious that I do love him.'

'I hope you wouldn't marry him just because you think

everybody's ganging up, you being as stubborn as me at times?'

'Now there's an idea.'

'Stop being silly.'

'Tell me, Lorna, you've convinced yourself that he must have committed those robberies, haven't you?'

Lorna's face said that she didn't want to answer.

'Come on. I promise not to bawl at you.'

Lorna sighed. 'We've never had a robbery, not that I can recall. In the short time since he, since Quinn's been here, we've had two. Couple that with the fact that I know him to be secretive – from his early letters to you – plus the mental illness. . .well, I'd pick him ahead of Johnny Cochrane or Bert Jones or Henry …'

'Shit, Lorna,' shouted Jennifer, forgetting her promise, 'it just amazes me how you can glide so smoothly from illness to theft. And there's absolutely nothing else to go on. I wonder what weight you'd be placing on the coincidence of Quinn's arrival had he no history of schizophrenia?'

'The same.'

'I doubt that.' Jennifer paused. 'If you think about it, there's another explanation.'

'Such as?'

'There's widespread hostility towards Quinn's presence here, right?'

Lorna nodded.

'And I'm certain some of our correspondence was read by others before it reached us.'

'Really?' said Lorna, sitting up. 'What gives you that idea?'

'Just something I heard.'

'That's pretty cosy. I suppose next you'll be getting strong hunches that Bert Jones robbed the Gills and Pete just because you hate Bert.'

'There's nothing I can prove against Bert, and as far as the robberies go I'm almost certain he's had nothing to do with them, although I can't tell you why I believe that either.'

'So come off all this thin ice.'

'It's obvious. Someone in the valley has stolen things to put pressure on Quinn to leave, or on me to ask him to.'

'Preposterous,' said Lorna, looking down to the river.

'Not when you think about it. In fact, it's more logical than Quinn having done the robberies, especially the Gills'.'

'It's not at all logical to me.'

'Okay,' said Jennifer, controlling her voice. 'Was the Gills' place wrecked, turned upside down?'

'Kevin didn't say so.'

'Right. So Quinn, a total stranger, first finds the Gills' house, gets past their dogs, then is magnetically drawn to the kitchen, to a cannister on the shelf where they keep their shopping money. Talk about striking it rich! No pulling out drawers, lifting carpets, turning mattresses? Now I know that Anne Gill keeps her Walrae money there, all of us do who share shopping runs. What's more, I could use a small chainsaw. Circumstantially, it's got to be me, not Quinn. Or Gladys Sampson, or you, Arvi or Sue, Mary. . .'.

'Come on Jen,' Lorna cut in, 'loyalty's one thing. If one of us was a thief, why haven't we done it before, over all these years? Because you don't shit in your own nest, that's why.'

'But it is not need or kleptomania that's behind these thefts, Lorna, it's ulterior motive. Someone either very badly wants to wound me, and has seized the chance, or, which is more likely, someone fears Quinn's schizophrenia to the point of paranoia itself. A spate of thefts is guaranteed to whip up resentment against him, evidence or not.'

'Why would anyone want to wound you?'

Before Jennifer could attempt an answer Lorna stood and called her daughter's name loudly, leaning over the verandah rail. 'Must be going, I've got some dough rising. I'm glad Quinn's been out walking in that it's given us a chance to talk a bit, even though it's been hard. We've been so close, you and me, and I'm missing it, a lot.' She was unable to look Jennifer in the eye.

'Me, too. But it's not a man that's come between us, Lorna, it's a spectre.'

Kate bounced up to them as they stood at the back door. She was chattering Splash, hens, mud. The contrasted states of the child she loved and of the man she loved compounded the fractured images in Jennifer's head. Not wanting to have to resort to walruses again, she held fast, and the wave subsided.

'So you'll let me know then?'

'You still want us to come, even though you feel about Quinn the way you do?'

'I admit that I *am* scared. No-one can be predictable when their mind becomes unhinged. I don't know, and you don't, how, and how often, that is going to happen, if he stays.'

Both women wanted the Parthian shot. Lorna had taken a step, Kate's hand in hers, when Jennifer added: 'On that basis I suppose anyone who has had any psychiatric illness should be locked up permanently? Be on the safe side?'

Lorna conceded the battle if not the war. 'Until tomorrow night, then. At least he and Henry can rant about trees and woodworking, even if we're bitching at each other.'

Kate waved her small unknowing goodbye.

Jennifer stayed in the doorway after they'd left, relieved to be alone. Her eyes climbed the slope. 'I'll bring you some food, some clothes. Stay the night up there with you if you'll let me.'

She set about her sad picnic: bread, a square of cheese, two peaches, a bottle of lime cordial, a knife. They could light a fire up there, boil the billy.

After packing the food and a jumper for herself, she changed into jeans. From Quinn's drawer she took a navy blue jumper and a scrunched khaki jacket; sometimes the nights up there at The Room were cool.

While she rummaged and wondered about long trousers Jennifer felt something flat and smooth between two shirts. An envelope. Withdrawing it, her pulse went into a steep climb. The envelope was addressed 'Jennifer Jade'.

The shock made her quickly look over her shoulder as though he had suddenly caught her with her hand in the till. She turned it over and over as she sat on the couch, put it down beside her and rolled a cigarette without taking her eyes from it.

At the top right where it might have said 'By hand' Quinn had printed 'By chance'. Very funny, Quinn. I wasn't snooping, I just didn't want you to really get the 'flu I've invented for you. She felt like a girl who has found her Easter eggs on Saturday. Busting to open; scared to.

Jennifer had smoked half the cigarette before she ripped into it. All the adrenalin she had floated upon so many times down at the letterbox on the Dirranbandi road had returned. Their letters had been the foundations for what they had built so quickly, their bedrock, as Quinn once punned in the dark after they had made love. Now, as she began, she had to hold the sheets tight to prevent her hand shaking.

Dear Jennifer Jade,
We're back to paper! If you are reading this part-work, then fate has planted footsteps upon me/us. I've written it on and off since I arrived. Forever changing bits, steadily wishing more and more that I could be writing to you solely from my heart, where all the good words are falling over each other to get out.

I want to try to be a little bit more honest about my problem, which by now I suspect has become partly yours. What I've written and spoken to you about schizophrenia has been pleasantly detached and theoretical until now, perhaps giving you the false impression that I'm well aware of the process and progress of distortion that an episode inflicts on me and, differently, anyone close to me. In truth I'm not. All that I have told you is book-learning or reports of my behaviour or that of others from those who have observed it. I have no knowledge of the roads my thoughts drive down when the illness is behind the wheel. Only guesses. I've tried to paint rationality and self-analysis over it all to imply that I can see right out to the edges of the canvas.

One of the reasons I have been unable to explain the machinations of schizophrenia is that it's idiopathic: cause unknown. Also because the bite is different with each person. Now I am worried that I may have gulled you into seeing my episodes as almost 'flu-like bouts that you, because you love me, can nurse me through. Well, I don't underestimate the strength of love, and the fact that yours for me is mirrored makes it up there with the Big Powers. But schizophrenia can rust love's girders. The person you love can disappear in all but body, can revile your attempts to help. I'm not aware of any such paradoxical emotions having stomped through my thoughways, but then I am not the fly on the inside wall of my skull.

Two days later: it's a savage bastard at times. I'm writing this in pessimistic anticipation, my love, trying to melt the icebergs of fear that I suspect will threaten to sink you if I have slid from the Quinn that you know (quite well) to the shadow neither of us do. More theory: one shrink I have read describes schizophrenia as destroying 'mutuality'. This is the equivalence of experience which enables people to communicate based on similar interpretation of what is supplied by the senses. The sufferer of schizophrenia can lose this mutuality with the world. He or she is alone in a different one. One baby born in each one hundred can be counted on to know these black holes, whether clutching at their sleek edges or lost in their infinity.

I've remembered an analogy Logan uses. He picked it up from a researcher called Broadbent, who refers to failure of the sensory filter, that capacity we all have to sieve from our consciousness the unessential. To act, to get anywhere, we need discrimination between the multitude of messages the senses bombard us with, or ephemera can overwhelm. It must also be capable of responding to new information, weighing it on the cerebral scales. We take it for granted, this filter. For me and those other one-percenters it becomes clogged or damaged. The message flow becomes chaotic, an inundation.

Hence, in my case, the instinctual attempt at withdrawal, the idea that stillness and separation from people and sensory stimuli is a safe cave. The world outside is too much for me to absorb; I shall live in my own head.

I think this is where Ned Quinn may be sitting as you are reading, Jennifer Jade. In many ways the lucky one. The self-isolation usually works, or is presumed to do so from the fact that my history shows many such episodes, more than hospitalisations. When it doesn't, and here I'm falling back upon guesswork, delusions can begin their march, voices their whispering.

Nuts and bolts: should I become unmanageable/odious/embarrassing/convinced that I'm Beethoven/all of these, then, Jennifer Jade, I may be heading for or newly arrived in the State of Florid (no, not Florida!). I suggest that you borrow Henry's 4WD (I don't trust your ute) and park me in the Brisbane psychiatric clinic, of which details are on the back of the last page. There's potted history and Melbourne phone numbers there, too, should you need help. I'm advised that I'm a sheep in Socratic clothing: easily rounded-up.

The anti-psychiatry movement will tell you that this is all horse-feathers, that sanity is in the eye of the beholder, even that the bulk of such 'illness' is iatrogenic, or doctor-induced. The devil and the deep blue bottomless sea!

Later still: why am I writing this? I think I felt bound to because of the huge distances you and I have covered in such a short time. Haven't we danced!

My fear is that if we continue as we have, then fall apart, we could be asking too much of scar tissue. We may leave open wounds upon each other. Bites from the wolf spider. A twice-burnt redhead?

Right now, with my prophesied computer malfunction, filter blockage, whatever it is, I want you to
think about this loophole. Say to me: Quinn, I love
you now, I know you have loved me, let's go away and
bury our bits of treasure separately. Bones for old
dogs to dream on. And I will kiss you and go, with the
Out of Africa sunset and the credits slowly rolling. . .
You once wrote that your head told you that I should
not come, though your heart wanted me to. Now, as
I write with my well-synchronised head, it tells me
that I should go, its voice sharp above the jeering of
my heart.

                                             love, Quinn

Darkness was stalking the ridge, dodging among the trees
as Jennifer climbed, bag across her shoulder. Somewhere in
the twilight an unseen crow repeated 'far, far, far' in its
unslaked voice.

She was becoming hot from the climb, yet occasionally
she shook. It must feel like this when the police call you out
to the morgue to identify. Pull yourself together, girl, don't
be bloody melodramatic!

When she crested the slope and took the path to the left,
the day was nearly done. As she silently reached The Room
there was just enough shallow light for her to see Quinn, or
at least part of his long legs. They protruded from the
crevice she called her cupboard. He had taken out the
sleeping bag, groundsheet, her camper's paraphernalia,
dumped them on the ground, and had backed himself into
the hole, only his gangling tucked-up legs visible.

She approached slowly, lowered the bag to the ground
and sat down a few metres from him.

'Hi. I've brought some food and drink, some clothing. It
might get cold later. We can light a fire if you like?'

No answer.

'I've read your letter, Quinn, the one you put in your

drawer with your clothes, intending me to find it if this happened. Remember? It explained a lot. Thanks. I suppose I can understand a small fraction of what might be going on.'

'I'm perfectly alright.'

Jennifer squinted, trying to see the face from which such an unQuinnlike voice had come. It was someone else's tone, half an octave out either way.

'I want to stay with you Quinn. I won't talk at all if it bothers you. Do you think a fire would be nice, some tea?'

'A fire's out of the question. Completely.'

'Fine, no fire. We'll see some stars soon. I reckon you can touch them from here.'

'What I'd like is no more pestering. These attempts to put me off my guard have been a bit obvious.'

Jennifer bit her lip. 'Right. One last question. Anything to eat? It's been a long day.'

'My ears won't be listening, my eyes won't be fooled again. If they want to visit, you can tell them to forget it.'

'Quinn! I love you. I'm Jennifer Jade. You wrote to me.' She moved closer and knelt on the ground in front of the hole in the rock. Sobbing. She put out a hand to touch a leg. He winced as though about to be struck.

'Don't worry, Quinn. I'll leave you in peace. I'll go down to the cabin and wait for you there. You know I'll be waiting, don't you?'

She took the bread, cheese and fruit out of the bag, arranged them on a square of paper; stood the cordial bottle up nearby; placed his extra clothes neatly on the dry ground. They would be useless with dew by midnight, but at least they were all easy to find, laid out like this, if he changed his mind.

Jennifer stopped herself from saying anything else; her words seemed to hurt more than help. She wiped her eyes and dusted herself off, delaying, trying to see what expression his face wore. She couldn't.

Turning her back on him she quickly and quietly left, the sandy ground of the path muting her footsteps. Half a dozen paces along it, she stopped and listened. She could hear nothing. Gingerly she took a few steps back towards The Room, pressing her back into the rock, darkness conspiring with her by filling the channel of the path more than the open room.

She could just make out Quinn through his movements. Craning her head she saw him lower his legs stiffly and slowly, inch himself awkwardly from the crevice in which he had wedged. She held her breath as he bent to the food she had arranged on the white paper, which held what little light was left. But he did not eat or drink. Quinn picked it all up by the four corners of the paper, as though removing a dead rat. In the middle of The Room he clubbed his left heel down and down, making a hole, the paper parcel swinging as he dug and shovelled with his boot. Satisfied, he knelt and slid the food off the paper, awkwardly enough to suggest that he was at pains to avoid any of it touching his skin.

He filled the hole and patted the earth back down with his sole then returned to the side of The Room where the crevice was. He bent forward, backed himself into the recess again and forced his knees up under his chin.

Jennifer tiptoed away up the path. When she turned onto the slope again she saw that she had forgotten to put a light on in the cabin; it was almost impossible to make out its shape. She hadn't brought a torch and the walk down was difficult. Like stumbling into a Black Hole.

Jennifer spent the night in the Condamine, even woke holding her breath. In dream, however, the river was not its placid self; it was hostile, tugging at her with whips of weed and willow, no longer tea-brown at its edges but black as the Styx, its mud not cream silt but rank sludge. Instead of breasting the current she had been fighting upwards for its surface, for air. There was something wrong with the air, too. It tasted of tin. Through watery eyes and ears she was also aware that the constant shoptalk had disappeared from the trees. No birds sang.

Waking was rescue; spars of sunlight graspable against the underwater night.

As she looked around at the firm ground of day – her clothes across the chair, coffee mugs on the floor, the latest letter from Quinn next to them, the emptiness on his side of the bed – consciousness did not seem such an improvement. Quinn was interred in his illness up on the ridge; the valley and Walrae were uniting in opposition; Lorna was expecting them for dinner.

Jennifer walked down to the river, the tail of the crumpled shirt she had slept in just covering her bottom. One of Quinn's. She knelt naked on the plank jetty and let the Condamine re-impress her; the vocabulary of its wetness, the way it absorbed some trees, reflected others, the gentle correspondence between it and the morning, insects humming the best of both worlds. Then she bent forward, Muslim to muezzin, and her red hair tumbled onto the surface.

It was good to have her head under, kneading the water to her scalp, feeling the sureness of the planks against her knees. She flung her head back and a mowhawk of spray flew into the air. Walrae's best shampoo shaped her hair into a wet meringue.

Jennifer soaped her body then stood at the end of the planks like an Olympic diver, flexing her toes over the edge, shifting the weights of her buttocks, raising and lowering her arms. Leaning forward a fraction she gave herself to gravity, gracelessly flopped. She pinched her nose and squeezed her eyes shut as the river flushed away the suds, the dregs of night.

Back at the cabin she spent time slowly, disentangling her hair before the undoubting mirror, drying it in the sun on the verandah while she ate toast. The longer she took the longer she could hold the hope that Quinn's own nightmare had died with the daylight and that they would walk down together from the ridge.

On the way up she cuddled the goat, held its hard head against her hip. As she moved the tether spike she knew that the bellblows of two metals would be signalling her movements to Quinn. She shovelled some chooks' droppings into a bucket, changed their water, broadcast grain. Stood and watched them for a while with her fingers hooked into the wire. The tall rooster's greens and browns and blacks looked polished for the parade ground, his comb and wattles raspberry ripe.

Clicking her heels, she saluted. 'Morning, Mr Soviet. She saw again Quinn's smile when she'd explained that the rooster's manner with the hens was all hammer, that his tail-feathers were perfect sickles.

She took long slow tacks up the slope and at the top paused for a while, looking back at the valley's plunging neck-line, the smooth skin of its merged trees. Then she turned abruptly left into the shade of the path that led to The Room

Jennifer pulled up short: the narrow entrance to The Room was blocked. Quinn had built a wall using the black-ened round stones which had contained her open fire.

Above these were cries-crossed light branches and sticks up to the level of her chin. Through the gaps she saw Quinn standing at the front of The Room, arms folded across his chest. He must have watched her slow ascent.

She did not know what to do. The barricade would not have stopped a child. A couple of kicks with her boot and it would have crashed back into The Room. But it had obviously been given a greater strength in Quinn's mind. She whistled. At first a fine tremor prevented any noise emerging, but then a thin sound escaped.

He swung around.

'It's only me, Jennifer. I've just come to see how you're doing?'

Quinn came to the barrier and peered through, as though she, not he, was fenced off, in the zoo.

'I'd like to come in, please.' She'd said it firmly.

Quinn began to withdraw the latticed branches with some effort, as though they were much heavier than sticks.

'That'll do,' she said when he'd removed a bit more than half the obstruction, 'I can step over this much.' She lifted her legs carefully; the stones would likely fall if she knocked them and something told her to flatter his misconception.

'You look much better today, Quinn. I see you've tidied things away a bit.'

He put his hands over his ears as she spoke. 'I can't take that noise!'

'Sorry,' Jennifer whispered. The bottle of water in front of the crevice caught her eye. She had left it full; now it was half-empty.

'Were you cold in the night?' She was searching his face for some spark.

'Of course not.' He had attempted to laugh but the sound was mirthless and his mouth stretched rather than smiled. 'I've told you, I'm perfectly okay. If people will just not shout we'll get along fine. I think I've probably got an ear infection. I'll be one hundred per cent by tomorrow.'

'That's great, Quinn.' Her voice was barely audible. They were standing in the middle of The Room, the early sun idling over them. He was not looking through her now. On the contrary, he seemed to be examining every freckle, line and detail of her face, avoiding only her eyes.

From a pocket of her shorts Jennifer withdrew two crumbly raisin cakes she had taken from the tin as she left the cabin. 'You like these. Are you hungry?'

'Should I take them?' he asked aloud. Jennifer noticed that while she was required to whisper, he spoke normally.

'They're fresh enough.'

He put out his hand and she placed the small cakes on his upturned palm, brushing his fingers with her own.

'Have them later if you want.' She could see that he was torn, that the cakes had become momentous. At last he put one in his mouth, the whole thing. Held it there like a communion wafer.

Jennifer heard herself exhale as he slowly began to eat. Caught herself chewing in unison, like a mother introducing solids. Quinn put the other cake in his mouth.

'I'll go now,' she said, 'but I'll come back later?'

He didn't answer. His lower jaw ground cake as though it was cow cud.

Jennifer reached up and touched the side of his face, running her fingers down his beard to the tip of his chin. He did not recoil, or respond. Her instinct was to kiss him, but she resisted. Turned and walked away, climbed carefully over the barricade. She wondered whether it would be there when she returned

As she made her way down the slope her step was surer, there were no tears.

He's a lot better, she told herself, or was she becoming inured? At this rate maybe they would end up with a *folie à deux*. She had laughed when Quinn explained the state in which a schizophrenic's partner can come to accept the delusions as reality. 'If you can't beat 'em, join 'em?' she had joked. Not so funny in hindsight.

She stopped to collect the eggs on the way down.

The cabin was unpleasantly hot as she busied herself tidying, making the bed, doing dishes. Housekeeping and a long session at the sewing machine would keep her a step ahead of maudlin. At some point she would have to walk up to the Vickers, to say that Quinn's 'flu was on and the meal was off.

It wouldn't have worked anyway. It was hard to think why Lorna had invited them, given the way she felt. Jennifer sighed. Their friendship had shifted. It was more than Quinn; Lorna had already changed before his arrival. Her impishness had gone, for one. Robbie's death had sucked hard at the pool of her youthfulness.

After the housework Jennifer pretended not to see the sewing machine and went up to Quinn's garden. That was how she now thought of the re-shaped land that banked down the slope in seven steps, all now behind post and wire. He'd told her there should be nine rows, something to do with Yeats, laughing at her insistence on seven. She'd said that apart from Seven being a good number, the garden would be unmanageable if he did not stop. The lowest bed had been raked to a tilth and marked off into small plantings: parcels of seedling broccoli, courgettes, pumpkins, tomatoes. The fastest vegetable, the radish, had already pushed up its tubers of alcoholic noses. She bit into one, its whiteness stiletto sharp.

Taking up the pole with its tied buckets, Jennifer shouldered down to the Condamine. The bamboo cut into her skin on the return, but it was so rewarding to cup the water onto the seedbeds, to dose it to all the almond, apricot and nectarine trees that would one day staircase down the right-hand side of the garden. She made four trips in the smelting sun, her forehead wet under the straw hat. Quinn had advised watering at sundown when the air had lost its thirst, but she didn't care.

Until lunchtime she hoed weeds, then went in from the broil, took off all but her shorts and washed her face and neck at the sink. Slumped in a deckchair on the verandah Jennifer let the dry breeze drink the drops from her back, from between her breasts. She made some tea, ate some biscuits and cheese. What would Quinn be doing? The Room became so hot when the sun was at its hilt.

Restless, she went inside again to put on a clean T-shirt then sat in a reserve of shade on the verandah with her sewing box. She was behind with orders but the needle was sluggish in her fingers and she soon put the embroidery aside. Subsiding to the bed, she read Quinn's letter yet again. A fly looped around the room, preventing her dozing from becoming sleep.

Having to go up to the Vickers' weighed upon her. Not so much the purpose of the visit; she had already prepared the way with the influenza lie. There was the inexplicable sense that she had let down her friend, had failed her. Also she was angry, numbed by Lorna's neanderthal response to Quinn. But it went beyond that. It was as though she was grieving.

By four pm the sun was still punching out jabs, crosses, upper-cuts. Jennifer sat in the doorway pulling on her old Dunlop Volleys, one shoe with a hole in the canvas where her big toe had worked through. As she did them up she was muttering, lacing incoherence with swearwords. She banged on her hat and set off for the Vickers' to cancel the booking.

The bush on either side as she walked buzzed with hot stories, glints from the beetle's green armour, mirrors curved on the crow's wings. From a gum by the river three black cockatoos stared down at her, their beaks open but silent, miming shriek.

Climbing the last rise of her track before it left the thick undergrowth and arrived at the Vickers' clearing, Jennifer heard mixed voices on the dry air. She stopped to get her breath and to wipe her face. The screen door banged then the voices grew distinct. Instinctively, perhaps because one of them was definitely Pete's, she cut off where there was a gap in the scrub and pushed a few steps into the bush, placing her feet carefully to avoid twigs.

It was unlikely that anyone would have come onto her track, but here she would never be seen. She wasn't sure if she was hiding because she didn't feel up to facing Pete, or because she wanted to eavesdrop, gather some intelligence from behind the lines. More the latter, she admitted. Pete's curt voice carried clearly to her.

'… he'll have to go for mine. Man's got to feel safe around his own home. None of us can now. Kevin Gill reckons we should confront him and Jennifer, say so.'

'Meaning what?' The disembodied voice was Lorna's.

'Some of us go up to her cabin, tell them how we feel and that the only solution is for him to sling his hook 'cos we can't live in peace. Sorry and so on, but that's the way it is.'

'I wouldn't be part of that.'

'You don't need to be, Henry. It'll still happen.'

'What about Jennifer?' Lorna again.

'What about her?'

'Well, it'll alienate her from us forever.'

Jennifer bit her lip.

'She'll get over it in time,' Pete answered. 'Plus if he stays and these robberies continue she'll be alienated anyway. From all of us.'

'Two robberies don't prove a plague,' said Henry. 'Anyway, there's no proof he did them.'

Jennifer closed her eyes and thanked him. Often she'd thought of Henry as wishy-washy, and even now his voice was not assertive. Once she'd accused him of being a fence-sitter in the face of strong argument the way some men are aggressive in strong drink. Now she made a promise.

'Even if that's correct' – Pete again – 'we know enough to want rid of him, the fact that he's been in the loony bin.

Be a constant worry. Be wondering if your kids were safe while you were away. How'd we feel if he went troppo? I'm not saying it'd happen, but why take the risk? I'm not saying it's his fault if he's a bit in the head, but they've got proper places for that sort. Look, he's only been here a matter of weeks, not as if this were his established home forgodsake.'

There was silence. Pete's voice again.

'What about you, Lorna?'

'I want him out.'

Jennifer's tears refused orders. So unequivocal. Tough as ironbark. None of Pete's whinge-tinged self-justification, just finality. The solution.

'There you are!' Pete must have been fixing Henry with those narrow eyes of his.

'Mind you,' Lorna came back either in deference to her husband or because her reply had been too bald-faced even for her, 'I'm unsure about the best way to go about it. Maybe we'd be better to wait until he commits another theft before confronting them? Whoever gets robbed will just have to wear it. Nothing really big has been taken, no engagement rings.'

'That's easy to say when it's not your shed ...'

Henry cut across Pete. 'Jesus, I hope neither of you is on the jury if I'm ever on trial.'

'It's not just us.' Lorna sounded angry. 'It's the Gills, too. And the Cochranes, Arvi and Sue, Bert Jones, Gladys ...'

'Well not me,' said Henry. 'What about Mary?'

'You know Mary.' Pete dismissed his wife. 'Head in the clouds.'

'Listen Pete,' said Lorna, 'wait for a bit. They're coming up here for a meal tonight. Henry and I should have a better feel of it after that. We might even find out something useful.'

Pete must have answered with his face or a shrug.

Part of Jennifer told her to run out and confront them, tell them she'd been eavesdropping and give them a blast for their bigotry. Or just throw her head back and scream. Instead she remained rigid with anger.

With the trio in the clearing making their farewells, in apparent agreement that nothing be done immediately, Jennifer almost gave herself away. As she moved her stiffening legs something bit the toe that stuck through her tennis shoe. Her mind's eye saw an Overton scorpion and she barely stifled a yell.

Instinctively she'd lifted her foot. There was no sign of a scorpion, nor a bull ant, but a single blob of blood grew until it ran off the end of her toe and lost shape on the dirty canvas of her shoe. She concentrated again on the fading sounds from the clearing.

Pete was making his way down the Vickers' path to the track by the river. He must have ridden his pushbike, managed to pass the cabin without her seeing him.

Jennifer relaxed her shoulders, shook each leg, moved back towards her own track. She stopped and glanced back to see if another angle revealed what had bitten her. Nothing moved; no sign of pincers or sting. Funny that, usually you could find the culprit. It helped to know just in case it was a tricky spider and you were circulating venom. She shrugged. There was no poison-pain. Own stupid fault for not wearing her boots, for keeping these broken shoes.

Back on the track she stopped once more and made herself count to ten. The urge to scream at Lorna had abated to seething. She instructed herself: go to the door, call Lorna out and simply say we can't come this evening. Got to hurry back because, because … well, I just do. Stay any longer, risk saying anything more, and you'll explode.

As it was, Lorna greeted her at the door

'Jen, come in. You look like a lobster. Have a drink.'

'No. Thank you.'

Lorna looked up quickly. The voice had been husky, empty.

'What's up, Jen?'

'We can't come,' Jennifer said in neutral, gently rubbing her pricked toe against the calf of her other leg. 'Quinn's better, but he's not up to company. Also, Kate might get his 'flu.'

'You don't look so flash yourself, girl. Are you sure you won't come? Might clear the air, one way or another?'

'No. Must be off now.' She turned to go, her mind a cauldron. As she stepped off the verandah she looked over her shoulder, the green of her eyes meeting the black of Lorna's for the first time. Jennifer stopped, turned around.

'How are you, Lorna?'

The feeling was back in Jennifer's voice. She did not know where it had come from. Lorna's answer was thin.

'Oh, hot and bothered. Like you.'

Jennifer saw that Lorna was burrowing, head down.

'I mean really?'

'What are you standing there and rabbiting about, girl?'

'Don't bluster me, Lorna. I'm thinking it's no more than a month since your Robbie died.' Her voice was as gentle as it had been with Quinn up in The Room. 'Perhaps it's time we talked about your … loss. I wonder if you've been gagging your grief? Have you been down to Robbie's grave?'

'No,' Lorna whispered. She broke eye-contact. 'Henry has. He goes all the time.'

'Don't you think …'

'What I think is that you should mind your business, Jennifer.' Now her head was raised. Her cheeks flushed and her eyes were shiny wet.

'I only meant …'

'Well, I don't want to talk about it!' Suddenly Lorna realised how she'd spat. 'Not now, Jennifer,' she said in her own voice. 'I'm sorry. And that you can't come tonight.'

Lorna turned her back and hurried into the darkness inside the house. Jennifer heard the sobbing escape before the bedroom door slammed shut. There was no sign of Henry or Kate.

Jennifer stopped for a drink of Condamine near the frog

willows. She stuck her right shoe into the river, swished her foot about. The small incision on her toe looked like a cut, not a bite. Must have been a sharp stick.

Her head was still dizzy after she had reached the cabin and stood by the kettle on the primus: all that spleen she had heard from her hiding place, the strange urge to question Lorna about her emotional state, to ask things simply for the way they diverted her fury … Lorna's fiery response and, before that, the way she had looked at her in the few seconds when they connected … What was she saying with those dark eyes, where did it scale between hatred and love?

Also, there had been an odd sensation when she was standing just off the track, listening. It wasn't déjà vu. Not the feeling of being watched. It was as though someone else before her had also stood in that same spot, had listened and had felt angry thoughts on a dry wind.

Jennifer sat on the couch, sipping black tea. In an hour she would go back to the ridge. She would not bring food this time. 'I'll take my faith in you instead, Quinn. I might be rewarded.'

It was as she doubled forward to put a bandage on her toe that cogs meshed within her confusion. Something about the ground where she had stood in the bush and looked to see what had bitten her. What? Maybe Henry had been digging in some rabbit holes? Burying the dunny? No, there were never rabbits so close to the clearing, and surely Henry wouldn't, to use that line of Lorna's, put his shit so near his nest?

There was nothing for it but to go back and look again. Heat or no heat. If she didn't go now whatever it was might vanish, that thing which had jagged her subconscious the way a rosethorn can steal a thread from a cardigan. It may just have been an aura, someone's bodily electricity incompletely dissipated.

Christ! What ridiculous demands her head was making upon her legs. Two trips to the Vickers', two to the ridge, on a hot day and after hoeing and watering. My god, girl, these thighs will be shrivelled to gristle! Carefully she pulled a boot onto the bandaged foot, snorted aloud to the crackling air around her. 'Jennifer Duncan, you're like a bloody bee in a bottle, banging off in all directions and getting nowhere.'

She marched off again in her protective boots. On the track she managed to sing inside her head the song that was written for the engine notes of the utility: *Show me the way to go home, I'm tired and I want to go to bed* ...

As the track began the climb from the river she concentrated, lifting her feet to walk almost noiselessly. Already she was beginning to feel stupid, the sun mocking the idea that she should expect some revelation in the army-green sameness of the scrub or the decay-coloured soil.

Breathing heavily, she looked for the place where she had left the track just short of the clearing. The scrub gave her no help, but she found her own tennis-shoe prints. So close to the Vickers' house! She placed her feet carefully then squatted down to think. There was no bloody aura, not even déjà vu from her own presence less than an hour ago.

The longer she looked, however, the surer she felt. The ground about her gradually came to be different. There was less leaf litter and fewer bits of twigs and bark. She picked up a straight stick and gently swept at the ground in front of her the way an archaeologist brushes the dirt from bone or shard. No bunker of bull ants or squad of scorpions. That possibility had already diminished given that her toe had not begun to throb or swell. She shifted her weight and sent one foot forward, sweeping like a metal detector.

Such a device would have told her more quickly, but Jennifer's thick rubber sole did the job. It caught on something sharp. She pulled her foot back, made a few jabs with the stick, switched away some crusty soil. Realisation hit hard as a falling tree, with the immediate opening of a huge emptiness. The tooth of the creature that had bitten her belonged to an extremely rare underground species.

A chainsaw.

Jennifer did not dig any further for some minutes, just sat there on her haunches staring at half a dozen teeth that curved to follow the tip of the bar. Now that she knew, she could determine the slight indentations about her where another foot had tamped the ground before respreading the leaf litter. Eventually she stood, allowing the bloodflow to resume around her knees. With a curl of dried bark she bent again and with little trouble unpacked the saw, dry dirt clogging the once-greasy ten-inch bar. It came out easily when she grasped the handle and jerked. In the cavity was a brown paper bag; she felt it but did not take it out.

Jennifer replaced the saw and covered it over again. She had to push it down hard. There was a slight convexity to the ground but sprinkled leaves and bits of bark helped to conceal it. She was in a hurry to get away, feeling strangely guilty again. Shit, Lorna, why couldn't you have dug a couple of bloody inches deeper?

As she reburied the cache her eyes summed up another patch of ground a few paces further into the scrub. The skin of soil was broken and in places the leafy detritus was bunched rather than fallen. Pete's tools.

She brushed her knees and elbows and pulled out the bottom of her shirt to wipe her forehead and cheeks. Stepping high and slow back to her track Jennifer felt the tremble in her legs. It was less noticeable once she was striding downhill on the ribbon of dirt.

When she had cleared earshot she began to gallop, physical distance everything.

Quinn had been like the boy saving the dyke, the whole of his body in the breach instead of a mere finger. Wedged in the crevice in Jennifer's Room the pressure did feel like a vast body of irresistible water. He had reached that vibrating point where one or two innocent drops of rain could tip the scales from motionless reservoir to kinetic torrent, a tumult sweeping all before it and devastating the landscape of his mind. That image of inundation had remained with him many times after he had levelled out from the nosedives of his illness. Once, in a poem that attempted to throw an anchor into the fathomless reaches of schizophrenia, he had the lines:

> *I think therefore I am*
> *the Caborra Basa dam*

He had called the poem *Look, No Sluice Gates!* The Caborra Basa dam, like all such man-made obstructions, had openings in it to bleed the great weight of the Zambesi's water whenever it became overbearing through flood. But the best Quinn could do with *his* dam was to lean against its wall with his small strength. That, and pursuing silence and stillness.

He would try to picture his mind as an infinitely wide sheet of mirrorwater, not a gnat stirring its taut surface, nor the disturbance of one bird's wings above it. If no dark clouds were attracted, if not so much as dew fell, then the watery weight might subside, evaporation and the leaching of distant dry land would lower the levels. Quinn would be able to tiptoe away, as one might from a mere migraine.

This was his strong side, the optimistic, stiff-upper-cere-brum view of it. Down in the gut the sensation was darker, the water more of an oleaginous slurry. The second his back was turned, sappers would be laying mines and attaching plastic explosives to the critical structural points of the dam, deto-nating them from remote safety. So in the silence Quinn would be listening, eyes radaring about him for betrayals of movement.

The smallest things could be vital indicators. The first time Jennifer had come up to see him, the way she had placed her feet had been of critical importance. If she should be wearing white, or those broken sandshoes, then he would know she was now an adversary. One lifted eyebrow could confirm a whole conspiracy.

Jennifer had been to visit him several times. He could not tell if she was being used. There had been some whispering to do with her but it was hard to distinguish individual words from the general muttering. He'd also known that if he had to speak then it would be best not to use her name. The food had been far too great a risk, of course. He had buried it so that the dirt would make it inedible. Hunger worked like a corkscrew in his belly and he might weaken, run the risk and eat. It was bad enough that he'd drunk the water; but then he'd smelled it, just wet his tongue at first, waited for at least an hour for a reaction.

His preoccupation was not with death. That would be too simple, the bait of finality too neat. No, it was the pervading fear of disablement, if he should allow his guard to drop. Disablement would lead to entrapment. Once weakened – by his own laxness, some chemical inducement, some ploy – he would be ripe for the picking. A mind there for the taking and using. This was exactly what those proponents of Socrates' second coming must have done the last time he was less than fully vigilant. The rule was that while you were aware of the threat it remained pending; once you were no longer able to perceive its proximity, it was too late. it had you.

Shutting himself off from Jennifer had been hard. This was why he had avoided those green eyes. What was required was an emotional heart bypass, some surgery to cut away the fact that he'd fallen in love. He tried to see Jennifer only through a window made of wax, a visual version of Ulysses' earplugs.

Hunger was so strong that he must have been in The Room for at least a week? His saliva had a grassy, chlorophyl taste. Recently, he was not sure how many days ago, he had succumbed to the acids in his guts and eaten some small cakes Jennifer had brought. Inexcusable weakness, but nothing untoward had happened.

In the heat of the day it was now acceptable to walk about The Room. Its design, the single entrance at the rear, the three impenetrable walls, the impossibility of approaching unseen up the slope towards the fourth – all these were reassuring. Locked in a flat in the city, thin walls, ply doors, breakable glass, you were far more vulnerable. The city offered anonymity, true, but here there was the feeling of fortress.

The nights were black and bleak, however. He would doze, jerk awake minutes later, curse himself for his exposure as he flexed contorted limbs. The past two nights he had sensed a slackening, an enemy retreat, and had stretched on the ground in the sleeping bag, the wall at his back. Risky luxury, but hunger was his watchdog; when it took him, sleep was light and twitchy.

This morning he had also risked looking Jennifer in the eye when she came up. Nothing happened. And throughout the day he'd kept out of the crevice, even re-packed her belongings into it. Someone had put sticks and stones in the pathway, he noticed, but it did not worry him. He would clear them away.

Defecation and urination had required the cover of night and several stealthy steps down the slope. Now at times, if the breeze curled around the rock and into The Room, he would get a whiff of his own manure. His stink somehow damaged the view down to the trees by the river. Given that he was apparently going to come out on top in this engagement, he decided to risk going out in broad daylight to properly bury his wastes, minimal though they were because of his fasting. Again, nothing untoward happened.

Although weak physically, Quinn was starting to feel stronger where it mattered more.

Jennifer had fallen back on the couch after bursting off the track. Her mind was incapable of forcing the huge lump of her discovery through the sieve of deduction. All she could think of was that Lorna was crazy; causes, consequences … nothing would proceed.

She had not the slightest idea what to do next. Except go down to the Condamine, throw herself in and let the river carry her far, far away from here. Flush her out of the valley. 'Just upped and went,' they'd say at Hamilton's bar. The story of the bush burial and the strange thefts would be incorporated into Walrae folklore over the years, the facts embroidered.

And you're the woman who boasted to Quinn of your strength! It was Quinn who had taken her thoughts beyond the acts Lorna had perpetrated with her wounded eyes and righteous anger. What could Jennifer Duncan, sole friend, soulmate, lover, what could she do if Quinn stayed up there, eating virtually nothing, not washing, presumably not taking his medication? She knew enough of drugs to realise that their potency had build-ups and run-downs. But how long could she responsibly leave him alone in The Room?

The day was almost done now, its blues turning from oils to watercolours, and she must go up to him. As a 'strong woman', a pillar of trust, understanding and resilience. Piss off, tears!

Jennifer patted water onto her face and washed all traces of earth from her hands and forearms. Before the mirror her hair returned red lights, was glossier than it used to be. Perhaps from lovemaking? She wondered as she brushed whether there was some hormonal formula which, without benefit of advertising, made it shine? 'Gone to your head, eh?' She managed to smirk at her reflection.

On the spur of the moment she decided to change, for Quinn. She reefed off her T-shirt and shorts, scrabbled in the wardrobe and found a pale blue sleeveless blouse and a denim skirt. The Blundstone workboots below made her comically hick, not chic, and she removed them. Fashion was low on Jennifer Duncan's list, but thinking about what to wear acted as a beta-blocker to images of Lorna. Taking a plastic dish of water to the back door she soaped away the circles of dust that ran like anklechains around each leg. Clean feet were a blessing. Suddenly she thought of Sunday-school Christ, had to bite her lip to fend off more tears. She concentrated on drying her toes then returned to the wardrobe for sandals. On the way out she stopped before the mirror again for a final inspection and to run a stick of clear salve around her lips. Now light responded from her mouth as well as her hair.

Splash's bleating to her departing back was dismissed with a wave. Jennifer lifted the front of her skirt in each hand as she walked up the slope. Straight up, for once, no zigzagging. Her mind was quite calm; the way people can be when first told that a family member has died in a car crash. It *had* helped to dress up; she felt clean and relaxed. The evening made it hard to be otherwise: feathering down on brushes of gold, broad strokes of pink, dove greys, revenant blues. She hoped Quinn's mind was working from the same palette, that he was lying on his back in The Room and swallowing with his eyes. This sky was a major tranquilliser.

At the top of the ridge she paused in the enveloping calm while her breath slowed. Then she walked purposefully through the canyon. The stone-and-stick barrier had not been repaired since the morning. Jennifer lifted her skirt to step over. 'Hellowwww,' she called, not loudly but keeping any waver from it. 'It's me, Jennifer Dumb Duncan.'

Everything had been tidied away: sleeping bag, ground-sheet, waterbottle. There was no sign of Quinn, apart from his boots, which stood neatly at the front edge where the land fell away. Jennifer's calm left her. The disembodied boots said death, even though the land sloped rather than plunged, the emptiness an optical illusion. She ran to the boots, picked them up in one hand, dropped them back. She cupped her hands around her mouth. 'Hellowww, Quinn, hellowww.'

The sound cannoned off the rocks and down the slope, but there was no sign of him. Where would he have gone without his boots anyway?

She almost fell forward in fright when a voice descended from the sky:

'Hello, Jennifer.'

Swinging around, she shaded her eyes. Quinn was atop the flat rock that made the back wall of The Room, wearing only his jeans, which were rolled halfway to his knees. He was skinny, his belly almost concave, but baked brown by his days in the sun. Jennifer thought he looked like a shipwrecked sailor who has discovered he is not alone on his island. More than his appearance, she had noticed his voice. It sounded like Ned Quinn, came quietly from deep inside him rather than high up in his neck.

'You really frightened me,' she said, still shading her eyes. 'It was weird just seeing your boots and no you. What are you doing up there, Quinn?'

'Just looking about. Getting the bearings of the surround-ings, seeing as much of this sky as I possibly could. How many days have I been in The Room? A long time?'

'Can you come down? I can hardly see you.'

She watched him move off to the right among the serrated rocks and towards the footholds to the path. She had been shouting at him, but he had not reacted against the noise. As he came across the firestones and into The Room she waded right in. 'Let's get your things and go back down to the cabin. It's about time you had a decent meal, don't you think?'

It had sounded like a sister trying to cajole a loveable but indolent younger brother. Beneath the facade, Jennifer's heart-rate was a sprinter's.

'Okay.'

His voice was flat, but when she gripped his hand in lieu of words he returned the squeeze briefly. She preceded him through the narrow entrance, keeping her mouth shut on the babble of excitement inside her.

'How do you feel?' Jennifer allowed herself quietly as they were on the slope, the colours now rinsed from the sky in the short space that separates greyness and night. He didn't answer, but said: 'I suppose you've been going through a really hard time, Jennifer?'

She was not about to tell him how bad, but was touched that he should feel for her, not mention his own hell. Best of all, his eyes were now the ones that always gathered her with their warmth. The sooner they reached the cabin the better; she wanted to bathe in the lights of those eyes again.

'You must be starving?'

'I am, but I'm more exhausted than hungry. I wasn't able to sleep much up there. Is everything … ?'

'Yes, it's fine,' said Jennifer firmly, the truth of the moment.

Part 4

On his return from The Room Quinn had drunk a pot of tea and eaten six slabs of toast. He said he was too tired to walk down to the river, asked Jennifer if she minded if he went to bed just as he was – dusty, with hair like Bob Marley's. Not if he gave her a hug, Jennifer said. Quinn put his arms around her and she held him to her laughing as he succumbed to a long yawn next to her left ear. She could feel the weakness in his body: he was on the point of falling over.

In bed, he smiled at Jennifer as she watched him from the couch. Then he was asleep. Fast as that.

She wanted to get in with him, to cling to her prodigal lover. But the pallor that underlay his tanned, bearded face warned her that she should content herself with watching him fall deeper and deeper into sleep, his face muscles relaxing and his lips parting over those strong white teeth. At the other end of the bed his large naked feet protruded from the sheets. Jennifer felt like bringing the bowl she had used for her own and washing them, lovingly. How daft! This apparent foot-fetish must be to do with the way she'd found the chainsaw?

Suddenly Quinn's coming down from the ridge, the hope that she might just slide softly in beside him and drift into her own sleep to the hum of his bodyheat … these simple plea-sures went roaring away with the word chainsaw. No longer, with Quinn tucked in and blissed out, could she shut off the afternoon's shattering discovery.

Quite quickly Jennifer realised that what she'd learned about Lorna was hardly worth having. She had begun to think Quinn would now be safe, that she could prove his innocence, whatever the cost. How naive. Were she to call Senior Constable Worthing, lead him to the goods after somehow explaining that Pete, too, had been robbed, he might well think that she had buried them herself to protect Quinn. Would he consider for a minute that she had stumbled on them quite by chance, while quietly eavesdropping on her friends?

Obviously something had broken from the moorings of Lorna's mind since Robbie's death. Quinn's arrival had become the mist behind which she was adrift. It occurred to Jennifer, for the first time, that Lorna could be *jealous* of her love for Quinn. It was also conceivable that Lorna subconsciously blamed her for the death of her baby son, was exacting bizarre payment. Even more worrying was the likelihood that, whatever had been the trigger, Lorna had absolutely no conscious idea of what she had been doing, that she might quite honestly be outraged at the suggestion that she was Overton's thief.

At the same time Jennifer wondered how her friend could have physically carried out the robberies. She took her mind back and, yes, Lorna had driven the Land-Rover into Walrae on the evening of the Gills' robbery. Invariably she called at their place to see if they wanted anything. Gills' dogs would have been accustomed to her. Lorna also was a frequent visitor to Pete's and Mary's place, and it was true that they were often away from their house – Pete attending his hives, Mary painting in the bush, their offspring practically living up trees and in all sorts of secret places along the river's banks. Lorna could have broken the lock on Pete's shed: force did not sound like Lorna, but certainly she was practical, quite capable of changing a wheel or of hot-wiring the Land-Rover's ignition if she'd mislaid her keys. If you could do that, you'd have no problem using a jack handle to lever open a cheap padlock.

Before Robbie was born, when the three of them had been reading up on home births, both Jennifer and Henry had silently absorbed the chapters on post-natal depression. The chemistry of the maternal vessel could become labile, even with an easy delivery, a healthy baby. Lorna's nine months of autonomic nurture had ended with a few tiny breaths. If depression could lurk behind a joyous event, how much more likely was it beneath grief, the more so given that it was suppressed? This blackness, the books said, could – in a way that she imagined was not dissimilar to what happened to Quinn when he crossed the boundary into florid country – sheer off into 'puerperal psychosis'. If Lorna was slipping around robbing her neighbours, all the while pointing at an innocent stranger, then she was … a case.

This speculation was getting her nowhere, and yet there was an urgent need for action. Lorna, whatever had inspired her, had delayed Pete and the others from sending a posse to her cabin. But for how long, especially after she had declined the dinner invitation that was the pretext for the delay? What if there was a third robbery … what if Lorna, knowingly or otherwise, was to hammer another nail into Quinn's chances of remaining with her? She and Quinn had not discussed how long his visit would last, when he would head south again to put his affairs in order. But both knew without the exchange of a word that he would not be resuming the life he had led at Ivanhoe High School, at his solitary city flat. Each of them wanted another throw of the dice.

Jennifer cut off these thoughts. What hope did the two of them have when other people kept changing the rules of the game? She was exhausted from the day's events. She couldn't think along a line of thought for more than a few sentences, her mind taking tangents that became cul-de-sacs of tearful tenderness for Quinn, outrage, hopelessness, self-pity. All her self-sufficiency had been spent this hot day; she was in need of a mother or a big sister, even a priest would have been better than nothing. But there was nowhere to turn for counsel.

Once she would have laid all her cards on the Vickers' kitchen table. Between Lorna's cheeky impetuosity and

Henry's warm thoughtfulness she would quickly learn the options, weigh up their opinions, find her right path. How do you ask your best friend for advice on her own psychotic behaviour? Or your best friend's husband?

Jennifer lit one of the lamps and placed it on the floor so that its waxy light would not bother Quinn. She suspected that even a pneumatic drill would not have stirred him, but it was something positive to do. She stepped over his protruding feet and went out to the verandah, shutting the door after her because sorties of moths would soon be dive-bombing the lamplight. Leaning on the rail she smoked a thin cigarette into which she had rolled a few flakes of Seven Sisters, a poor substitute now for human ones.

Three lungfuls into the Sisters she got the idea. There just *might* be a source of no-frills advice on the best way to save the man she loved from the woman she also loved, the woman she loved from herself. Jennifer would not put it like that, but there *was* somebody she could go to and ask for help. Right here in Overton. Right now.

By the time Jennifer pulled the utility off the track which hugged the Condamine and onto the even bumpier one which ended at the Joneses' unpainted weatherboards, some of the inspiration had left her. The headlights were swathing into the bush like a drunken samurai. It would have made less noise and a lot more sense to have walked down, tiptoed up to the house to see how the land lay. But Jennifer had done more than her share of walking, more than enough snooping. Apart from which, she did not feel like trying to outsmart that brown dog, which, Hilda had told her, frequently was off the chain at night. No, to hell with it. If Bert proved difficult, if she couldn't get Hilda away on her own, well, she'd invent a pretext, something like running out of kero …

Hilda was standing in the doorway as the headlights made the last lurch around the bend that stopped at the house. She was holding Browner by the collar, his front legs off the ground, his teeth visible in the Holden's beams. The night's silence rushed in as Jennifer cut the engine. She left the headlights on and got out, called across the roof of the car, one foot still in it.

'It's me. Jennifer.'

'Knew it was. Misfirin' motor.'

'I'm sorry to turn up out of the blue, out of the black … Hilda, I need to talk to you. Maybe you could come over and we'll sit in the car, I mean if that would be more convenient?'

'Here on the verandah's where I was sittin' when Browner and me heard you comin'.'

'It's just that … it's private.'

'Private on the verandah, but. Bert 'n the boys 've went into Walrae. They'll be back from Hamilton's so noisy 'n full of theirself you'll hear 'em soon as they come over the rise past Pete's.'

Jennifer switched off the lights, paused while her eyes adjusted. Then walked towards the four panes of barleysugar light that eked from the kitchen onto a small section of the verandah. She heard Hilda swear at Browner, the dog yelp.

'Siddown here.' Hilda pointed to a bentwood chair and Jennifer realised it was herself, not the dog, being addressed. 'Tea,' Hilda said, and was gone into the kitchen. Browner lay on his belly, chin on the ground, eyes computing every thumb movement as Jennifer rolled a cigarette and wished Hilda would hurry.

At last they were in a triangle, Jennifer in the chair, Hilda on the boards, her back supported by the door frame, Browner all ears.

'We've talked privately before, Hilda. Confidentially. Well, I want to explain something very difficult for me about these robberies. I need some advice, I reckon, but it has to be from someone I can trust to keep it quiet. Forever.'

In the dark the glow of Hilda's cigarette moved up and down a few times, which Jennifer took for assent.

She told about the eavesdropping, the discovery of the chainsaw, gave a potted explanation of post-natal depression. Said how she feared what a third robbery would do. The only bit she baulked at was a full description of Quinn's illness. She did say that he had become very confused, couldn't think straight, how she felt that the pressure of blame and suspicion were probably contributory. Finally, with Hilda's silence starting to embarrass her, she asked: 'What would you do, in my position?'

'It's a spot, but,' was all Hilda said. Maybe Jennifer was asking too much?

Hilda sucked up some tea. 'First off,' she set the mug on the boards, 'I'd put the stuff back.'

'What"

'Yeah, sneak the saw and the money back to the Gills. Shove 'em on the seat of Kevin's truck or somewhere. Pete's stuff, too. He won't 'ave a new lock yet.'

'But … what would be the point?'

'S'pose if people get their stuff back … they aren't goin' to be so hostile. Second, when yer mate learns the stuff 'as been put back by somebody, gone from where she buried it, gunna get one helluva shock. Even if her nickin's sub, sub …'

'Subconscious?'

'Yeah, even if it's that. Might snap 'er round.'

They sat in silence for a while, with only the sound of Jennifer blowing the surface of her tea.

'It's a bloody good idea, Hilda. At least …' Jennifer's voice faded away. 'I couldn't do it! No way could I go creeping around the Gills and Pete's at night. I'd trip over something … not to mention Gills' bloody dogs.'

'Dig the stuff up, girl. Right away. One bag Gills, one bag Pete's. I'll get 'em back. Bloody Gills' dogs, eh!' Hilda chuckled.

Jennifer involuntarily pictured herself sitting down with a witch. She felt ashamed of the thought in the face of such uplifting generosity.

'I don't know if I've got the strength to go and dig the stuff up now, it's been such a day.'

'Ain't got no choice but, Jennifer.'

It was the first time she could recall Hilda using her name.

'Then I should come with you to replace them, too.'

'Rather on me own.'

'You're a clever lady, Hilda,' Jennifer said, relieved to be relinquishing part of the mess.

'Henry Vickers,' said Hilda.

'What about him?'

'He don't bullshit about. Ain't so keen to string up yer Ned?'

'Not like the others, that's for sure.'

'You talk to 'im?'

'Well, yes …' What was Hilda getting at?

'How about takin' 'im aside, on yer own like. Tell 'im the truth, even how you found what his missus done?'

'What could I expect Henry to do? I could hardly ask him to expose his wife as a thief.'

'Never said that. But yer want no more robberies, right? Well, if Henry knows 'is missus is off the rocker, he can have a good eye on 'er, even get some doctoring. Main thing is to be keepin' 'er hands outa other people's sheds 'n trucks.'

'Getting between a husband and wife is very risky, Hilda. I can't even be sure how Henry would react, to me or to Lorna. He's taking the baby's death pretty hard himself, no doubt. We'll think about it. But even if I don't tell him about the robberies, I could try to talk to him about the change that's come over Lorna …'

'Better get a move on.'

The audience was over. Jennifer stood, Browner lifted his head.

'I can't begin to …'

'Get them bags 'n all down 'ere. I'll be waitin'.'

Hilda went into her kitchen. Browner followed.

Quinn remained deep in subterranean sleep when Jennifer returned to the cabin. She sat on the couch again and watched him for a few minutes. He looked quite beautiful, she decided. Like one of the Apostles, almost: black hair wild on the pillow, big aristocratic nose, the way the fingers of the hand that had flopped on the floor pointed upwards as though holding an invisible apple. She smiled. Apostles? What do you know about apostles, for heaven's sake? First the washing of feet, now this. That's the second old-time-religious reversion you've had today. If God's mercy were truly infinite he'd let a girl go to bed. You're thinking like this because that's what all religions evaporate to: the salt of right or wrong. Around here it's getting hard to tell the difference.

Jennifer got down on her hands and knees next to Quinn's head. She put her face about three inches from his, felt and heard his breath sailing in and out, long lulls between. Let her lips rest on the triangle of cheekskin between nose, eye and beard. She stood carefully, the end of her tongue against her top lip. There was the smell and taste of the man in her bed. She let her head hang back, roll from shoulder to shoulder. A sudden yawn made her straighten again as she swallowed air.

Under the cabin, she hunted with the torch for flour sacks. Around the rim of the torch she bent a circle of cardboard, kept it on with a rubber band. This stopped diffusion, held the beam to a solid bar so that up close to something little light was given away. With two folded hessian sacks and the garden fork, once more she headed up her track.

The spot was easier to find this time. After stepping carefully into the scrub she laid the torch on the ground and, as a further precaution, put some pieces of bark over its end, making the light look like a flake of glowing meteor. Before she began to dig she stood quite still. There was no sound at all from the Vickers' house and she could see no lights from where she was. From far up the slope came a soft whinny, almost a repressed laugh, from Lorna's horse. Thank God the Vickers didn't have a dog.

The tines of the fork slipped into the broken ground and the chainsaw came out quickly; she put it in one of the sacks, its flour mixing with yellow dirt. The paper bag went in with it. She forked the earth back before doing a little dance with her boots to compact it, using the back of the fork to remove any footprints.

The second hole yielded Pete's belongings just as easily. By the time she had finished retrieving the axe, wirestrainers, tin shears, wrenches and a few other tools, Pete's sack was the heavier of the two. Again she expunged her solemarks but she decided not to fill in the hole; Lorna, if she did return, should be aware that things were not the way she left them.

Heading for home, her body bent forward against the weight of the sacks, she felt like one of the Seven Dwarfs after a day at the mine. And I know which dwarf, Jennifer thought to herself. Dopey! The alleged thief is asleep in my bed, the real one is oblivious and probably tossing in her own bed, and I'm clumping through the bush at night with a ton of toolery so that it can be returned secretly to its rightful and righteous owners by another party, also innocent! I'm not so sure who's mentally ill around here …

The sacks clanked to the ground next to the utility. She returned to the work area under the cabin, replaced the fork then went back carrying a small broom and pan and a can of turpentine with a rag in its bung. With the cardboard guard removed from the torch she set about cleaning the tools. She was not quite sure why she was doing it. Was it something to do with removing any traces that might lead back to herself? Or was it because the owners were tool-lovers and might be as upset by abuse as theft? Briefly she wondered whether the sacks might incriminate her, but then everybody in the valley would have a few from McConnachies'. She tied string around the necks.

It was nine pm by the time she started nosing the utility

back down to Hilda's. The bush was silent and she drove extremely slowly, to make as little noise as possible. People who were near-deaf when you were talking to them nevertheless had a way of knowing when a car was miles off, even picking a local's from an intruder's.

Jennifer was still feeling a fool. It occurred to her suddenly that Hilda had no way of carrying the sacks to their respective owners' houses. The round trip from Joneses' to Gills' to Pete and Mary's and back was probably ten or a dozen kilometres; the sacks were far too heavy. Hilda didn't have a car, didn't drive.

She thought about stopping, slinging the sacks into the Condamine. She was so tired. But there was Hilda, stepping out from the bush near her turn-off, waving her down. Browner's eyes seemed to have gone blood-red this close to the headlights. He didn't bark.

Hilda was already lifting the sacks from the back.

'Which is which?'

'Pete's is the heavier one. But Hilda …'

'I'll dump the stuff, bring the bags home, burn 'em.' She was in charge.

'But Hilda! It's bloody miles, there's buggerall moon, the Gills have got those maniac dogs, you can't possibly carry so much on foot. Let's just hide the stuff, bury it again somewhere, sling it in the river even?'

'Second best,' said Hilda derisively. Part of her answer was to step back into the bush and return with a bicycle. She began tying the sacks between its handlebars with baling twine. 'Flamin' car'd 'ave Gills' dogs tearin' their chains out,' she explained as she worked. 'Bike's dead quiet. Browner'll come along and 'ave the Gills' dogs yappin', stir 'em a bit. Gills know that sort of barkin' aint real warnin' stuff, die down soon enough. Browner'll give just about the toodoo so's no-one hears Hilda slingin' a saw and some dollars into Gills' truck. Your mates Pete and Mary? We'll be like mice, won't we, Browner?'

Jennifer had never heard Hilda so voluble. She was talking to herself and the dog, really. Quite excited by her part in the conspiracy, totally relaxed about travelling about the bush in the dark. Jennifer could not help wondering whether Hilda had done it before, if she didn't sometimes stand in blackness outside people's windows looking in to get an idea of what a family might be. Possibly she had even stood below Jennifer's own cabin, fiercely lonely.

One day, she decided, she would persuade Hilda to sit on her own verandah with her and share some Seven Sisters. Just the two of them it would have to be. Quinn would understand.

She realised that Hilda was talking to her. 'G'won then. Off 'ome. Have yer gone asleep standin' up, girl?'

'Sorry. Sorry, Hilda. Are you sure …?'

'Said I'd do it, didn't I? Go back to that feller of yours.'

Hilda stood by her bike as Jennifer slowly turned the utility using the opening to the Joneses' track. She drove off towards bed. In the rear-vision mirror all was black behind her.

Reversing the ute up the steep slope at night was difficult. Jennifer used the headlights to pick out landmarks that told her angle and distance. After chocking the front wheels she reached through the window and punched the knob to kill the lights. Silence and darkness encircled her, she could feel them on her face as she walked slowly across the slope to the cabin, which was leaking warm lamplight.

The silence followed her inside. She took off her dress-up blouse, unzipped the back of her skirt. The front of it, she noticed, looked like one of Mary's artistic smocks: flour, grease, turpentine. It fell to the floor from her hips and she flicked it with her foot into a corner. Did the same with her knickers. She turned down the wick and blew out the lamp.

Now only Quinn's faint breathing told her he was in her bed. She fumbled for the sheet on her side, slid in. Her body did not touch his but she could feel the warm sleep emanating from him. Briefly she thought of Hilda and Browner somewhere in the dark, of how quickly the news would get around tomorrow.

Lying on her back, she let out a long yawn. The jawy noise must have disturbed Quinn. He rolled on his side towards her, a long arm curling across her breasts. Just the right weight.

Jennifer woke alone. It was nearly eight am and Quinn's side of the bed was cool. It made her sit up sharply and knuckle the sleep from her eyes, but then she relaxed back onto the bed, smiling. Rolling over to his side she smelled the dented pillow, the creased top of the sheet. Made her think of grilled steak. Or crisp bacon? There was also an edge of nutmeg to his odour. It honed her appetites. Even though Quinn must have been dirty after his confinement in The Room, there was nothing stale to his scent, nothing foxy

Looking from the verandah, the boards warm under her feet, there was no sign of him near the jetty. She gathered a towel, also warmed, from the rail and tied it above her breasts.

Quinn was on the bend about a hundred metres to the right of the jetty, doing his compromise crawl, balancing his strength to the river's. Jennifer threw her towel on the bank and jumped, her toes touching the silty bottom. When she surfaced Quinn was still ploughing his furrow, head down. He had not noticed her. She breaststroked slowly upstream, occasionally dunking her head to let the current pull her curls back from her eyes. When she pulled alongside Quinn he was still swimming, breathing every four strokes but on the opposite side to her. Treading water, that part of the river too deep to stand, she watched for a while. Then she moved closer, slid her hand under the surface and touched his side.

The shock cost Quinn all rhythm. He contorted like a snake on the surface of the river and his eyes stood out on his dripping face as the current began carrying him off. Jennifer could not help laughing at the change from sinuous swimmer to thrasher and splutterer.

'Jesus Christ!' He was now holding his place again, down-river from her. 'My head was miles away.' He stopped to cough and breathe. 'And you creep up. I thought for a moment. That a carp had latched. Onto me. Like a piranha.'

'Sorry,' Jennifer grinned, clearly not so. 'I couldn't resist it. Anyway, you looked as though you might have gone on lumbering through the water all day, leaving me there like some tiring pilot fish.'

Quinn had moved towards the far bank and was standing, recovering, in waist-deep water. Jennifer steered herself towards him on the current, her hair now curling back around her face like a scarf in a tailwind. She could see that Quinn was waiting for her. Their eyes were reeling each other in.

When he caught her, as the river pressed her to him, she said, 'Welcome home, Quinn.' Her voice had meant to sound smooth, but it came out croakily. He kissed her on the mouth and sent his hands from the nape of her neck to the rise of her bottom, the water making them fluent down her back. Jennifer felt a tremor in her legs. Quinn lifted his mouth from the wet hair around her neck.

'Come with me.' Unlike hers, his voice was deep and unbroken.

She waded after him holding his hand and they scrambled up the dark earth bank. There was a shelf of flat land before the start of the climb to the opposite ridge of the valley, which Quinn had combed with his eyes from The Room. Still being led, Jennifer watched the movement of his back and his ribs, the way his skin fitted its frame, tight as a wetsuit. She could not see the front of him.

Quinn stopped suddenly and before she knew what he was doing bent and slid an arm behind her knees, the other around her back. When he straightened she was being carried over the grass like a bride. She was shocked that he was able to walk with her, given his lean body and her more Roman proportions. 'You'll break your back, Quinn!'' she protested, but he was not staggering, there was no strain in his face. In fact he stopped, kissed her lightly on the lips, kissed each wet breast, then continued.

It was about twenty-five metres that he carried her, to a grassy clearing in the tall trees, a spot Jennifer could not help thinking was similar to the place further up on the other side where Robbie Vickers had been buried. But there were no willows here, only straight eucalypts with human-smooth skin. Quinn had bent on one knee and was lowering her carefully onto her back on the grass. She realised how remarkably strong he was by the fact that his breathing was easy.

'You Tarzan, me Jade,' she said, laughing nervously.

She had her hands on his shoulders now, reaching up. The world had slowed drastically, as though his mouth was approaching from a long way away. Drops of water were still running off their skin, slowly raining onto her from the black wetpointed curls of his hair. The grass beneath her, and the earth it grew from, were soft as the pressure upon her increased.

'Quinn?'

She was going to ask him if he too felt a dizziness. But the question got lost, dissolved in the murmuring of the long black Condamine. Everything got lost.

Breakfast on the verandah was also like good times revisited, the impossibility of going back to beginnings. Each of them had a plate resting on their knees, the centre of which was an orange glow. Boiled eggs. They were both on their second, stabbing fingers of toast into the lava, brushing them lightly through ground pepper and salt at the rim of the plate, trailing glutinous smears of yolk and butter. Then they were blowing on black tea. As they chewed and slurped it struck Jennifer that sated lovers fill these lesser appetites so offhand-edly. For a long while food shouldered talk aside.

'I'm not sure how many days I was up there,' Quinn said at last, straightening things up, lifting the conversation from the level of oh and ah and the suck of lip on flesh and food. 'Five days? A week?'

'Three and a half,' Jennifer answered quietly. She had put down her plate and was brushing away toast crumbs that had taken refuge in her navel. Her breasts looked flaccid in the bright morning sunlight, she thought, the nipples now pale and dormant. Never had she allowed herself such abandon as just now beside the river, but for all their carnality she knew as they sat there, twin Cheshire cats, that they had touched upon something deeper this time.

'Both of me must have been keen to return to you,' Quinn joked. 'That's pretty short.'

'How long can they last, these, ah, minor ones?'

'Sometimes weeks, a month? By which time they are no longer what you'd call, ah, minor. Those are the times when I can't seem to block the voices. The timing for this one wasn't too brilliant, was it? Sorry.'

She reached for his hand to silence him. 'As long as you keep coming back, I'll be waiting at the edge. To be honest, I couldn't be with you if you stayed like that permanently, off on some far distant horizon, because, well, that's not the Quinn I love. It's a stranger.' Jennifer just managed not to look away. 'Anyway, now that it's happened once it'll be less frightening for me. I s'pose the hardest part of it will be to learn patience, to wait like some sailor's wife for your return. I think what I feared most was that when you did get back from those rough seas things would be different between us. Maybe that your illness could attack the roots of what we feel. This morning you've reassured me that it doesn't. Next time I'll try to cling to that.'

Now she did turn her eyes to the river. 'I'd sort of half-rehearsed what I just said, Quinn, but somehow it sounded better when I was saying it to myself. The thing is, I've come right off the back burner, Quinn … all this emotion boiling through me. I still trust the totems about me, with my sort of wounded animist faith, only now I've got this great gush of feeling for you. I'm not used to such … for a man … don't think I've ever been. It's like being electrocuted, but living through it.'

When at last she managed to look back at him Jennifer was biting her bottom lip, two tears trailing lines of light down each cheek. She was laughing at the same time.

Quinn, who usually found words more easily, also had brimming eyes. He was about to say something, but understood from her face that he didn't need to, that she knew. So he put his finger to his lips, showed her that he was silencing himself. Reached for her hand. They sat for a long time like that, looking into their perspectives of simple bush, human complexity.

'The robberies?' Quinn said at last.

'No more.' Jennifer's voice was flat. 'With luck they're over and we'll be left in peace.' As she spoke she knew her that's-that approach would not work.

'Tell me what's been happening,' he said quietly.

'I have. No more robberies.'

'Listen, I don't want to be protected.'

'Maybe it's not you I want to protect.'

'You've found out who did them?'

'This is pushing me, and yourself, Quinn. You've been through great pressure and stress in the past days and I don't imagine misplaced blame has helped exactly. Wouldn't it be better if you let me deal with it and didn't get involved? After all, I've had to handle it while you've been … away.'

'I need condescension even less than I need stress, Jennifer.' They were his first sharp words to her.

'Sorry,' she said, stung.

'Forget it. Pure motives, but I have enough problems with reality as it is.' He bent sideways in his chair and kissed her on the cheek.

'Okay then,' Jennifer sighed, 'fasten your seatbelt.'

It took nearly an hour to tell, with Quinn interrupting for

clarifications, occasionally to say 'shit!' or 'bloody hell!' Once or twice he laughed.

'What a remarkable woman,' he said, almost to himself, when Jennifer at last finished and slumped back in her chair.

'She's a good woman,' Jennifer said defensively. 'It's hard to comprehend post-natal depression, but it can and does ...'

'No, no, I meant Hilda Jones. I'd like to meet her.

'Don't hold your breath. If I described myself as once-burnt, then I suspect Hilda lives in eternal flame. I don't think she's ever had reason to see men as other than selfish and dangerous. Must be pretty devastating to come to that conclusion on the basis of the man you married and the two sons you bore. I suspect romance does live on in old Hilda, but in some sealed compartment. She saw a glimmer of it in our plight, I like to think. That would explain why she was willing to run risks to help us, or me anyway. But experience has treated her too harshly. To convey romantic love to Hilda would be like trying to explain the smell of lavender mathematically.'

His grin made her blush. 'Alright, alright,' she said petulantly, 'I won't mention love or romance, not even lust, for the rest of the day. So there!'

He laughed. 'Jennifer Jade, you know I'm teasing. But to stick a pin in our mutual swooning, we've got to do something about Lorna, about all of this.'

'Like what? She'll hear today, probably has already, about the return of the stolen goods. That may put the brakes on, it may not. As for the Cochranes, Arvi and Sue, the Gills, Hilda's Bert, Pete particularly, plus the upstanding burghers of Walrae ... they'll be on a fraying leash, if I know this place at all. One or more of them is acting quite independently of Lorna, anyway, I'm positive of that.'

'I don't like sitting here with my fingers crossed, waiting.'

'If the valley forces you out,' Jennifer whispered, 'I'll go, too. I mean, if you want me to that is. Not just because of you but because I wouldn't want to live here if that happened.'

He smiled at her coy solemnity. 'No, it mustn't come to that, Jennifer.'

Before she could reply Quinn had turned away. 'I think I should act now. You've done more than enough, you and Hilda. Something pre-emptive. I have the impression that there is more to this hostility towards me than the thefts, particularly in the case of Pete. I seem to have come into his focus as a circling albatross. And yet they will use the thefts as the best way to see me off, to circulate their displaced fears.'

'You may be right,' Jennifer interrupted impatiently, 'but whatever excuse they find for their hysteria about your illness, the end result is going to be the same: they want you out.'

She got up. The day was strutting towards noon, carving the shade on the verandah to a patch just big enough for their deckchairs. The egg-streaked plates glazed in the sun. She gathered them and went inside to make more tea. Quinn watched her breasts move inside her shirt as she bent for the plates, his concentration breaking. He wiped his forehead with his arm as she left, frowned over the verandah rail.

At the sink Jennifer stood and listened to the primus flame ticking on the base of the kettle. She was thinking about his reaction to her offer to leave, how he had accepted it with his eyes but refused it with his mouth. She had meant it, even though it was unplanned. Why wouldn't he want her to go with him, if it came down to it, if he loved her? Too much running away in his life? Indebtedness to her? God, she'd made her feelings for him explicit enough. Both of them had been behaving as though the world had only a few more days left.

Through the small kitchen window she saw some movements above the bare ground at the back of the cabin. Feathers. Downy white brushstrokes floating on the dry dirt. Shit, she hadn't fed the hens, or Splash for that matter. A hen had flown the enclosure and become fox breakfast; or worse, the fox had found a way inside, in which case there would be carnage.

First she would take Quinn his tea. It was as she stepped out the back door to empty the leaves from the pot that Jennifer saw just what sort of a fox had preyed upon her. The small white hen lay little more than a step from the door; she almost trod on it. No teeth had touched this bird.

Its neck had been cut cleanly, the head placed about six inches from the body, as though a section had been removed. Jennifer let out a small 'aahh', bringing her hand to her mouth too late to stifle it. Over her shoulder she saw Quinn's back was still to her. He hadn't heard. Next to the decapitated body the fox had written in blood in the dirt. With stick or finger, in capitals. 'GO'.

The blood had already gone almost black.

Jesus! It must have happened while she and Quinn were consuming each other in the clearing by the river. She'd left to join him soon after eight am. Some bastard had gone and slaughtered a chook, painted in its blood, almost under their noses. Possibly the person had brought the dead hen with them? She cocked her head to look at it, was pretty sure that it was not one of hers.

Virtually everybody in the valley had chocks. Not Lorna, though. Not Lorna. Jennifer couldn't help scanning the slope all the way up to the ridgeline, as though the perpetrator wouldn't have long gone. You must have come that way, she thought, you'd have been seen if you'd come by the river.

Again the urge to scream. Instead she would have to hurry, fling both parts of the poor hen into the trees and bury them later, rub out the putrid message. Quinn could walk inside from the sun at any minute.

But she stopped herself. Quinn should see this. He'd really meant what he said about her attempts to protect him from truth, no matter how unpleasant. What about rubbing out the bloody word, just let him see the hen? Its meaning was obvious enough? No, she must let him see that, too. So many chilling things had happened to her in the past few days that she really would have to think about her future in this haven she'd vowed, once upon a time, never to leave. Regardless of what happened to Quinn.

But she did not really convince herself: what she did want, she had to admit, was for him to see that they were in this together. Him and her. 'The two of us,' she said sadly to the white hen.

She stepped past it and flung the tea dregs, went back inside and poured boiling water onto new leaves. While they brewed she marvelled at how calm she was. Apart from that little squawk, more surprise than anything, here she was making tea, contemplating the long-term, her head going through all the potential culprits' names like a tired policeman. She tried to stop herself, but she kept seeing Pete's narrowed eyes, hearing again his voice as she'd listened to it harping at Henry. She saw the distaste on the faces of both Gills that night when she and Quinn had gone to the Vickers'. Or that florid-faced, open-flied, lascivious Bert Jones? Possibly Hilda had blown it last night? Been caught going down the track by her tanked husband and sons, made to say what she was doing with sacks of stolen, dusty tools? Surely not. Hilda was too clever for that. Hadn't Quinn just now described her as 'remarkable'?

'Quinn? Can you come in here?'

Pouring the tea her hand was steady, but Quinn picked something awry in her voice, and was inside immediately, standing there before her, tensed torso and raised eyebrows.

'What's happened?'

She nodded her head to the door. 'Careful where you step.'

Her eyes followed him She heard him groan as he stood in the doorway, saw his head go up to scan the bush the way hers had. He did not turn back to look at her but walked out. A minute later she heard the blade of the shovel slide on the dirt, then again.

When he returned from burying the hen Quinn came and put his arms around Jennifer from behind. She was still standing by the bench, staring at her tea as though it held answers.

'Jennifer Jade,' he whispered in her ear, 'I'd decided before the chook, but this confirms it. I want you to take me into Walrae. There's an afternoon train today, isn't there? I think we'll have to go almost straight away to catch it?'

In the pause that followed there was the moan of a blowfly that had come in for a few laps of the room now that the drawcard of chicken's blood had gone. Then Jennifer swung around, breaking roughly out of Quinn's embrace.

'No, Quinn! I won't let these weeks, this morning, be wiped out by a sick woman and some other lunatic who throws rocks and necks hens. We love each other. Don't we? It's *never* been this way for me. You said the same … all those wild things you were yelling down by the river, do I have to repeat them? Were you making them up or what? Cock talk? Bullshit you were! I love you, Quinn. I want my chance to be with you. Don't go slinking off on the train because of, because of …'

He took her face in his hands, rubbed the end of his konky nose against the freckles of her smaller one, the nostrils of which flared with anger and despair.

'I was hoping you might give a speech like that,' he said quietly. His eyes were wet. 'I s'pose I almost tricked you into it, for which I'm only partly sorry. I'm not wimping off wounded, my Jennifer, that's not the way I'll leave you. What I'm suggesting is a strategic withdrawal. You take me to Walrae, forlornly farewell me onto the train. Bigotry rules. But I come back. Which only you know about. I get off the train at Dirranbandi. Unobtrusively. You hang around Walrae, show your sour face while you do some shopping, then drive to Dirranbandi and meet me. We return here about nightfall, me well hidden, head down on your soft lap. Could be very enjoyable!'

'Stop it Quinn!' Jennifer was blushing from the innuendo he'd put in the last word, plus the passion which had exploded from her. She put her arms on his shoulders, rested her forehead on his chest while she gathered her thoughts. Annoyingly, she felt like taking him over to the bed.

'Very clever, but what's in it for us?' she asked eventually, looking into his face. 'We probably could fool a lot of people for quite a while if we hid you back here, if you didn't work the garden during the day, only swam in the moonlight etc. Or you could hide out almost indefinitely in The Room.'

Involuntarily, she shuddered. 'But you wouldn't want to be my secret forever, and what will be different once you're sprung? Won't the bigots come straight back out of their hives?'

'It gives us some initiative, at least. May provoke some reactions. What if Lorna committed another robbery while I, apparently, had an alibi? Surely that'd make one or two people scratch their heads?'

'But if you go the day the stolen stuff has been returned, won't people be even more convinced that it was you?'

'I don't see why. A thief would hardly bother with all the risk of returning things if he was departing. He'd say sod the bastards, let 'em go look for their precious belongings. Wouldn't he?'

'Dearest Quinn,' Jennifer sighed, 'they think you are much worse than bad. In their eyes you're mad.'

He appeared not to have heard her

'I've done nobody harm. If there were to be no more robberies, surely people would come around? In time? If they got to know I'd been living here all along and the earth hadn't opened and swallowed them? We're not exactly hoping to be asked to dinner parties, are we? Just left alone would do us fine, wouldn't it?'

Jennifer thought he sounded so sad. Like a small boy who can't recover the innocence older eyes have seen him briefly lose, who is desperate for just a pat on the head. 'What makes me so angry,' she said, but she was no longer arguing, 'is that Lorna at this moment is just as distraught as you were in The Room, even though she can veneer over it. In fact the more so *because* she can keep up the front. Yet my own reaction to her, which the valley would share, is one of trying to understand, of sympathy. If her post-natal depression doesn't go away soon, if Henry can't hide it and the people of Walrae and Overton find that she's distrait, they'll all say 'never mind, poor girl lost her baby, a terrible thing, she'll come round in good time, plenty of rest … blah, blah, blah'. Even Molly The Ferret would understand, join the queue with casseroles at the Vickers' door. People offering to mind little Kate, suggesting a holiday for Lorna and Henry. Why should female hormones deserve such tolerance while your chemistry is spat upon?'

'Because, Dearest Jennifer, my schizophrenia does not have the shield of a dead child. It is endogenous, born into me. A birth defect.'

'You should be put down!' Jennifer smirked. She had said it to stop him because she did not like the deadness in his voice when he said these things; it scared her. 'All I meant was, don't be putting too much faith in human nature around here. Apart from the unlikely champions of Hilda and Henry, all you've got – all we've got – is blind hatred. But anyway,' she forced her tone upwards, 'let's do what you say. At worst it'll kill off the afternoon rather than us sitting about waiting for something to happen. I'll enjoy hissing my way around Walrae, performing for the pointynoses, as Lorna and I call them. Pack your bags, Ned Quinn, pack your bags. I'm riding you out of town.'

Quinn kissed her, rushed off to his chest of drawers. He began stuffing clothes, a towel, some books, anything to bulk out the rucksack.

Soon they were side by side in the utility, round and hot like a baked high-tin loaf as it lurched towards the river and gathered speed for the kick start. Quinn saw small pearls of sweat on Jennifer's upper lip as she waited before lifting her foot from the clutch. From the corner of her eye Jennifer could see that despite the gimmick of their trip, despite the fierce heat in the car, Quinn's face was pale, frowning.

Quinn had thought of walking out of Dirranbandi, meeting Jennifer on the Walrae road as she came to collect him. But it is a long, lonely streak of dirt: she told him nobody ever walked it. Anyone driving would therefore have a good long look at him, and even before they'd got back to the cabin the word would be dispersing, fast as soluble aspirin.

Instead, they'd plotted, he would move from his seat before the train reached Dirranbandi. As it stopped he'd slip straight to the pongy lavatory on the platform, lurk in a cubicle for five minutes or so. Then drift off on his rubber soles when the station had resumed its silent waiting. He could avoid the main street by following a route Jennifer told him about, going down through the memorial park where the Aborigines drank in dark clutches. 'No-one will ask *them* if they've seen a stray schizophrenic,' Jennifer had said as the utility walloped towards Walrae towing a cone of dust, hard-pushed for the train.

Jennifer told him about a creekbed that in wet times fed the Culgoa just on the Walrae side of Dirranbandi. She imagined he could sit under the wooden bridge and wait for her out of the sun, away from eyes and mouths. He'd even got a book and his glasses, a bottle of water she had rammed into the pack as they'd hurried from the cabin.

'This is bloody crazy,' Jennifer yelled across the noise of the motor more than once. But they were both laughing, having a good time the way children do when preparing to run away from home, before the pennies begin to drop. Quinn had cheered up now, and the caper was worth it just to see the light come back into his face. His arm stuck out the window as though they were doing a permanent left turn, his fingers clenching and opening to grab chunks of the fast dry air. 'The answer, my friend …' he sang in a nasally voice, but much deeper than Dylan's, '… is pissing in the wind, the answer is pissing in the wind.'

Jennifer frowned.

'Well,' he grinned, 'it beats bursting your bladder.'

'What happens,' shouted Jennifer, 'if I can't keep a straight face when I'm making my film-star farewell? Do we shake hands or have a long, succulent platform kiss through the train window? We should've sat down and scripted this thing properly, Quinn … *Last Train to Dirran-bandi* … *Murder on the Dirranbandi Express*. You'll have to pay for a ticket right through to Brisbane, you know, that'll be the first thing the pointynoses will ask Wal: where did he book to?'

'Sure. One-way ticket to ride.'

'Of course,' she said, 'I mightn't come to Dirranbandi this evening. How do you know I'll turn up? You could be sitting there under the bridge like a hairy troll. Forever!'

'Oh, in that case, I'll have to walk back.'

'To Melbourne, or to me?'

'Dunno,' he laughed. 'Do not know.'

'I'm closer.'

At the Walrae station the script almost wrote itself. Wally Hunt looked up when he asked Quinn what sort of a return ticket he wanted, how long he'd be gone. 'One way,' Quinn had mimed so quietly that Wal had to ask him: 'Come again?'

That was the only time Jennifer had to fight laughter. In fact, most of their one-act play cut too close to the bone for either of them to like it much. Quinn kept his head down, staring at the tacky asphalt as they waited in the spiced shade of a peppercorn overhanging the platform. They were visible from the stationmaster's window, standing a few paces apart, not touching, not smiling. Three passengers were waiting under the other peppercorn beyond the station building, brown suitcases secured with stout leather straps.

The train wormed in from the distorting strata of heat only a few minutes after they'd bought Quinn's ticket. Its engine and two carriages hummed and vibrated fatigued metal, the smell of hot diesel lacing the empty air. Quinn didn't board straight away, Jennifer hissing that they should give Wally some time to organise his 'up freight' and his 'down freight' as he called the few parcels and boxes that came to and left Walrae. As a bonus they saw Molly The Ferret further up the platform, come to collect the limp canvas mailbag. Two of the best mouths in Walrae would be disseminating their story by this evening. Molly inclined her head towards Jennifer, less in the way of a greeting than to get a better eyeful of the southern letter-writer, the weird bird.

It wasn't until Wally started blowing his whistle and holding out a grubby white flag on a stick that Quinn quickly bent for his rucksack, slung one strap over his shoulder. He was holding out his hand to Jennifer, staring her in the eye, expressionless. She accepted his hand, then took a step and kissed him lightly on his left cheek, the side Wal and Molly were on. Then he was gone, and the train began moving inch by inch for Dirranbandi.

No wave from the dust-pocked window. No wave from the Duncan woman as it slugged off into the haze. Later on Molly would observe to the more intimate of her contacts – intimate and contacts given their broadest possible interpretation – that the Duncan Woman had tears on her face as she had pushed brusquely past her through the platform gate. Jennifer herself did not notice this until she looked in the utility's rear-vision mirror. She was only aware that the charade was no longer at all funny, that enormous losses can begin with a handshake.

On the seat of the Holden Quinn had left an envelope. Jennifer inhaled sharply as she saw it, white as those hen feathers, addressed simply 'JD'. When had he possibly had time to write to her? Surely for his departure he'd just had the flash of inspiration, teased her into it, crammed a few things into his rucksack, then they'd rushed off? But here was a premeditated envelope glaring at her on the seat in sharp sunlight. Had Quinn camouflaged real disappearance? He had acted his part on the platform so well … the handshake, the no-turning-back.

Jennifer was sweating in the soupy cabin of the utility, her nerves producing their own humidity. Not so long ago she had ached to get letters from this man, mocked herself for wanting them so much as she stood oh-so-casually next to Lorna's horse by the letterbox on the Dirranbandi road. Now this … underhand note, sitting there like a default summons. She didn't have to open it? Pretend she hadn't seen it? If he had truly gone from her, she would forever drive around in the utility with it sitting there as a plain white reminder of love found and lost, a dirtying ghost.

'You are an idiot, woman,' she said aloud, quickly looking outside. The main street was deserted. She picked up the envelope, turned it over. Unsealed. Holding it against the windscreen she could see there was one sheet of folded pad paper and some notes, perhaps $50s? The money exacerbated her doubts; settlement of account? No dues, no debts, and thanks for the memories? Slowly she let her fingers withdraw the paper, leaving the two $50 notes. Her green eyes galloped along the handwriting:

Jennifer Jade,
Some cash for board and lodging.

    I had no idea that you would lodge in me the way you have, quick as a spear. Sometimes I imagined that a love such as ours would feel like a wound: a slicing shock, then the long ecstasy of healing. I do feel this way now; a clean steel has cut right through some part of me, its point now resting against my core and jangling me alive. I am seeing and hearing things (real things, don't worry!) so acutely that I could count all the needles on a conifer, all the ants in a colony. The sheer amount of sky overwhelms iris and lens. And my ears! I listen to gurgles and slashes of the elastic Condamine miles upriver, hear the cry of a cockatoo even before it has uttered from the beakcurve. My hands irresistibly feel the trunks of saplings, stroke the sides of stones as though Braille reading animist scriptures. Hyper-perception? Or is it that love can melt wax, re-cut fingerprints, act as caustic soda to the mind's old furniture?

Yet hidden in the darkness a dull force seeks to divert the spear and twist it, to make this clean wound gout blood and vital organ. Your strength and mine cannot fight this indefinitely, any more than some literal wounds can stay gangrene. There comes the point of surgical cut. I have pictured the hot train as a knife, have thought that I should let Dirranbandi hold me for its few minutes, then pass me on to the bigness of Brisbane, and point south.

I know, however, that I won't run away, almost that I can't. I have had to do a lot of running: reality escapes me, I escape the reality of the consequences. This will be my last stand. If you agree, of course, and bearing in mind how last stands often end.

I have had to write this because my love for you has bowled me like knees against the surf: a great wave of moving excitement that lifts me off my feet and leaves me weakly spluttering, articulate as a fish. So happy.

Your Ned Quinn

Jennifer bought milk and butter at Lance's store and some shellgrit and layers' pellets at McConnachies'. At the garage she got petrol and put more oil into the utility's wretched engine. Her springless walk, the monotone of her unenthusiastic answers about the weather and the state of the roads, most of all her eyes ... the clues were being absorbed wherever she went. It was scary to think how people got their information, how easy it was to manipulate the signals and codes upon which firm opinions are based. Here she stood, face blank and heart amok, and no-one could see below her surface. Only when the young man from McConnachies' yard asked her how the fishing was going did she drop her guard. 'Good, thanks,' she answered warmly, 'Quinn's getting us some top meals with that gear.' But all the lad had done was to say as he'd departed, 'No worries, see you later then.' He was also wearing disguise; Jennifer couldn't know that as he went back to stacking bags of cement on the outstretched arms of a forklift he was fantasising running his hands through the tangly red hair of the woman who lived in a cabin in the bush, of catching fish for her.

The first hitch in the escapade came when Jennifer was about a kilometre before the turn-off to the valley track. She had been intoning 'show me the way to go home, I'm tired and I want to go to bed', this time with feeling. The erogenous peaks of the morning with Quinn by the Condamine had flattened to this unarousable plain around her as she drove, heat and light slowly haemorrhageing from the day. She felt uneasy about being apart from Quinn, about his silly disappearance, the thought of having to hide him to keep him. She did her utmost to hold his letter at bay; she had not allowed herself to read it more than that first rush through. She would later hide it away in a safe place, even bury it in a tin. As much as the words exhilarated, they frightened her, their contingent, knife-edge tone, the fact that he must have gone off quietly to write them – having carefully planned the false departure that had appeared to be so spontaneously daft.

The smokesignal of dust ahead of her switched her mind to safer, more immediate concerns. The bullbar and squat body, almost the same colour as the dust it trailed, soon told her that the Vickers' Land-Rover was going into Walrae. A few minutes and she would have passed the turn-off and been an anonymous blur on the Dirranbandi side. Now she would have to stop and talk with them, strained though the neighbourliness had become. The narrowing of the dust plume and the fact that the Land-Rover had moved from the middle of the road confirmed it was slowing.

Thank God. Henry was alone. They talked from where they sat behind the protection of their steering wheels, facing opposite directions. An impromptu roadblock.

'Could've picked something up for you.' Jennifer looked sheepish. 'Sorry. '

'That's alright. I'm going to get some painkillers for Lorna. More headaches. Have you heard about the robberies?'

'Heard what?'

'Pete's gear's been returned. So's Gills', even the money. I thought you two would have heard about it. Pete told us. No idea how, but he thinks sometime in the night. Kevin Gill said he saw his stuff on the seat of his truck first thing, can't figure out who could have got there without his dogs raising the dead. Three of them chained within metres of where he parks that truck. Weird.'

'Any ideas who?'

'Beats me. No-one's got a clue. I don't know if it will help you and Ned or not. Obviously some people are going to say that this is precisely what a crazy guy would do, which conveniently overlooks the fact that those Gill dogs wouldn't shut up for a stranger, would they. Surely schizoid legs are as good to bite? Where is Quinn, didn't see him as I passed the cabin?'

'I've just taken him to the train.'

'What?'

'You're one of the first to know, although not by much I suspect.'

'You mean ...'

'Henry, for lots of reasons I don't want to talk about it now, I just can't. Please don't ask me to. No doubt you'll be regaled in Walrae with the news that he bought a one-way to Brisbane. Some day I'll explain it to you, I think I owe you that, but not yet. It's best this way.'

Henry shrugged. 'I didn't think you'd ... so soon ...' But he stopped himself, seeing the blank refusal in Jennifer's face. He shook his head and stared over the steering wheel, as though the dancing distance might provide some answers.

'How's Lorna?'

'Fine.'

'No she's not, Henry. Don't bullshit me.'

'You don't want to talk about Ned. It hurts, doesn't it?'

'Henry, everybody has been doing too much talking about Quinn. Lorna's here. Your wife, my neighbour, my closest friend, we've *got* to talk about her. She's sick, Henry. Don't you realise ...'

'I live with her Jennifer, for God's sake, of course I bloody well know she's ... unwell.'

'Sorry, I didn't mean to imply that you're an insensitive brute. I just don't know if you realise what state a woman can get into after ...'

'I read the same chapters as you, Jennifer.'

'Well you know she needs help then. How is she filling her days when she's not out doing ... what's her manner like when she's not obsessed with getting rid of Quinn?'

Henry overlooked the re-direction.

'She mopes. Says hardly anything to Kate, barely tolerates me being round her. You know how tactile and cat-like she is normally. When she's not weepy or silent there's the impression that she's struggling to keep the lid on an enormous anger. It shows when some little thing goes wrong, like dropping a cup or a plate, and she bangs her fist on the table and storms out of the house cursing. Not just a tantrum, wild anger. If I suggest she's not herself since Robbie, that maybe we should get some grief-counselling or see a doctor, it gets worse. She said to me on Sunday: "If you like bloody doctors so much, why didn't you have one here to deliver your son?"'

'Oh, God no.'

'I can handle it. I know it's not my Lorna talking, but it does cut. I can't *make* her seek medical help, I don't think her behaviour's what the books describe as psychotic, it's more depression. The best she's said to me, with her eyes full of tears, was a few hours after that doctor remark: "Don't worry Henry, I'll get better." I guess I have to just sit it out? I wonder whether, now that Ned's left – I know this sounds terrible – could you have Kate at the cabin for a few days? It'd help her if not Lorna? Katey misses you, she's told me so.'

Jennifer sighed. 'Henry, things seem to have become so complicated around here. There are crossed lines everywhere, people going round thinking and acting on wrong information, half-cocked and full of toxin. I believe Lorna is worse than you think. In fact that she *is,* part of the time anyway, in what those books called a "florid state".'

Henry was looking ahead through his windscreen again, eyes narrowed. Jennifer sensed he could tell she knew more, that he did not dare to ask for evidence in case she had it. Jennifer did nearly take the risk, but Henry's face looked so crumpled. She couldn't do it. Not here on the arid plain with him headed for painkillers. It would take such a long time to explain how she'd found the stuff. Would she have to tell him what she and Hilda had cooked up?

Coiled like a snake beneath her indecision was Lorna's devastating remark about the doctor. If Lorna was blaming Henry, she would also be blaming her. Probably more so because she had been acting midwife; Henry's role mainly hot water and towels, looking out for Kate. Which brought her back to Henry's request. How could she possibly refuse to mind Kate when he had been so privately supportive of Quinn and her? But how could she say yes? Kate would see Quinn, it would be impossible to ask a child to become a co-conspirator.

'Yes, of course, Henry,' she said at last. She and Quinn would think of something. 'I'd love to have Kate for a few days. Bring her down in the morning.'

Henry looked so relieved. He reached forward and started the Land-Rover's engine.

'I do think,' Jennifer raised her voice above it, 'I do think you should watch Lorna closely. I know you've got to go to Walrae, but from now on I think you should try not to let her out of your sight, hard though that'll be for you. Just a feeling I've got.'

"I don't think she's suicidal, let's not get carried away.'

'No. But I believe she needs watching nevertheless. Call it female intuition if you must.'

Thin laugh. 'I'd better get moving. 'Til the morning?'

Henry was waiting until the utility started, just in case. 'Thank you, kind sir,' she called as she hooked the column shift towards her into first and moved off.

'The answer is pissing in the wind,' she began crooning. 'How many roads must a woman drive down …?'

From the valley turn-off it is a forty-five-minute drive down a ruler of road to Dirranbandi. Jennifer saw no-one else; the only life hidden in ant hills or departed from a goanna or snake pasted flat to the road. How strange were the odds that, in all this space, creatures could be caught between a fast tyre and unyielding ground.

She was barrelling down the road at the utility's limit, which made no sense; a breakdown would be the last straw, and it was not as though she had a train to catch now. Quinn would not have been waiting under the bridge all that long, given the slowness of the train, the fact that he had to get from the station to the outskirts. It was still light enough for him to be able to be reading.

Jennifer forced herself to ease her foot on the accelerator. 'It's only,' she had to admit to herself, 'that you have a nagging doubt that Quinn didn't get off at Dirranbandi.' Like everybody, he would have wanted to avoid a sticky goodbye, but Quinn did not have it in him to devise this game, to have her drive to a dry creekbed to find nothing there but … dry creekbed. That sort of man could not write that sort of letter.

Quinn heard the utility as a murmur from the beaten-down horizon, just the way, he smiled, he'd had his sleep interrupted by an engine that day when he had walked out to Jennifer's valley from Walrae station. He had found the bridge easily and felt a bit of a fool sitting there under it, the rounded stones in the middle of the creekbed like the crest of an enormous spine exposed after centuries of burial. Not a soul had passed him walking from the town; no cars had crossed the bridge.

For a while he had read, but found his concentration wandering up and down the sandy creekbed. He drew in it with a stick, forming a stumpy-tailed goanna, then put lots of dots around it as Aboriginal painters do. With his thumb he carved a thick border around his artwork. Had there been some good soft rock, he thought wickedly, he could have cut the design into it and signed it 'Trolkwin, Split-jantjara Tribe, 1923'. Some peripatetic scholar of the primitive, stopping his grant-funded 4WD to take a pee, would be fooled for a minute or two.

Quinn was feeling that way. Down-in-the-mouth bitter. While the train had lurched drunkenly towards Dirran-bandi he had been flat as the plain. He'd had to talk himself out of the premonitory sense the enacted station farewell had printed on them both. Earlier in the day when he had gone off and written that letter he'd put on the seat it had left him feeling almost post-coital, as if he had released his very strongest emotions in one great emission. He was happy to have shown Jennifer the depths to which she had penetrated him, but neither had he veiled his sense of bleakness or the truth that, however they loved each other, their chances were slim. An affair flying as high and as fast as this needed fine trimming for it to bank and sweep and soar the way it did. Surely, Quinn stopped scratching in the sand to think, neither the swallow nor the eagle have such distractions from flight. He swished his stick to erase the sacrilegious sand goanna, his gritty self-pity.

The noise was much closer now and Quinn stood and hitched a strap of his pack over one shoulder. He scrambled up the dry creek bank, still holding his opened book, his thick-framed reading glasses halfway down his nose. Above the bridge the sky was faded denim, studded with a few early stars. Standing at the rail Quinn sucked at his teeth and spat some saliva down to the creekbed. 'There's something to be getting on with,' he said, then began walking towards the car he could now recognise as Jennifer's.

She let it roll very slowly then stop about fifty metres short of him. On that slopeless ground there was no need for the hand-brake; she got out quickly, leaving the engine running, and stood by the door. Quinn's white teeth against the blackness of the beard emphasised his approaching smile. He was not hurrying, just walking in that lazy-hipped blackman's way of his. No arrogance, she thought, quite unconscious of his smooth movement. When he was half a dozen of those easy steps from her she threw her arms wide. Quinn did the same. They collided. A clutched pair, tightly silent.

As they at last leant back from each other enough to fit in a kiss, his glasses slid right down and they had to pin them between both noses to stop them falling to the ground. Their kiss broke into laughter as Quinn reached up to rescue them.

'Do you want to drive home?'

She couldn't think how else to greet him, could not,

here on this dry road, divulge all the relief and longing she felt. But then she knew that he knew. She almost said she felt about as articulate as a fish, but stopped herself. The letter – this one would always be *the* letter – had become a most private possession.

'Nope,' he said, eyes travelling around her face and fox-red hair like a photographer composing the frame, 'me driving is not what I'd planned, Jennifer Jade. Remember, this is a mission to be carried out with military precision: it calls for you to drive disconsolate to your cooling cabin, me out of sight with my head on your lap. Just in case one of the citizens of the valley is out strolling in the ebb of this strange day.'

'Sounds acceptable to me.'

They didn't say much as Jennifer headed the utility back in the direction of Walrae. Quinn was sitting up, his left arm again out the window in the torpid air, his right running along the top of the seat, with his hand slid up under her hair and his long fingers putting the lightest pressure on the nape of her neck. Once or twice he looked back over his arm, but there were no dust-trails fore or aft.

When they were about half way to the turn-off he asked: 'Any reactions as you went about Walrae?'

'No. I did manage to look hangdog and silent. Wally and The Ferret will be hard at work right now.'

She told him then about having run into Henry Vickers, how he'd given the news of Hilda's nocturnal raids, how they had caused considerable confusion, which probably wasn't a bad thing.

'The immediate problem,' Jennifer said, clearing her throat, 'is that Henry asked me then and there if I could mind Kate for a couple of days, to give Lorna a break. Bizarre, I know, but ...'

'I hope you said yes?'

'Couldn't think what else to do, given that Henry has supported us. Kate's a delight, but what are we going to do about our plot? She's got a big mouth for a three-year-old.'

'When's she coming?'

'Henry's planning on bringing her tomorrow morning. I could go up and ask him to postpone it for a few days?'

'No, don't do that. I'll stay up in The Room while she's there.'

'But I don't want …'

'I'm fine, Jen, my head's sharp, and all mine. Like you, I can swallow a lot of solitude.'

'I'm thinking of me, Quinn, I want to hear you working in the garden, see you sloping down to the river with that walk of yours, talk with you, eat with you, have you beside me in my bed, our bed, every night … and maybe in the daytime too!'

He laughed. 'I want those same things. You now know how much I do. I'll sit up in The Room and contemplate all that they mean to me. I can do some writing, the odd Aboriginal painting in the sand.' He saw her querulous look but pretended not to. 'It's only for a few days. Does Kate have afternoon naps?'

'Always.'

'Good. You can come up and see me some time.'

'I'll bring food.'

'I wasn't thinking of my stomach.'

She looked out her window as they turned off the road to the start of the valley track. It annoyed her that after all their intimacies, and the ease with which she felt able to initiate them, she could still blush.

'I thought you said you were going to keep your hairy head out of sight?'

'Yes, Mam,' he answered, at once twisting in his seat and folding his top half down to his right, resting the back of his head on her lap in the space between the steering wheel and her belly. His knees were angled against the glovebox, just below the line of sight as long as no-one came too close.

'Hello up there,' he said dreamily, 'I like the look of you

just as much from down here, the way your hair is moving around your neck as we bump along.'

Jennifer laughed and ran a hand into Quinn's hair, pulling it back from his eyes.

'Both hands on the wheel! Observe combat silence!'

'Yes, Sir!'

As she drove on Jennifer wondered whether they would reach the cabin before she had to resort to headlights. The trees around them seemed to be sucking down the day, and all blue was gone from the sky she glimpsed through leaf and branch.

Quinn had turned his face towards her as though he was going to sleep for the last few kilometres. But he wasn't; she felt his right hand where her jeans bit into the curve of skin just above her navel. He popped the stud and slid his whole hand in against her flesh, the zip descending to its limit with a giveaway noise.

'Quinn,' she said, but was unable to think what to say next. After a pause she added: 'Should the general be interfering with my privates? While I'm driving?'

'Shhhsh! You're under orders, remember?'

His lips brushed her belly as he spoke, a thumb lifting the elastic of her pants. His mouth continued to mime talk across her skin.

Jennifer re-gripped the wheel as Quinn nuzzled the red hair that began as a wide horizontal line set against light freckles, then tapered. Two beards together in the bush, she couldn't help thinking, and laughed awkwardly. For his part Quinn was thinking of the way a beeline is set so clearly against the slope of a mountain, the sharp definition of the growth. He wanted to tell Jennifer that she smelled of good earth, but he didn't dare risk speech. Instead he lifted a hand and held one of her breasts.

'I might crash, Quinn,' Jennifer said huskily, against the rules. At this speed, barely holding second gear, it wouldn't much matter if they did. She wanted to take her hands from the wheel, feed her fingers into Quinn's hair and press his head to her.

But she didn't. She drove slowly and silently on, obedient. Only half aware that her breathing had become deep and quick.

They didn't pass a soul.

It was going to be a day of visitors, Jennifer sensed, and she did not relish having to cope alone, apart from Kate Vickers' small presence.

She and Quinn had tumbled straight onto the bed when they'd returned from the Dirranbandi diversion, little needing to be spoken. They had agreed that they would rise at dawn, go together to the river, then he would pack away his things and store them in the old wardrobe under the cabin while she prepared a stash of food for him to take to The Room. He would set off early, every trace of him gone before Henry arrived with Kate.

Apprehension woke Jennifer as the first colours were making insinuations against the sky. Propped on one arm she had gently kissed Quinn's face and nuzzled his beard until he'd opened his eyes.

A few soft hours later, single again, Jennifer heard Henry and Kate talking as they came off her track. Standing in the doorway she saw the father with a rucksack, the child with a balding bear in a headlock under one arm. She lifted the running Kate, squeezed her.

'You're bit sad and mummy's bit sick,' Kate announced as though her presence required justification. Henry shrugged at Jennifer, at his daughter's tight editing of his windy explanation.

'I've packed a heap of clothes, toothbrush, hairbrush, some toys.' He worked his arms from the rucksack's straps.

'I staying for long, long time, Jenjen.'

'No you are not,' Henry quickly corrected as he followed them into the cabin. 'I've told you, I can't manage without you for more than three days.' Jennifer had turned; he raised his eyebrows to ask if this would be alright.

'Three days is fine. I'll bring her back myself. You two take a seat on the verandah.'

When she brought out a tray with a pot of tea, a glass of pineapple juice, some raisin cakes, Kate was nestled in her father's lap, her thumb in her mouth. The two of them were staring at the river, forlornly.

Henry tried to be positive. 'Things should calm down for you now, I s'pose.'

'Not calm at all, not here and here where it counts,' Jennifer said quietly, touching her forehead and chest. 'You and Hilda are the only ones who have survived as friends as far as I'm concerned. Mary, too, I suppose. But Bert Jones, Pete, the Cochranes ...'

'My mummy's your friend,' Kate said, an alert full stop to any discussion.

'Of course!' Jennifer reached for Kate's hand. 'Could you get off daddy's lap and do something for me? Walk up the hill and see if your friend Splash has got enough water, give her a cuddle?'

'Orright.' Kate climbed down, unenthused.

After she had left, Henry looked back to Jennifer. 'Lately that's all she's been getting from us ... go outside and play, go and pat the horse, go anywhere so you don't hear your mum and dad arguing. She's not silly.'

'I'm sorry, I'll make up for it after you've gone. I didn't feel I could talk about Lorna in front of her.'

Henry waved his hand. 'Like all kids, she reacts to atmosphere.'

'You could say that about a lot of people around here.'

'I suppose you could. But somehow you are going to have to find a way not to let bitterness start breeding in you like a cancer.'

Jennifer laughed harshly. 'It's too early yet for me to be properly bitter. But I admit I'm developing some malignant feelings. Oh yes.'

'You and I have to talk around the edges of things nowa-days, don't we?'

'We do, Henry.' The hardness had fallen from her voice. 'I am really sorry about it, but there are parts each of us has to hold back. Because of our different relationships to Lorna. I'm not even sure our ends are the same, let alone our means. What did she say when you told her about Quinn?'

'I didn't. Which must seem odd given how hard she and others have been working to get rid of him. I can't properly explain why. I'll tell her this morning when I get home. I suspect it was because she behaved so strangely when she heard the news that Pete's stuff and Kevin Gill's had been returned. It was Mrs Cochrane who came and told her. Lorna just kept repeating: "How could that happen, Mrs C? How could that happen, Mrs C?" On and on like a needle stuck in a groove. I had to intervene and make some goose of an explanation to the old sponge-ear: "Lorna's not well, Mrs Cochrane. All this talking's not good for her." I think I was less tactful than that. Then, when Mrs Cochrane leaves, Lorna's looking at me with that fury in her eye. "Some bastard!", she starts off. "Some bastard!" On and on she went with that, steadily becoming less coherent, muttering to no one in particular about "slippery people".'

'Poor Henry. No wonder you wanted me to have Kate for a while. Did she mind?'

'Lorna? No, not at all,' Henry lifted his gaze from his boots. He was rubbing the tips of his fingers into his temples. 'Her mind seemed distracted when I suggested it. Something has shifted Kate from her place at the centre of Lorna's life. It's hard to bear thinking about. I suppose I didn't want to see her reaction to the news that Quinn has left, the look I fear I will see in those dark eyes. Maybe triumph, but maybe nothing? Deep down I think I'm scared that Ned's departure won't provide Lorna's return.'

Jennifer knew as he talked that she would not be able to offer Henry any comfort, she was already misleading him about Quinn. She listened as he stumbled on about how inept was mere love to deal with whatever was consuming his wife, how all that they'd banked between them over the years seemed to have been devalued in some huge currency shift.

Jennifer heard him say something like 'Her big loss seemed to parallel your big gain', but, though she knew Henry needed and deserved some measure of reassurance, much of what he was saying was falling away from her ears. Her thoughts rising smokily to the ridge, to her handsome, haunted lover. She was aware that she was almost smiling, could not summon the effort to forge solemnity. She had to bite laughter off at her lip as it struck her that Quinn's head was like a bank – with all the doors and windows open. She pictured him sitting up in The Room, perhaps looking down on the small square of cabin roof.

Quinn had packed a gardening book and the novel he'd been reading under the bridge outside Dirranbandi, Hesse's *Steppenwolf*. She would rather *she* was the disappeared one, the clandestine lover reading in anonymity in the warm early sunshine. A nobody. She remembered the excitement on Quinn's face when he'd found on her shelf the other book, *The Vegetable Garden Displayed*, first published by the Royal Horticultural Society in 1941. She had bought it at a Walrae fete, for the old black-and-whites of the bygone Englishmen tending their measured vegetable allotments in jackets, waist-coats, ties, braces, stout boots. Their wartime skies and seasons and soils bore no kinship to Queensland, but Quinn insisted on reading chunks aloud to her, finding some poetry in its uselessness for their own stepped garden. 'Listen to this,' he'd say: 'The most troublesome disease is club root or finger and toe. The remedy in severe cases is to lime the ground with a dressing of 28 lbs per square rod of ground chalk or lime-stone.' Or, still on cabbages, he would run off the names of 'trustworthy cultivars': Wheeler's Imperial, Early Durham, Myatt's Early Offenham, Fillgap, Greyhound, Golden Acre, Primo, Christmas Drumhead, Winningstadt, January King ...'

The interfering sound of Henry's voice forced Jennifer to grip the verandah rail, to focus her back from whence she had floated.

'Sorry,' he said, embarrassed, 'I've been wallowing in it. I switched you off.'

'No you didn't, Henry. What you said at the start was important, necessary for me to know. I think I snuck off into dreams of cabbages and kings because I'm at a loss for constructive suggestions.'

'Cabbages and kings? As in walruses and carpenters?'

'Sort of,' Jennifer lied with a smile. She was thinking she should suggest to Quinn that they re-name an Australian cabbage variety Hilda Jones, a truly 'trustworthy cultivar'. Later she might take Kate down to the Joneses' for a visit, bring a small bag of Seven Sisters as a token of thanks. A toke of thanks.

Kate had returned from her diversion up the hillside and was noisily drinking the juice she had earlier refused, one proprietorial hand on her father's knee while carefully watching Jennifer over the rim of the glass.

'Mummy coming for a visit, too,' she said quietly, putting the glass down on the open slats of the verandah.

Jennifer and Henry looked at each other.

'I seed her,' Kate said.

'Mummy's having a sleep, Kate, remember? You kissed her in bed before we came down to see Jen.'

'She waked up,' Kate insisted. 'I seed her.' She pointed to the back door. 'Mummy say tell daddy.'

Henry was quickly on his feet. Jennifer stayed put in her chair, hastily arranged Kate's hair with her fingers, used a thumb to wipe the cake clues from the corners of her small, compliant mouth. Feeling oddly guilty, she was about to hoist the child onto her knee; but now Henry was walking across the cabin towards them, one arm around Lorna's shoulder, and Kate scuttled to them, reached for Lorna's hand, which was allowed if not given.

Jennifer stood to greet her neighbour. 'Hello, Lorna.' She was surprised at the lifelessness of her own voice. 'Can I make you a cuppa?' she tried again, this time at least managing an upward inflexion.

Lorna looked so well. From what Henry had said, and knowing what Lorna had been through, and up to, she had expected that her friend would be haggard. But she wasn't. Lorna's eyes were dark as ever, but the whites were clear. Her short black hair was glossy in the sharpening sunlight.

'No, thanks,' said Lorna, sitting in the chair Henry had vacated. He stood between them with his back to the rail, Kate leaning into his long legs, watching her mother. It was clear that Lorna had rushed down the track; she was catching her breath. Jennifer sat down again.

"I didn't expect this,' said Henry to fill the hole. 'When I asked you if you wanted to come with us you said no ...'

'We've been robbed.'

Lorna's voice was neutral, her eyes triumphant.

Henry caught Jennifer's look, but she turned away. For his sake.

'I said we've been robbed. Didn't you hear? Henry?'

'I heard, Lorna.'

'It's your bloody stuff. Tools again. I couldn't sleep after you and Kate had left. Got up and got dressed. To take my mind off ... for something to do I started to work ... on that chair I've been fixing. Needed some more upholstery nails. So I went out to your workshed. The door was open. I got a fright because I know you hate that. Possums get in.'

She was speaking in spurts. Henry imagined it was from running down the track; Jennifer heard each curt sentence as a spit of venom. Henry held up both hands, fingers spread, to wicket-keep his wife, to stop her careering to the boundary. Jennifer held her breath, aware that if she exhaled she might begin to yell.

'Everything's a mess. Tools all over the place. In the dirt on the floor. I started looking. For things I knew you had.

Like that plane I gave you last Christmas. It's gone. So's your spirit level. And, and I couldn't see that machine you cut tough stuff with. The whatsit …?'

'Angle grinder?'

'That's it. I reckon he's taken that. Too.'

'He?' Jennifer's voice was an angle grinder itself. 'You saw the thief?'

Henry tried to stop his wife stepping onto the mine.

'Look,' he said, his face and his voice stretched pale, 'I really don't think anyone has come all the way up our valley to knock off a handful of my tools. Maybe … probably you were upset and you went in there and let out some anger. That's okay, we'll clean up …'

It was as though he'd not said a word. Lorna's eyes were locked to Jennifer's. 'No,' she said, trying to hold her runaway words on a rein so they were less staccato, 'I did not see your man. But, tricks or no tricks, we all know it's him, don't we? Surely now you're not still going to carry on with the pretence? Three robberies! How long can you go on denying it, how long can Henry keep his head in the sand?'

Jennifer felt winded, as though a fist had expelled all the air from her abdomen. Hatred, she thought, this is naked hatred where we had been dressed up in friendship. She tried to say something, but nothing came. At last she managed a whisper:

'What's become of you, Lorna?'

There was no answer. The four of them remained silent on the verandah, angry heat licking about them. Jennifer realised that her question was too big.

'Why have you turned on me so?' she asked, gently now. 'Me who has always been so close to you? Like sisters, you were always saying. Is it because . . .'

Henry interrupted again, unable to bear to go where he knew Jennifer was heading. Now he demanded his wife's attention, dragging her eyes away from Jennifer's face. 'Lorna! Lorna! Listen to me for a minute. Jennifer's right.

She hasn't changed, I haven't changed, it's you. These robberies …'

'Don't tell me *you* are also going to convince yourself that they didn't happen?

'… Lorna. Ned Quinn's gone.'

She looked up at him sharply. Then to Jennifer.

'He got the train yesterday,' Jennifer explained, then turned away, unable to watch Henry's tortured face, Lorna's panicking eyes.

'One-way ticket to Brisbane,' said Henry's empty voice. 'All Walrae knows about it, the whole valley. I heard when I went in to get your painkillers yesterday evening. I'd intended to tell you last night, but you were so …'

'Therefore how,' Jennifer took over, trying at once to work out whether anything but Robbie's death could have opened such a gash in Lorna, 'how could Quinn have taken things from Henry's shed if he was on the train to Brisbane? It doesn't make any sense all of this, does it, Lorna?'

They were staring at her now. Kate, too. Lorna looked to Henry, back to Jennifer, but not at Kate.

'Obviously,' she began quietly, 'he must have done it before he cleared off. His parting shot against us. Don't you keep looking at me like that, Jennifer Duncan, as though I'm crippled! It's your Mr Quinn who is cuckoo, not me.' Now she was shouting. '*You* insisted on him staying when nobody wanted him here, when he'd begun to prove our worst fears. *You're* almost as crazy as *he* is. Why don't *you* go, too? See how long *you* last?'

'Lorna!' Henry shouted. Jennifer saw tears on his face. 'Ned Quinn did not rob us. I was in and out of that shed all day yesterday. It was exactly as it always is late in the afternoon. By that time Ned had to be well the other side of Dirran-bandi. You must accept that. Jennifer took him to the train, Wally sold him the ticket, he got on the train. The Ferret herself can tell you that. Lorna? I don't know what happened with Kevin Gill or with Pete, but the three of us know …

Lorna? Don't make me spell it out?'

Lorna stood. 'I'm not listening to any more of this. I never thought I'd live to see the day my own husband accused me. I don't suppose it has occurred to you, Dear Henry, Dear Henry, that the Mr Quinn you, too, are so obviously bewitched by may have had an accomplice? You wouldn't want to think of that. Or *who* that accomplice might be? Just *who* it is who would really like to throw the attention off her lover boy and onto someone else? So then she can bring him back? God, Henry, you amaze me sometimes. Come on, Kate, mummy is taking you home. She has to clear up a big mess in the shed, and you can help her.' Lorna looked up at Jennifer. 'I'm certainly not leaving her here with you!'

Kate took the few steps to her mother. 'You all better.' She buried her face in the folds of Lorna's skirt.

Lorna patted the head of her purblind blood ally. She threw a look like a handful of nails at Jennifer and strode back into the cabin and out the back door, Kate's hand firmly in her own.

Henry could not look at Jennifer. Head down, he went after his wife and daughter, who were by now walking as fast as Kate's legs could manage towards Jennifer's track to their house.

Quinn was surprised. He was parked just below the crevice into which he had squeezed his body when he was less his own master. The sun was now too hot to sit in but there was a relief of shade along that wall and he had been sheltering in it, so immersed in Hesse's fiction that approaching footsteps intruded only when they were almost upon him. For an instant his instinct was to flee, to flit over the slope to his right then lose himself in the strange planet of rock formations he now knew well.

It vanished with Jennifer's voice calling his name, announcing herself. Surely he could not have been reading so long? He had not expected her until mid-afternoon, if at all. They'd agreed that if Kate did not take her usual nap Jennifer would wait until the child was bedded down for the night, at which time she would flash her torch on and off at the back door to signal that he should come down. They had at once begun to look forward to it, laughing in embarrassment at the need to be clandestine.

'You'd think we were committing adultery,' Jennifer had joked.

On the way up she had tossed the truth from hand to hand like a pebble. She did not want to tell Quinn what had happened; she did not like the fact that she was increasingly censoring her accounts to him of what was going on around them. She could simply tell him that Lorna had come down, been angry, taken her daughter back home. Forget the rest? This would be the truth, if not the whole truth. No! She could not wrap Quinn in a cocoon; the world would be too hard for him to face when eventually, as he must, he flew into it.

As she entered The Room from the path Jennifer gave a reflex shudder. The place was less the sanctuary than it had always been. She wondered how long it would take before she would cease to associate it with Quinn's episode. It now made her reluctantly aware of the certainty of another derangement. When? One day. But then his quick, raised eyes caught hers, and the pleasure of seeing him was a clean page. She laughed at the slight surprise on his face, and the sound fell all over her doubts.

'Couldn't stay away from you!'

'Oh yeah?'

She stood and enjoyed Quinn's smile. The sun was burning into the back of her neck where she had lifted her hair into a ponytail and exposed usually hidden freckles.

'What are you gawping at, Jennifer Jade? And where's Kate? Didn't Henry bring her? After all our dawn preparations?'

'Oh he brought her alright. Poor old reliable Henry. But Lorna came down and took her away again.'

'Christ!' He patted the dusty ground beside him and Jennifer stepped into the shade.

'Hold onto your hat,' she said as she gratefully sat beside him. 'This is going to take some believing.'

She told him the lot. Only holding back on the cut of Lorna's eye, the edge to her voice, which were too hard for Jennifer to convey.

'Seems we're out of the frying pan,' Quinn said quietly when she had finished, mother, daughter and dogged father Vickers going back on the track to their house.

'Meaning?'

He was drawing slowly in the dirt with one finger. Their bent legs were touching, their backs against the hard stone wall. He was looking at the ground.

'Well, Henry will probably manage to keep Lorna from talking to the world about this, my latest robbery. But only for as long as she believes that I departed. If she learns that I was lurking here all the time, I'm right back in the fire. Or, maybe, given the state she's in, Henry won't be able to hold her even now, she'll convince those who want to be convinced that I snuck up to their shed for a last klepto fling before I got the train. Even more good riddance. When you think about it, Hilda's returning of the stuff you stumbled upon to Pete's and the Gills … it hasn't done any good, has it? You and she might as well have dumped it in the Condamine.'

'I suppose we'd hoped that it would throw the hounds off your scent, given that no stranger could have accomplished what Hilda did, that it had to have been done by an insider.'

'That wasn't meant to sound ungrateful to her, or you. I just meant that, however ingenious, it didn't have the intended effect. And now what? Do I hide up here like a tropical Yeti? Or do I come down and we tough it out, presumably after we've driven down to Dirranbandi, and staged my re-arrival?'

'I think we should just do nothing for a space. You come back to the cabin and we get on with our own quiet life. We don't need anyone else, do we? I don't. Apart from each other, we've got the garden, and the river, books, this private Room. You could duck out of sight if we hear a vehicle approaching, maybe you could rig up a tripwire on my track, so that there'd be an odd noise of a tin can or even a gunshot into the air if somebody came down it. Mind you, I don t expect Lorna or Henry will be dropping in for tea for a while. Then, in what Henry calls the fullness of time, the cancer in this place will dissolve and disappear of its own accord. Eventually somebody will work out – or I'll tell them – that you've been here … and that the sky hasn't fallen in. I'm not suggesting that Walrae will turn on the tickertape, or that I'll gloss over the way some people have behaved, but we may just be allowed, well, to exist?'

Quinn looked up at her with a wan smile and quickly kissed her forehead. Then his eyes dropped back to the ground, to the snakes and ladders he'd been drawing, wiping away, re-drawing.

'If you ever get sick of embroidering clothes for rich children, you can start selling encyclopaedias.'

She put her fingers into the snakes of his hair. 'Don't be unkind, Quinn. I just don't want you to let yourself be eroded by all this. We mustn't let some malicious overreaction undermine what we have. It's such a rare thing to be in love.'

Jennifer paused. She had taken her own breath away. Now her voice was lower, controlled. 'I don't want to be tying you up, Quinn, pressuring you. I only meant that …'

'I know what you meant, Jennifer Jade.' He was holding her eyes now, bright above her reddened cheeks. 'I know.'

His right hand reached for hers folded in her lap. His left hand still drew its language in the dirt.

Jennifer reluctantly let him slide away. Her hands dragged down his back as he rolled from the bedclothes and stood, naked and stretching his arms high above his head. They had slept in; the cabin was already awash with easy light. Jennifer did not want to relinquish the hum of two skins, the exclusiveness of bed. He could go to the river alone; she would lie here a few minutes more, sheeting her contentedness.

There was a chance he'd be seen, but a slim one. Quinn now swam a long way up from the jetty where some willows, missing Europe, wept right down to the water, screening him from the track. Here the Condamine talked over a bend of rocks on one bank, subsuming the rustle of his strokes in its pressing conversations.

Curled in the bed Jennifer watched as he pulled on shorts, slung a towel around his neck. She knew that he knew she was watching him. He picked up the soap near the door, turned and winked at her.

Around the side of the cabin, a few paces down, and Quinn saw the figure on the track.

It was too late to jump back. The dog had spotted him instantly.

He strode quickly towards them, waving his arm in a gesture that said they should come up. The figure in blue overalls directed a finger at the brown dog as if ordering it to sit. When Quinn got within a hundred metres, she began to walk away, Browner trotting by her legs but still watching Quinn.

'Mrs Jones. Hilda. Hang on!'

She stopped and toed the ground with a boot as he caught up.

'Ned Quinn.' He held out his hand as he reached her.

Hilda did not look at him, but she extended her hand and he took it, briefly felt its dryness.

'Don't go,' he urged. 'I'm having a swim. Jennifer's up at the cabin. She'd be upset if you didn't call. Definitely!'

He looked up at the cabin and there was Jennifer standing at the verandah rail, watching them. As though to confirm his invitation, she was waving.

'Go on!' Quinn cajoled. 'She's very fond of you, you know. And both of us have reason to be in your debt. Surely you can stop for a cup of tea?'

'I expect I could,' said Hilda, looking at Browner.

'Go on up then,' Quinn said quickly. 'I'll be there in a bit.'

'I didn't reckon you'd bunked off on that train.' She might have been addressing the dog rather than the back of her neighbour's lover. Quinn smiled but did not turn around. He headed for the Condamine; Hilda and Browner began walking up the slope.

Jennifer, surprised that Quinn had even got Hilda to stop for a how-do-you-do, rushed back into the cabin, began pulling up the bedclothes, burying socks and underwear. She was lighting the primus when Browner gave a single bark at the door.

'Stay!'

The kelpie dropped to its belly and Hilda stepped inside.

'This is a nice surprise,' Jennifer said warmly. 'I suppose you must have been pretty shocked to see Quinn still here?'

Hilda didn't answer at once, concentrating on the cigarette she was rolling.

'Not so much. Reckon I was more so when the word got about that he'd hopped on the train, which it did quick enough. Felt like comin' up to see you, to ask what was up. Chickened out, I did.' She got onto safer ground. 'You two birds are goin' to have to be a bit smarter if you don't want nobody to twig he's back, specially the Vickers on their way past.'

Jennifer shrugged guiltily. 'You're right. Usually we've been more careful than today. Neither of us likes his having to play fugitive, to hide. In one way I'll be glad when the word does escape that he's back, as it must.'

'Not through me it won't.'

Jennifer smiled her gratitude and got up to make the tea. When she returned she went through the whole story with Hilda – how Quinn had slipped off at Dirranbandi, how she'd gone to collect him from a creekbed. Hilda cackled a couple of times. She did not show it but she felt privileged to be sharing knowledge no-one else in the valley or in Walrae had. She, whose view, so Bert had said often enough, nobody gave a rat's arse for.

'Got some information from my old man,' she volunteered when Jennifer had finished. 'For what it's worth.'

Jennifer raised her eyebrows.

'Well, Bert was pissed last Sat'dy night, which isn't news, and he was goin' on about how everyone reckoned things'd be gettin' back to normal now, and how it was good that the old families and the new ones had pulled together to give your Ned the heave-ho. I told him he was pullin' somethin' else, but of course he don't listen to a word of me. Anyway, he was rabbitin' on about this plan they'd had to make sure your feller wasn't in two minds, as he said it, about stayin' in the valley. And he let out that it was Arvi who put the rock through your window, and old Cochrane who give you the treatment with the dead chook. They was goin' to keep sendin' you what Bert calls messages. So now you know who done them acts. As I say, for what it's worth. At least you know your friend Lorna didn't do none of that.'

Jennifer nodded slowly. She was thinking that it would almost be better if Lorna *had* been responsible; at least that would have contained the madness around them to one person.

Browner gave a desultory bark and the women looked up to see Quinn entering the room. He'd slicked down his hair with a comb and had stopped underneath the cabin to put on trousers and a T-shirt in deference to man-shy Hilda. His feet were bare and white from the river.

'I don't need to introduce you two?' Jennifer asked.

'Nope, we know each other,' said Quinn. 'I suppose Jennifer has explained to you my disappearing act?'

'Yep.'

'Maybe we didn't think it through, but at the time it seemed to offer a breathing space, a cheeky way to take the heat off, a bit like your effort with the stolen stuff.' He sat down on the decking, drops of the river showing through his T-shirt like rain.

'How long can you two lie low, but?'

'As long as we have to,' Jennifer cut in before Quinn could answer. But Hilda wanted his opinion, made it clear by looking at him.

'I have to tell you I don't like it,' he answered quietly. 'Not much good at being devious, at listening out for noises so I can hide myself like a leper. I've spent enough of my life fighting battles inside my head, trying to make certain voices go away. Trying to make myself disappear physically … it's getting to me, since you ask. Not such a good idea, even though it was my own.' He laughed hollowly. 'It's making me feel quite fractured.'

'Reckon it would and all.'

Jennifer shut up now. If she was surprised at Quinn's openness, she was amazed by Hilda. The woman rationed her monosyllables with the only men she ever saw, Bert and their fatherlike sons, and here she was engaging in conversation with a 'city' man, asking him questions. Quinn was more gifted than she had thought.

'It don't hurt to have that one in your corner.' Hilda waved her cigarette in Jennifer's direction, talking now as though she and Quinn were alone.

'Not wrong, Hilda. Not wrong. But at the same time I feel that me being here isn't doing *her* any good.'

Jennifer was about to speak for herself, but she swallowed and managed to remain silent. Was Quinn sending her letters via Hilda, using her to deliver what he found too hard to say when they were alone? Quinn looked at her briefly and smiled, then turned back to Hilda rolling her third cigarette.

'Jennifer's life was stable before I came, Hilda. She was self-contained, she had learned the gift of solitude and had an intimacy with the Condamine and the trees and the ridge, her animals. Not unlike you, in your different ways, I imagine. Nowadays she has a bigger vegetable garden and my love, but the price is upping all the time. Occasionally the very bush itself seems to have become alien; a hissing of dislike to this valley, a pressure-cooker effect. It's in the air, as they say. I could feel the deathly vapours of it that day I caught the train in Walrae …'

'Youse could always leave?' Hilda's voice never had any inflection, everything came out blunt as tree-stumps. She did seem to have felled Quinn's self-pity, however. He was grinning at her.

'Meanin' the both of you, 'course. This place ain't all that much more special than other bits o' bush I've heard about. Like they say, it's a big country.'

Jennifer wasn't sure whether she was more astounded or offended by these two oddbods, discussing her like she was the cat's mother.

'Oi! What about you two asking me what *I* think? Eh?'

'You'd go with him, I believe. Wouldn't you?'

'Yes, I …'

'Well then. What about an escarpment?'

Quinn spluttered into his tea. 'An elopement?'

'One of them, yeah.'

'Because,' said Quinn firmly, before Jennifer could try her oar again, 'because, Hilda, if we went somewhere else we'd just carry the same seeds to different soil, I can tell you. If

Jennifer and I can't make it here, isolated, only one family needing to pass our door, as good as cut off from the world, well where could we? It gets down to the fact that I'm high-risk. Geography can't change that. Jennifer's told you about my schizophrenia?'

Hilda nodded. She caught the look in Jennifer's eye and qualified her assent. 'Well, I get it that sometimes you go out of yourself, like everythin' gets blurry.'

Quinn smiled at the tobacco-faced woman. 'It does that.'

'Can I ask one thing, but, respecting your illness? Been thinkin' about it, like everyone else seems to be. But I don't read.'

Quinn looked positively delighted. 'A woman who will return stolen goods on her bicycle in the middle of the night? On behalf of people in love? She can ask anything.'

'When you're off out of it could you, like they reckon, get violent? How some men do when they're drunk? Try and kill somebody?'

'Not me, Hilda.' Quinn said it so calmly that it made Jennifer bite her bottom lip. 'There are a lot of stories about schizophrenia because it isn't properly understood, even by doctors. It's happened. People with acute psychotic episodes *have* gone off the deep end of disturbance into violence, but other everyday conditions of rage and jealousy and fear and greed have killed far, far more people. With schizophrenia there's more often an implosion than an explosion. With me, I tend to want to *save* the world. At the same time, I'm frequently deluded into thinking that someone or thing wants to do away with me. No, Hilda, it's only Ned Quinn I've ever tried bumping off.'

'I don't like any of this!' Jennifer snapped the seance between Hilda and Quinn with her own anger and fear. 'It's escapist and defeatist and it gives in to the forces of bigotry and barbarism!'

'That's a mouthful. Nearly as big as what his was.' Hilda's grin revealed teeth colour-coordinated with the stretched leather of her face. 'I s'pect you're saying you and him shouldn't be quitters?'

'Exactly! If we've got to make what Quinn once called a last stand of it, fine! The Cochranes can bring up as many dead chooks as they like, Arvi can smash all the windows out, Pete can put bees down the chimney, your Bert can …'

'Don't you worry about 'im,' Hilda interrupted sternly. 'I'll be knowing anythin' *that* one gets up to.'

'I don't give a shit what they get up to. We'll bury the chooks; we'll reglaze the windows; we'll smoke out any bees. In time, especially if the robberies are over, they'll run out of spleen if we sit tight. People will find something else to gossip about and to hate. If we run away that will convince them that they were right, and I couldn't stand the thought. Anything but that.'

'Hope you're right, girl,' said Hilda standing. 'Better be gettin' back. Ta for the tea. What you might need is to have Browner around for a time? He's a real 'earing haid, Browner. Tied up on a good rope, course, or 'e'd be back at my place before you could say Hamilton's Hotel. Could try 'im for a week, if you like? Bark if anyone comes within cooee. Can hear a motor or a footstep helluva long while before you two will. If someone wanted to know why 'e was here youse could say you was holdin' 'im for me.'

'Thanks, Hilda,' Jennifer smiled, the anger gone. 'We'll take you up on that if any trouble starts, but not for now. It wouldn't be fair on poor Browner.'

'Anyway, ta for the cuppa.' Hilda's neutral voice belied the fact that she had engaged in more conversation today than in the past six months combined. Jennifer had noted how she'd even volunteered to Quinn the secret of her illiteracy.

Quinn was also on his feet. 'It'd be good if you called now and again, Hilda, wouldn't it, Jen? You've got good eyes and ears, and both of us trust you. Jennifer's not exactly overburdened with friends since my arrival.'

Jennifer walked out with Hilda. Quinn noticed her stop at

a kitchen cupboard to press a small paper bag into the bib pocket of Hilda's blue overalls. He stayed on the verandah and watched them walk down to the track talking, Browner circling them as though they were slow sheep.

Quinn went out to the vegetable garden before Jennifer returned. He knew she would have something to say. Several minutes later her voice cut through the rhythm he'd fallen back into with the pick, slugging its blade into the ground like a slow heartbeat.

'Hoy!'

He straightened his back in the hot silence of late morning. 'What?' He called down the slope to where she was standing, leaning against the doorframe.

Jennifer shook her head from side to side, red hair swishing.

'Prince bloody Charming!' she bellowed up the hill. He saw the flash of her teeth before she went inside.

Quinn was in the garden same time the next day … same temperature, same immobile, immeasurably high blue sky … when he got word that someone was coming. Towards the middle of the day the parrots were as good a burglar alarm as Browner would have been. In the heat they were silent if undisturbed, cranky when bothered. Right now the smoke-dry insults of sulphur-cresteds announced that someone was on the track from the Vickers' house. Quinn stopped digging and grinned. The birds sounded as though they were shouting 'Bastard! Bastard!'

He loped down the hillside and poked his head in at the back door. Jennifer was sitting on the bed, knees bent, feet tucked under her bottom and her back straight. Needle in hand, she was somewhere between embroidery and meditation.

'Visitor from the Vickers.'

Quinn's voice jerked her from thought, began unfolding her legs.

'I'll just disappear through the eye of a needle,' Quinn said enigmatically.

Then he was gone.

He had more than enough time; it was minutes before Henry stepped off the track. He'd been whistling for the last few hundred yards, tunelessly signalling his approach, inured to the harsh noises of early-warning cockatoos.

Quinn had anticipated this sort of thing happening. Depending on where the approach came from, he had

various slip-aways planned. He could get from the top
right-hand corner of the vegetable plot to the shelter of the
beeline in twenty seconds. A few metres in and he was safe
as a grain of sand on a beach. From there, if necessary, he
could climb unsighted to the ridge, where he could travel
fast in stony silence. With enough warning, say an engine
on the rise in the track past Pete and Mary's, he could
descend to the Condamine, eel his way along the banks and
bends, loiter still as a brown trout in its black-tea shallows.
He had not told Jennifer but he'd even taken precautions
in case he got caught short on the exposed terraces of the
vegetable garden; he'd dug a pit the size of a rough grave
into which he could drop himself from all but birdsight.

For now, knowing that it must be Henry, Lorna, Kate, or
any combination thereof, he slipped below the cabin to the
open-faced room where tools and food bins and hanging
capsicums mixed their sweat with the vapours from a
44-gallon drum of kerosene on the dry dirt floor. He'd
rigged a camp stretcher behind the row of rat-proof
garbage bins containing flour, rice, sugar, bran, wheat.
They ran beneath the workbench Henry Vickers had used
when he built the place. Here Quinn lay on his back, hands
behind his head and ankles crossed, physically very relaxed,
the way workmen are when they stop for smoko.

His thoughts were less so; he could not concentrate
them, straining though he was, on Henry or on Hilda, even
on the vegetable garden he'd just come from. His mind
kept triangling between threes, coursing and flashing like
neon in an advertisement tube. Lighting up, moving on.
Whatever he thought of, it would ricochet off two other
irrelevancies. Jibberishing between inane points of reference, he thought to himself. Then that idea, too, would
recur and disappear, triangle into a pair of other thoughts.

Quinn was glad he was lying here where he could over-
hear most of any conversation inside the cabin. Whatever
was going to be discussed above him should at least concen-

trate his mind, block up some of these jerky tangents and cerebral cul-de-sacs. He knew this threadless thought as a precursor. 'Like someone's unravelling your knitting,' he had once written to Jennifer. Often what came in above such loosening was the sound of voices. Insinuating their way in whispers at first.

He heard Henry's knock, Jennifer's inviting him in, Henry's boots above where he lay. Henry was alone. While it was never raised, his voice carried well. Quinn heard all but a word or two of their entire conversation.

'I'm sorry about the other day ...'

'Don't be, Henry. How is she?'

Quinn heard the springs as Henry sat on the couch, the clunk of pottery mugs on the kitchen bench, the brush of Jennifer's bare feet on bare boards.

'Worse, if anything. She's stuck with that madness about my shed. She's even told people here and in Walrae about it, how you and I seemed intent on exonerating Ned at any cost. Deliberately in front of me, almost a challenge. I know it's academic given that Ned's gone, but I've wondered if she isn't keeping it up as a way of punishing me?'

Jennifer groaned.

'Anyway, I'm taking her and Kate to Brisbane tomorrow. That's what I'm really here to tell you.'

'To her sister's?'

'Yes. Officially a break, a chance for Kate to see her aunt. In truth because I know you're right, Lorna needs help with her head.'

'But she still doesn't agree?'

'Well, no. But I think she will. She knows deep down that she's in trouble and she no longer swears at me when I raise the subject. I've said *I* probably need counselling about Robbie. And she's the mother, so ... Lorna listens to her sister. I'm banking on Karen to help me persuade her.'

There was a silence above Quinn.

'I was wondering if you might milk the cow, take care of

the horse and the cat? Possibly do some watering? I don't like to ask, but …'

'You know I will, Henry. How long will you be gone for?'

'Two weeks at least. I'd say more likely three. If it's too big a task I could see if Hilda Jones would do it, or even get Gladys Sampson, but she's so vague. Perhaps Arvi and Sue might move in, they're pretty mobile …'

'Shut up, Henry! I'd do it for six months. I'm so deep in your debt from over the years. Not another word!'

'Thanks.'

'Now for the bad news, Henry.'

Quinn wondered what Jennifer was up to, whether she'd remembered that he might be lying where he was. Her voice became cold as a coroner's.

'Since you're going for help for Lorna, I'd better tell you that she also took the things from the Gills, broke into Pete's shed. I know this for sure, but I just haven't been able to bring myself to tell you until now. I could explain to you how I got to find out, but it's too long a story unless you don't believe me?'

Quinn could not hear the next few words from Henry, his voice had fallen away. He thought he caught the word 'suspected'; certainly Henry wasn't proclaiming disbelief.

'That's right,' Jennifer continued. 'One day I'll even tell you how the things got returned, but it's not important now. If you do get Lorna to see someone in Brisbane you could possibly have a private word with them about it. I wouldn't raise it with Lorna, certainly not now. If she's still trying to pin your shed on Quinn, there's no point in bringing in Pete and the Gills. What's more, she may genuinely not know that she did those stupid things.'

Suddenly her voice lost the reins. 'Post-natal depression seems to work like a passport; schizophrenic derangement, now that's a different fucking trip.'

'Jennifer …'

'I'm sorry, Henry. I'm sorry.' She was immediately back

in control. 'I mustn't be haranguing you. You've got your hands full. Anyway, there's more.'

'You're not going to tell me that Lorna put that rock through your window, too?'

'No,' Jennifer laughed icily. 'I know who did that. What I am going to tell you in strict confidence is that Quinn hasn't gone.'

'What ...?'

'Fraid so. He's been here all along. We faked his departure. He got off at Dirranbandi. You remember when we met on the Walrae road? I was on my way to pick him up.'

'Holy shit! Where is he?'

'At this moment? Hiding somewhere. Like a bloody prison escaper. He heard someone coming, warned me, disappeared. Into the trees. Down along the river?'

'Christ! If Lorna and some of the others learn that he's back ... that he didn't even leave in the first place ...'

'They'll eventually find out that he's here, of course. I don't see that they need to know that he didn't go. If you and I don't tell them. Quinn and I may have to stage his return, I don't know, I haven't discussed it with him.'

Suddenly Quinn felt uncomfortable. Now that Jennifer had told Henry, there was no reason why he shouldn't join them, speak for himself, as he'd done with Hilda. The intensity of the conversation had enabled him to focus his thoughts, but he felt stretched. Before he could make up his mind to move, the talk from above pinned him.

'How's he coping?'

'It's hard for me to say, Henry. I so much *want* him to cope that I'm not in a good position to be distinguishing wishful thinking from reality. Ha! Well, he's fine as ever to talk to, witty and warm. Just the way I like him. But since our stunt with the train I've been aware that he's feeling the pressure. This is what really infuriates me: the prophesies that Quinn will go loopy become almost self-fulfilling. He doesn't say anything but he's told me in letters that there's a possible link between stress and the trigger mechanisms for his leaps into perceptual chaos. Logical when you think about it. It's making me so angry – I mean that those bigoted, ignorant voices whispering away in the back-ground in Walrae and the valley will increase the chances of another of Quinn's "episodes" coming on. Throw in Lorna. I *know* she's none of those things normally, otherwise you and I wouldn't love her as we do, but right now, in her own state …'

'Thank God she thinks he's gone. At least what you're doing now offers some respite. As long as no-one gets to know he's about …'

'Exactly. But I'm worried about how Quinn will fare when they do. Will it all start up again? Where will Lorna stand? Can Quinn resist persecution from without as well as within? I just don't know, and I sense that *he* doesn't either. It must be difficult enough for him knowing that if he nosedives right out of reality his new-found lover will have to somehow cart him off to a psychiatric institution in Brisbane. I've learned that I will be up to it, which came as a bit of a surprise to me, but surely that's enough for Quinn and me to deal with, to be left alone with, if not supported?'

'Well, once the heat dies out of all this you know I'll support you, so would the Lorna of old. And she'll be back.'

Jennifer's voice softened. 'People do surprise you, don't they?' Quinn could sense that she was thinking of Hilda Jones.

'Have you thought of going away? For a time, not permanently?'

'Neither of us likes the idea of running. I think Quinn's done a bit of it in his time, that he believes it would just be postponing things, the way we are now, I suppose.'

Jennifer sighed loudly enough for Quinn to hear. 'You can't run away from schizophrenia any more than you can from post-natal depression. Like income tax, you can only put off the day of reckoning, and there are penalties to pay for that. The difference for Lorna is that her condition is temporary, that if people around here get to know about it – and some of them must have noticed that she's been strange lately – they'll willingly attribute it to the trauma of Robbie's death, they'll be queueing up with Samaritan casseroles. Fuck them! All I want is to be left alone to live oh-so-quietly in the bush with a man I love. His schizophrenia should be his fight, and mine. No-one else's apart from doctors when we're losing it ...'

Quinn shut his eyes. Part of him knew right now that he was, as she sweetly put it, 'losing it'. But he could also picture the colour in her eyes, the sway of her hair. She was a dogged lover, was Jennifer Jade Duncan. It was good to know, as Hilda had remarked, that someone like her was in your corner. Even if you were losing. Especially if you were losing ...

Jennifer and Henry were not saying anything worth listening to now. It was departure talk. Henry had stood up, was shuffling his boots on the floor as he explained things about the animals, said that he would leave a list on the table up at the house, his sister-in-law's phone number etc etc.

Briefly Quinn heard a third voice in his left ear. More a whisper, indistinct but definite. He knew too well its sibilance.

'Oh no you don't, Two. Oh no you don't.' He didn't say it aloud.

He focused on the vegetable garden, made his head mentally take the seven steps up the terraces, back down again. Over and over. In a few minutes, giving Henry time to be well onto the track, he'd slip back to where he'd been working so that Jennifer would not know he'd been imprisoned beneath her words. He would adopt the mantra of the swung pick, the rise and fall of it, the climb and cut of it, the muteness of shaped wood and steel.

Quinn tried to stop right there, to keep the image clear. But the first bloody voice was too quick, flashing up on the screen three picks, like a coalminer's family crest, arranged in a rough triangle.

Part 5

In the fortnight after the Vickers left for Brisbane Overton Valley did its best for Jennifer and Quinn. Golden-oldie crooning days: Blue skies up above … up a lazy river in the noonday sun … Waking in the tumescent dawn; staying up late into the buttery lamplight; sleeping with sudden deepness between these poles; eating; touching – the rareness of an economy that balanced demand and supply. At least this was to become Jennifer's memory of that pause, a smooth stone in the pocket of her future.

They were not constantly beside each other, often they didn't exchange a word for half a day. Quinn was throwing himself into the vegetable garden as though it was a paid job with a fixed completion date and penalty clause. Jennifer only once suggested he slow down. In a voice either innocent or lascivious – she could not tell which – he answered that he was on a 'working honeymoon'. He knew precisely how to extract her blushes.

The seven wide steps of terracing were almost finished, each drop shored with angled walls of stone from the ridge line. These Quinn transported on a device he'd christened a 'tropical sled'. It was a wheel-less, high-sided contraption like a stretched billycart upon which he heaped broken stone way up on the slope then pushed and nudged down to where he wanted it. He'd crowbar its ironbark runners over rougher ground or around obstacles.

Sometimes it would gather too much speed and lurch onto its side, spewing stone. Quinn would whistle air as he re-stacked it. Once a load escaped as a minor landslide, halted only as it bombarded the top line of chickenwire which defended the terraced land. Splash and the chooks had set up a chorus as though the sky was falling in. Jennifer watched Quinn whistling quietly to himself as he restrung the damaged sections.

She had been observing him carefully, which is to say she took care that he did not see her doing so. He was quieter, much quieter, but she decided that this marked a calm preoccupation with the rhythm of his work rather than any inner turbulence. It was difficult to judge – the right sort of silence was such a gift to share. They would have to talk over the ways they were going to cope, but not now, not in this still air

No outsider was sighted, but Quinn always looked up at loud cracks or thumps in the surrounding bush, listened to the telegraphed warnings of birds. Once he had to restrain the urge to skip into the trees when a small plane from one of the cattle stations flew over. He and Jennifer did laugh about how his terracing and rock carting would be explained to people who believed that she was alone. Jennifer joked that Lorna would demand to feel up her biceps. Such asides, predicated upon windshifts, were as close as they got to grappling with the future. They were like the stones travelling on Quinn's sled before he had fitted and tamped them into the retaining walls: unstable. The possibility that Lorna might return in the same state in which she had departed was left alone, a moving pendulum.

Jennifer worked alongside him when she felt like it, tilthing and treading the shifted soil, cutting drains so the terracing would cope with the wet season, bucketing up water peasant-style from the Condamine to succour the seedlings. Each morning and evening she would take the track to the Vickers' to attend their cow. Often she would ride Lorna's horse back with the morning milk, return on it in the evening to let it out in the yard. She also made

bread, sewed and embroidered commissions for her anonymous Sydney babies, set the excess milk from the cow on
the slow course towards cheese.

It was the baled cow, her warm milk singing into the
stainless steel bucket, to whom Jennifer first spoke a Carte-
sian sentence she had been trying for several days to utter,
without success. Her forehead resting against its piebald
side, hands fluent on the long teats, she said softly:

'I think … I'm pregnant.'

The cow ground on with her cud, not missing a beat.
Jennifer smiled to herself; it had been quite easy to say.

When it was too hot to work Quinn and Jennifer would
sometimes siesta together in the hammock he had made
and slung under the cabin – not far from where he had
listened to her and Henry talk. Other days they would take
books down to the river, doze on its grassy banks, make love
under its dusky surface, their flesh flashing like the under-
sides of trout. Once they even did so above it, climbing
naked up and out on an overhanging she-oak. Copulating
like monkeys, with more passion but less agility, Jennifer
holding a branch in front of her, Quinn behind holding
her everywhere he could. Afterwards they joined hands
and jumped, thigh muscles tingling and their laughter
recklessly loud about them as they hit the water.

In the evenings Jennifer might sit on her own on the jetty
smoking thoughtfully while Quinn fished the river from the
peninsula of the first bend upstream. They would gesture –
he would semaphore bites with a raised thumb – while main-
taining silence religiously, allowing the bush and its inhabitants to bed down or bestir for the approaching night.

A few times they doubled up on Lorna's horse in the
evening and Quinn watered the Vickers' fruit trees and
vegetables while Jennifer milked and fed. She showed him
around the inside of the house, eerie with the odours but
not the noises of her friends. Quinn's woodwork-teacher

eyes admired Henry's bush carpentry. He had also climbed all over Henry's windmill and tankstands and followed the pipe down to the Condamine. One night in the cabin he interrupted Jennifer's sewing to show her his own adaptation for the terraced garden above the cabin, using a hydraulic ram implanted in the river's body like a pacemaker. He told her a windmill was a hare, a hydraulic ram a tortoise. She would hear its clunking heartbeat from her bed. Jennifer had laughed at his boyish enthusiasm and admired the sketch.

She'd asked a few intelligent questions, but something bothered her about it; perhaps the way he'd printed 'Jennifer Duncan's Water Supply' neatly above the dated drawing.

The sketch did force them to deal with one formality. She asked him how much the equipment, tanks etc would cost. Quinn had already made estimates. He told her casually that he would like to buy it, if that was acceptable? He also wanted to provide a shed and more fencing.

'I've got money sitting in Melbourne. I'd rather it was lifting water up here for you.'

'For us.'

'I saw there was a bank in Dirranbandi. I'll write to my brother and ask him to make some transfer arrangements.'

'Alright. Thank you. Did you write to the school again?'

'Yes, it's all underway.'

They looked at each other then went back to needle and pencil, momentous matters dissolved into mere details.

Half-way into the third week of the Vickers' absence Jennifer went into Walrae and rang Lorna's sister's place in Brisbane. She prayed that Henry would answer. She wanted to find out when they were returning. Both she and Quinn were beginning to tense any time they heard a non-animal sound, imagining internal combustion noises. More than once Quinn had stopped using tools or shifting rocks to make sure he was not drowning out a returning Land-Rover. Looking up from the kitchen window she would see him frozen in intense concentration. They didn't discuss this jumpiness, but Jennifer did let him know that she was going to ring 'to see how Lorna is'. She wanted to commit herself to telling him how the land lay, to prevent herself burying the news if it was bad.

It was Lorna who picked up the phone.

'Hi! It's me. Jennifer; in Walrae. Everything's fine. The animals are well. No dramas at all. How's Brisbane?'

She almost didn't stop talking, she wanted to put off hearing Lorna's voice, the tone. The two women had not seen or spoken to each other since that day on the cabin verandah.

'Thanks for ringing, Jen. Brisbane's alright, I suppose. Same as it ever was. I want to get back home, very much. Henry says to tell you we'll be there four days from now, that's on Sunday. In the evening.'

Jennifer could have kissed the telephone. The voice sounded distant and tired, but not hollow. The fact that Lorna used 'Henry says' made Jennifer smile. That wasn't the way Lorna talked, it was always 'we've decided'. If she was taking her husband's advice perhaps it showed that she'd been getting professional help? Jennifer strode in.

'How are you feeling, Lorna? I don't mean physically.'

A sigh travelled several hundred kilometres.

'I'm better,' she said eventually. 'Much better, Jen. I feel terrible about the way I've treated you, my best woman friend. Henry tells me I've trampled all over that friendship. I'm still not quite sure how badly, to tell you the truth. Excuse me a sec …'

Jennifer could picture Lorna holding the telephone away from her, heard the muffled duck-honk of nose into handkerchief. Then she was back.

'Sorry. I seem to be crying all the time at the moment. I went … Henry and Karen dragged me to see a psychotherapist the day after we got here, whenever that was. I took an instant dislike to her, our chemicals didn't mix, as you'd say. We got referred to a psychologist who does a lot of grief counselling, and he's been a big help. I've been going every second day.'

'What does he say about your … condition?'

'Apparently I blamed myself for Robbie's death, then I transferred it to Henry and, more so, to you. Henry says I've been quite loopy at times. I believe this guy when he says I was trying to punish you … through Quinn. Which is why I made up that story about Henry's shed.'

There was a pause, but Jennifer was at a loss to fill it. She daren't ask.

'You still there?'

'Yes, I'm here, Lorna.' Jennifer could hear soft crying again.

'Do you think you're ever going to be able to forgive me?'

Jennifer's laugh was brittle, she couldn't doctor it. 'You sounded just like Kate then. I hope we can weather the storm, Lorna. Really I do. Are you taking any medication?'

'Tranquillisers. Just for a while. Henry is bringing me back here after a fortnight or so at home so this fellow can see how I'm progressing. If I hadn't been so difficult Henry could have brought me to him much sooner.'

'Henry's been fantastic, Lorna. I hope you know that?'

'I'm sure he has, I'm sure. I suspect he's still sheltering me because I don't really follow all that's happened since, since Robbie died. It's going to take me time … I think a big wall of sadness shuts out everything.'

'I know, Lorna, I've hit the same wall, remember? Look, we probably shouldn't talk any more right now. I'm only a friend, not a psychologist, and, what's more, I'm running out of coins. I'm so glad the old Lorna I know is making a comeback. Will you tell Henry I rang? Please tell him that everything's okay at this end. Got that?'

'I will, I will. Everything's okay at this end. I mean your end …'

'Bye.'

'Bye …'

Lorna had started crying again and her voice had trailed. Jennifer was surprised to find tears running down her own face.

It was not until after they had finished eating on the verandah that evening that she got to tell Quinn what had been said, what her impressions were. After clearing the plates into the kitchen she returned with coffee and an already rolled Seven Sisters number, which wreathed its smoke into the level evening.

'So,' she began when she felt that the drug was erasing clumsiness, 'Lorna is definitely on the way back. In both senses.'

Jennifer was standing at the rail, Quinn sitting very still in a deckchair, his head tilted forward and his long fingers resting on each temple.

'What did she say?'

Jennifer went through the phone call word-for-word. The only omission was how she had skipped and laughed after hanging up. Right in the middle of Walrae.

Quinn did not react at all, verbally. He kept his fingertips at his temples, clicked his tongue against the roof of his mouth for a while.

'We were due for some good news,' Jennifer said, catching some of the smoke from her mouth in her nostrils and inhaling it again. 'I don't know whether Lorna will ever learn what a mess she's been or what damage she's done, but I think there's a good chance that you'll eventually get to meet the Lorna I told you about in my letters, not the witch she was turning into.'

'I'm not so sure about psychologists, let alone psychotherapists.'

'But, Quinn, he's got her to start unravelling her grief, to have some insight.'

The last word made Quinn laugh harshly.

'Would you rather we didn't discuss it?'

'There's not much else to say. Wait and see, cat and mouse.'

'Alright. At least we know we've got until Sunday. I suggest we continue our charade for a little while after she returns. We should take Henry's advice on that, don't you think?'

Jennifer could see the unease behind Quinn's eyes, but it puzzled her. This *was* the best news they'd had for a long time, the *only* good news if you discounted the discovery of the hidden Hilda Jones.

Jennifer now used Hilda to get out of the mess she, or the Seven Sisters, were making of the evening, which had started to carry winged traffic. Moths, even smaller aircraft, reconnoitred through the near-darkness. Occasionally bigger wings sheared away, half-seen, as bats and owls began their hard day's night.

'I thought I'd call in on Hilda on the way into Dirranbandi tomorrow, see if she wants anything. But not if you want to come, Quinn, I'll give her a miss … and her poxy husband.'

At the mention of Hilda Quinn's face looked calmer. He drew his fingertips from his head.

'No, you call in on Hilda, Jen. I don't fancy ducking around Dirranbandi in case somebody from Walrae is there and spots me. You can post my letters, and I don't need to open an account until I hear back from my brother. He'll still be addressing my mail to you, by the way. No, you go alone. I want to finish that last bit of wall. You might even persuade Hilda and Browner to go with you?'

Jennifer was relieved. 'I reckon Hilda would come if you were! You've won a heart there, Mr Quinn. Arvi and Sue and Pete and Mary claim that between the four of them they have never heard Hilda Jones say more than two words, whatever the occasion. But for you she comes in to drink tea and have deep-and-meaningfuls? Hmmn?'

Quinn waved her cheekiness away, grinning. Jennifer was pleased with the outcome. Had he decided to come with her to Dirranbandi it was she who would have had to do the ducking and weaving.

The trip was ostensibly to visit the auto wreckers on the far side of the town, where the guts and bones of deceased cars and trucks sit in the hot sun of the plain. She was to try to cannibalise another carburettor. Quinn had done some running repairs to the utility, but its fuel system was on its last spurts. He had given her a long explanation of its problems as she'd leant across the opposite mudguard watching him work, the raised bonnet acting as a sun umbrella. She loved hearing the banter Quinn would set up with himself while his hands were busy. His mental sphincters stopped their clenching, and he became beautifully silly. A shield, she imagined, to block out infrared thoughts.

Once while tinkering with the Holden's engine he'd conjured a song. Made her sing it through with him in an overripe, boozy Australian accent, tuneful as a blowfly, until the pair of them fell down greasy and laughing on the ground. It was, insisted Quinn, the Queensland version of *American Pie*:

> *Boy, boy, miss the Aussie meat poy*
> *Drove me carbie to the barbie*
> *We was covered in floys*
> *Them good 'ol boys*
> *Were drinkin,' Bundy and droys*
> *Singin' this'll be the doy that I doy*
> *This'll be the doy that I doy.*

There was an outside chance Jennifer could snaffle a replacement carburettor at the Dirranbandi wreckers, and he had explained to her carefully what to look for in terms of wear and tear. She was dubious about his faith in her mechanical eye. Jennifer also needed to consign a stock of her nighties to the coast, just as easily done from Dirranbandi station as from Walrae. But the real purpose of her trip was an appointment with the Dirranbandi doctor.

To Jennifer's surprise, and delight, Hilda agreed to come the next day. She had left the engine running and bipped the horn outside the Joneses' house – unnecessarily, given the racket Browner was making as he tested and re-tested his chain. Bert Jones and Charlie, the eldest of the two sons, came around the corner of an outbuilding, saw it was Jennifer, turned and went back to their business. Hilda emerged from the kitchen wiping her hands on a towel. She yelled at Browner to shut up, leant both hands on the passenger-side window sill.

'Morning, Hilda, I'm going to Dirranbandi. Want anything?'

'I do need some stuff. Will you write it, stop for a cuppa?'

'Sure. I don't s'pose you fancy coming along for the ride?'

'Dirranbandi?'

'Why not, I'm going, aren't I?'

'Haven't been there for, oh, three years.'

'Suit yourself. It's not exactly going to the races, I know.'

'I'll come.'

'Good on you, Hilda!'

'Give us a minute.'

Jennifer took the risk, turned off the engine. The unexpected silence brought Bert back into view. Jennifer watched Hilda walk across to him, exchange some words, return to the house. She played eye games with Browner while she waited, uncomfortable at the thought that Bert Jones might decide to come and speak to her. But he didn't, and Hilda stepped back into the sunlight a few minutes later.

Jennifer could not recall when she had last seen Hilda wearing anything other than overalls; now she was decked out in a plain cream blouse with an old-fashioned rounded collar, clean grey cotton slacks, thick white socks and tan leather slip-one. She had wisely not addressed her face with lipstick or makeup, it was too sun-dried sultana for that, but she had wet and brushed her cropped salt-and-pepper hair. Jennifer thought she looked like a pageboy who had been smoked over a fire. She pretended not to notice Hilda had changed.

'Can he come?'

For a second Jennifer panicked, then she saw that Hilda had nodded in the direction of her dog, not her husband.

'Tie 'im in the back?'

'More the merrier.' Hilda would like to have someone to talk to later, at length, about her Day in Dirranbandi.

The dog clearly understood English. No sooner had Hilda bent to release the catch of the chain than Browner bounded and sailed into the back of the ute without touching the side. Hilda tied him there with a short rope.

'Cross your fingers,' Jennifer said. Hilda put crossed, nicotined fingers on the dashboard. Jennifer shuddered at the possibility of having to ask Bert and Charlie to push-start them. She turned the key, and the ute started first time.

'Bloody Rolls,' grinned Hilda.

Neither of them said much while they made their slow progress down the valley track. As they passed the entrances to Mary and Pete's, Arvi and Sue's, the Gills', the Cochranes' and others, Jennifer couldn't help feeling embarrassed that she was not doing the neighbourly thing, calling to see if anybody needed supplies. Then she felt stupid for even considering this. When they reached the

Walrae–Dirranbandi Road and turned left, when she had settled the utility into 45 mph and looked in the rear-vision mirror at Browner, high on the rush of air up his wet nostrils, she told Hilda the truth.

'Apart from this carburettor business and putting my parcel on the train, I've got an appointment with Dr Urquhart.'

'You crook?'

'Not exactly. I'm pretty convinced that I'm pregnant though.'

'Hooley Dooley!' Hilda had been looking out at the flat red geography of the plain, the meanness of the scrub such a contrast to the valley's fecundity. She turned to Jennifer and gently punched her on the shoulder.

'What's 'e reckon about that kettle of fish?' She was grinning.

'Quinn? I haven't told him. You're the first to know, if you don't count Lorna's cow.'

Again Hilda felt privileged by these odd neighbours who both seemed to have taken to her.

'Why not?'

'Well, I may not be, that's why. I'm pretty sure I am, but there doesn't seem much point in telling him I might be going to have his baby. It could just add to the stress he's already under because of what's been going on, with Lorna and everybody.'

'A woman usually knows if she's got a bun in the oven. Did straight away with my two lumps. You ain't a chicken for your first, no offence.'

'Not my first, Hilda. I had a little girl who died in a car accident.'

'I am sorry. I shouldn't be jokin'.'

'You weren't to know. I knew I'd conceived with her, and I feel just the same way now, all these years later. Fancy having a baby at thirty-eight, no I'd be thirty-nine by then, if I really am. I don't know if I'm more thrilled or scared.'

'Were you plannin' on havin' one?'

'Not at all. Before I conceived my daughter my ex-husband and I had been trying to have a child for several years. We'd been to clinics, specialists, you name it, and the verdict was that I was all but infertile. We thought it was a miracle when I got pregnant, so did the doctors. I'd discussed all this with Quinn, who has never had kids, and, well, we weren't being too careful. Obviously.'

'Looks like you might 'ave a second miracle on yer hands, eh?'

They both laughed, Browner chipping in from behind the glass with a few fast-disappearing barks.

'I'm busting to tell him, Hilda. It's been really hard keeping the lid on it. The other day he was saying how his terraced vegetable garden was going to produce more food than we could possibly eat ourselves, and I was dying to say: "What, all three of us?" Had to bite my lip.'

'Sounds to me like you ain't so sure 'e'll want a bub?'

'I think he will, Hilda. I hope he will. I know he worries about the impact of his illness on me, and that he will probably say defensive stuff like he's not fit for fatherhood. But I'm ready for any of that. The truth is, he's such a good man, so clever and so patient and so loving that he *should* have children. The world needs dads like Quinn.'

'Oi, it's not *me* you gotta sell this bub to, girl!' They laughed together again. 'Your mate Lorna? Goin' to have to tread a bit careful there.'

'I know,' Jennifer said quietly. 'I might not tell her, or anyone, until my belly gives me away.'

'Always does,' said Hilda sagely. 'Always does.'

They continued in silence for a while. Now that she had broken her news to a human being, Jennifer too needed time to re-absorb her feelings, to wonder whether or not she had been talking her confidence up. After a few more flat red kilometres had been reeled off she coughed, and, without turning to look at her passenger, asked:

'If I am ... and if it's a girl ... and if Quinn went along with it ... how would you feel about there being two Hildas in the valley? You and Hilda Quinn?'

She did not answer straight away. Then Hilda said: 'It'd be an honour, girl. And thank you. But I c'n feel it in me bones that if you are in the club, and I reckon you sound silly enough to be, then what you've got in there is a little feller. Couldn't call a bloke Hilda.'

Jennifer drove straight down the main street of Dirran-bandi and out the other side. The wrecker's domain is a large tin shed on the road to that other resting place, the district cemetery, and, a kilometre further on, another graveyard: the Dirranbandi tip. Hilda got out and spoke to the proprietor before Jennifer got the chance.

'G'day. After a carbie for that thing there.'

The man looked them over, then the ute. 'Come in, ladies, we'll see what we can do for youse.'

They did get a carburettor, although Jennifer had little idea whether or not it was, as the man repeatedly assured Hilda, 'good as new'. Hilda had told him, hands in pockets and inclining her head towards Jennifer: 'Her old man'll skin her if she gets home with a lemon.'

'No worries. That carbie's a goer, I'm tellin' ye.'

Back in the main street of Dirranbandi they decided to part. Hilda, with Browner on the short rope, went off to shop for her own things, for once not being obliged to reveal her inability to read or write in the process. Jennifer headed for the station first, a few odds and ends of shopping, then Dr Urquhart's surgery. They would meet in the Farraday Tearooms at four pm.

When they did so, or when Jennifer arrived at the lace-curtained tearooms at 4.15, Hilda got up from the table where she'd been slowly and awkwardly sipping her solitary tea. When Jennifer saw her and began crossing the large room, Hilda was already revealing her tea-toned teeth. Jennifer's face told her everything. Hilda extended her hand. 'Congratulations, girl.' She shook Jennifer's hand hard and then changed her mind and gave her neighbour a quick, rough hug. As they sat Hilda said loudly: 'Let me shout you a bun.'

Jennifer's laughter bashed about the room before she managed to recover her voice. She gave Hilda a full account of what Dr Urquhart had said, how he'd tested her urine and told her the news with his typical detachment. He'd explained the increased risks of foetal abnormality at her age but had said, after examining her and after learning that she had carried many years before, that she was fit and healthy and 'built for childbearing'. He began to say that if, on the other hand, she and 'the father' felt they did not want to proceed …

Jennifer told Hilda, as her tea arrived, that she'd closed that conversation straight away. As expected, Dr Urquhart had lectured her on smoking, about which he felt so strongly that he said he did not want her as a patient if she thought she could smoke and create a life at the same time. Jennifer swore that she would have one last joint this very evening, and thereafter not another for the seven and a bit months left. Scouts honour. Dr Urquhart had also wanted to give her a full explanation of the plusses and minuses of hospital versus home birth, advocating the former because of her age, but she had cut him off there, too.

'Hospital,' she'd said. 'One hundred per cent hospital.'

The GP just shrugged and carried on, made an appointment for her next visit.

'I'm real pleased for you,' Hilda said, waving to the waitress for the bill, 'real pleased.'

Quinn was sitting down writing in the cabin when Jennifer returned, tired but aglow. Hilda had left her to her own maternal thoughts most of the way back. The sun was descending like a losing arm wrestler on their left, resisting the table-top horizon.

They embraced briefly in the doorway, Jennifer laden with shopping. Quinn went straight out to the ute upon her telling him that she and Hilda had gone together and scored a carburettor. He returned with it, studied it care-fully as he held it up to the verandah window.

'The fellow promised that it was "a goer" and that I can return it if you don't like it. Hilda just about threatened his life.'

'No, it looks fine. Fine. I'll put it in first thing in the morning.'

'I've got news ...'

They said it together, perfect sync, although Jennifer's voice and eyes were alight, Quinn's were not.

'You first,' she laughed. 'I bet I know what yours is: you've finished the seventh terrace?'

'I have,' Quinn said quietly, with none of the zing that he'd had a few days earlier when he'd told her that this garden was going to be the eighth wonder of the world. 'But that's not it.'

'Alright, Hitchcock, I'll bet you can't guess mine either. Tell me.'

'Two things,' said Quinn, in the level voice that seemed to steer him lately. He might have been a woodwork teacher imparting the steps in making breadboards. 'The first is that I've been seen. Spotted.'

'Christ! How?' At once Jennifer wished she'd shown less shock, given it less significance.

'I was down at the river. Fishing, not swimming. Two hours ago, I suppose. Everything was sweetly quiet. No bites, but it was fine just to be sitting there listening to the river telling me that my back wasn't really hurting so much after finishing that last terrace. I looked up and there were two boys standing on your jetty, staring at me flat out. Mary and Pete's youngsters, from what you've told me of them. I imagine they'd come to see you. I called out that you were not here. As soon as they knew I'd seen them they were off like frightened bunnies. No doubt mum and dad had a full description within the half hour … no doubt the bush telegraph has been working overtime.'

'Oh,' was all that Jennifer could manage. She had begun preparing their meal, stopping and looking at him occasionally as he sat on the couch. 'What's your other news, sunshine?'

'That I'm going. For a few days. I don't feel up to a posse of objectors right now, not the way I am. Also the Vickers will be back on Sunday. I'd be in and out of my various hideyholes like a jackrabbit. So I thought I'd take a small pack, food, water, book or two. Go for a bit.'

'Up to The Room?'

'Possibly. Why do you ask that?'

'Nothing. No reason. I just wondered where else.'

'Oh, I might hike about a bit. I think exercise helps, and I can't work freely on the garden after today.'

'My poor Quinn. You are stretched, aren't you? Your voice and your eyes tell me, even if you don't. One minute you can be so soft with me and so beautifully stupid, then I see that you've got your heels in the ground and your back to the wall. It's just that if you were in The Room you'd be quite safe sitting there reading, and I'd know where you were. The thought of you drifting around the bush, with me unable to come to you, to watch over you as I've done once…I don't like it.'

'It's not safe for me to tell you exactly where I'll be, Jennifer.'

He was looking right at her now, but his eyes had no give in them.

'You may receive certain information, however.'

Quinn was holding his fingers to his lips and he flashed those eyes left and right quickly, signalling.

Why was he saying they could not continue that line of discussion here and now? Jennifer held the tip of her tongue between her teeth. She nodded to show that she was on side.

'Promise me one thing, Quinn. Quinn?'

'Sure,' he said, his eyes flickering around the room, clearly relieved that she was not going to debate his departure.

'Tell me you won't reduce or stop your medication?'

'Not a problem,' he said, shutting the subject. 'Now, you tell me your news.'

Jennifer bent down below the kitchen bench and crashed some pots together in the cupboard. When she stood straight again her eyes had been hastily wiped, and the skin on her left forearm pinched so hard that it stung fiercely.

'My news is that I've decided to give up smoking. From tonight.'

It's all very well to be lurching about the bush like Voss,' said Two, 'but he at least occasionally went in straight lines.'

'Leave off!' Quinn barked, loud enough to cause a shriek above his head that fired up every hair on his body. The cockatoo wheeled from the green canopy into the blue.

'Let's sit down and take some time to work things out,' One said above Quinn's right ear in her naggingly conciliatory way.

'If I could choose between you,' said Quinn aloud, his voice back below cockatoo threshold, his eyes on the elephantine skin of a she-oak, 'I'd be hard fucking pressed.'

'The point remains,' laboured One, 'that you have to have a strategy, one doesn't just charge off into the fray, any more than Napoleon did.'

'Oh, One doesn't, doesn't One?' The hiss from the left was furious at the implication of precipitant flight. 'When the opposition's pincering in on you, safer ground is your first priority. Christ, haven't we agreed on that often enough before now? It's dandy to say we must have neat strategic goals, but we weren't going to have *any* plans if they got to us first, now were we? There's nothing I've read in Napoleon's rule book against strategic retreat. Living to fight another day, it's called.'

One didn't answer, but that was normal enough; both of them had the habit of going at each other through him, the way heated politicians still address their invective through the Speaker.

Quinn sat down on a round stone mushrooming through the dry floor. A matching blue-grey lizard revealed itself as it screwdrivered off into the leaf litter.

'You should have stamped your boots,' sighed Two. 'Let a snake know you're about and it will use its discretion and glide off. Surprise it, and the thing fangs instinctively. I think each snake we see must be read as signifying another enemy. So far we've sighted two, obviously representing Pete and Kevin Gill. I'd say we'll get up to, oh, seven. Maybe eight? Then we'll know precisely where we stand.'

'Sod the snakes,' said Quinn, 'stuff the enemy. I don't want to know.'

'Have a drink of water,' said One. 'It's hot, we've got disagreements, but you do need to conserve during daylight. Even snakes do. It's accepted that the nights are going to be the most dangerous, when we'll have to be on duty.'

'There's no doubt,' said Two, in rare accord, 'that they'll be operating by night. No doubt at all. There are silent-bladed helicopters which can fly in darkness, using infra-red. Fine, fine, smile as you will, but if you are not vertically hidden at night you may as well be standing out like dog's balls. Which is the other half of it: dogs by day, you can bet on that alright. That's why I badgered on and on about removing all traces of clothing from the cabin, burying them. Remember, dogs by day, and don't rule out quiet choppers by night.'

'Browner knows my smell alright,' Quinn told the branch of a dead eucalypt that nevertheless was moving on some hidden air, slowly scratching his photograph of the sky.

He sat very still, fingertips held to his temples, elbows on his knees. The incessant talk was draining. Even when both voices were not engaging him he could hear their constant undertones and asides, like a dinner party in another room. Other voices sometimes bubbled above those of the hosts One and Two as the conversation rose and fell into and out of meaning's grasp. The silence of the bush about him made the battle easier in that no humans required answering, but its contrast also served to heighten the intrusions in his head.

Quinn stopped mimicking relaxation and took one of the two bottles of water from the rucksack between his legs. He'd filled them from the Condamine the previous evening, Friday that was. Somehow he would have to remember the days as they passed. Now it must be Saturday; tomorrow the Vickers would be back. By then he would not have seen Jennifer for nearly three days.

He thought about writing down the days on a piece of paper. It seemed an onerous task. It would be nice to have a measure of distance, though, the way it's handy to know how long a tunnel is when you are boring through it in a train. What could be wrong with just trying to record the passing days?

'Everything,' said Two. 'I still say you shouldn't have promised her that you would call back before the end of one week. This may be a much longer haul.'

'Am I meant to eat twigs and gumleaves?' Quinn cut him off. It made more sense that he should talk to them internally, but he found this increasingly difficult. As though his head wasn't big enough to run three overlaps. He could maintain silence in the middle of a crowded street or on a train, but even then sometimes half a sentence would jump off his tongue. The volume at which it did so was also tricky to manage. Dr Logan had told him that he'd once shouted: 'If *I'm* bloody Socrates, *you* shut up and listen!' This was not the sort of blurt, Logan teased afterwards, to impress psychiatrists or policemen.

Here, not far below the ridgeline opposite the Vickers' house, it did not really matter that Quinn appeared to be talking to stones and trees, to the odd teased cloud. It stopped the blurring of the triumvirate. Even though Two had that whining pomposity and One kept her voice insistently neutral, if he didn't articulate his own words it made it much easier for the others to edge him right out, to leave him a subservient waiter at the dinner party.

This had been another of the growing list of reasons why

he shouldn't stay around the cabin: he did not want Jennifer to hear. When his utterances were robbed of context, well, they did sound strange. He could enlist banter or song to disguise the truth that the voices were there, the way he did, say, when working on the car or with the stone walls, but it was a huge effort. If he could speak out freely he would keep a better grip on the world.

'If I don't go back I'm stuffed and you know it, Two.' Quinn's eyes were following a large blackcurrant ant hauling a crashed hoverfly backwards over a twig. 'I've only got food for two days or so, and even then I have to be careful.'

'We're going to have to discuss the food,' Two diverted him again. 'I'm not happy about that side of things.'

'There's a point,' interposed One, 'and I know how sensitive we've become about it over the past weeks, where Jennifer will start taking matters upon herself. By which I mean organising search parties of her own. Well-meaning, but …'

'I am *not* staring at the bloody trees!'

Quinn had shouted again at Two's suggestion, concurrent with One's painful attempts at tact, that he was staring at a particular stand of scribbly gums, and why was he doing so? What had caught his eye?

'The best thing,' he said as though addressing his boots, 'is that I slip back, say on Tuesday, and placate Jennifer, get another swag of food.'

'Not face-to-face,' insisted Two. 'Back on nightfall, into the food bins under the cabin, some vegetables from the garden to eat raw, a note left under the door for her to see in the morning. Something like: "Am fine. May be back in another week, may head for Melbourne." If she leaves it lying around and the enemy spots it, so much the better.'

'You don't think The Room …?'

'Out of the question!' The answer was so abrupt that Quinn was uncertain whose voice it was.

'If Jennifer knows you're there, others will get it out of her, use her,' Two explained as though a schoolteacher burdened by slow-learners. 'We've got to float a bit, be alert. There's every reason to believe that these pathetic valley people are decoys, that there's very big outside influence at work here. Say no more. The other critical thing about The Room is that it's wide open at night, meaning that what you think is a low-altitude star may very well indeed be a high altitude silenced helicopter.'

'There's a crevice in one wall,' Quinn said wistfully, only half-hearing his voice as it declined down the slope into the absorbent trees.

'Oh, sure,' said Two sarcastically, 'tall man beats tech-nology by folding himself into a hole in a rock.'

The day was like the discussion: all heat and getting nowhere. Through the trees Quinn slitted his eyes at the sun, guessing it to be stationed at four pm or thereabouts. Either One or Two had told him not to wind his watch, he couldn't recall which, or why. Inside his shirt he could feel two drops of sweat merge and slide down his side. His forehead and eyebrows needed wiping with the back of his arm.

Suddenly, as though he had been waiting for an opening, Quinn whacked a palm across each ear, so hard it hurt. At the same time, his elbows still on his knees, he began to rock. He was raising the toes of his elastic-sided boots, crunching them down, then doing the same with his heels. This made his torso roll back and forward, the dull beat travelling from his boot-soles up through his legs and arms and into his ears. He might have been one of those travelling teenagers cupping the earphones of a cassette recorder, moving to private music. The reverse was true: Quinn was trying to exclude, not amplify.

'When we've finished this little performance,' said Two clearly through the noise made by Quinn's boots, 'perhaps we could move on, eh? Staying in one place for any length of time is an open invitation.'

'What we can get along with,' encouraged One, 'is finding

a good bivouac. Last night's arrangement of wedging yourself up the tree was good, but there is that problem of being spotted from above.'

Quinn, his feet now stilled, spoke at his rucksack: 'Not to mention the difficulty of trying to pull on a sleeping bag when you're twenty feet up a gum tree, or worrying about whether you'll drop off literally.'

'There's a lot to be said for that state,' said Two cheerfully. 'Keeps you alert, one eye open like a watchdog.'

'Christ! Listen, the pair of you, I need some fucking sleep!'

'What we need now,' One ignored Quinn's anger, 'is to close that rucksack, climb up to the ridge and reconnoitre for a nice ledge of low rock for tonight. Kill two birds with one stone, if you'll pardon a little cleverness: protection from certain dew and from possible overhead surveillance.'

Two was an absolute arsehole, Quinn managed to think to that little bit of himself he was fighting to hold onto, like it was Iwo Jima. He was standing now, closing the rucksack as One had suggested. Two was paranoid alright, his voice moaned like a jar of mosquitoes, he butted his crackpot ideas into every thought you struggled to keep for yourself. But in many ways, the longer it lasted, the more tolerable of the pair he became. One was so effing virtuous-calm on the surface, slippery as a forum of foreign ministers underneath all her saccharine diplomacy. She reacted to his anger like a fencer, feinting, letting it flash over her left shoulder. Her smile was unbreakable crockery.

'Bitch!'

Quinn had, before moving off slowly up the slope, brushed the ground with a small branch of leaves he carried stuck into the back of his pack for the purpose. He'd erased the toe-and-heel indentations made by his boots. Two had even insisted that he thoroughly brush the rock upon which he'd sat. 'Many a person has been undone by a stray cotton thread, lint from the pockets.'

'Of course, of course,' Quinn dusted away at it violently.

'Quite right. Do you want me to chase up the fart I did half an hour ago? Shouldn't I spit and polish the bits of sky I've left my eyeprints on?'

'Don't make jokes about the sky.' Two ignored the bile almost as well as One would have. 'The sky is a serious problem. All I can say is that there should be a hell of a lot less of it. It opens too many avenues.'

Jennifer was working in the garden, a Ruth amid the alien vegetables, when she picked up the coming-and-going sounds of an engine working its way úp the track. She chipped up a few more of the weeds that lurked among the silverbeet, then rested the hoe against the wire fence and kneaded the muscles above her bottom.

On her way down she stopped in at the cabin. In the mirror she stared at herself for a while and finger-combed her hair. 'You're pale, woman,' she said to her reflection. Several times in the past three days she had clutched at the thread of verse Quinn had alluded to in one of his early letters, the one where he was guessing what she looked like. The first one? She had been forced to learn the poem as a schoolgirl: *O what can ail thee, knight-at-arms, Alone and palely loitering? The sedge has withered from the lake, And no birds sing.*

'Yep,' she said to the mirror, 'palely loitering.'

It had not made much sense to her as a parroting Australian child. All these years later there might not be sedge to wither from the Condamine, the valley's birds *did* sing alright – although when you thought about it galahs and cockatoos were less ode-inspiring than nightingales or skylarks – but only now could she really feel for Keats's love-wracked knight. She was *La Belle Dame Sans Quinn*.

During the hiatus since he had left, Jennifer had decided that if anyone, anyone at all, asked her a single or a hundred questions about Quinn over the next few days, her answer would be the same: 'He's not here.' No more, no less. The curtness would paper over the ache she felt at his absence and the fears she held for him. She was furious with herself for having left a gaping hole in their lives by not managing to tell him that their baby was inside her.

By Saturday evening she had already forgotten her agreement not to go after him. Twice she had climbed up to The Room to see if he had changed his mind. It was quiet, safe as a bank … and empty. On the second visit she had left a note under a small stone inside the crevice where Quinn had curled up. 'I am carrying our baby. I love you, Quinn, J. D.' She doubted that he would read it there, but it was a nice feeling, made her remember putting treasure maps inside bottles as a child, casting them into the holiday sea. When she woke early on Sunday morning she sat down with coffee on the verandah and wrote about ten identical notes. She spent the whole morning, sometimes crying, sometimes laughing at herself, going about all their favourite spots and leaving a note on a friendly tree or rock. About half of them she placed at points along the Condamine where he had fished or where they had made love. She did not climb up the heavily treed ridge opposite because neither they nor anybody else ever went there. But she had watched Quinn pack and knew that he would have to visit the cabin or the river for water. He might be upset that she was betraying his presence in the area – but surely he would see that the chance of someone else coming across a note was remote, particularly now that Mary and Pete's boys would have been very firmly instructed that Jennifer's place was off-limits. No, what was more worrying was the likelihood that he would not believe what she had written. Conception might become yet another conspiracy.

When he recovered, he would be as thrilled as she was. She knew that in her very DNA.

Jennifer reached the track just as the Vickers' Land-Rover was clearing the trees on her left. She had her hands in the pockets of her jeans. Tighter at the waist now, but her secret still quite safe. Given that Lorna knew the saga of her 'infertility', she would not even become suspicious for ages. Jennifer was quite composed. 'Alone and palely loitering', she said through a smile forced in the Land-Rover's direction. She could hear Kate yelling over the engine noise.

The Land-Rover stopped fifty metres short of her and she could see Henry reaching back and opening Kate's door. The child sprinted along the track, small arms pumping like an athlete's. Jennifer trotted towards her and then crouched so Kate's outspread arms could fly into her own.

'I missed you, Jenjen,' Kate panted. 'Guess what, daddy bought me a torch in Brisbane. My own one. I wanted a dog, but he said I have to be olderer.'

Jennifer kissed her on the cheeks and forehead, said all the right things about how much she'd grown in three weeks, stroked her bouncy black hair.

Henry had slowly driven up to them and now he and Lorna stood by, their daughter doing all the icebreaking. Jennifer at last lowered Kate and went to Lorna. As they lightly embraced and exchanged small-gift smiles, Jennifer saw Kate's dark eyes measuring the rapprochement.

Jennifer stepped back and tiptoed to kiss Henry on the cheek. 'I'm glad you people are back,' she said. 'Your cow and I were running out of things to say to each other.'

'I'm going to be much better, Jen, Lorna said. Again Jennifer thought she sounded like a repentant Kate. 'I'll take it easy for a while...easier on you and Henry, too.' Her laugh was nervous.

'Good,' said Jennifer, smiling.

'Goody,' said Kate.

In the seconds while Lorna bent to pick up her child Jennifer flashed a look at Henry. He read what her raised eyebrows asked and smartly gave a negative headshake. 'Right,' Jennifer acknowledged to herself, 'you haven't mentioned Quinn's presence.' She saw Henry's eyes rake the slope. They stopped at the completed vegetable garden, making calculations about the man-hours that had gone into the terraces since they'd left. His eyes moved on then returned to Jennifer's. The faintest movement of her head told him that Quinn was not in the immediate vicinity, and that he should say nothing to draw Lorna's attention to the garden.

'I've left some eggs on the table,' she turned quickly back to Lorna, 'and there's some bread I made yesterday. Not as good as your own. I lit the stove late this morning, so I hope it'll still be going.'

'Thanks for all this,' Lorna said quietly. 'How are you keeping yourself?'

'Fine.' Jennifer could hear her own crispness. 'The main thing now is for you to continue to look after yourself, and, if you don't mind me suggesting it, you should avoid some of the people around here until you're stronger.'

'Point taken,' Henry quickly answered on Lorna's behalf. 'Thanks for looking after everything. It's been a long hot drive from the coast and I think we'd better start preparing this young lady for an early night in her own bed.'

Kate looked less than thrilled. 'I want to stay with Jenjen,' she pouted.

'No!'

He's snappy, Jennifer thought, watching Henry direct the child back to the Land-Rover. She wouldn't really have minded; Kate would have broken the silence during the evenings, at night she would have contributed the fractional reassurance of someone asleep and breathing.

Apart from her promise to Quinn, Jennifer had already backed down on the one she'd made to Dr Urquhart. Temporarily. One joint on the verandah late into the night was all. Not another puff during the day. She would quit entirely as soon as Quinn was back. Surely hard-line Urquhart would accept that a mother-to-be also needed to be able to sleep?

Sitting on the verandah, the lamps off inside because they magnetised moths, Jennifer patted her belly. 'Sorry about this, mate. You poor spaced-out little foetus, you.' She wondered why Hilda thought it would be a boy. It didn't feel like one to her, somehow. What sort of names would Quinn fancy for a boy?

There was a rationed moon up, big but filtered by the high clouds that travelled by night. Its light glossed then darkened the slivers of Condamine Jennifer could see from the verandah, as though, she smiled, God was toying with the dimmer switch. Then there was a bolder light by the river, a lump of fallen moon. Jennifer stood and stared over the rail. Instinctively she trod out her half-smoked joint.

Quinn hadn't taken a torch. It was one of the things that had led to their parting words being less than warm. She'd tried to insist that it was ludicrous to be alone without matches or light in the bush, plain unnecessary hardship, but he'd ignored her. Now it was clear that there was a torch in someone's hand down by the river. It was not being shaded; frequently she saw the full circle of its beam as it was directed up towards the cabin.

Jennifer remembered the size of the rock that had sailed through the window. She imagined one flying out of the darkness straight at her face. Or maybe a still-warm headless hen? She shuddered and rubbed at the goosepimples making coarse sandpaper on her forearms. She was about to step back inside, desperately trying to convince herself that Kate had managed to persuade Henry to take her possum-spotting with her new toy, when there was a panting noise from the darkness below and ahead of her, a matter of metres away.

Browner's belated whine of recognition only just stifled Jennifer's scream. The dog added one small, back-of-the-throat bark as though Hilda had warned him: 'Don't scare the pants off of her.'

'Browner, you yellow-eyed bastard,' Jennifer hissed over the rail, as though she too needed to be careful, 'fetch your boss up here while I re-swallow my heart.' She still hadn't sighted the dog, but she imagined she could see him circling fast back down to the track, nose-to-ground. She quickly lit the lamp and turned the wick up, overwhelming the moon's pale efforts. The primus was also alight under the kettle when Hilda tapped at the door.

'You nearly gave a poor woman a miscarriage, Hilda.' Jennifer directed her neighbour to the couch. Browner had taken a metre or so of liberty into the room, lying with his chin on his extended front legs; low-profile, high-beam eyes.

'I thought youse two might've turned in for the night,' Hilda said to explain why she had stood by the river with her torch and despatched her envoy. 'But then it can't be much after half-nine.'

'Quinn's gone bush.'

It was good to be able to say it to someone, bluntly the way Hilda talked.

'A bit …?'

'Very much so.'

'Shit,' said Hilda, although she sounded more angry than concerned. 'I come up here, as I s'pect you've figured, 'cos about the last thing you'n your Ned want might be on the go.'

'More protests from the vigilantes?'

'The what?'

'The anti-schizophrenia paratroops.'

'I get you. The same lot.'

'Bad news has long legs, doesn't it? The boys spotting him fishing?'

'Yeah. Pete and my Bert was over at Arvi's about it this mornin, plus me boys. All five of the Cochranes was there, the Gill tribe, three or half a dozen others. Bert come back and blabbed it all to me. 'Course he don't know I'm a double agency, whats-you-call-it.'

Hilda really did look like a witch when she laughed, Jennifer decided.

'At least the Vickers weren't back then.'

'Oh, they wasn't going to contact Lorna. Bert said everyone reckoned she was raggy-arsed enough over her kiddie dying, and all.'

Jennifer turned down the wick of the lamp that was sending quavers of fine black smoke from its flue. While she poured the tea she couldn't exclude the momentary idea that Hilda might be enjoying all this, playing a supporting role in a soapie.

'Are they going to look for him? Ride up and down the ridges in a posse?'

'Well, girl, they don't know 'e's bangin' about the bush. Far as they know 'e's warmin' your bed.'

'I wish he was, Hilda, I wish he was.'

'It weren't your news what got to 'im?'

'No, Hilda. I'm afraid you're still the only one who knows. I was about to tell him when he announced that he was going to camp away for a while … so I didn't get around to it.'

'I see. Well, I couldn't get exactly what they're up to. Bert said if I wasn't comin' along he wasn't going to bother tellin' me. He did say Mary was arguin' to leave sleepin' dogs lie, and how she reckoned her boys mightn't have even seen Ned, how they were always comin' 'ome with tales of Boogeymen they'd spied on. But he said most of 'em this morning claimed they'd already been startin' to get suspect that you and Ned might've pulled a stunt. They reckoned that'd account for the breakin' on Lorna's shed. Who else coulda done it, like? There was some talk of callin' in the police, but that didn't go down so well, Bert, Pete and none of them Cochranes being all that fond of coppers. Don't s'pose anyone c'n do much more than try and freeze you two out, play dirty tricks, like. Lot of hot air about, if you ask me. Thought I should tell you, but. Few of 'em went into Walrae after, to Hamilton's, so it'll be round the town alright.'

'Thanks, Hilda. I feel like buying a shotgun and sitting up here on the verandah with it across my knees.'

Hilda had finished her tea. After she rolled a cigarette for the road she stood, as did Browner. Her voice dropped very low. She was trying to make it sound gentle, but it emerged croakily: 'If you ain't seen 'im back by tomorrow p'r'aps we should have a scout about for 'im? Not so much worried about them hot air bags, but your fellow mightn't be too good on his own in the bush, bein' crook. Ain't sayin' to disturb 'im, but me and Browner c'd go out on our own a bit, 'ave a quiet look-see? Up to you, girl, and hope you don't think I'm tryin' to poke me big nose where it don't belong. Say so and I'll pull me head in.'

Jennifer put an arm across Hilda's shoulder. 'I don't reckon I've ever heard Hilda Jones say so much in one go,' she teased. Hilda's eye contact was locked to her dog's. 'But yes,' Jennifer said, suddenly quiet herself. 'I guess it'd be a good thing if you think you and Browner could discreetly locate him and report back to me.'

'Wasn't plannin' on chattin' with 'im. You got somethin' Ned's been wearin' what hasn't been washed? Browner's had a good sniff of 'im, but it'd freshen up 'is nose.'

Jennifer walked out into the cloud-shredded moonlight with Hilda and Browner, took the torch when they were under the cabin. She reached into the old wardrobe and emerged with some of Quinn's scrunched underwear, which Hilda took and gently rubbed along the top of her dog's nose. 'That's 'im. That's 'im,' she whispered warmly. Browner wagged his tail.

She handed the things back to Jennifer. 'Funny place to keep his gear.' Hilda couldn't resist. 'He put it there hisself?'

'You think that's funny, eh? Do you know where his clothes were when I found them?'

'I don't.'

'Stuffed in plastic bags and buried in the garden, pretty roughly, in the space between the Lisbon spring onions and the Pontiac potatoes. I found them yesterday after I saw bits of that plastic growing through the ground like new leaves.'

'Jesus wept!'

On Wednesday night, six days out, Quinn was kneeling in weak moonlight high on the opposite ridge midway between the cabin and the Vickers' house. On the bare ground in front of him were the small piles he had made from the contents of the rucksack. He now did this each night; made six piles, checked each one six times. When he had completed the routine he would pull on the sleeping bag and slide his long body under a slab of rock which hung only a metre off the ground. Before zippering himself up he would use both arms to scoop the dead-dry sandy ground in around the edges of the bag; this kept him warmer as well as helping to hide him.

The small piles of possessions had the opposite effect, advertising his presence, and their exposure meant that they were invariably dewy by morning. But to Quinn they had become a barrier, sound as a trench or a tank trap. The piles were evenly spaced about half a metre apart. One mound was his boots and socks, which he was now having to pull on wet each dawn, the second was his knife, the one he kept surgically sharp for fish, his handkerchief and the bit of branch he used to obliterate his tracks. The two waterbottles, one empty, made up the third pile. Food was fourth, although this was now down to a plastic bag with about two cups of dry muesli, a plastic container of brown sugar and two oranges. His waste pile, the one Two insisted was critical, was a large round stone sitting atop empty plastic bags, orange peel, the torn label from one of the drink bottles, any detritus that might reveal his presence to searchers, including threads and lint from his clothing.

The sixth pile was the rucksack itself, inside it only two T-shirts, underpants and a second pair of shorts. Jennifer had put his medicine containers in the zippered sidepocket. He no longer took them out to inspect them. Had Two not been so insistent about not leaving traces Quinn would have buried the containers under a rock. The three of them had agreed … when was it? Didn't matter; the stuff was contaminated and could only make him feel worse. A promise was a promise, but Jennifer would quite understand if she knew his medicine had been interfered with in an attempt to make him feel drowsy.

It was necessary to be sharp. Even if his medicine hadn't been tampered with, any pill-induced sluggishness might allow them through his guard. Yesterday, or the day before, he had definitely heard movement below him, down near the river. It had been at dusk and he'd cocked his head to catch the thump of kangaroo. But there was a bark. One quick bark, not very loud, then complete silence. A snake might have frightened the dog? Sometimes when he had been working in Jennifer's garden he had seen a stray mongrel wandering on its own, half-feral. But, as One pointed out, the bark had sounded as though it came from this side of the river; the animal may have been on a lead. On his scent.

Quinn had been to the river many times, always an hour or so before the sun was doing the day's first light fantastic on its surface. He would tiptoe down barefoot, slowly and back-wards, brushing away at his tracks as he went. He'd fill the two bottles, return to his stashed rucksack. If he washed he always got into the water with his clothes on, not swimming because of the noise he might make or the fact that he'd disturb the mud and discolour the water downstream. He'd sit like a boulder, the current cleaning away his sweat and smell. Two had suggested it to make things harder for the dogs.

What felt especially good about sitting in the Condamine in his clothes before sunrise, and what had probably made Two sound reluctant in his endorsement of the practice, was that Quinn found it restful.

'This is the only calm I can get,' he said to One as he sat in a bend in the river on Wednesday morning. He always went to a different spot. For long periods he would stay completely submerged, his fingers clasped into the muddy bottom to hold him there. It was a stupid thing to be doing, Two argued, because in the stillness you could hear his heavy breathing each time he was eventually forced to come up for air.

'You're just scared I'll drown myself,' said Quinn, his panting voice sliding across the surface. 'And where will that leave you, eh?'

The river did tend to lift his spirits, even though it was the most dangerous and exposed part of his days. In the water's embrace he could briefly think of Jennifer, especially when he had his head under. One had argued patiently that it was best that he didn't, that he put her out of mind until the struggle was over. 'Then you can go back to her,' One said calmly, 'when the work's done. Possibly it would be best if you regarded her as a journey's-end factor rather than a present additional load, or interference.'

Quinn didn't argue. He even came up more frequently than he had to for air, placating Two with quieter breathing. But he was at his slipperiest in the water, and the others knew it. At times he could manage agreement or fake dispute with both One and Two while simultaneously slotting fragments of the red-headed woman into the seams of his thoughts. For instance, he might throw up a tangent solely to engage them in dismissing it, allowing him a gap to dwell on Jennifer. Once he was able to think how he could try to make it up to her after he had come through all this. Another time he got an erection sitting there in the darkness of the river.

'For Christ's sake,' Two had said, 'if there's anything to undo these sort of operations its randiness. Sex is the classic unraveller of vigilance. Until the campaign is won, couldn't you keep that limited mind of yours above your bloody navel?'

'I was thinking of my vegetable garden,' Quinn laughed as he got up and began climbing the bank in a crouch. 'You don't know how good it feels!'

The sun was pushing off the bedclothes of night and there was a grey light about him as he retreated up the slope to the hidden rucksack.

'All this water running off you is a bastard,' whispered Two. 'It's leaving marks on the ground like someone's dragged a struggling carp up the bank. I think, when we get back up the top, we're all going to have to discuss moving on, getting many kilometres of ground between us and the pursuers, even if they are also out on the plain. Force the issue a bit.'

'Proximity to food, yet distance from the eight snakes,' said One, slightly contradictory in her tone. As though in appeasement she added: 'And, yes, the overhead surveillance.'

As he hooked the straps of the rucksack over his sodden T-shirt, Quinn's expression was either a grimace or a twisted smile. Another bonus of these dark dips in the Condamine was that they enabled him to pull the wool on both his hectoring inhabitants: they could not spot the difference between drops of water running onto his face from his hair, and tears.

Hilda often went off on her own in the early morning or late evening, so her husband and sons took no notice of her doing so regularly during that week. They would have thought something was amiss had they seen her with Browner on a lead, but she slipped the rope around his collar only when they were well away from the house. Browner didn't like the idea at all, it went against every article of his constitution, but Hilda muttered that she wanted him to work, not lurch off on every whiff of fur or feather. Silence was important, she explained, and Browner trotted huffily by her side.

They had called at the cabin a few times, partly to tell Jennifer that there was nothing to report, more so because Hilda wanted Browner to get his face into the wardrobe again, to inhale Quinn. Several times Jennifer asked to accompany them, but Hilda was adamant. It'd double the noise, she'd insisted, and would distract Browner from what he was meant to be doing.

They worked over many miles of ground, first the steep going along the same side of the ridge that her own house, Jennifer's and the Vickers' were built on. It was a matter of travelling very lightly on your feet, letting your ears and nose and eyes have every chance, staying in touch with the dog. To begin with Browner kept wanting to take her up to a strange walled-up sort of a place on the ridgetop above Jennifer's. Quinn had obviously spent time there, but Jennifer explained that there was no way he'd be in this place she called The Room.

Browner also took his mistress to several bends and

nooks along the Condamine. Jennifer's identical little notes to Quinn spooked Hilda and she would stuff them in the bib pocket of her overalls. Although she couldn't read them properly, she had a pretty good idea that one of the words was 'baby'. Back at home she slipped them into the wood stove when she was alone. Later, much later, Jennifer would press her to try to remember exactly how many notes she had gathered, whether any had been marked in any way. Unfortunately she couldn't be sure, although she understood why Jennifer was asking.

They had started working slowly along the opposite slope on the Tuesday, and Hilda could tell by Browner's increased interest that Ned had been about, even though he had left no sign of his presence; no ashes, no buried excrement, not so much as a thread. One possibility was that Jennifer's man had gone up and perhaps over the opposite ridge, could've even doubled back somewhere and walked to Dirranbandi and the railway line. When she'd suggested this, however, leaning in at the back door of the cabin watching Jennifer feed a seam to the singing needle of her machine, that red hair of hers had shook utter certainty. 'He's about, Hilda.'

Henry had called the morning after. Jennifer had known that he would, read it in his eyes as he'd stood there by the idling Land-Rover on the day of his return from Brisbane. She could not face him, couldn't hear his gentle voice explain how they would keep Lorna in cotton wool or how people were calling to offer help because she'd been, as Hilda told her Molly The Ferret was putting it, 'sickened with grief'.

So Jennifer had written a note to Henry and pinned the white envelope to the back verandah post. Her senses had become so acute in recent weeks that she knew from the birds when he was less than halfway down the track, her track. At the time she had been feeding Splash and the hens. All she did was stroll back to the cabin, shut the door and wait.

Sitting dead still on the floor next to the couch, her head in her hands, Jennifer heard Henry's boots moving about outside the door. There was the sound of him whistling over his bottom teeth as he read. Later she saw that Henry had pinned it back to the post with a big brown tick on the envelope, from him licking a finger and jabbing it in the dirt. The note had said only that she was exhausted and would like to be left alone for a few days, after which she would come up to visit the three of them.

Hilda's behind-the-lines intelligence was that Jennifer needn't get jumpy until the weekend, probably on the Saturday afternoon. That was when a few people would come up to the cabin to see her. Hilda had been unable to ascertain from Bert exactly what it was they planned to say. The impression she'd gained from her husband was that he and some of 'the others' thought that there was, as Bert put it, 'too much namby-pambying going on'. She suggested to Jennifer that all that would happen would be 'some rantin'. They would probably ask to speak to her alone, not knowing Quinn's plight, or as Hilda called it, his 'predicament'.

'I'll bet,' Hilda had said fiercely, 'one of them pig-keepin' Cochranes will do the talkin'. Message will be that everybody wants to get back to bein' neighbourly, and they're willin' to wipe the slate and all, providin' you pack Ned off fair dinkum this time.'

Jennifer appreciated that Hilda was rehearsing her; she had tried it herself several times. It was impossible to keep the spleen from her voice or the colour from her cheeks when she tested her reply: 'Ned Quinn isn't here right now or he'd speak for himself. He wants to be here with me minding our own business. I want him to. He is going to stay. You good people can like it or lump it. Afternoon.'

Hilda advised against the like/lump part, said she should substitute the fact that, whatever they wanted to believe, she knew Ned Quinn had not harmed any person in the valley or in Walrae. Jennifer had said she would think about it.

Hilda and Browner spotted Quinn very early Thursday morning, the day Jennifer had planned to gird herself and pay a social call on Lorna.

Without Browner, Hilda would have missed him. But she had felt the tension in the dog through the rope twisted around her wrist. Browner had stopped and cocked his head.

All about them was stillness. The river was perhaps fifty metres below them but frequently hidden. Where they stood the slope was just beginning its long haul up to the far ridge and the trees were heavy and dense. There was still overnight coolness coming out of the ground. Before setting out Hilda had seen Bert and the boys off at first grumpy light, away for the day after a truckload of firewood. Now it must have been about seven am, and the canopy above her was still effective against the low-slung sun.

Crouched beside her dog, Hilda scanned, pinching her eyelids half-shut to concentrate for the discordant colour or movement that would confirm a sighting. 'I'm like one 'o them bloody birdwatchers,' she whispered into Browner's ear. 'Can't see nothin', but. Hear nothin'.'

She tried to follow the line of the yellow eyes, but Browner turned and surprised her by licking her cheek.

'Geddorf!' Too loud for secrecy.

'You're havin' me on, boy.'

Hilda stood, annoyed at the false alarm. Probably he'd sniffed a late-breakfasting 'roo.

Then Browner pulled hard. Almost got away from her.

'Alright, alright, I'm comin.' She was whispering again.

The leaf litter was dry and laced with brittle sticks, so she moved forward slowly, leaning back against the pull of the dog.

Browner barked twice, and she kicked his rump.

'Cut yer bloody mouth, willya!'

Browner stopped again as they passed a tall stringybark. Hilda looked right, then left.

Just below the level of her chin she saw Ned Quinn's bare feet.

Hilda had a lot of difficulty climbing the tree. There weren't many low branches, and Quinn was a tall man. Also she had the shakes.

For a while she had not been able to look up. She had led Browner to a thinner tree about ten paces off and tied the rope to it. 'Drop 'n shut up,' she'd ordered. Browner obeyed, despite the quavering voice.

When she turned and forced her eyes she thought she'd half-prepared herself, but it was worse than the bleakest limit of imagination. Hilda lurched a few paces back towards her dog then fell to her knees and vomited her breakfast. For a while she propped on hands and knees, just breathing. At last she got back up and with one of her boots sprayed dry dirt over her mess.

Turning back to the hanging body she realised this time that she could not see Quinn's eyes; his hair had fallen forward, obscuring them. She was grateful for that.

'I'm gunna cut you down, lad,' she said aloud.

'Can't leave you like that. Can we, Browner?'

Now she saw that Quinn had used the webbed straps of his rucksack, which was on the ground nearby. Each strap had been pared neatly down the middle to knot together enough length. Hilda thought it looked very thin to be supporting the weight of a big man.

After several attempts, Hilda got up the tree to the branch. The contrived rope was looped over it only about a metre out from the trunk. Looking down from just above him she could see three brown ants on Quinn's right cheek, and could smell the foulness on his trousers where death had released a small amount of waste.

Hilda had her pocketknife out from her overalls, but she hesitated.

'I've got to cut yer down, boy. But between you and me I'm real frightened to hear you hit the ground. Real frightened.'

Her left hand was losing its grip on the trunk, so she had to go ahead with it. Placing the blade on the top of the makeshift rope where it looped, she shut her eyes, and cut. She would never discuss with anyone, not even Browner, the noise of Quinn's body as it slumped on the ground.

Quinn had landed on his back, with his legs bent under him from the knees. Down from the tree, breathing heavily, Hilda was relieved to see that his eyes were shut.

'Before we tell that poor lady of yours, I'm gonna straighten you up a bit, Mr Ned Quinn. I don't s'pose you'll mind Hilda doin' it?'

As she went about the job Hilda realised that Quinn must have killed himself that very morning, perhaps about the time she was preparing breakfast for her three men. His clothing was wet, so he had been in the river not long before he did it. She found that she was able to pull his legs from under him; that his body bent when she lifted his ankles and dragged him several metres from the tree. His mouth was slightly ajar, so she closed it by pushing his jaw with her overalled forearm. Frightened to feel his skin.

The ants had disappeared with the fall.

When she got stuck for things to say to the body Hilda kept repeating aloud as she went about arranging him: 'You poor silly bastard. You poor silly bastard. You was goin' to have a bub. You poor silly bastard.'

It made her cry.

At first she thought of trying to drag him right down to the river's edge. That way she could have let Jennifer believe he'd drowned. The slope of the land would have made it possible, but it didn't seem proper to try to trick

Jennifer. It'd be an interference she'd no right to make. Also Jennifer only had to look at that bruise on the right side of his neck. Why was she so sure Jennifer would be coming to see the body? Couldn't answer that, but she *was* sure. She'd handled plenty of dead animals in her time, but, crikey, a thinkin' man. What's more, one who'd been real nice to her straight off. Whole thing was police business alright, but shit to that. No way she could have left him up there for Jennifer. Plus it was better to be cut down by a friend than a copper.

The flood of confused thought helped while Hilda went about getting Quinn as clean and comfortable-looking as she could manage. She'd gone to the river for some water to sluice the stains from his legs. She emptied the few things from the rucksack and used it as a bucket. The fact that Quinn was already wet from his last swim made it easier.

Finally she lifted his head – the fear of touching him now gone – and pushed a cushion of dry dirt under his hair. With his head raised a bit Quinn's adam's apple was less prominent. Some leaves and small pieces of bark on the right side of his neck hid the only mark she could see on his body.

On her way back Hilda stopped again at the river to wash her hands and face and to splash a few scoops of its coolness over her own neck.

She waded across on a rocky bar, already making plans.

Hilda saw that her hands had resumed shaking.

Browner had been left tied to the tree to keep guard.

Burial was Jennifer's idea, but Hilda had already thought of it herself.

When she stood and knocked at the back of the cabin, she'd had to say remarkably little. From the verandah Jennifer had seen her trudging up without her dog. In the doorway she looked Hilda up and down, saw how wet she was and how that 53-year-old face looked suddenly a lot older.

'Is Quinn dead, Hilda?'

'He is, girl. Browner 'n me found him just now.'

Jennifer didn't react in any way that Hilda could see. She was staring over her head at the vegetable garden.

'I can't say nothin', Jennifer.'

'Can you leave me for a bit?'

'Yeah. Don't mind if I go up and sit with yer goat f'r a while? Come and get me when yer ready.'

Jennifer nodded then quickly shut the door.

Hilda sat cross-legged on the cropped ground next to Splash, fondling the animal's ears. Its hard pellets were uncomfortable on her lean bum through the damp overalls. She wished it was Browner with her, but the goat was better than nothing. Without something living and warm to touch right now she might have broken down, gone all wobbly.

The hot sun was drying her overalls. After a while Hilda moved to squat in the shade of the tin shelter, Splash trotting along with her, face sad as a donkey's.

It was more than an hour before Jennifer called to her from the cabin. As she got up and trod her cigarette Hilda realised how tired she was and saw that she had barked the skin off the back of her left hand.

The two women spoke only practicalities for the rest of the long day. Not one warm word passed between them. Twice Jennifer broke into dry sobbing, but each understood that any attempt at comfort would be worse than wasted, almost offensive.

Months and years later neither of them could comprehend how they behaved as they did. 'I suppose we were in shock,' was all Jennifer could suggest.

The only sharpness came when Jennifer asked Hilda which tree it was.

'That's no matter now,' she'd snapped, 'and I can't face discussin' it, what's more.'

Hilda stood several paces back while her neighbour knelt beside her dead man and slowly massaged his forehead and both temples. Jennifer then bent and touched her lips on his. After that, Hilda remembered later, she had become all efficient and businesslike. Her only other question was to ask why his clothes and hair were wet. Hilda explained that Ned had obviously gone for a last swim in the Condamine. Fair enough to leave it at that.

The one time that day when Jennifer held her eye was as she stood up from the body and said:

'I want to bury him, Hilda. You can help if you like. It'd have to be a lifelong thing between you and me?'

'I agree.'

'Also it's dangerous. Totally illegal.'

'Said I agreed, didn't I?'

Between them they dragged Quinn's long body about one hundred metres further up the slope, just on the high side of an outcrop of grey rock. It was all they could manage and they sat exhausted on the ground for several minutes before either of them could speak. Without asking, Hilda had put a black T-shirt from Quinn's rucksack over his face and upper chest while they dragged him, each holding a wrist. Jennifer had not objected.

It took more than three hours before they finished. Jennifer had returned from the cabin with a pick and shovel over each shoulder, and they had taken turns in the dry, shaley ground.

Hilda insisted on doing much more of the work, especially when it came to standing knee deep and shovelling. Mindful of unmentioned pregnancy. Jennifer demanded that it be a really deep grave, only relenting when Hilda complained that she could almost stand in it unseen.

Not a word was said over the filled grave.

They spent another hour smoothing and clearing up, brushing away the smallest footprint, leaving the ground unmarked and scattered over again with dry leaf litter. So much so that Hilda suggested Jennifer might want to come here and she'd be unable to find it again if they did not at least put a small rock nearby, say ten paces to the right? Jennifer had refused, saying only that it didn't matter if she could not find it, that it wasn't necessary.

They washed their faces and arms and hands in the river as they returned, they washed even the faces of the pick and of the shovel. Jennifer carried the deflated rucksack under one arm – the only way she could because of its missing straps. Hilda did not ask what she would do with it, its few pathetic contents.

After wading the river they stopped on the track.

'Eventually Quinn's brother may ask questions,' said Jennifer. 'I'm sure he will, he was a good brother. I'll just have to tell him that Quinn went away because things didn't work out for him up here. Finally he'll become a missing person.'

'Yeah,' said Hilda.

She looked up at the ridge behind Jennifer's cabin. Already the sun was past it and heading for the other horizon. Not long before Bert and the boys would be home and expecting food. She wouldn't be able to cook, not a thing. She would lie down sick, for once.

'You oughtn't be on yer own tonight, girl. Not much I can …'

'Oh yes, I ought to, Hilda. Tonight I ought to.'

'Can I come up in the mornin', then? Talk a bit?'

'Yes please.'

Jennifer bent down and patted Browner on the head.

EPILOGUE

There was no mention in the *Walrae & Dirranbandi Advocate* but Jennifer made inquiries and paid for a small insertion in *Grass Roots,* even though the magazine staff could not recall having run a birth or death notice before. After giving the date it read:

BIRTH
At Dirranbandi Base Hospital.
To Jennifer and Ned, a daughter,
Hilda Jade Quinn.
Mother and child doing well.